THE PASSENGER FROM
SCOTLAND YARD

THE PASSENGER FROM SCOTLAND YARD

A VICTORIAN DETECTIVE NOVEL

By H. F. Wood

WITH A NEW INTRODUCTION BY
E. F. BLEILER

DOVER PUBLICATIONS, INC.
NEW YORK

This Dover edition, first published in 1977,
is an unabridged and unaltered republication
of the second edition of the work as published
by Chatto and Windus, Piccadilly, London, in
1888. E. F. Bleiler has written a new introduction for the Dover edition. Two illustrations
have been added to the Dover edition.

International Standard Book Number:
0-486-23523-8
Library of Congress Catalog Card Number:
77-76586

Manufactured in the United States of America
Dover Publications, Inc.
180 Varick Street
New York, N.Y. 10014

INTRODUCTION
TO THE DOVER EDITION

i

THE last third of the nineteenth century is a barren period for the detective novel. Between *The Moonstone* (1866) by Wilkie Collins and *The Hound of the Baskervilles* (1902) by Arthur Conan Doyle there is very little that is worth remembering, even as a statistic in the publishing industry.

Not many adult detective novels were published during these thirty-five or so years, and to list even the better-known authors is simply to chronicle mediocrity and worse: Fergus Hume,Anna Katharine Green, Julian Hawthorne, Thomas B. Aldrich, F. du Boisgobey, Lawrence Lynch, Major Arthur Griffiths, Dick Donovan, and so on.

The reasons for this hiatus involve mortality and economics. By the end of the first decade of this period most of the older practitioners were no longer writing detective fiction. Dickens died in 1870, leaving *The Mystery of Edwin Drood* unfinished. J. S. LeFanu died in 1873. Wilkie Collins was written out, and struggled along with potboilers and social novels. Mrs. Henry Wood, after *Within the Maze* (1872), turned to domestic fiction, as did Miss Mary Braddon. The second decade, 1881–1890, produced two famous longer works, *A Study in Scarlet* (1887) and *The Sign of Four* (1890) by Doyle, but oddly

THE PASSENGER FROM SCOTLAND YARD

BY
H·F·WOOD

STREET & SMITH, PUBLISHERS, NEW YORK

American dime-novel publication of *The Passenger
from Scotland Yard.*

enough these are not true novels, but detective short stories tacked onto historical romances, in the manner of Gaboriau. During the third decade-plus, 1890–1902, a younger generation appeared, but all its creative energy went into short stories, with the result that there are many good short stories in the 1890's, but almost no novels. Here economics played a role: *The Strand, Pearson's Magazine, The Windsor Magazine* and other variety magazines paid well for short stories.

There are only two exceptions to this arid scantness. The first is *The Big Bow Mystery* (1891) by Israel Zangwill. It is still read, and occasionally reprinted, mostly because it is the first important sealed-room novel. The second exception, a much finer work, now almost forgotten, is *The Passenger from Scotland Yard* (1888) by H. F. Wood. This was a well-concentrated, nicely written, highly imaginative novel that was unique in its period.

ii

About the author of *The Passenger from Scotland Yard*, H. F. Wood, very little can be said at present. Contemporary bibliographic records like Allibone occasionally refer to him as H. Freeman Wood, but these same records also often confuse him with Sir Henry Trueman Wood, a British Kodak tycoon and writer on aesthetic and scientific subjects. Even worse, the British H. F. Wood has also been confused with H. Firth Wood, an American compiler of humor anthologies. The result of this syncretism is that the book listings under H. F. Wood's name in the general reference works are often wrong and are not to be trusted.

A search in the British birth records office in London reveals that a Harry Freeman Wood was born in Bradford, West Riding, England, in 1850. For the moment it is assumed that this is our H. F. Wood. Nothing is known about Harry Freeman Wood's antecedents or his later life, but it is possible that he was connected with the Wood family of wool staplers in Bradford, from whom arose the great late-nineteenth-century surgeon, John Wood. It must be admitted, however, that the writer H. F. Wood in his last two books used the name H. F. Wiber Wood, and that no trace of the name Wiber is to be found on the birth record of Harry Freeman Wood. The writer H. F. Wood was a newspaperman by profession. For some years associated with the London *Morning Advertiser* and the *Glasgow Herald,* both major newspapers, in 1895 he served as their special correspondent in Egypt, covering the British occupation of Egypt after Arabi's putsch.

The bent of Wood's fiction indicates that he was a cosmopolitan traveler, and that he was intimately acquainted with Paris and French ways. My guess is that he lived in Paris for a large part of his life. There is also a possibility that he was in the United States in the late 1880's, shortly after the appearance of *The Passenger from Scotland Yard.*

Of H. F. Wood's later life nothing is known. He was presumably alive in 1915, when his last novel was published, but this is his last appearance in records. There is no English record of a marriage, a death, or a will of either H. F. Wood or of Harry Freeman Wood of Bradford. Since in England such records are centralized with admirable efficiency, the probabilities are that H. F. and Harry Freeman are the same person, and that this person died outside England after 1915.

H. F. Wood wrote seven books, three of which are detective stories. His first and best book, *The Passenger from Scotland Yard* (1888), went through at least two printings in Great Britain, and was reviewed favorably by even such "highbrow" journals as *The Spectator.* It was pirated almost immediately in America, where it was issued by several different publishers. It was sometimes retitled *The Night Mail* and sometimes attributed to William Ward!

Wood's next two books were sequel in small ways to *The Passenger from Scotland Yard.* These were *The Englishman of the Rue Caïn* (1889) and *The Night of the 3d Ult.* (1890).

The Englishman of the Rue Caïn centers around an attorney who is trying to track down a missing legatee in Paris. He learns that the legatee has been murdered and discovers that an old flame of his own seems to be involved, either as murderess or accessory. On the attorney falls the ticklish task of both uncovering and covering up the crime. Associated with him is Toppin, the Paris representative of Scotland Yard, who had played a secondary part in *The Passenger from Scotland Yard*.

The Night of the 3d Ult. is set in London. In a low rooming house, which also doubles as a sporting arena, an unidentified lodger is found murdered. Two detectives are concerned with the crime, though in different ways. Detective Sergeant Vincent Erne is trying to locate the murderer, so that he can embarrass his superiors, against whom he has a grudge for having taken him off the case. The private detective Aaron Vowcher, who appeared briefly in *The Englishman of the Rue Caïn*, is investigating commercial frauds and locating lost persons connected with the victim. The investigations of both detectives lead them into ever-widening complexities.

Unless there is some minor periodical publication in England that has not been identified, *The Night of the 3d Ult.* was published only in the United States. This suggests that Wood may have been in America at the time. Due to peculiarities of American copyright law, if Wood sold his manuscript to an American publisher, he would retain British rights and could collect further monies. If he had published first in England he would probably not receive payment from American publishers, since there was no copyright protection for British books in the United States. Such arrangements would best have been made personally.

Both these novels, *The Englishman of the Rue Caïn* and *The Night of the 3d Ult.*, are very unusual for their day in attempting to convey the social circumstances surrounding murder. They are adult in language and background, and attempt sophisticated characters. In this respect they anticipate the interests of the Edwardian-Georgian detective novel that came into existence in the

This is the only edition of my book "The Night of the 3rd ult." published in the United States with my sanction, and the only American edition by which I shall profit.

H. F. Wood

Specimen of H. F. Wood's handwriting, presumably authentic.

early twentieth century. For Wood detectives were human beings who loved and hated like other men, had their own lives beyond detection, and might suffer downfall because of their emotional constitutions. *The Englishman of the Rue Caïn*, for example, anticipates the central situation of *Trent's Last Case*.

There are also many original and unusual touches in these two novels, just as there are in *The Passenger from Scotland Yard*: oddities of background, strange personalities, and quirks of plot that show a strong, original imagination. Toppin, Erne and the somewhat slippery Vowcher are among the most skilfully constructed detectives in the literature. About the ending of *The Night of the 3d Ult.* I shall not speak, except to say that it is almost brilliant.

Yet despite these occasional virtues, these two novels, as wholes, are much inferior to *The Passenger from Scotland Yard*. *The Englishman of the Rue Caïn* wanders too much into rodomontade and the ultimate motivations are not credible. The really interesting detection in *The Night of the 3d Ult.* is pushed into the background all too frequently by domestic subplots which grow only vaguely out of the criminal situation. Both novels, too, have sensational aspects which are by no means as well handled as in *The Passenger from Scotland Yard*. The *Athenaeum* summed up these novels well: great originality but wrong-headed cleverness.

Wood's other work is much less significant. His social novel *Avenged on Society* (1893) is of no great interest. *Egypt Under the British* (1896), a journalistic apologia for the British presence in Egypt, draws on interviews and is vivacious, but it represents a trivial moment in history. *Under Masks* (1908) is a collection of short stories, a couple of which contain crime elements, but the author's main interest seems to have been travel background à la Mérimée. Wood's final work, *War's Forget-me-not* (1915), has not been available to me, but it was reviewed as a confused thriller about a conspiracy to conquer England. There is a remote possibility that Wood wrote an eighth book which was perhaps published some time before 1890. The title page of the (American) Lippincott edition of *The Englishman of the Rue Caïn* lists a book entitled *The Prologue to a Drama* as by Wood, but no trace of such a book has been found.

iii

H. F. Wood is a one-book author, but this is not damning praise: most authors never reach this level. *The Passenger from Scotland Yard* is not simply a historical monument, but is a fine piece of work. The murkiness surrounding the original crime and the gradual revelation of the main characters concerned with it; the slow emergence of the second, more important crime, the murder on the train; the wary counterplots of detectives and criminals in the seedy hotels and gang covers of Paris; the curious relationship between Scotland Yard and the Sûreté offer a new range of themes to the reader.

Particularly remarkable are the train sequences and the characterizations in this novel. I know of no other passages in English literature that convey so sensually the presence of a Victorian train-ride—its miseries and discomforts, its amenities, its strange physical structure, and its dangers. In characterization there are the depth structurings of Detective Byde and the wonderful criminal trio, Innocent Benjamin, Finch and Sir John. Two of them, at least, rank among the great personalities of detective literature. There is also the wonderful evocation of Paris of the 1880's. In short, despite occasional minor flaws, *The Passenger from Scotland Yard* belongs among the classics of the detective story. In my opinion, it is the best detective novel between *The Moonstone* and *The Hound of the Baskervilles*.

New York, 1977   E. F. BLEILER

CONTENTS.

CHAPTER VIII.

CHAPTER IX.

CHAPTER X.

CHAPTER XI.

CHAPTER XII.

CHAPTER XIII.

CHAPTER XIV.

CHAPTER XV.

CHAPTER XVI.

CHAPTER XVII.

CHAPTER XVIII.

CHAPTER XIX.

CHAPTER XX.

CHAPTER XXI.

THE

PASSENGER FROM SCOTLAND YARD.

CHAPTER I.

THE night mail for the Continent stood ready to glide out of the London terminus, the leave-taking friends assembled in small groups upon the platform before the carriage doors were reiterating last messages and once more exchanging promises to 'write,' when a hard-featured, thick-set gentleman who had been peering out of a second-class window drew back with a slight exclamation of annoyance or disappointment, and sank into a corner seat. Hardly a moment had passed, when the rattle of the guard's key was again heard in the lock, and the door fell open to admit a fifth passenger. 'Just in time, sir!' muttered the guard, banging the door after the new arrival and relocking it. He immediately signalled with his lamp, a whistle rang out sharply, and the night mail for the Continent started from London.

The new-comer installed himself unobtrusively in the nearest vacant place, and at once muffled himself up in a travelling-rug and a voluminous wrapper or two. Presently there was little to be seen of his face but a pair of gray eyes and a Roman nose. He sat with his back to the engine, in the corner opposite the thick-set, rubicund, hard-featured gentleman, and the latter had from the first followed his movements with a singular interest. In fact, the new-comer might have been justified in remarking with some impatience upon the odd scrutiny of which he thus became the object. He seemed, however, to be quite oblivious of his fellow-passengers. It was nothing to him, apparently, that the gaze of those blood-shot blue eyes should be roving continually from the cloth cap which he wore, with lappets over the ears, to the bulky hand-bag he kept upon his knees, and the plain walking-stick he had deposited in the receptacle overhead. The walking-stick had knots or rings along its length, such as are suitable for concealing the juncture of the handle and the sheath in ordinary sword-canes. Its owner kept his eyes lowered, for the most part, as though he wished to be as little observed as he was himself observant, and as though he feared to be drawn into conversation by even a chance interchange of glances. But, now and then, he might have been detected in a rapid survey of the entire compartment; indeed, at the end of one of these lightning-like excursions, his gray eyes encountered the blood-shot, inquiring orbs of the passenger opposite. It was already some time since the train had glided out of the London terminus, and dashed through the suburban stations on its way to Dover.

'A curious case—that diamond robbery in Park Lane!' said the red-faced, thick-set gentleman aloud. He appeared to be addressing the remark to the company in general, but he still watched the features of the latest arrival amongst them. That personage moved slightly as he heard the remark, but proffered no response. He merely closed the keen gray eyes, and buried his chin deeper in the warm travelling wrap. The rest of the company turned interrogatively towards the speaker. 'A strange case,' he repeated, studying the closed eyelids in front of him; 'the man who planned that robbery and got away with all those diamonds must be a clever man at his business, and no mistake. He'll want some catching, that man will! But I think I know a man as clever as he is—and quite clever enough to do the catching for him.'

'Dear me, now!' returned a passenger in a sort of attire which, without being clerical, had a clerical look, 'I have seen no mention of the occurrence in the newspapers. May I ask you, sir, to what affair you make allusion?'

'Well, I shouldn't be surprised if none of the papers had yet heard of it,' answered the other; 'but they'll hear of

it to-morrow morning, I dare say. We're due at Dover at
ten o'clock, and we don't stop on the way, bar accidents.
But when we do run into Dover Station, I dare say we
shall see what we *shall* see !'

He drew a spirit-flask out of his pocket, and took a pull
at it. His questioner had been about to put some further
query, but checked himself at the sight of the flask. A
suspicion that the man had had recourse to it before was
easily discernible upon his countenance. In the far corner,
a short, spare, youthful passenger, lost in the folds of a
roomy ulster, turned towards the window and composed
himself for sleep.

' Yes, you may say what you like about the failures of the
police,' continued the person who had begun the conversation, 'but *I* say that the London detective force are a body
of remarkable men, and *I* know something of their ways
and what they do, sir, I can tell you. Know something
about them ? I should think I did !'

' Bless me, now, really ?' said the clerical gentleman,
evidently quite interested. ' And what may be the nature of
this robbery you refer to—this diamond robbery in Park
Lane ; an extensive affair, now ?'

' Twenty thousand pounds,' replied the other, ' that's all !
Twenty thousand pounds' worth, at a fair figure.' He
screwed up the spirit flask, and fixed his gaze obstinately on
the closed eyelids opposite. ' Gone out of a safe in the
strong room, where they had been placed for one night
only : and no traces !'

' No traces whatever ?'

' Nothing. But, all the same, there are certain circumstances which—well, if they do happen to be upon the right
track, they'll owe a good deal of it to me. For I don't mind
telling you that as a tradesman living in the neighbourhood of
Park Lane and serving the house in question—Mr. Wilmot's
house—Stanislas Wilmot, diamond merchant in Hatton
Garden—wealthy old boy—as a tradesman, I say, serving
the private house in Park Lane regularly, I happen to have
been situated better than most people for knowing what was
going on inside it. However that may be, the man was
a clever one that planned this robbery.'

' Well, well, well ! But tell me how this Mr. Wilmot,
with premises in Hatton Garden presumably suited to his

business, came to transfer so large a quantity of valuables
to his private residence?'

'Because the quantity of valuables was large. The consignment had only been delivered at his office on the
previous day, although he had been expecting it for a week
or two. Well, he doesn't like to trust his clerks, and he
doesn't like to trust the housekeeper in Hatton Garden, or
the watchman, or the strong-rooms there, and so he prefers
to take extra good stones, passing through his firm, to
the little private house he occupies in Park Lane. Oh, it
isn't the first time he has run the risk, by a long way. He
knows what he's about, though, as a rule. There's always
a special constable on duty just about there, in the lane;
and the strong-room in the private house is as good as you
could wish to see. He's an old swell, a widower; and you
can often see him riding in the Row with a young lady
he has adopted—Miss Adela, a poor relation of his wife's.'

'The thief, or thieves, then, broke into the private
premises during the night?'

'Who can say? The old boy brought these diamonds
home without saying anything to anybody. In the presence
of his butler, he deposited them as usual in his strong-room.
The next morning they found both the locks intact, but
the diamonds were gone.'

'Is he sure he locked them up?'

'Sure? Of course he's sure! And so is his butler.'

'Ah! A confidential servant, now, the butler?'

'Yes, sir, a confidential servant.'

'Quite so, just so! a confidential servant.'

'Oh, I can answer for the butler. I can answer for him
as I can answer for myself.'

The clerical gentleman smiled sweetly, and inclined his
head. If, with Master Dumbleton, he 'liked not the
security,' he did not allow his mistrust to be manifest.

The train rushed onwards to its destination, covering
mile after mile at the same headlong speed. It was the
third week of December, and the weather was detestable.
Driven against the carriage windows by violent gusts of
wind, the rain showered like hailstones upon the panes
of glass. As the passengers flashed through the stations on
their route, the lights, appearing to them for an instant only,
were all blurred and indistinct. Three occupants of the

compartment we have travelled with were doubtless fast
asleep. The clerical gentleman had not lapsed into
slumber, that was clear. His lips occasionally moved as
though he were engaged in the rehearsal or construction of
a discourse. He opened his eyes dreamily from time to
time, and at one of these moments his gaze met that of his
communicative, red-faced neighbour.

'Going to cross the Channel, sir?' asked the latter.

'Yes.'

'Calais or Ostend, sir?'

'And a tolerably rough crossing it will be,' pursued the
other. 'Are you going by the boat, yourself?'

'I think I shall stay a night or two at Dover. My
business takes me across the water every now and then,
but a day sooner or later does not signify. West End
tradesmen are largely supplied from the Continent, and I
deal regularly with certain houses myself. Business has
been bad, however. Those who do cross to-night will find
it nasty in the Channel, I can tell you.' He unscrewed his
pocket-flask. 'And there'll be some fun at Dover, if the
man shows fight.'

'Bless me, now? The affair you were referring to?'

'Why, yes. I don't mind telling you'—the speaker
stared once more at the closed eyes and the Roman nose
directly opposite him—'that they've got the man suspected,
or, rather, that they will have him. On all the northern
lines the police are on the look-out by this time. It was
thought he would make a feint of taking refuge on the
Continent, and that he would go north instead. But *I*
believed he was bound for the Continent in reality, and
unless I am very much mistaken he is in this train. The
butler has been at Folkestone or Dover since this morning,
and the local police were wired to watch the night mail.
The butler will identify him, but there may be a confederate
in the case. A detective who had seen him in suspicious
company was to run down by the night-mail—this very
train.'

He winked most expressively as he uttered these words,
and nodded with great vigour in the direction of the Roman
nose and veiled gray eyes. The clerical gentleman lifted
his eyebrows and pursed up his mouth in the profoundest
astonishment. As a kind of confirmation and rejoinder,

the other smiled upon one side of his rubicund visage, and again nodded and winked.

'Bless me!' ejaculated the clerical gentleman. 'And the man whom you suspect, now—who is he?'

'A young fellow of good family, named Sinclair, private secretary to old Stanislas Wilmot until three months ago, when he was suddenly dismissed. He knew all about the old boy's business dealings, and has been seen several times in the neighbourhood of the house during the past few weeks. He gave it out that a gentleman abroad had engaged him as private secretary. We can see very well what that little manœuvre meant. A great pity, for he was generally liked, and quite a superior young gentleman. Miss Adela and he—well, well—I say nothing.'

'But how could he have got into the strong-room?'

'That's just what *I* said. The butler thinks he must have got in simply with the keys; and as Mr. Wilmot's keys were not out of his possession for a single moment, while the diamonds were there, he thinks the young fellow must have had duplicates. It seems that the keys were once mislaid for a few hours, before Mr. Sinclair went away. You can soon take a pattern for duplicates, can't you? Great pity, sir. The result of fast life, however, from what the butler tells me.'

'Suppose the young man really had had these duplicates made, with dishonest intention; they might, likewise, have been stolen from himself, or "borrowed" in just the same fashion?'

They stared at each other for several seconds, and then looked round the compartment as if for the opinions of their fellow-voyagers. There could be no doubt that they were all three fast asleep.

Suddenly the carriage began to vibrate with a succession of shocks. The train was slackening its pace. Two of the other passengers woke up immediately.

'Something on the line,' observed the clerical gentleman —'or else we are going to pull up at a roadside station.'

'A roadside station!' growled his red-faced interlocutor, 'and what for? We are not far from Dover, and we shan't be punctual as it is.'

He let down the window.

The train reached the first lamps of a small country

station. It was moving at so slow a rate that at any
instant it might have stopped. Voices outside could be
heard, calling backwards and forwards. ' Wire to Dover,'
shouted somebody, and a second or two afterwards the train
took a fresh impetus.

' I don't know what it is,' muttered the red-faced gentleman, putting up the window again, ' unless it refers to the
Wilmot affair. Perhaps young Mr. Sinclair has been
detected in the train under some disguise. The two guards
were in communication.' He mopped his cheeks with his
handkerchief, and wiped the clinging rain-drops from his
coat. ' A pretty crossing !' he added—' a pretty crossing,
to-night, for those who've got to make it. Going to Calais,
sir ?'

He put the question abruptly, to the passenger whose big
blue spectacles seemed still to be bent upon him.

' Yes, I am going across,' was the answer, in somewhat
affected tones ; ' as I suppose we all are ?'

' In this weather !' exclaimed in unmistakable Cockney
accents the youth ensconced within the ulster. ' Not me !
Cross in a gale of wind like this, and with the rain a-coming
down in bucketsful ! Not if I know it, for one—not *me*,
Mr. Wilkins !'

He delivered these phrases in the manner of a soliloquy,
and it was to be conjectured that the Wilkins he apostro-
phised was but the creature of his fancy, a familiar who
received habitual confidences. He shrank further into the
festoons of his shapeless garment, and turned his face again
towards the window-curtain.

' We are surely travelling at a dangerous velocity,' resumed the clerical gentleman, clearing his throat with a
cough which recalled the platform of public meetings. ' The
hazards of this life should be always present to sober-minded
men. Now, my very excellent friend opposite concurs with
me, no doubt, upon many topics, sees matters with my eyes,
and probably with greater clear-sightedness ; and yet there
is one topic upon which assuredly we look with different
vision : my friend smiles, and I think he comprehends my
meaning—yes, my dear friend, the question—the great and
burning question—the vital, national, indeed, international
question, I may say—of alcohol !'

' To every man, what suits him, say I,' responded the

other, feeling once more for the spirit-flask. ' What suits me, sir, on a wet night, when I can't take exercise, is the old prescription out of Scotland—a wineglassful when you feel to want it.'

' Ah, that widespread and too potent fallacy ! If we could only vanquish and expel, for ever and aye, the error which that argument disseminates, what a vast stride towards the precious victory, what a splendid benefit conferred upon civilization ! The globe, sir, would re-echo with one long sigh of glad relief ; for the extirpation of that single error would bring us promptly within sight of the goal.'

' In the teetotal line, sir ?'

The red-faced gentleman, as though unwilling to wound the susceptibilities of his neighbour, relinquished his search for the medical prescription which suited him.

' A pioneer in the great cause,' assented the other. ' Let me offer you my card ; we may be companions for the rest of the journey, should you decide to cross to-night.'

He produced a mother-of-pearl card-case, and with a deprecating gesture handed over a rather exaggerated oblong slip of pasteboard.

'Bro. A. Neel,
Lecturer,
I. O. T. A.'

So ran the card.

'I. O. T. A.?' repeated the person to whom it was handed.

' International Organization of Total Abstainers,' answered Brother Neel sonorously.

' Just think of that !' murmured his questioner, with a vague expression of alarm. ' Been going on long, sir, this international movement ?'

' Not a great length of time, but we have already accomplished results of an exceedingly encouraging kind.' He glanced at the card passed to him in exchange for his own. ' All we need, Mr. Remington, is activity in proselytising, and intelligent assistance from the rich. As fast as our funds permit it, we shall open a new branch in some Continental centre. At present we have half a dozen branch establishments on the Continent, the most important of them being the branch at Paris. In fact, we

make Paris our headquarters for the Continent. You
are probably acquainted with our offices in that metropolis?'

'No,' replied Mr. Remington, his bloodshot eyes still
fixed upon the initials of the international society.

'Well, we intend to achieve great things. As a first
measure, we attack the railway officials on the principal
lines, the international services. "Attack" is my way of
putting it, you know.'—Brother Neel endeavoured to look
jocular as he threw in this parenthetical remark—' And we
have enlisted a fair proportion of them on this side, and at
Brussels. We find that there are cases—especially the
guards and engine-drivers—which tell admirably in our
half-yearly reports. Wherever we extend our operations
we find the public most willing to support our movement,
and our agents write that they are zealously aided by the
English colonies in all the Continental centres. People
travel so generally nowadays, you see, sir. And how much
woe and ruin may be wrought by one—but one, inebriated
engine-driver! And this was the reflection which occurred
to me when I noticed the hazardous velocity with which
we were travelling. Ah, my dear friend, I quarrel with no
man's views; I do not demand that my brother shall live as
I live, but neither can I live as my brother lives—hourly
conniving at suicide, moral and physical. Oh, cast the
tempter from you—hurl away that accursed bottle, hurl it
far away! You will pardon me my earnestness, dear
friend?'

'Oh, I know the prescription that suits *me!*' said Mr.
Remington, with a gruff laugh, ' and you'll excuse me, sir,
but when you get into the Channel you might feel to want
a wine-glass of it yourself. Hark at the wind.'

He lowered the window, and a keen gust at once swept
through the compartment. The night was too dark for them
to discern the few swaying trees along their route, but faint
lights began to flit by, and presently the motion of the train
became less rapid. 'Dover!' announced Mr. Remington,
in an unsteady voice. He ought to have experienced small
need of any further recourse to the spirit-flask, but he took
a final pull at it. If the oblique regard despatched at him
by Brother Neel meant anything, it meant ' A wine-glass
and a half, this time.'

The night mail drew up at the Dover ticket-station.

'There they are!' exclaimed Mr. Remington, leaning out of the window. 'And they've got him! There's a force of the local police waiting on the platform.'

'Bless me!' responded Brother Neel, 'and so they've caught the thief? Bless me!' He gazed at the other three passengers with surprise at their indifference. 'Twenty thousand pounds in precious stones, now! Could we not catch a glimpse of the prisoner?'

'The door's locked,' returned the other, somewhat excitedly, trying the handle. 'They'll have to pass this way, however, to leave the platform, and then you'll see him. Yes, here they come. They are not losing time, at any rate! Just as I thought: it's Mr. Sinclair they've arrested. Well, but what does that mean——who's that?' He put his head in for a moment, and glanced at the passenger who had been the last to enter the compartment at the London terminus. 'There's a man in plain clothes directing the constables,' he added; 'that must be the detective who was to come from London. They're making no noise about it, anyhow! You'll see them march by.'

A tramp of footsteps was heard on the drenched platform, and the helmets of the foremost constables could be seen from the interior of the compartment.

'I'm sorry for you, Mr. Sinclair,' called the passenger who had recounted the story of the missing valuables. 'You've been led away; and I'm sorry for you.'

'Oh, Remington—is that you?' answered a young man's voice, in firm and distinct tones. 'Well, they have arrested the wrong man, I can tell you!'

'The wrong man!' echoed the other, looking after the constables, as the tramp of footsteps died away. 'Yes, they all say that.'

Mr. Remington had to make room for a ticket-inspector, who now appeared at the carriage-door and threw it open. The gentleman with the Roman nose woke up at the same instant as placidly as he had slept. He produced a through ticket, like his four fellow-travellers. The official tore out the first leaf, 'London—Dover,' in each case, handed the little books back again, and vanished.

'Going across to-night, sir?' inquired Brother Neel of Mr. Remington.

'I hardly know, till we get down to the pier,' replied that individual, looking towards the sky, although there was nothing to be seen. 'Shall you cross to-night, sir?'

'I have not quite made my mind up,' answered Brother Neel, with a glance towards the carriage window, which, however, only reflected their own figures.

A minute or two of cautious progress, and the train came to a standstill on Dover Pier. But no porters presented themselves to unfasten the doors.

''Ere, let us out!' exclaimed the youthful gentleman inside the ulster. It was his place that lay nearest to the platform at Dover Pier, and he let the glass down with a run, and peered out for the information of his companions. 'There's something else up,' he remarked; 'they're visiting all the carriages.'

A guard, whose cap and overcoat were dripping with rain, suddenly made his appearance at the open window, scanned the five passengers hastily, prepared to pass on, and then checked himself.

'Is there a passenger here from Scotland Yard?' he asked, with some hesitation.

No one replied.

'A passenger here from Scotland Yard?' he repeated, holding up the envelope of a telegram, which large drops of water had smeared and blotted. No one replied.

'I beg pardon,' said Mr. Remington hurriedly, to the person opposite, whose proceedings had inspired him with so deep an interest from the outset, 'but are you not the gentleman in question?'

'I?' returned the other, speaking for the first time. 'From Scotland Yard? I? What an idea, to be sure! Certainly not.'

The guard lingered at the entrance, gazing from one to the other.

'My name is Pritchard,' continued the personage interrogated, 'and I am travelling through to the south of France. Pray let us take our places on the boat.'

The official unlocked the door. As the five occupants of the compartment scrambled down the steps, they saw him visiting the next carriage to their own.

'This way for the Calais boat!—Ostend boat that way, sir!—This way for Calais—boat waiting!'

Male and female voyagers, clad from head to foot in heavy cloaks and capes that protected them from the wet and cold, but impeded all their movements, struggled as best they could through the vehement wind and streaming rain. The lamps of the Pier Station lighted up their paths, as, hampered with packages, rugs, and shawls, they followed the directions of the railway servants posted about the platform for their guidance. Disconsolate comments in broken English met the ear, mingled with staccato sounds in objurgatory French. The passengers were not numerous. In the third week of December the traffic across the English Channel is usually excessive from the Continent to England, but slight from England to the Continent — the home, peculiarly, of Christmas festivities being Britain. 'This way for the Calais boat!—take care, sir—take care, ma'am!' The stone steps down to the gangway of the vessel glistened in the scanty rays of two lanterns held by sailors. The gangway itself swung with the gentle rise and fall of the Channel boat; it was pretty certain that the weather would be 'dirty' outside the harbour. A black shroud, however, seemed to cover the whole scene beyond and to hide it from the view. One by one, with infinite precautions, the voyagers groped their way on board the *Astarte*. The last of the stumbling figures in Indian file appeared to be Mr. Pritchard, with the through-ticket for the south of France. No; there was yet another: a gentleman who had at length arrived at a decision about making the passage that night— Mr. Remington. And one more form approached—this time, the last—at some little distance in his rear; that of a gentleman who, likewise, had eventually been able to make his mind up—Brother A. Neel, of the I.O.T.A.

CHAPTER II.

The *Astarte* had received her mail bags and the passengers' luggage, and lay alongside the pier, gently rocking as if impatient to put out. The through-guard of the train was in conversation with the captain of the boat.

'It put me in a difficulty,' said he. 'How was I to find out the man they wanted? The message to me asked for

a reply at once, and so I wired back that there was no one
from Scotland Yard among the passengers.'

' Why didn't they name their man ?' inquired the Captain.
' It seems a strange proceeding—unless—well, we never
know : it might be a repetition of that affair.'

' So I thought, for a moment. But it seemed more likely
to be a mistake, or a piece of neglect. They must have
meant the telegram for the plain-clothes man who came
down from London, and who arrested this young fellow,
Sinclair, at Dover town station. Or perhaps there were
two plain-clothes men down by the train, travelling apart,
and the telegram could be delivered to either of them. Well,
I can't undertake to conduct their business for them. The
message was addressed " Passenger from Scotland Yard,"
to my care, Dover—" Guard of Continental night mail,
Dover station "—with a word to myself. I have just wired
back that a plain-clothes man had apprehended a Mr.
Sinclair on a charge of diamond robbery in the West End,
and that I had sent their telegram after him by a messenger
into the town. That's all I could do.'

' Who identified this Mr. Sinclair ?'

' The butler of the house, who was waiting on the platform with the constables.'

' Do you know what I think about it ?' demanded the
captain, after a pause. ' It looks to me as though they've
sent down one of their big men after somebody, and above
all wanted to keep his name quiet. Suppose that something
happened after the train left, which it was most important
he should know. How were they to communicate with him?
They did not wish to disclose his name, we will say, because
it would have handicapped him, especially if he were following clever people, or if he were " made-up " in any way.
Shouldn't be at all surprised if I've hit it.'

' No one came and asked if a telegram was waiting ; and
I had to go and inquire in the compartments where the
passengers looked at all likely people. It's pretty well
known now that somebody else from Scotland Yard was
believed to have run down by the night mail.'

' They must have seen that at Scotland Yard in send-
ing off the telegram ; but of the two evils no doubt they
chose the less. Very likely their man was one of the passengers you asked. Of course he would not acknowledge

the telegram if he were watching his man; he would risk it.'

'There are a good many "ifs" about that, captain; but we do see such rum things, you and me, going backwards and forwards, that I dare say you are not altogether far out. But, now you mention it, how do we know that the message came from the Scotland Yard authorities at all? Suppose a gang of criminals know that one of their number is being followed by one of the best men from Scotland Yard; what is to hinder them from wiring to the detective, in the name of his superiors, to stop him at Dover, and so enable their own man to get away with whatever he has got about him? The one envelope was inside the other; and I only know the words of the message to myself as through-guard.'

'It might be as you suggest; only, in that case, your reply would not have been arranged for?'

'Not as a blind?'

'By Jove,' said the captain, after shouting an order to the engine-room, 'I should like to know what the business really is. For all we can tell they may be tracking American dynamiters! So long as they don't blow my boat up, I don't care.'

'How's the sea outside?'

'Bad!'

Everything on board was now tight and water-proof. The captain nodded to the guard, uttered another direction, and ascended to a more elevated post. The joints of the shining machinery slid round, and the *Astarte* gave two or three preliminary throbs.

'Off at last,' muttered to a companion one of the few passengers who had remained on deck, 'we're twenty minutes behind time.'

He was enveloped in a mackintosh which fell almost to his feet. The collar, turned up, rose over his ears, and the cloth-cap he wore, furnished with lappets and a broad peak, completely hid the upper portion of his features. His companion was a much shorter gentleman, and underneath the broad brim, pulled downwards, of a soft felt-hat, it was impossible to distinguish his head. Perched on the summit of a roomy upright ulster, the soft felt-hat looked as though it crowned a tailor's effigy, of the kind which, with tickets suspended from their necks, grin at us from the plate-glass establishments of the cheap clothier. A casual observer would not have supposed these two persons to be acquaintances. In spite, however, of their attitude towards each other—the attitude of strangers—they presently exchanged observations in extremely low tones.

'Are you sure he's on board?' asked the taller of the two anxiously. 'I was too much occupied with my man to be able to look after him. Are you quite sure?'

'Certain,' murmured the other. 'I watched him go downstairs into the cabin, and take a berth.'

'Well, you had better go down, too, Bat, and keep an eye on him. Change some money with the steward at the same time. We shall want some French money on the way.'

'Go down!—not me! The "tec" may have slipped you, and gone down himself. I don't want him to know me by sight as well as I know him—what do *you* think! Suppose I just went into the lion's den at once, without making any more fuss about it? Not me!—It's——awful, up here—but you don't catch Bartholomew walking into the arms of Morpheus—no, sir! It would be like stepping into the Old Bailey dock right off. Not me, Mr. Wilkins!'

'I tell you I've not lost sight of the detective. He is in one of the private cabins—the last on this side. I'll watch him till we get to Calais. You had better go down, and see what our man is doing—whether he is drinking. Some one else may be after it. We ought to get half an hour at Calais. Come to my table in the station-restaurant.—Why, what are you afraid of? There's nothing against you.'

'No, but there soon may be.' The speaker reeled against the bulwarks, as the *Astarte*, rounding the harbour entrance, encountered the first of her foaming assailants, and lurched with the shock. He grasped a rope to save himself from falling. 'Come, you had better go downstairs, Bat,' repeated his companion, who, though apparently the better sailor, held on perforce to the same rope for a moment.

The *Astarte* made straight for the white ridge of a black mass opposed to her. There was a loud crash, and over the deck flew an invisible shower of salt, ice-cold spray. The *Astarte* left the dim, white ridge behind her, and the black mass rolled sullenly away; and then she sank, dreadfully down—down—into a yawning furrow, where for an instant she stood quite still, as if to collect her energies for another such antagonist.

'Perhaps you're right, Sir John,' said Mr. Bartholomew faintly; 'I could do with a drop of brandy from the steward.'

The two figures parted, the sack-like ulster steering an erratic but precipitate course in the direction of the cabin staircase.

Sir John continued hardily at his post. The breaking surf and howling wind appeared to disturb him less than the occasional approach of a surprised seaman. As the *Astarte* drove upon her way, the marine birds riding exultantly on the waves would fly up in front of her and dart across the deck, or swoop along the vessel from stem to stern, cleaving the gale with their muscular, forked wings.

On the lugubrious, indeed pathetic, scene below, it would be both undesirable and invidious to enlarge. When the limp felt-hat and draggling ulster had climbed to the foot of the brass-edged stairs, and forced an entrance into the cabin, there was no mirth at the piteous mien of the youth upon whose insufficient frame those articles hung. The steward and his assistant were too busy to attend to him at once. The necessary fluid, however, procured and gulped down, and consciousness having been partially recovered, Mr. Bartholomew addressed himself to a review of the company around him. A callous, jesting personage, presumably a commercial traveller, sat at the table in the centre, with some cold boiled beef before him, and a bottle of stout, and with a London evening newspaper propped up against a loaf of bread. The *Astarte* plunged and recoiled, shivered and righted herself, and at times it might have seemed to the dispirited voyagers that the Phœnician goddess of the moon would brusquely dive with them into the very bowels of the earth.

Mr. Bartholomew, scrutinising one after another the recumbent forms, allowed his eye to rest for a moment on the inflamed visage of Mr. Remington. That gentleman was ensconced in an easy-chair, at the raised extremity of the cabin. He, too, had been examining the company from his point of observation, and his gaze met the cautious glance directed towards him by the new arrival. Both countenances immediately assumed a bland expression of unconcern, and each proceeded with the apparently interrupted survey of his neighbours.

'Anything in the paper, sir, about the diamond robbery in the West End they were talking about at Dover?' asked the steward, as he rested from his labours. 'There was quite a to-do down at the station. A ticket inspector told me that the police took the thief directly the mail touched the town platform.'

'Not a word about it,' replied the commercial traveller, carving the cold boiled beef; 'the whole thing must have been kept precious quiet. Sometimes that is the best way; and if they have really put their hands on the right man the Scotland Yard people have done the trick, this time, about as neatly as you could wish to see.'

'Smart work,' said the other. 'I heard there was twenty thousand pounds' worth of valuables. Do you suppose he had the diamonds about him, sir?'

'I suppose so. I suppose that was one of the reasons why he was making for the Continent. However, they'll find that out when they search him at the lock-up. It seems he had no luggage in the van—nothing but a portmanteau which he kept with him in the carriage. They ought to have concluded the search by this time.' He looked at his watch. 'I wonder whether they were family jewels—necklaces, bracelets, and so forth—or whether they were loose stones! That makes a deuce of a difference, you know; people always exaggerate the value of their own family jewels; but there's this about brilliants set in precious metal of some design or other—you can trace them if you don't let too much time slip by.'

'So you can, sir; whereas loose stones——'

'Whereas, how can you identify loose stones? You may have one or two of exceptional size, and those you may be able to swear to, though I shouldn't like to risk it myself, even then, not being a diamond-cutter or polisher, or an expert. But take a few loose brilliants of the average size; how are you to identify them if they have passed out of your possession for a day or two? Here are two rings that I've worn, one for ten, the other for fifteen years. This one looks very well, doesn't it? It's set with "roses," and I've had it for fifteen or sixteen years; well, it's not worth very much. This other—see how beautifully the diamond is cut,

and it's a deep stone—I've been wearing constantly for
certainly ten years. I could identify that ring, as it stands,
amongst a thousand, and it's worth some money. But take
the stone out of the setting, tell me it has been put with
others of the same size, and bring it back to me—I wouldn't
like to swear to its identity. Very likely I couldn't pick it
out from half a dozen other loose stones, cut in the same
shape, or thereabouts.'

' I've often noticed that ring, sir, when you've been crossing by the boat. Don't you think it might be a temptation
to dishonest parties ?'

' Oh, nothing has ever happened to *me*. And I shouldn't
advise anybody to try it on ; I don't travel unarmed.' The
commercial traveller was a man of powerful build, and he
laughed boisterously. ' Talking about diamonds reminds
me,' he went on, ' of a friend of mine, a brother " commercial," who used to travel in the diamond trade between
Amsterdam and the United States. There was a tremendous
duty on diamonds going into the States, and my friend, who
was an Englishman, used to be always trying to get some
through the Custom House free of duty. So long as his
firm would let him bribe, he was pretty successful, but the
bribes began to mount up to almost as much as the duty,
and they found out there was no satisfying those
fellows out there. The firm stopped the bribes, and after
that they regularly persecuted him, out there, whenever he
landed. Well, he rather liked this for a time, but human
nature could not stand the life they led him, and in the end
he gave up the business. What I am coming to is the last
thing he did. He had brought a valuable consignment from
Amsterdam. The Custom House people felt convinced he
was declaring much too small a quantity, and so he was.
They ransacked his luggage, tested the sides of his trunks,
made him open secret compartments, and tried the lining of
his clothes, but all in vain. At last, with one of their
apologies, they required him to partly undress, to see
whether he was not carrying a diamond-belt. He expostulated, and wanted to resist, but they begged him to take
into consideration his past successes. He yielded, and they
could find nothing. But he had a strengthening plaster
across his shoulders, and one of the officials noticed the
corner of it beneath his vest. "Hold on," says he, ' I

guess we've not done yet." They tested the surface, and sure enough between the plaster and his shoulders were the little protuberances they had suspected. They got the plaster off with hot water, put it away with the stones underneath, and took his address for summoning him at the police court on the charge of defrauding the revenue. The summons never came on, however. On examining the stones they had seized, the officials discovered that they were all imitation.'

' And where had he put the real ones, then?'

' The genuine stones were closely packed in a large old-fashioned silver watch—or, rather, what looked like it—which he carried carelessly with a common watch-guard. But, of course, he did not keep them long in his possession.'

' Well, well, well!' exclaimed the steward, admiringly.

Again the glances of Mr. Remington and our young friend Bartholomew met, and were instantly averted. A vague sort of mutual cognisance appeared thenceforward to exist between them—a cognisance betrayed by, as much as anything, a distinct effort on either side to abstain from observation of the other. Interminable seemed the rumbling of the vessel, together with the thundering of the surge against her sides. Amidst the most dolent of manifestations, the steward adjusted a pair of spectacles, and took up the evening paper for his own perusal.

A mariner in a suit of tarpaulins came down the staircase, and imbibed something at the counter.

' Are we far off?'

' Just there, sir.'

' Thank goodness!'

' *Dieu merci !*'

' What a beastly crossing!'

' *Ah, monsieur, quelle traversée !*'

Ten or twelve minutes afterwards the crashing gradually died away. The *Astarte* neared the shore—the coast of France. Overhead, a great clattering became audible; and within the cabin, several of the experienced passengers prepared to gather up their hand-packages.

' Long coming over?' inquired one of his neighbour.

' Two hours and a quarter,' was the reply ; ' but what can you expect in weather like this? It will be worse to-morrow.'

Clambering up the gangway to the top of the pier, the

voyagers had no sooner passed the ticket-inspectors—simultaneously clutching their hand-packages, clasping their hats, and producing their tickets—than they found themselves besieged by the bands of loafers, who, even between midnight and 1 a.m., obstruct the distressed Channel navigator, accost him with cries of ' Portaire,' and endeavour to wrest from him his phantom hand-bag or attenuated portmanteau. Master Bartholomew entered the spacious refreshment-room in the centre of a group, They were the latest arrivals, and, after a second's hesitation, he carelessly shaped his path towards an almost unnoticeable table at which a single person had just installed himself. Master Bartholomew dropped into the vacant place opposite.

' How do you feel?' asked the other, without looking at him. It was the Mr. Pritchard who was bound for the south of France. He neither lifted his eyes from the wine-list, nor moved his lips as he spoke.

' Feel?' responded Bartholomew feebly. ' This is a nice business old Clements has sent me after. Why couldn't he come after it himself! You could have done it between you, and I'm sure *I* needn't come so far as this, and go through so much, to find a good piece of work. If he hadn't paid all my expenses, and guaranteed me something handsome when it's all over, I'm —— if I *should* have stirred a step! I've been over to Chantilly races and the Grand Prix of Paris, to pick up some of the winners, but I never came over before at this time of the year. 'Ere, waiter!—*gassong !* —give me a small bottle of brandy—what do they call it?— *connyac!* I'll show them how to speak French! Let's hope we *do* get something for our trouble, Sir John.'

' Keep your voice down—and don't appear to be saying much to me. Is your man here?'

' Here? Yes, I should think he was here—and drinking enough for you and me and him together! Makes me thirsty to look at him—unless he's only pretending to drink. He's just over there—don't you see?—but there's something I don't like about it. Looks to me as though he's " tumbled." See him?—there !—he had his eye on both of us. Where's your man?'

' Don't know,' replied the other rapidly, attacking the comestible deposited before him. ' Watched the private cabin as long as I could without attracting attention, but he never came out of it that I could see. Wonder whether he knows anything! Oh, he's a clever gentleman, that one is—equal to all the rest of them at Scotland Yard put together! He's a clever gentleman.'

'He's A1 at the game, and no mistake,' answered Bartholomew impartially.

'So much the worse for us.'

'Oh, I don't know! He may be as clever as you, Sir John—perhaps cleverer—and he may be cleverer than me, but he ain't more clever than you and me combined, with Grandpa' thrown in. If we bring it off, and Grandpa' meets us at the station, as old Clements arranged, it'll be all right.'

'It'll *have* to be all right. They had better not give us any trouble, because they are not in England here.'

'No; and *we* ain't in England either. Don't you be in a hurry over it now. If we miss it to-day we'll get it to-morrow. And, mind, no putting anybody out in this! I told old Clements I wouldn't be in any putting-out business, and that wouldn't suit his book either. Where's that *connyac ?*'

There seemed less than ever of Mr. Bartholomew in the roomy ulster and the soft felt hat. No regard for his personal appearance, however, troubled him. With a zest at least equal to that of his companion, he fell-to upon the regulation Calais restaurant dish of succulent roast fowl. They were both thus engaged silently when the through guard of the train approached Mr. Pritchard, or 'Sir John,' and touched him on the shoulder. Mr. Pritchard did not start, and did not look up; but he suddenly left off eating, and turned rather pale. The guard then bent down to him and whispered confidentially.

'Beg pardon, sir,' said he, ' but if you *are* the passenger from Scotland Yard, as that gentleman fancied, here's another telegram from London. I wired to them from Dover, and this is a reply to my message—a further telegram, sent on to Calais, "Care of through guard, night mail." The message to me here says they don't mean the plain-clothes man who stopped at Dover, and I am to try and deliver this at once. No one else has seen the telegram, sir, because, from what that gentleman said, I thought perhaps it might be you.'

Below the level of the table, out of the general view, he held the blue envelope of the French telegraph office.

Mr. Pritchard cast a rapid glance around him ; and young Mr. Bartholomew considerately rose from his seat to procure himself a roll of bread from the adjacent *buffet.*

‘ Well, yes,’ replied Mr. Pritchard in an undertone, ‘ I *am* from Scotland Yard, and the telegram must be something urgent for me. I’m on a difficult affair—keep it quiet who I am—they’ll make it right with you at head-quarters for the trouble you have been put to. When do you make the return journey ?’

‘ By the next night-mail from Paris,’ answered the guard, unconsciously imitating the quick, subdued utterance of his interlocutor.

‘ Present yourself at head-quarters as soon after your return as you like. But keep away from me, or you’ll spoil my game.’

‘ Beg pardon—the same case ?—Park Lane ?’

‘ Et cætera.’

As the guard discreetly sidled away, Mr. Bartholomew rejoined his companion, and they continued their repast for a minute in silence.

‘ Can’t you open that —— envelope, Jack?’ at length demanded Mr. Bartholomew impatiently.

‘ When I get a chance, I can,’ said the other. ‘ Now, then—follow your man !—there he goes. I’ll settle the bill.’

Mr. Remington, who had very deliberately quitted a table at some distance from them, now lounged in the direction of the doors with a somewhat unnecessary show of nonchalance. He had scarcely crossed the threshold when Mr. Bartholomew, whose expression of face had become quite wondering and artless—the natural timidity of unprotected, diffident youth, bewildered by unfamiliar surroundings in a foreign land—slipped the half-empty bottle of ‘ connyac ’ into a recess of the drooping ulster, and sauntered likewise towards the restaurant entrance.

‘ *En voiture pour Paris ! En voiture, les voyageurs !*’ intoned one of the French railway servants. The summons created the usual bustle among the passengers. Profiting by the opportunity, Mr. Pritchard deftly tore open the envelope and surreptitiously perused its contents.

'This is second message to you *en route*,' ran the despatch. 'Have wired Toppin, our man in Paris, to meet
your train, and act under your directions. Look out well
on the road. Ernest Vine, *alias* Grainger, *alias* Jack
Smith (Golden Square case, two years ago), and Bartholomew Finch, *alias* Walker, West End pickpocket, left
by night mail with tickets for Cannes. Reason to believe
they are on business. Find them out if possible and don't
lose them. One of Soho gang is watching your house.
Yourself supposed to be in London; we have thought it
best to wire you in this way, trusting to guard's discretion.
You are nominally told off for London duty.'

'*En voiture pour Paris !*' The passengers hurried towards
the platform.

CHAPTER III.

THE train for Paris was drawn up on the far line of rails,
and Mr. Remington, surveying the carriages, halted on the
edge of the platform, to avail himself of the shelter, overhead, from the pouring rain. As he stood thus, apparently
engrossed with the selection of a suitable compartment,
two or three fellow-travellers passed him, opened their um-
brellas, and stepped out briskly across the metals, and through
the pools of water, in search of the corners in which they had
deposited their hand-packages. Mr. Remington scanned each
figure that moved by him, and did not seem to have secured
his own place in advance. *En voitu-ure!* He threw a searching look on all sides, and strode from the edge of the platform
on to the iron way. He had not noticed an individual who
was studying in a very bad light a pictorial map of France.

Mr. Remington exhibited no little fastidiousness in the
choice of a compartment. Did he wish to travel alone, or
was it the difficulty of lighting upon a well-filled compartment, that embarrassed him? On a long night journey it
might be desirable to make one of a numerous company.
That, however, was just the condition which it appeared
impossible to realize. The passengers were not numerous,
and there was no lack of empty compartments. But in the
first endeavour which he made to secure a single place in a
row of occupied seats, he apparently discovered some per-

sonage whom he was seeking to avoid; whilst in a second essay he saw that the allotted number was already complete. From identical reasons, doubtless, others among the passengers had preferred to travel in a numerous company. A couple of porters pushed by him wheeling a truck. They had done their portion of the labours involved by the arrival of the night-mail, and were diverting themselves, as they trudged along, at the expense of certain voyagers whose sorry plight had attracted their notice. Mr. Remington's indecision proved sufficiently manifest to excite the remark of these facile satirists. They commented on it in the usual vein of the French working man, one of whose characteristics is a total incapacity to attend exclusively to his own occupation.

'Is he slow, *hein*, that clumsy Englishman!' 'The rest of them will be in Paris by the time he has made his mind up.' 'Paris can get on without him, *allez!* Let him stay here, and pay us a glass each; we're good enough society for him, I should think—a pair of honest Republicans, and thirsty!' 'What! Isn't this moisture sufficient for you— a night like this?' 'Ah, *ouate!* The more water there is, the more liquor you want to make it palatable. Pay me half a pint, and I'll be godfather to your next.' '*Farceur, va!*'

Mounting hastily the steps of a carriage in response to a further summons from the railway officials, Mr. Remington found himself face to face with Brother A. Neel, of the I.O.T.A.

'Aha!' exclaimed the latter cordially, 'fellow-travellers, after all, sir! I did not see you on the boat, and thought you might have decided to stay the night at Dover.'

'Well, I made up my mind to come on at once,' replied the other, to all appearance satisfied with his companion. 'I shall get back the sooner. We are more than five hours from Paris, and I can sleep better travelling at night than in the daytime.'

'In that, you are like myself,' said the first, pleasantly.

Another passenger ascended the steps, and took a place with them. It was Bartholomew Finch, *alias* Walker. Behind him came a French official, who demanded their tickets : '*Paris—Paris—Paris—bien!*' The official swung on one side, slammed the door, and passed along the step to the neighbouring compartments.

'They don't lock the doors, I observe!' said Brother Neel.

'No; they just let down a latch outside, below the handle. That secures the door, without imprisoning the passenger.'

'All that's necessary—and more convenient,' remarked Brother Neel.

The engine emitted a despondent squeal, and coughed asthmatically. Its bronchial tubes had obviously suffered from exposure to severe weather. Once on the high road to Boulogne, however, there was no fault to be found with its notion of express speed.

'Been this way many times before, sir?' inquired Mr. Remington.

'On business of the "Iota" I usually make the journey by this line,' replied Brother Neel effusively. ' "Iota?"— ah, yes, I forgot you were not one of us; that is our familiar appellation, our pet name, I may say, for the Order in which we are enrolled—International Organization of Total Abstainers; don't you see?—an easy abbreviation, which forms at the same time a sort of affectionate sobriquet, don't you know! one of those endearing nicknames which are so often met with among the members of harmonious families. And what is our great, our noble Order, but a family upon the widest, the most humanitarian scale! The administrative affairs of the "Iota" do occasionally require my attendance at the Paris branch. But that is not the motive of my present visit. No; there are certain special aspects of the drink traffic, in the French metropolis, which are capable of emphatically illustrating and enforcing the truths of our great cause, and which for our purposes have never yet been adequately studied. I have a mission to collect material on those aspects of the drink traffic, for our lectures and pamphlets and public demonstrations. Ah, this is a weighty, a colossal question, sir, it is indeed! Think of the correlation between alcoholism and crime! I wish—I wish I could induce you to enrol yourself in our valiant army.'

'Very sorry, sir; but it wouldn't suit *my* constitution! Let those do it whom it suits. *I* don't complain, and I don't want to interfere with them.'

'Dear me—dear me!—what a sad and dangerous, what a

terrible and infinitely perilous frame of mind! I would
wager, now, that the unfortunate young man whose apprehension we witnessed at Dover was addicted, now, to the
use of alcohol. I would wager it! When shall we rend
our fetters, and free ourselves from this gigantic incubus,
which is oppressing the heart's blood of civilization, over-
shadowing its mighty pulses, and trailing in the dust and
mire the snow-white name of Christianity?'

The tumultuous imagery of Brother Neel's rhetorical
enthusiasm appeared to extinguish what powers of rejoinder
lay at the disposal of Mr. Remington. Their only companion in the compartment began to nod, as though he had
dropped off into a doze. Mr. Remington eyed him sharply,
and presently allowed his own lids to fall. Brother Neel
stared vaguely at the notices in three languages which apprised the isolated and imperilled traveller of the means
provided to him for ensuring his personal safety, and which
likewise threatened him with penalties for making use of
them. The temperance lecturer moved his lips now and
then, raised his eyebrows, frowned, and slightly tossed his
head, as though he were again rehearsing perorations.
Thus they ran on till they reached Boulogne, the first of
the four stoppages on their road to Paris. They might have
counted upon remaining undisturbed throughout the journey;
but Mr. Remington, who had got up to consult his time-table
by the light of a station lamp, was obliged to give way to
allow ingress to a new-comer, It was Ernest Vine, *alias*
Grainger, *alias*, again, Mr. Pritchard.

The night-mail sped out of Boulogne-sur-Mer and turned
inland, leaving for good the sand-hills of the coast. Its
next destination was Abbeville; but in spite of the considerable distance to be traversed, Mr. Remington's faculty
for sleeping in night journeys by the train seemed to have
deserted him. His thoughts were evidently as much absorbed as ever by the personality of Mr. Pritchard. His
eyes resumed their restless examination of the hawk-like
countenance which, this time at any rate, faced, not himself, but another of the travellers—the undersized tenant
of the ample ulster. The new-comer had sunk unobtrusively into his place, just as he did at the outset of the
journey. The cane which he deposited in the rack, above
his head, had decidedly the aspect of a sword-stick; the

small black bag upon his knees might have held conveniently
a pair of handcuffs and a revolver; it seemed almost a pity
that he was Mr. Pritchard, bound for the south of France, and
not, as the observer had too readily suspected, the passenger
from Scotland Yard. Mr. Remington drew forth his pocket-
flask, and took a plentiful draught.

'Abbeville!' shouted a porter, as they ran into a dismal
station, hardly anything of which was visible in the darkness of the night. 'Abbeville, Abbeville!' echoed faintly
down the platform. The train came to a standstill; Mr.
Remington folded his rug over one arm; and in another
moment the door was hanging open, and there were only
three passengers in the compartment. The celerity with
which he had accomplished this exit was remarkable in a
gentleman of his size. With an almost equal celerity, however, Brother Neel stepped out after him. The temperance
lecturer had, indeed, hesitated an instant, but a glance at
the two travelling companions who were left to him apparently sufficed to lead him to a prompt decision.

When Brother Neel alighted on the Abbeville platform
the French guard was already signalling the train onwards.
He made for the only other carriage-door which hung open,
and found himself again alone with Mr. Remington. The
night-mail dashed away in the direction of Amiens.

'I did not like the look of those men,' said Mr. Remington, somewhat embarrassed.

'Nor did I myself, I am bound to confess,' replied Brother
Neel; 'and I thought I would follow your example. One
may be doing them an injustice; but—well, there! I did
not like their look.'

'Not that *I* ever make these long journeys with large
sums of money about me. I buy in rather extensive
quantities, but I always pay my dealers in Paris by draft
on an English banking-house which has a Paris branch.
I never travel with much more than the small change
absolutely necessary. In fact, I lost over the last transaction in the Paris market, and trade has been so bad
that I had thought it hardly worth while coming over to
buy.'

'Dear me! And do they consider this line to the North
at all insecure? I mean—the cases of outrage, and so
forth, on the French railway systems—the cases we have

read of in the public press : are they associated, now, with
this line at all ?'

'The Northern line ?   Oh, no.   I should say that the
southern and eastern railways of France are more dangerous, but there was a mysterious case some time ago on a
western line ; it was never cleared up.'

' A case of—— ?'

' Murder !'

' Bless me—now, really ! Well, well.   It would not in
the least surprise me if that Mr. Pritchard, as he calls himself, were a detective-officer after all, though I don't know
why he should deny it.   But those men love to make a
little mystery ; it attracts attention to them, flatters their
vanity, and makes them appear important even when they
have achieved nothing.'

' You seem to know them, sir,' said Mr. Remington, with
a smile.

' Oh, very slightly, very slightly, I assure you.   But one
of our dear friends—not a colleague in the I.O.T.A., but a
brother lecturer in the temperance cause, a worthy, dear
friend, he was, and an able—almost fell a victim some few
years ago to the malice and obstinacy of one of these men,
and none of us, I am sure, are ever likely to forget the
event.   For my part, I must say that I regard the com-
panionship of detective-officers as little less compromising
than that of criminals.   Who knows where detectives have
sprung from ?   They do say that ex-thieves make the very
best thief-takers.   Imagine honest people at the mercy of
an ex-criminal !   The painful case of my worthy dear friend
inspired me with an aversion for the entire class, although
there are members of the detective force enrolled in our
organizations.'

' Well, if that man isn't from Scotland Yard I'm greatly
mistaken.   He has quite the cut of it ; and they go wrong
so often—as in the case you speak of—that I am glad to be
out of his company.'

The conversation drifted into general topics.   While thus
engaged they were both startled momentarily by the sudden
appearance of a head at the window.

' Oh, the ticket-inspector, of course !' exclaimed Mr.
Remington, laughing jovially.

' What—once more ?' said Brother Neel.

'The last time on the journey,' explained the other.

The inspection of the tickets was performed as usual by the French guard of the train, who passed from compartment to compartment, opening the doors easily and closing them again quietly, as the mail rushed at its fastest rate towards Paris. Brother Neel remarked upon the possible danger of this operation, on a night, as he said with striking originality, ' dark as Erebus ;' but Mr. Remington assured him that the process was the simplest thing in the world, and that there were details in the construction of the carriages which expressly facilitated it.

' What other stoppages lay before us ?' asked the temperance lecturer.

'Two more, between this and Paris,' replied his companion, ' Amiens and Creil. At Amiens we get from five to fifteen minutes, according to the time of the train, and we're late to-night, or rather this morning. At Creil we only touch.'

Mr. Remington forthwith disposed himself comfortably for a nap. Brusquely opening his eyes after a silence of ten or twelve minutes, he found his travelling companion so intently observing him that he became all at once wide awake again. Was it curiosity, calculation—or what— that he read for an instant, an instant only, in the square face opposite him? Brother Neel met his anxious and surprised scrutiny with the air of bland attention which appeared to be his professional manner. Mr. Remington changed his position, and did not again close his eyes.

They ran into the spacious Amiens station. ' Just time to cross to the buffet,' muttered Mr. Remington, after listening to the announcement of the porters. He descended from the carriage, but did not cross to the buffet. He loitered on the platform for a moment, and then proceeded to a different carriage altogether. The fresh compartment he chose, however, appeared to have been selected by other people, also desirous of seeking other places. Mr. Pritchard, flanked by Bartholomew Finch, *alias* Walker, clambered up the step, and deliberately took the two corner seats at the entrance. Calling to a railway official that he had mistaken his compartment, Mr. Remington had just time to descend again, and grasp the handle of a neighbouring door. The official grumbled at him in his native tongue, and helped him up as the train began to move.

'It's no go till we get there,' pronounced one of the two persons he had so promptly deserted, Mr. Finch, *videlicet*— 'he has "tumbled" to something—that's sure!'

'He can "tumble" to what he likes, now,' responded the other. 'I'm going to get it before I leave this train.'

''Ere—mind what I said,' urged Mr. Finch; 'no putting him out!'

'No putting him out? Well, how do you think we are going to get it?' savagely retorted Vine, *alias* Grainger, speaking nevertheless in a very low tone. 'Do you suppose he's going to put his hand into his pocket and pull out a velvet case with £20,000 worth in it, and pass it over?'

'Well, you can wait a few hours, or a day or so, can't you? Anyhow, I won't be in this if there's to be any putting-out.'

'Perhaps you'd like to wait until the property has gone out of his possession, and they have all three of them shared the money? Perhaps you'd like to pick his pocket nice and comfortably, and get his purse with a ten-pound note in it, instead of the small fortune Clements promised? There are three of them in this, and it's as clear as day. The secretary hangs about the house in Park Lane shortly before the night of the robbery. The robbery takes place, and the secretary goes away in a suspicious manner. The other two then put the police on him; the butler pretends to have reasons for believing that Sinclair means to go by Dover to the Continent; they send him down in the morning, and he waits for the arrival of the train with the plain-clothes man who has followed Sinclair in the hope of dropping across confederates. At Dover, he identifies the secretary, and the police make the arrest. Of course the secretary has been searched by this time, and they've not found anything; and, of course, as to the robbery in Park Lane, he'll have a perfect *alibi*. By the time Sinclair had been released, in default of evidence, the property was to have been got rid of; and *this* is the man who was to have got rid of it. I thought at first that this man and the butler were doing it between them, but I see all three are in it. Wait a few hours! And what about Byde—what chance should we have when we get to Paris? There's a

man I *will* put-out some day, if he causes me much trouble
—Mr. Inspector Byde! He hasn't recognised either you
or me, but it was a lucky thing I got that telegram. It isn't
the first time I've been taken for a detective, but it's the
first time I said I wasn't one. We shall have to look sharp
about getting out of the Paris station. If Byers isn't there
to meet us we must get away without him.'
  ' Grandpa's certain to be there, if he said he would.
What is the other place we stop at?'
  ' Creil,' answered the pseudo Mr. Pritchard, referring to a
small train bill; ' and after Creil there is a clear run of fifty
minutes to Paris. We must do it between Creil and Paris.'
  The night-mail had not altogether made up its arrear
when it emerged from the darkness enveloping the entrance
to the northern terminus at Paris, and placidly stole into the
feebly-lighted station. Beyond the barrier, where the railway servants posted themselves for collecting the tickets,
there was the customary assemblage, even at that early
hour, of persons awaiting the arrival of their friends. The
few passengers descended gladly enough, and straggled
along the platform towards the ticket-gates. The supposititious Mr. Pritchard passed through among the first.
Not far behind him came Mr. Finch in one of the folds of
his flapping ulster; and then followed a knot of dazed
voyagers, confused with the abrupt change, but making
blindly for the nearest exit. After these marched Brother
Neel, erect and deliberate, not to say portentous, but pale
from the fatigues of travelling. The railway officials
lingered at their posts for a few seconds, and then, one
after the other, closed the gates of the slight barrier. All
the voyagers had evidently passed through. Mr. Remington,
however, had not been one of the voyagers who had passed
through.

CHAPTER IV.

AMONG the persons assembled at the Nord terminus, to
meet the passengers by the overnight London mail, there
was a rather tall, fairly good-looking young man, of decidedly British aspect, who, instead of joining the group
just outside the barrier, had preferred to remain within the

spacious but barn-like waiting-room, from whose glass partition he could easily survey the arrivals, without being
distinctly seen himself. From the point at which he was
placed, the end ticket-collector stood almost within arm's
reach, although, of course, they were separated by the
partition. The lamps which aided the collectors in their
work, facilitated the scrutiny directed by this sturdily-built
young man upon the faces of the voyagers, as the latter
approached, delivered their tickets, and filed past. So
absorbed was he by his occupation, that he did not perceive
a trifling incident of which the waiting-room was the scene,
and in which he himself appeared to play an unconscious
part. Had he been free to observe that incident, he might,
no doubt, have deemed it worthy of attention, slight though
it seemed. An elderly gentleman who had come up in great
haste, as if in fear of arriving too late for the passengers by
the train, was hurrying across the waiting-room, when he
caught sight of the solitary watchman at the glass partition.
The elderly gentleman immediately pulled up short, and
retraced his steps with redoubled speed. Turning to the
left, he trotted into the station courtyard, where the cabs
and luggage-omnibuses were beginning to bestir themselves,
and, veering again to the left, he got to the outer doors
as the first of the departing travellers passed through
the hands of the revenue officials. The latter proceeded to
put their usual questions to the possessors of hand-packages.
Vine *alias* Granger was requested to exhibit the interior of
the small black bag. Whatever might have been its contents, they were clearly not contraband goods, and the
owner of the bag at once turned to the right and moved
towards the station gates. Mr. Finch followed closely upon
his heels, wearing an air which seemed to say he knew he
was in a foreign land, and unprotected, but that he rather
knew his way about, for all that.

The elderly gentleman stayed for a few moments facing
the threshold, scanned one or two of the figures pushing out,
and then in a disappointed manner returned in the direction
of the courtyard gates. A porter called to him that the
majority of the passengers had not yet issued forth, but the
other was apparently hard of hearing. ' Old imbecile !'
added the porter, looking after him. At the station gates
the elderly gentleman overtook our two acquaintances, and

passed them hastily. He traversed the wide street, made for the corner of the Rue Lafayette, dived into this thoroughfare, and presently arrested his course in front of a cab which stood drawn up by the pavement. The cabman had descended from his box, and was stamping his feet and striking his gloved hands together. The elderly gentleman opened the door of the vehicle, and told the man to drive to the Central Markets. As he held the door open, Vine, *alias* Grainger, or Pritchard, came up with Mr. Finch.

'After you, grandpa,' said Mr. Finch politely.

'Now then, Bat, jump in,' growled Vine, *alias* Grainger. 'We don't know who's behind us.'

'I'm behind you, for one,' returned Mr. Finch, with cheerful humour. 'In you get, grandpa—age before honesty! I'm going to try a glass of this hot stuff.'

A vendor of steaming black coffee had installed himself some yards away.

'Jump up, will you?' repeated the other fiercely.

'Look here, Bat,' said their elderly companion rapidly, 'we don't want any of this—game!'

'All right—all right,' responded Mr. Finch imperturbably; 'but if Mr. clever Sir John here ain't brought it off, as he says he ain't, I want to know what we've got to be in a hurry about.'

'Not brought it off! Do you mean to say you've not brought it off, John?' inquired grandpa anxiously.

The object of his query had already seated himself in the cab, and for all answer urged the other two, with an oath, to mount beside him.

'Not me!' responded Mr. Finch, with calmness. 'A nice thing this is! Here's a man I'm sent to do a bit of business with, and, when we get the chance to do it, he says he thinks he can manage it better by himself. I let him go and do it, because so long as it's *got*, whether he does it or I do it, I have my terms from old Clements, don't I! Well, I bar putting-out, and he agrees; and then he gets out of the compartment to go and do it, and I never see him again until we both get out at Parry, just this instant. And then, when I ask him about it, he says he ain't brought it off. A nice thing this is! I thought I was working with a clever man. If he ain't brought it off, what are we to run away for? Where's the man we've come after—why

ain't we following him? What could you want better than
this !'

He glanced upwards at the sky. The rain had ceased,
but it was still quite dark. Grandpa put his head inside
the cab.

'Have you missed it, yes or no ?' he demanded curtly.

'Yes,' was the reply, emphasised with an imprecation.

'Then where is he ?'

'Where is he !' The speaker made a gesture which was
lost in the gloom. 'Stop here as long as you like,' he
added savagely, 'but don't blame me if you get taken.'

'Why, John, you alarm me ! Get in, Bat; we'll have an
explanation as we go along. There's evidently something
very wrong with this affair.'

The vehicle started on its journey towards the Central
Markets.

'Yes, we've got nothing, and appearances are all against
us,' resumed Vine, *alias* Grainger; 'but I know where to
look for it, if we can get clear now, and find the man
out afterwards.' He sprang up from the seat and looked
through the small pane of glass at the back of the carriage.
'I thought so !' he exclaimed excitedly; 'there's a cab
following us.'

'Why, who can be in it ?' said grandpa.

'Byde of Scotland Yard came down from London to
Dover. He hid himself on the Channel boat, and we haven't
seen him since. I'll lay a thousand he has come through,
and if he's in that cab he'll never leave us.'

'Won't he !' said grandpa, rendered extremely serious
by the name his companion had pronounced. 'He won't
leave? Oh, oh ! we shall have to be severe with Inspector
Byde. But, before I take steps of any kind, I must know
exactly how this matter stands; because, if you're not
dealing fair and square with me, you don't go any farther in
my cab. Inspector Byde may be after you, and the whole of
the French police as well, for all I care ; I don't move a step
for a man who doesn't deal fair and square. When I under-
took this business with Clements, I stipulated that there
was to be nothing previously against either of the men who
were coming over. I am not going to be compromised for a
single moment, remember that plainly. If you were not
wanted for anything up to eight o'clock last night, when you

left London by the mail, why should you be running away
from Inspector Byde, or anyone else, this morning? How
can it matter to either of you who is in that cab—come?'
Mr. Finch kicked viciously at the foot-warmer lying in the
well of the conveyance. Sir John made no answer.
' Surely,' pursued the elderly gentleman, in a softer tone,
' surely you are not thinking to bamboozle grandpa? Is
that it? Is that a sort of little game that *you* would try
on, Bartholomew Finch, *alias* Walker, late of the Old
Bailey, and formerly of Clerkenwell Court-House?'

' Me?' replied the youth thus interrogated; 'not me!
Bamboozle *you*, grandpa? Not me!—no!—not me, Mr.
Wilkins!'

' Well—is it a sort of little game that *you* would try on,
Mr. Ernest Vine, of Clements and Company? Do you
think I should stand that, John—do you think any man of
my years and experience could put up with it? I give you
half-a-minute to turn it over in your mind.'

Sir John sat up straight with a jerk, and pulled off the
fur-tipped glove of his right hand.

' Get us home,' he exclaimed sullenly, ' and I will tell
you the whole story. Does that look like bamboozling
you?'

He opened his right hand wide. The fingers and palm
were smeared with blood.

' We must throw this cab off at once, if it's really following us,' said grandpa promptly. He stood up and glanced
through the small pane of glass. ' Yes,—we are being followed. However, we'll soon set that little matter right.'
He twisted the button which sounded the bell-signal to the
driver. ' Stop at the first wine-shop or café you find open,'
he called, in ready but Britannic French.

A little farther on the cabman pulled up in front of a
small wine-shop, which apparently had not long before been
thrown open. Grandpa stepped out of the vehicle and bade
his companions follow him.

' What's this?' demanded Sir John suspiciously.

' The shortest way. All you have to do is to follow me,
and look sharp about it. I dare say I can get you out of this
for the present, but whatever happens *I* mustn't be seen.'
Grandpa muffled himself up so closely that his short white
whiskers and fresh pink cheeks almost entirely disappeared.

Darting across the pavement into the wine-shop, he gave an order at the counter, and took his seat in a nook removed from general observation. He then directed Mr. Bartholomew to watch the movements of the other vehicle. 'It can only be a case of precaution, whatever it is,' he added, 'or we should have been stopped immediately.'

An unwashed waiter in his shirt-sleeves brought the blotting-pad and writing materials of the establishment. While grandpa proceeded to address an envelope, the waiter returned sleepily for their glasses of hot black coffee. He was blinking and yawning, and stumbled against Mr. Bartholomew Finch as the latter sauntered from the threshold towards his companions.

'The cab has pulled up a short distance away, and no one has got out of it,' he reported.

'There's no doubt about it, then,' said grandpa.

He was manifestly taking great pains to disguise the handwriting of the address, but there his trouble ended. The sheet of paper which he folded and enclosed within the envelope was blank. The postage-stamp requisite he obtained on paying at the counter. Remounting the cab, grandpa gave the order to continue towards the Central Markets.

'They're after us,' announced Mr. Finch, who had applied his eye to the small glass pane.

The approaches to the Halles were impeded with the carts and waggons which, laden with all kinds of provisions, wend their way every morning to these vast Central Markets. Grandpa shouted a precise direction to their coachman, and they soon found themselves involved in long lines of vehicles converging towards a particular point. Reaching a large corner tavern, thronged with market-gardeners, butchers, poulterers, and other people whose avocations brought them regularly to the Halles, the cabman slackened his pace, but a further order was shouted to him to turn the corner and to come to a standstill at the other entrance.

'It's almost unnecessary,' murmured the spry, elderly gentleman, as he peeped once more through the square of glass; 'they seem to have lost us as it is.' Obeying his instructions, nevertheless, the driver turned the corner, and drew up at one of the tavern entrances on the other side. Grandpa promptly hopped out of the carriage, and closed

THE PASSENGER FROM SCOTLAND YARD.

the door the moment he had been followed by his companions. 'Go back to the Gare du Nord,' said he, handing the coachman the envelope he had stamped and addressed —'go back as fast as you can, and post this in the station letter-box; it will be in time for the foreign mail if you post it there at once.'

The gratuity with which he accompanied the payment of the fares must have been considerable, for the coachman whipped his horse generously, and at once set off with an edifying show of zeal. The incident had been managed with despatch, and grandpa drew the others after him into the midst of the groups encumbering the pathway. The market-people, imbibing their *petit noir*, or their morning nip of rum, were noisily discussing prices, or joking, and fencing at bargains. As the cab just quitted made its way through the labyrinth of country carts and barrows, the other vehicle appeared at the corner, hemmed in for an instant by a couple of heavy waggons. Both windows of the cab were down, and the three watchers could distinctly see the whole of the interior. The vehicle had but a single occupant. He was gazing anxiously about him, and presently leaned out of the far side to indicate the departing cab to his own coachman.

Vine, *alias* Grainger, and Mr. Finch, stared at each other with astonishment.

'What has *he* got to do with us?' demanded Bartholomew; 'I never saw him before!'

'It isn't Byde, that's one thing,' returned Mr. Vine; 'and so long as he isn't Byde, I don't care who he is. Do you know him, grandpa?'

'I have that distinguished pleasure,' replied their elderly friend, shooting his shirt-cuff; 'yes, my boys, I do know the gentleman, although up to the present time of day the gentleman does not know me. That is Toppin—Mr. Toppin —Detective Toppin: a praiseworthy, active, and conscientious officer kept in Paris by Scotland Yard. Toppin is full of ardour, and will no doubt improve. But he is not yet what we understand by a "flyer;" no—Toppin isn't a flyer! He'll follow that cab—oh, he won't lose sight of that cab! —he'll follow that cab, I dare say, till the cabman takes it home to-night. He'll go right back to the Northern terminus, Toppin will—right back to where he came from!'

'How do you know he came from the Northern terminus?'

'Because I saw him there, my little dears! He was there to meet your train, and if, as you say, Byde was a traveller by the night-mail, he was most likely there to meet his eminent and respected but not necessarily infallible colleague, Inspector Byde. And you may take your oath, boys, that Byde has sent him after you—perhaps on the offchance, perhaps not. We can make our minds up when we hear your little story, John.'

'That's all very well, Byers,' said Vine, *alias* Grainger, with another look of suspicion, 'but what did you put in that letter?'

'A sheet of notepaper with nothing on it,' responded grandpa—'and on the envelope I put a fancy address, in a disguised handwriting. Suppose the man goes back to the station and drops it in the letter-box—no harm is done. Suppose he simply drops it in the first letter-box he comes to—no harm is done. Suppose he forgets to post it altogether, as he may do—for I didn't ask him for his ticket—and intoxicates himself on the tip I gave him—no harm is done: and Mr. Toppin will have to do the best he can. Well, now, we needn't drink anything here; in fact, we couldn't get attended to, if we wanted anything. I will take you to your hotel—a snug little place, out of the way. —There's blood on that handkerchief of yours, Jack—keep it out of sight!'

CHAPTER V.

WHILE Mr. Byers—to adopt the name under which grandpa had been interrogated by Vine, *alias* Grainger— was inscribing an apocryphal address upon the envelope containing a blank sheet of paper, a gentleman who had just taken up his quarters at the Terminus Hotel, nearly opposite the Gare du Nord, proceeded to indite an epistle which threatened, on the contrary, to extend to rather formidable dimensions. He was one of the travellers by the night-mail from London, and he had a letter to send off by the return post, he informed the obsequious waiter of the hotel café; for this reason he would be glad of writing

materials at once, and would defer partaking of the refresh-
ments so glibly enumerated until his important missive had
been sent on its way. Oh, but monsieur had plenty of
time! Monsieur could post at the station letter-box just
across the road up to a few minutes before the departure of
the mail. With that fact he was perfectly well acquainted,
replied the monsieur : that fact alone had impelled him to
put up at the establishment, seeing that when he had
breakfasted there once before they had served him a beefsteak which was a calumny upon the Continent. Ah!
monsieur was English?—American? 'Bring me the largest
sheet of paper in the establishment.' A very large sheet of
paper—certainly, monsieur. Oh, he knew England well,
the waiter did, having passed a year in Battersea to learn
the tongue—Battersea—monsieur knew that quarter, perhaps? A very nice quarter. Oh, yes, very nice, very
handsome! A large sheet of paper, was it not? Immediately, monsieur! White paper or blue?—because if
monsieur wanted blue they had none. Ah, it did not
matter?—blue, green, or yellow—precisely : monsieur being
in a hurry. There was nearly an hour and a half yet before
the departure of the morning mail—plenty of time! Where
he was in Battersea they served great number of beefsteaks
—steak-and-potate—and great quantity chocolate, and ices.
The air of Battersea was not too active, and suited him ;
but having learnt the tongue he came back to a situation
to speak English towards English and American visitors,
though monsieur himself spoke French very nice—oh, yes,
indeed, very nicefully!

The caligraphy of this early arrival at the Terminus
Hotel was of a character that might have secured for him
the second or even the first prize for penmanship in the most
genteel of suburban collegiate schools for young gentlemen.
How beautifully regular the lines!—how fine the up-strokes!
—and the down-strokes, how symmetrically swelling and
how firm! And the fingers that guided the pen through such
elegant small-hand and such even text were those of a
middle-aged man who did not in the least look like a
schoolmaster, or like any other sort of person accustomed
to set copies for his livelihood. The phrases, too, which he
had uttered in the language of the country had almost
merited the encomium they had received. They were un-

doubtedly of a quality to earn the French prize at the suburban collegiate school. The gentleman in question wrote his letter and spoke his French a little laboriously, perhaps, but then he did not make a single blot upon the paper, and in what he said there was not one grammatical mistake.

He began by placing the superscription on the envelope; and it ran as follows, after the name of the recipient with a sub-line beneath it : ' Criminal Investigation Department, Great Scotland Yard, London, S.W.'

The exact terms of the epistle itself were the following : ' Wilmot (Park Lane) Affair.—This case has taken an unexpected turn. In accordance with my instructions yesterday afternoon I endeavoured without delay to ascertain the movements of Samuel Remington. He made no attempt to avoid observation, and talked freely with neighbours on the subject of the robbery. He expressed great sympathy for the friends of Sinclair, and deplored for their sake the impossibility of keeping the affair out of the papers.

' Remington has been in the habit for some time past of visiting Paris for the purposes of his business two or three times a year. He was regretting yesterday that his periodical journey to the Continent should compel him to absent himself for a few days at this juncture, and owing to the slackness of trade would apparently have relinquished the journey had it not been for a substantial order telegraphed to him by a country client. With the assistance of Sergeant Bell I found that an order had, as a matter-of-fact, been telegraphed to him. The telegram, however, came from Dover, a coincidence which the Department will appreciate. Sergeant Bell undertakes to obtain the name given by the sender, and this part of the inquiry I have left in his charge. Remington made appointments in London for the end of the week. I found that his present visit to Paris was a month in advance of his usual visit at this time of the year.

' He left his residence at 7.15 p.m., and I followed him to Charing Cross. He had no luggage but a valise. He took a return ticket to Paris, and I looked after him and got a seat in the same compartment. It was evident that he did not suspect me of watching him ; at the same time he seemed to be uneasy, and, from what I could divine, had

expected to see someone at the station who did not put in
an appearance.

‘ Three other persons presently entered the compartment
at short intervals. The first I fancy I must have seen
somewhere ; he had the look of a flash thief, but I had no
reason for suspecting him. The second I did not know at
all ; but the third, who arrived just before the departure of
the train, I feel certain I have met at some time or other.
It was annoying to be unable to fix his identity, though I
felt that if my impression with regard to this man were
right, it could not be recently that I had come across him.

‘ Remington compromised himself repeatedly on the way
down. From the first he seemed to be convinced that he
was being watched by the man I have just referred to—the
last of the other three passengers. In his anxiety to test
the correctness of his suspicion, he broached the subject of
the robbery himself, and during the conversation which
ensued upon it hardly removed his eyes from the man’s
face. Sinclair was promptly taken into custody at Dover,
and Remington professed to condole with him as he went
by on the platform. At Dover Pier Station the guard of
the train came to our compartment as well as to others,
with a telegram addressed to the ‘ Passenger from Scotland
Yard,’ care of himself, at Dover Pier. As Remington plainly
had no notion whatever of my own identity, I thought it
better not to claim the telegram—to risk its loss rather than
open his eyes, especially as it was competent for me to wire
for its contents directly I got free. I therefore allowed the
message to go by. I trust that the course I took may
occasion no inconvenience, but I was strengthened in the
resolve I arrived at by certain symptoms on the part of two
among the other travellers. It will be remembered that
the case placed in my hands was one of the vaguest suspicion only. If Sinclair was the thief, and Remington was
really his confederate, the former had probably hidden the
diamonds among common goods and thus forwarded them
by parcels delivery to an address in Paris, where Remington
would call for them. Such, as I understood it, was the
theory. With Sinclair denounced by Remington, the latter
would not readily be suspected of complicity with him. No
evidence would be forthcoming against Sinclair, and in the
meantime Remington would get the property off his hands.

I hope the Department may agree that I was right to preserve my incognito.

'Following Remington on board the channel boat, I fancied I saw grounds for believing that he was, in fact, being watched by the man above referred to, whom I likewise detected in secret communication with the (presumably) flash pickpocket who had travelled in the same carriage. I was uncertain how far I might be known to one of these individuals, if not to both, and for that reason decided to keep out of sight if possible during the rest of the journey. On the assumption that the theory we have acted upon was well founded, it appeared to me that these two individuals—about whose character the more I saw of them the less I entertained a doubt—had by some means or other got wind of the object of Remington's journey. It appeared to me that if I should trace Remington to any Paris address where a package was awaiting him, I should most probably discover that he had been likewise traced thither by those two men. But while I was concealing my own whereabouts from them I inevitably lost sight of their movements a good deal. At Amiens, looking along the train, I saw Remington descend from his compartment, but only for a moment, the stoppage being of less than the ordinary duration.

'On our arrival at the Northern terminus, Paris, I watched each passenger through the gates, the two men I speak of with the rest. To my surprise, Remington did not pass out. Toppin, however, at once came up with both the telegrams despatched to him by the Department, the second containing the substance of the message to myself which had miscarried. It was then that I recollected the man who ostensibly proved the alibi in the Golden Square case, two years ago—Vine, *alias* Grainger. I had just time to point him out to Toppin; and in view of the reiterated directions by telegram, Toppin hastened after Vine and his companion, to make sure of their whereabouts in case of need. I now await his return.

'While the last few travellers who had brought heavy luggage with them were going out of the gates, after the examination of their trunks by the Custom House officers, a porter ran to the entrance of the platform with the news that a dead body had been found in one of the carriages.

From Boulogne the passengers had not been numerous, and a considerable proportion of the compartments were unoccupied. On our arrival at Paris, therefore, several of the doors remained closed until the porters went through the train, and it was while this operation was being performed that the corpse was discovered.

‘ Conjecturing from Remington's non-appearance that the body might be his, I made myself known to the English through-guard. He was astonished when I showed him my card, for, influenced by a remark made, tentatively, perhaps, by Remington at Dover Pier, he had taken the man Vine for an officer of the Department, and, upon finding a second telegram at Calais, had privately addressed himself to that individual. Vine profited by the error to obtain possession of the message, enjoining the guard to say and do nothing that might hamper him in his imaginary mission. Of the contents of that second message I am necessarily ignorant, but presume it warned me of the departure of two suspicious characters by the night-mail, in the same terms as the telegram care of Toppin. Consequently, Vine and Finch have known, since the stoppage at Calais, that the Department is aware of their leaving by the mail, and that a special detective-officer has been told off to act with Toppin, of Paris. They may or may not guess at a connection between my errand and the Wilmot Case ; and, on the other hand, one can only guess at present that between their own errand and the Wilmot case there may have been some connection. The theory implicating Remington was one of the vaguest, when submitted to ourselves ; how can it have passed into the cognizance of men like Vine and Finch? Upon this point an idea occurs to me which, when matured, I will communicate to the Department. It is unfortunate that the inadvertence I describe should have happened. Under the circumstances, however, it was perhaps natural enough. It was vital that my presence should not be known to the party or parties ; the Department wished urgently to communicate with me, but preferred to avoid mentioning my name ; Vine was mistrusted by Remington, and was indicated to the guard as possibly the passenger he was looking for ; and the guard subsequently inquired in private of Vine himself whether such was not the case. That Vine should have answered falsely in the affirmative implies, to my mind, that he and his companion had come on business.

' It seems that the searching of the early morning trains, on the descent of the passengers, is often performed in a careless manner, and has sometimes been postponed for fully an hour. In the present instance the searching had begun some ten or twelve minutes after the delivery of the tickets. The news of the discovery was carried to the police commissary attached to the terminus; and it was only by the aid of the through-guard that I was enabled to get a view of the body before the arrival of that functionary. As I expected, the dead man was Samuel Remington.

' The deceased was in a recumbent position, with his head supported by a shawl rolled up to form a pillow. He was lying on his right side along the seat nearest to the engine, with his feet only an inch or two from the door. In the left temple there was a bullet wound from a firearm of small calibre, and I should say that he was perhaps asleep until the moment before the injury was inflicted. The features were not distorted, but wore an expression of surprise; his right arm was doubled-up under him, and his left arm had been thrown back, and lay extended behind him. The flow of blood had not been copious, but there were blood-stains about his clothes and elsewhere. His travelling cloak and undercoat were unbuttoned, one of the cloth buttons of the latter garment lying on the seat, at the back, as though the coat had been wrenched violently open. He wore a sealskin vest, of which only the top buttons were unfastened; but a left-hand breast-pocket in the lining of the vest had apparently been turned inside out, and was torn at one of the edges. I had not many moments allowed me for seizing these details. My examination was quite irregular, and I was stopped as I attempted to carry it further. But I was able to note that rings were on the fingers of the right hand, which was ungloved, that the watch and chain had not been taken, and that there was money—to what amount I could not ascertain—in the pockets. With regard to the breast-pocket, it was noticeable that the torn edge was at the left or upper corner, not at the right or lower corner. By a better light it would have been possible to pronounce at once whether the threads

had been recently severed or not; but, apart from this, it
would seem as though the material must have been torn
from above, clearly not by the deceased himself, who, in
depositing articles in this pocket or withdrawing them,
would use his right hand, and of the two corners would
usually catch the right or lower one. I need hardly add
that there were no evidences of any struggle.

'Summing up the situation, the case would appear to be
one of murder, with the purpose of gaining possession of
some object believed to be in the custody of the deceased.
What was the nature of that object? It might be the Wilmot
diamonds; but if they were actually in his possession, the
original theory brought to us is upset. To test that theory,
Sinclair's movements should be minutely investigated from
the night of the robbery to the occasion of his arrest. If,
as we understand, and as appears probable, Remington can
have had no personal communication with Sinclair, did the
latter leave a package for Remington at some place agreed
upon, or did he send him any parcel through the ordinary
public channels? Remington may have considered a bold
course the safest one. Travellers do not as a rule suppose
that their neighbours may have £20,000 worth of valuables
in an inner waistcoat-pocket; and if he had decided to bring
the property over himself, his murderer must be found before we get again upon the trace of the Wilmot diamonds.
At the same time, the original theory may be the correct
one, after all. He may not have had the valuables about
him; and the murder, if committed for the purpose of
obtaining possession of them, may have been committed in
vain. The inner pocket of the vest may have been found
quite empty.

'Suspicion evidently points to the two men named in your
messages—Vine, *alias* Grainger or Smith, and Finch, *alias*
Walker. They are, of course, in Paris, and for all I know
may be at the present moment within a stone's-throw of the
hotel at which I am writing. What their familiarity with
Paris hiding-places may be I cannot say. In all probability
they have come here furnished with an address. It is extremely fortunate that I should have been able to place
Toppin so promptly upon their track: and this we owe to
your telegrams. Toppin will have seen them safely housed,
and then, by his relations with the French police, will secure

their arrest on suspicion. I am only just in time to catch
the return mail.'

The writer sealed up his long epistle, procured the necessary postage from the waiter, and directed that wondering
personage—who now appeared freshly-shaven, and with his
dingy flannel-shirt hidden by clean linen that was rigorously
white, with bluish tones—to keep an eye upon his travelling-
rug, etc., while he ran across to the late letter-box at the
terminus. He consulted the railway clock, dropped the
missive into the foreign box with a sigh of satisfaction, and
stepped into the telegraph-office to wire a message that his
'report was following by morning-mail.' While standing at
the desk he also scribbled a note in these brief terms, and in
quite an inferior handwriting :—

'DEAR MARY,—Tell the boy to watch Clements, of Tudor
Street. He is to try and find out if C. receives letters bearing Paris postmark, or foreign telegrams. Should C. appear
to be leaving for Continent, the boy is to wire me above
hotel. Give him what money he may want. He may see
some one from the Yard on the same tack, but that is to
make no difference. C. will be on the look-out for the Yard
people, and may prove too slippery for them. Don't forget
the dog's medicine.'

An address was already printed on the crumpled envelope
in which the foregoing note was enclosed. Mrs. Byde was
the name of the accipient, and she lived in Camberwell.

The passenger from Scotland Yard, returning across the
muddy street in the gray light of the winter morning, seemed
to be able to pick his way among the puddles and to look
on every side of him simultaneously. His friend the waiter,
surveying him from the doorway, as he approached, apparently found it difficult to classify the customer whom the
early mail had brought to the establishment that day. The
phraseograms he would habitually pour forth before the
Cockney who arrived to him an hungred, faltered and died
away upon his doubting lips. 'Chop-and-steaks-and-potate,'
'Cole-rosbif-and-pickells,' 'Fright-sole-or-gril-kidneys,'
'Hamannegs,'—these and other simple viands, richly
anointed with margarine, had always been favoured by the
aristocracy of Battersea on Saturday nights, the Sabbath,
and Bank Holiday. The waiter had derived therefrom a
poor impression of the English noble as a critic of the culi-

nary art; and so he commonly informed those members of
his family sphere who had not hitherto enjoyed the benefits
of travel. But the gentleman who had come that morning,
and who resembled externally any other kind of burly
gentleman from Battersea—a little on in years, perhaps—
had just at this moment a glacial air which froze upon the
waiter's tongue the cockney commonplace he usually reserved for English travellers with shabby hats and copper-
coloured horse-shoe scarf-pins. Inspector Byde had not
arrayed his person with the elegance of a Bond Street
fashion-plate, that was sure. It was clear he had no arrangement with his tailor by which he exhibited and
advertised, in return for a discount, or a drawback, or
' liberal treatment, sir,—oh, we know when we're dealing
with a gentleman, sir,' the harmonies of that artist, or his
symphonies—under the reader's reverence. No ; the inspector has the quickest of perceptions of all outward effects,
as his colleagues in the force know well. Who like him can
adapt mere nothings to the uses of disguise ? Who so completely can appear the clownish peasant, the sportive stock-
broker, the atrabiliary meeting-house Jeremiah ? When
left to himself, however, Inspector Byde takes refuge in his
oldest clothes, and lets his bushy beard grow. And yet you
would never confound him with Sergeant Bell. The waiter
swallowed his phraseogram of ' tea—coff—choclate—bottell-
beer,' and called down the pipe privily to the cook to give
his best care to the forthcoming order.
    The order, indeed, which presently followed that warning
was conceived in the happiest vein of gastronomical pro-
priety, not unblended with zest. Inspector Byde would
sometimes say at home in Camberwell that when they had
sent him abroad, on business of the Department, he might
have failed to bring them back the criminal, but he never
failed to bring a new dish to the Camberwell kitchen. He
used to add that he was a better cook than detective ; but
this was not the opinion of Mrs. Byde, who could not relish,
do what she would, the *tripes à la mode de Caen* which he
occasionally essayed, and who did not believe that the
mixture of tomatoes, butter, eggs, parsley, and garlic, with
pepper and salt, so often prepared in a frying-pan by the
inspector, after that brief trip of his to Marseilles, could
possibly be otherwise than baneful to a Protestant digestion.

And the valued Caledonian downstairs, who could vie with anyone in roast meats and boiled, objected strongly to the master's presence in the kitchen. Inspector Byde gave his order like a cook and a gentleman; and his ' Frenche he spake full fayre and fetisly.' He had not attended evening classes at the local institute for nothing ; and he would have rather thought that their local institute, at the corner of the terrace, ranked as high as any ' scole of Stratford-atte-Bowe.' Whenever he landed upon the soil of France, therefore, he conversed with perfect readiness in the three dialects, agreeably intermingled, which he had managed to acquire; the first from the bankrupt Bordeaux hosier, who, established in a London villa, instructed the local youth of both sexes and adults; the second, from the estimable Swiss pastor with whom he had once stayed for the benefit of his health ; and the other from the Marseilles warehouseman to whom he had been referred for certain information of departmental interest. He found that he always secured attention when he spoke to the natives in their own tongue.

As he waited for his breakfast, Mr. Byde looked round for a newspaper. Finding none to his taste, he plunged his hand into a capacious coat-pocket and produced a few articles which he examined, one by one, and then ranged on the table. There were two pipe-cases; a small book, like an education-primer ; several envelopes and sheets of note-paper, between a pair of card-board covers ; and a clumsy leathern case for spectacles. The spectacles were blue and large—so large and so densely blue that each lens might have been mistaken for a saucer in a tea-service of old china. Mr. Byde breathed on the glasses and re-folded them, and extracted a piece of lead-pencil from another pocket.

The waiter must have journeyed to and fro more often by a great deal than his service could have required. Every time he passed the table over which the strange gentleman was bending he craned a little to one side, as if he sought to catch a glimpse of that gentleman's occupation. Perhaps he fancied that the new arrival might be caricaturing the manager of the establishment, who was now displaying his portly person at the counter, or that his own—the waiter's —oval countenance, shaded by short and shining curls, had aroused the admiration of the intelligent stranger, who might be transferring the picture skilfully to paper. Making ready at length to lay the snow-white tablecloth, he saw that both his impressions were erroneous. The stranger was tracing figures which he could not for the life of him identify with any objects in that restaurant. He drew the same figures repeatedly on different scales, and two or three of them had been traced upon the marble-slab of the table itself. It looked like sorcery, especially when the designer of the lines and circles printed letters of the alphabet here and there, and muttered to himself; but the gentleman was perhaps an architect?

As a matter of fact it was the problem of an equilateral triangle, to be described on a given finite straight line, that Mr. Inspector Byde had been industriously solving upon the marble-slab of the café table. From that exercise he had proceeded to a solution of the problem : To draw, from a given point, a straight line equal to a given straight line.

'Let A,' muttered Mr. Byde, as he printed letters of the alphabet here and there, ' be the given point, and BC the given straight line : it is required to draw from the point A a straight line equal to BC. From the point A to B draw the straight line AB. Postulate 1 says that a straight line may be drawn from any one point to any other point; so that I at once go on to describe upon it the equilateral triangle DAB., producing the straight lines DA, DB, to E and F; in accordance with postulate 2, which states that a terminated straight line may be produced to any length in a straight line. From the centre B, at the distance BC, I describe the circle CGH, meeting DF at G, inasmuch as postulate 3 declares that a circle may be described from any centre, at any distance from that centre. I next, from the centre D, at the distance DG, describe the circle GKL, meeting DE at L. Now it follows from the definition that BC is equal to BG, and that AL and BC are each of them equal to BG. And as things which are equal to the same thing are equal to one another, AL is equal to BC ; wherefore, from the given point A a straight line AL has been drawn, equal to the given straight line BC.'

Inspector Byde surveyed his handiwork with approbation, and added, most conscientiously, ' Q. E. F.' He also demonstrated how, from the greater of two given straight

lines, a part may be cut off equal to the less; which being
accomplished, he again pronounced a somewhat unctuous
' Q. E. F.' He had not soared to lofty mathematical
eminences, as the reader will no doubt have observed.
Indeed, he had never been able to push his researches into
the eternal truths of Euclid's elements farther than proposition 12, the scholastic advantages which he had almost
religiously procured for Master Edgar Byde, the sole scion
of his house, and possibly a future ornament to the Yard,
having been as a rule beyond his own reach, notwithstanding the popular institute at the corner of the terrace. But
the inspector could do eight out of those twelve, he flattered
himself, as lucidly as anyone, and five of them he knew by
heart. Was this bad, when you were a busy man, and self-
instructed? He could not bring himself to seek assistance
from his erudite son; but he borrowed Master Byde's old
school-books, and retained them—having paid for them
himself—ard frequently consulted those portable volumes,
in secret. The dog's ears through the education-primer at
his left hand indicated the giddy pinnacle to which his son
had climbed in regions of pure geometry; and of those dog's-
ears, together with marginal illustrations of the horse, the
locomotive-engine, the steamship, and the most prominent
features of the least amiable of the teachers at his son's
school, Mr. Inspector Byde was very proud.

It was when there was nothing of particular urgency to
occupy his mind that the inspector resorted to his rudi-
mentary diagrams. Some people will sketch impromptu
forms when they are fancy free, will tear pieces of paper
into the minutest fragments, gnaw at their finger-nails,
whistle for the gratification of their neighbours, or pick
their teeth with the specific implement to which a length-
ened usage may have attached them. Inspector Byde filled
up odd quarters of an hour by proving a few familiar
theorems and solving a cherished problem or two which
Master Byde would assuredly. have disdained. It must
have been all plain-sailing, for the moment, in the Wilmot
affair. The passenger from Scotland Yard went on to
prove that the angles at the base of an isosceles triangle
are equal to one another, and that, if the equal sides be
produced, the angles on the other side of the base shall be
equal to one another, also : the corollary resulting from

which demonstration being that every equilateral triangle is likewise equiangular.

The waiter bustled in from the street, evidently burdened with a piece of exciting intelligence. Did monsieur know? There had been a dreadful deed in the train by which monsieur had travelled—a murder. He had just learnt all about it from his colleague at the restaurant next door but three. Frightful, was it not?

'What, you have heard of it already, at this end of the street?' said the inspector. 'Bravo! things are smartly done in Paris, aren't they?'

'Yes—but they can't make out some writing on the slip of paper; and I am to go to the commissary's office to see if I can read it.'

'A slip of paper?'

'With writing on it, monsieur—writing in English—that looks like an address!'

CHAPTER VI.

IT was to a private hotel in a by-street lying between the Faubourg St. Honoré and the Avenue des Champs Elysées that Mr. Byers conducted his two companions on the morning of their arrival in Paris. As he explained to them, the quarter was sufficiently populous and sufficiently Britannic for their introduction into any portion of it to pass unnoticed. A good many of the stable-boys, grooms, and coachmen, in fact, who were to be encountered in that quarter came from the various counties of the British Isles, and Mr. Bartholomew Finch might easily have been mistaken for some among that class. He would not readily have been taken for a personage with many grooms and coachmen in his service; nor could his presence, as a guest, in marble halls or gilded drawing-rooms have failed to strike the observant menials waiting upon the company as a circumstance of the most suspicious order, not to say—if a genuine quotation from the servant's hall may be permitted —a promiscuous abnormality.

The physiognomy of Sir John, however, lent itself at once to any sort of society, high or low. We who are acquainted with his antecedents can state that his origin

was of the most vile, that the associations of his early years
were brutalising and sinister, and that all his life he had
profited by crime, although he was never known, by men in
Soho who are cognisant of everything, to have personally
engaged in its actual perpetration. The scandal in high life
which had ended so disastrously for a Spanish hidalgo who
had settled in Mayfair, had commended the Montmorency
Vane who had the intrigue with the hidalgo's wife to the
most favourable notice of the enterprising firm of Clements
and Company. That distinguished Spaniard had espoused
an American beauty—indeed, the 'belle' of Boston; and
really a very handsome and widely ill-educated young lady—
who had thrown over an ingenuous townsman (the Presbyterian auctioneer, who afterwards committed suicide) for the
sake of a Castilian invalid and title. When she took her
walks in Hyde Park, Montmorency Vane would follow at a
distance; sometimes a copy of verses, written upon vellum
stamped with a coat-of-arms, would reach her by the post.
From her window she had occasionally detected him watching her residence with the jealousy of true love. He would
shroud himself in a dark mantle, and pose in the attitude
of the mysterious stranger. He told her subsequently that
he had royal blood in his veins. Montmorency Vane turned
out to be Vine, *alias* Grainger. He was not a party to the
divorce suit, but in the impounded correspondence there
were notes which bore his name and seal. It proved a
great shock to the 'belle' of Boston who had jilted the
Presbyterian auctioneer—a young man of great promise and
fine prospects, and the support of his mother and sisters—
to find that her own maid had formed the veritable attraction. Through her own maid the mysterious stranger knew
of all her movements; and it was a humiliation from which
she never recovered to learn that 'her purse, not her person'
—as her counsel declaimed afterwards, tautophonically but
with noble indignation—had been the object of his persistent
siege. But it would be of no use denying it: about Vine,
alias Grainger, or 'Sir John,' there was a something which
imposed upon the wisest among the fair. Wherever he
went, the sex were gracious with him; and he hardly went
anywhere without turning to pecuniary account this gracious
disposition of the sex. He would borrow the savings of a
lady's-maid, or steal them from her; or he would live in a

magnificent manner for a week or two upon an instalment
of hush-money extorted from her mistress.

In London, people usually found it so difficult to ' place '
Vine, *alias* Grainger, that they often transferred their attention to his immediate neighbours as a means of making
up their minds with reference to himself.   You might have
taken him, in London, for a music-hall vocalist, or a billiard-
marker ; for a betting-man, or a professional philanthropist;
a bill discounter, or a noble viscount who, with no money in
his pocket, no balance at the bank, and not even a few blank
cheques to show in a deceptive cheque-book, goes behind the
scenes of theatres and invites the chorus-girls or ballet-dancers
to supper.   Vine, *alias* Granger, fitted into Parisian life quite
naturally.   In Paris he would at once become an excellent type of the Continental loafer who talks international
politics with the bias of John Bull, and never learns the
language of the country.   Only card-sharpers would have
played *ecarté* with him on a first acquaintance.   And yet
there are men of the same external type in Continental
cities upon whom mistrust would constitute a keen injustice : perfectly honest gentlemen—the cousins or brothers-
in-law of wealthy British residents—who subsist upon the
charity of their relatives and are not to be surprised in any
species of indecorous act.   As for Sir John, he might have
had no polish, but he used an impenetrable veneer.   He
could put on a dazzling show of gentility, and had always
found it answer ; gentility being, upon the whole, more
advantageous to the individual than refinement.   At any
rate, the ladies were always prepossessed in his favour—
especially those who prided themselves upon their gifts of
penetration.

When grandpa arrived at the Hôtel Clifton with his
charges, the damsel who presided over the small counting-
house had only just descended.   The raw air made its way
in with the three visitors, and the damsel gazed upon them
at first not too pleasantly.

Mr. Byers reminded the young person that he had engaged an apartment on the first floor for a couple of friends
who had just come up from Italy.   It was a double-bedded
room, and his two friends, who had travelled for some days
unbrokenly, would wish for absolute quiet.   Until they got
over their excessive fatigue, and felt a little better in health

—the doctors had forbidden them to travel northwards, but
the demands of business were imperious—they would prefer
to take their meals privately, in their apartment. Breakfast might be served at the ordinary hour, but in the meantime mademoiselle would send them up hot grogs.

Mademoiselle seemed to have intended to receive the
strangers haughtily—these foreign travellers presumed upon
their wealth. She thawed, however, beneath the casual
glance of Sir John, and informed him, responding to Mr.
Byers, that everything should be done that could possibly
be done to secure them comfort and tranquillity.

The first proceeding of Mr. Finch, on their installing
themselves in the apartment on the first-floor, was to look
out of the window and estimate the distance of the drop.
Mr. Byers examined the recesses and tested the walls.
Satisfied that they were secure from any risk of being overheard, Mr. Byers dragged a chair up to the mantelpiece,
and warmed himself at the log fire.

' Now, John,' said he, ' there must be no reticences in
this affair, you know. Let us have the remainder of the
story, just as it happened, nothing more and nothing less.
Whatever it is, out with it. If you've gone farther in this
than we like, we can back out, can't we, and say no more
about it ? We're men of business : you're safe with me,
and I'm safe with you. You've taken me up to the last
stoppage but one. At Amiens you had made up your mind
to get the property between Creil and Paris ? Is that it ?'

' That's it, grandpa,' confirmed Mr. Finch.

' Well,' began Vine, *alias* Grainger, slowly, ' I dare say
you'll want to wash your hands of this business, Byers,
when you've heard how it stands. As for Bat, if I am
implicated, he's implicated too. Appearances might be
against us at a pinch, but, after all, there's nothing they
could prove. If you left us, Byers, if you said you would
have nothing more to do with it, *I* shouldn't be surprised ;
but I know we should be safe with you ?'

' My character ought to be pretty well-known by this
time, I should hope,' returned Mr. Byers distantly. ' I've
done business with as many hard-working thieves as anybody, and I should like to know who could have sent men to
penal servitude if *I* couldn't—and some of them richly
deserved it for their ingratitude ; but I bear no malice, and I

remembered their wives and families. Safe with *me !*
What do you say, Bat?'

' I say that I want Mr. clever Sir John to tell me without
any more palaver what the ——— I'm " implicated " in, that's
what *I* say,' growled Bartholomew.

' Perhaps you'll blame *me* for what has happened?'
resumed the other. ' It was no fault of mine. How could
I know? You're well off that I changed my mind at the
last moment ; if I had kept to the original arrangement, *you*
might have been in this condition, too !' He took out his
handkerchief, and contemplated the stains of blood for
an instant, without any signs of emotion. ' My plan was
for Bat, here, to follow me along the step into the compartment where Remington had gone. It was very easy ; the
night was pitch dark ; there were only a few people in the
train ; Remington had a second-class ticket, and could not
be more than three or four compartments along ; he had
been endeavouring to get a compartment to himself ever
since we left Calais, and could hardly keep his eyes open ;
and by trying it after Creil, the last stoppage, we ran
a good chance of finding him half asleep. I may want
to cut things short sometimes, but no one can accuse me of
ever mixing myself up with violence. I did not desire any
violence ; I detest violence. If the boys would take a leaf
out of my book, they wouldn't be sent to " penal " quite so
often, I can tell you, or be settled by the black cap, leaving
their families to go upon the parish rates.'

' When the boys ain't such favourites with the ladies,
they have to do the best they can,' commented Mr. Finch,
rather rudely, as his companion paused—' me, for instance.
Not that *I'm* a partisan of violence—oh, dear no, not me !
Though I like to cut things short, as much as other people,
and what I want to know at the present moment is, what
the ——— I'm " implicated " in !'

' Supposing we had found him on the look-out, what could
he have dared to do? He had the property about him, and
would have immediately known that we knew it. If he had
shown fight, without making any noise, we were too strong
for him ; if he had called for help, or signalled to stop the
train, he was at our mercy, because he had the property
on his person, and we could have denounced him. What I
meant to do was just to tell him quietly what we had come

for, to recommend him to make no fuss, and to get it from him peaceably. We might have handed him something over for the trouble he had been put to, and had a drink with him when we arrived in Paris. That was my combination. It was straightforward, wasn't it—a straightforward plan, and pretty good?'

'The A B C of the game—that's all!' replied Mr. Byers.

'The A B C of the game, no doubt,' said the other coolly; 'if two things had not happened; if, to begin with, Mr. Bat, here, had not kept me arguing, after we left Creil, that it was better to wait until we reached Paris, and then watch our man and get the diamonds from him " comfortably "— "comfortably!" I told him to stay where he was, but to keep a look-out on the nearside of the train, up as well as down.'

'A look-out! You couldn't see your hand before you; and as for hearing anybody, you couldn't have heard it thunder, with the row the train was making. I admit I wanted to wait until we got to Parry, but as you had made your mind up to bring it off in the train, why couldn't I have come with you? No; you would have your own way—you said that that would spoil it.'

'Because, on second thoughts, if I could have caught him with his eyes closed, or asleep, it would have been quicker for one to do it than two; and then, with a bit of cloth across my face, I could have got away without his guessing who had pinned him down so artfully, and robbed him. And if he had struggled, he would have been hurt. The property could have been passed on to Bat, and I could have finished the journey in one of the empty compartments, just in case of accidents. Well, wasn't that pretty good?'

'I want to know what I'm implicated in,' said Mr. Finch gloomily.

'Murder,' replied his colleague deliberately. 'And as we were followed from the station on spec., and before it could have been discovered, Byers would be in it, too, if he could be identified as one of the three. When I got on to the footboard, on the off-side of the train, I found it was easier work than I had thought. There was no danger of the guard coming along again to look at the tickets, and even in broad daylight the passengers could not have seen me unless they had had their heads out of the window. As it was, the windows were all closed, and where there were passengers, some of the blinds were drawn. The train was going very fast, and swung now and then, but I found it easy enough to creep along. Everything was there ready to your hand. I thought I had gone past the compartment, owing to the drawn curtains, but presently I got to our man. There was an empty compartment on each side of his, and nothing could have seemed better. The lamp had burnt very low, but I could see that he was lying along the seat nearest the engine, with something under his head for a pillow, and his feet almost touching the door I meant to open. I did not think he could be asleep, with the knowledge that he had this property about him; but it looked as if he had come to the conclusion that all was safe, as we were getting near Paris; and that he was dozing. I had the door open in a second, and in another second I had him by the throat. He did not resist, and I shook him to see whether he would speak. He did not speak; but as I shook him I felt something at the side of his throat, moist and sticky. It was blood. I turned his head gently towards the light, and there was a small wound at the left temple. I tried the pulse. Our man was dead.'

'And that is how you got those stains on your handkerchief and your hands?' said Mr. Byers, breaking the silence which ensued upon this announcement.

'That is how.'

'Then there ought to be marks on the door, as you closed it after you, on going back; and a mark or two, perhaps, on the handles as you went along to your own compartment again?'

'It had not quite left off raining, as I crept back, and the rain must have washed away any traces of that sort. I entered almost the first empty compartment I came to, and that is the reason why Bat and I did not meet again before giving up our tickets at the terminus.'

'When did you get those nasty stains on your handkerchief?'

'When I wiped my wrist, afterwards, in the compartment alone. Whoever had done it could not have been there very long before me; and you can take your affidavit that I didn't stay there very long, either. It was quite sufficient for me to see that sealskin vest unbuttoned, and the pocket in the lining turned inside out.'

Neither Mr. Byers nor Finch, *alias* Walker, made any response.

'A child might have floored me when I found out what had happened,' resumed the narrator. 'I could scarcely believe it. I was so upset, that I nearly let go my hold as I went back along the footboard. The disappointment was enough to make you jump under the wheels.'

Mr. Byers gazed into the log-fire. Finch, *alias* Walker, tilted his chair back and studied the arabesques around the ceiling.

'Such a thing never happened to me before,' continued Sir John; 'and I wish I could have come across the party who forestalled us !'

'Why?' said Mr. Byers.

'Why?'

'Yes—why? *He* wouldn't have been likely to be dozing, you know. And you had no weapons—that is, you had no fire-arms?'

Sir John looked at his questioner without replying at once. He then transferred his scrutiny to Mr. Finch.

'What does this amount to?' he demanded presently, rising to his feet. 'Does this mean that you doubt my word? Which of you doubts my word—come?' Mr. Byers whistled softly to himself, and stirred one of the blazing logs with his foot. He companion followed with a fascinated air an arabesque in faded blue. 'Bat knows what I had, besides the sword-stick which I left in his care. If I had any fire-arms, where are they now? And why should I want to put the double on you? There would have been more than enough for all of us, and for three times our number. The stones were undervalued, Clements says. Why should I want to put the double on? Besides, you can satisfy yourself. Search me !'

'John, I am surprised at you,' remonstrated Mr. Byers. 'Your attitude just now was unbecoming in the extreme. Menaces! And with regard to searching, *we* don't search one another—not exactly! If we did not trust to one another, business could not possibly go on. What do *you* say, Bartholomew?'

Pity he didn't jump under those wheels—when he got

those marks about him—that's what I say,' responded Mr. Finch. 'He hasn't yet found out that he smeared his own undercoat with the stains from his hand—and look at it! Search him? He'll have to search himself if he wants to go out into the public streets with *me.*'

'Well, now, of course he will take the necessary precautions; that is another question. Make up your mind to this; you will both be suspected, *prima facie*, by the persons—friend Toppin, his colleague, and the rest—who know of your presence in the train; and that, of course, involves myself. Unfortunate—most unfortunate! What we have to do now is to find the property, because then we find the gentleman who did this business, or we get upon his track. If we succeed in taking over the property, we can soon get the gentleman indicated to Scotland Yard. Search *you*, John! Oh dear no! The gentleman I should like to search, from what you tell me of the proceedings on the way, is either' — grandpa paused in delivering judgment — 'Byde himself——'

'Byde!' exclaimed Mr. Finch, this time really astonished.

'I wish I could think it was Byde,' muttered Sir John.

'Or the talkative man, what's-his-name, in the temperance cause; and in my opinion that is the party we shall have to look for.'

'You've hit it, grandpa,' said Mr. Finch.

'My own idea, Byers—the temperance man!' said Sir John emphatically. 'To find the property, we must find that gentleman : though, if it were Byde——'

'Oh, he's quite deep enough to have thought about it,' observed Mr. Byers, 'but let us do him justice. There's no man at the Yard who's cleverer than Byde, but there's no man who's more honest. I did know one of them, a great linguist, Greek by descent—he's now away, doing fifteen years—who would not have hesitated a very long time about putting a knife into Remington—not a bullet: too clumsy—getting the valuables, and having you both arrested before you were fifty yards outside the station. It is greatly to be regretted that there has been any violence in this affair ; but the person who was there before you, John, was not a regular hand. No regular hand would use a firearm, would he?'

'Of course not. That's exactly what I said to myself,' exclaimed Sir John.

'I'll give a prize to any lady or gentleman who will bring the address of our dear friend from England to Mr. Bartholomew Finch, Esq., in the course of the afternoon,' remarked Mr. Finch.

Vine, *alias* Grainger, tried to recall the title of the organization upon whose beneficent influence Brother Neel had been expatiating. He failed, however, despite all his attempts. Mr. Byers, who had immediately brightened up, declared that it did not matter in the smallest degree. He would procure a list of the associations of that character which existed in Paris; they were not numerous, and John might be able to recognise the name, if he saw it. Only they must lose no time.

'It's lucky I'm with you in this, my boys,' concluded Mr. Byers, rising from his chair, and looking for his hat. 'Without me, what a nice mess you would be in! As it is, I undertake to unearth your temperance friend, and to put you in the way of getting quits with him. That part of the work will be for *you* to do, and if you do it effectually he will only get what he deserves for his dishonesty.'

'Those temperance preachers!' reflected Mr. Finch aloud. 'I wouldn't like to go into a crowd of them with my watch and chain on. I wouldn't even toss with them for drinks. Give me the man that likes his twopenn'orth of gin—that's the chap I can trust!' He sipped noisily at his grog.

'Leave the arrangements to me,' continued Mr. Byers —'and don't stir out of doors. I may come back at any time—perhaps not till this evening, perhaps not till to-morrow. Don't be alarmed if my absence should be prolonged. I must see how the land lies, and bring you back something definite. Ah, what clever boys we are from London, are we not? What should we do — whatever should we do—without poor old grandpa, who has practically retired from business?' After which playful thrust, and before departing, Mr. Byers instructed his juniors in the methods of filling up fallaciously the police sheets of the Paris hotels.

Sir John and Mr. Finch found that the hours hung heavily on their hands throughout the day. They had their meals served in their apartment, and, as invalids, did their best to restrain their appetites. When they were not eating, or taking a nap, they played at cards, although each knew that the other habitually cheated, and each preferred to play with his own pack, reproaching the other at the same time for his want of confidence.

A curious incident occurred later. Overcome by their fatigue, they dropped off to sleep almost as soon as they had disrobed themselves and retired to their respective couches for the night. Their regular breathing presently became louder, and continued both loud and rhythmical : the profound sleep of the good man and the weary was indubitably theirs. But Finch, *alias* Walker, seemed to be subject to somnambulism. Still breathing in the vigorous cadence to which we have alluded, he gradually slid out of the high mahogany bedstead he was occupying, and went through a series of movements which might have appeared surreptitious, if detected by Sir John. No light was burning in the room, but the rays of a street lamp just caught their window and faintly illuminated the interior. Mr. Finch had the air of stealthily proceeding towards his companion's garments. Yes, it was certainly towards this point that he had directed his course, for he was now engaged in the examination of the pockets, and, that process over, he very carefully inspected the lining of the small black leather bag. Had he mistaken these objects for his own? The spectator who might have adopted this conclusion would have most probably revised his judgment when he perceived the somnambulist turn in the direction of Sir John. Arrived at the latter's bedside, he stood there apparently surveying his relaxed features and listening to the measure of his notes. Such a remarkable fixity of attention, such obedience to a paramount idea, will not astonish any persons learned in the phenomena of somnambulism.

Finch, *alias* Walker, extended his left hand, and began gently—oh, most gently—to insinuate it under the pillow of his sleeping partner. The digital dexterity of Mr. Finch must have been from his earliest years cultivated to the acme of perfection. An ivory paper-knife inserted between the bolster and the mattress could hardly have caused a slighter derangement than the advance of that supple palm ; it was impossible that the motion should wake the sleeper.

' When you've done !' suddenly remarked Vine, *alias* Grainger, in a tone of expostulation.

' Ah, that's exactly what I thought,' replied the somnambulist imperturbably. ' I would have laid a thousand on it. A nice man to come away with, this is ! Shams sleep the very first night—puts the double on, with a pal. All right !'

' No offence, I hope ?' inquired Sir John ironically.

' All right—all right !'

' I was dreaming that I had found the man we want,' continued Sir John, in the same tone.

' And I was dreaming that I had found the property !'

' You had better dream that over again, and take a note of the address,' retorted Sir John.

CHAPTER VII.

INSPECTOR BYDE had finished his breakfast; and he had also finished questioning the waiter on the presumable ingredients of a sauce which helped the thinking faculty, he said, and which he would have been pleased to see acclimatised to Camberwell. He was now reclining with a certain majesty upon the red velveteen cushions of the café attached to the Terminus Hotel. From the half-dozen articles he had brought out of his pocket previously, and arrayed upon the table, he selected the leathern cases that contained respectively a large pipe and a little one. The indecision with which he regarded their competing charms might have seemed trivial in a person of his years—and quite unworthy of a man so justly respected in so serious a vocation—to anyone unacquainted with his ways. The inspector had two pipes, because he had two moods. His present mood, however, was after all not the anxious one; it was the mood of roseate calm, sanguine tranquillity. He therefore took up the smaller calumet ; and, after loading its wooden bowl with tobacco of a golden hue, he smiled long and placidly at a gay advertisement exposed upon the wall in front of him, without becoming in the least aware of its poematic and pictorial purport.

Thus absorbed, he undoubtedly did not notice a manly

form which appeared before the entrance to the café from
the street, which crossed the threshold dubiously, and which
at length advanced straight towards him. The manly form
halted at the inspector's table, and sank into a seat. It was
Toppin.

'Take a nip,' said Byde laconically, after a sharp glance.

He pushed the tray, with the diminutive decanter and
glass, across the table to his colleague.

'They've got away,' announced Toppin, looking very
crestfallen.

'How was that?'

Toppin explained that about the movements of the parties
he had been commissioned to follow there had been nothing
suspicious until they left the Halles. They had driven to
the Central Markets and had come away again, and it was
only when they were returning from that point that he discovered grounds for suspicion in their behaviour. The cab
was evidently pursuing a circuitous route, inasmuch as the
coachman turned back from the Halles and partly retraced
his steps. Pulling up at an ordinary district post-office,
which was not yet open for the day, the cabman had descended from his place to drop a missive of some sort into
the box. No one but the driver had descended; of that he
felt quite positive. The cab had then gone off to a different
locality altogether. He was careful to keep the vehicle in
view, and when it stopped once more at a tavern, he was
certain that, in this instance also, the driver was the only
individual who alighted. After a slight delay the journey
was resumed at a quick pace; and what was his astonishment when eventually the vehicle pulled up at a cabstand,
and took a station at the extremity of the rank as though
no party or parties were inside it! Hardly knowing whether
to show himself or not, he hesitated for some time to approach the vehicle. When he did go up to it there was,
sure enough, but a single occupant—the coachman, who
had made himself comfortable inside with the object of
enjoying a nap. This man was half asleep and half intoxicated. All he could elicit from him with regard to his
last 'fare' was that they were people who did not know
their own mind, and that they had discharged him at the
Halles.

'I don't believe this,' wound up Mr. Toppin, 'but I've

taken his number.   If they threw me off at the Halles, it
must have been done as quick as lightning.'

'And to have been done as quick as lightning, it must
have been done because they saw you following them,'
answered his colleague.   'I should recommend you to go
and find them again.   It's very likely they'll be wanted.'

Inspector Byde then briefly informed Detective Toppin
of the new aspect which the case of the Wilmot diamonds
had assumed.   The discovery of the murder had been made
soon after Toppin's departure on his errand of watching the
two suspicious characters to whom their attention had been
called by the telegrams from Scotland Yard.   It was a great
pity the men had eluded him.

'I did not think it could be so urgent,' pleaded Toppin.

'Well, now, what would be the procedure here in a matter
of this kind?   What will be done with the body?'

'That depends a good deal on the police commissary
attached to the terminus.   It would be left to his discretion
whether the body should be removed at once to the Morgue,
or be retained during the day at the station, for the purposes
of the inquiry.   A commissary at one place might decide
one way, whilst another commissary might decide the other
way.   It might depend on the circumstances of the case;
but it might also depend,' added Toppin, recovering his
assurance as he gave his colleague these particulars, ' upon
the intelligence of the commissary or on his ambition.   If
he wants to bring himself before public notice he might keep
the body where it is as long as possible in order to have the
control of the investigation.   If he wants to avoid trouble
or extra work he would send it on to the Morgue at once,
having made his notes and taken all the necessary evidence
on the spot as soon as possible.   The matter is left a good
deal to his discretion, but there are other functionaries to
be borne in mind too.   There is the *juge d'instruction,* or
magistrate, charged with the preliminary investigation of a
crime; and I believe the Procureur de la République would
come in at this early stage.   It is difficult to say where the
jurisdictions of these officials begin and end; they don't
always appear to know themselves.   And even if their
functions are well defined and don't conflict, I have known
of jealousies among these officials which have hampered
criminal investigations from the outset.'

' But for the identification of Remington—how will they
manage, supposing that nothing to identify him should be
found upon the body?'

' Why, you can identify him yourself!'

' Yes; and that's what I particularly mean to abstain
from doing. And you will greatly assist me, Mr. Toppin,
by forgetting absolutely, so far as the French authorities
are concerned, all that I have told you as to Remington and
the Wilmot affair. You do not know the name or business
of the deceased; you learnt his case from the ordinary
channels, remember—the newspapers this afternoon, if you
like; and you place yourself at the disposal of the French
police to take measures for ascertaining the identity. Now,
what I want to know is will this corpse be publicly exposed?'

' Yes; that is why it will be removed to the Morgue—for
the purposes of identification.'

' Very well. It goes to the Morgue, where anyone can
enter and see it. Now, do you think the body will be
taken to the Morgue, for public exposure, by this afternoon?'

' This afternoon? Yes; certainly. It may be on its
way there now. If you desired to examine the scene of
the occurrence, before the corpse was moved, I could have
arranged that for you with the commissary of the station.
But I am afraid you would be too late now; and then you
don't wish me to appear in the case just yet.'

Did Toppin suspect his colleague of a wish to keep him in
the background? Was all the credit in this case, which
promised to turn out a first-rate affair, to be monopolised
by a man already covered with distinction like Byde?
Toppin seemed to think it hard that this could be possible.
What could Inspector Byde, with all his foresight, perse-
verance, and ability, accomplish in a place like Paris, if he
had not at his elbow Toppin's knowledge of the Parisians
and their city, and Toppin's intelligence !

' I took all the notes I want, I think—as to the appearances at the scene of the occurrence—before the commissary
was out of bed. I want to know about what time the body
would be exhibited for identification. That, however, we
can soon calculate on learning when the transfer to the
Morgue has taken place, if it should have already taken

place. Anybody about here would enlighten us as to whether the commissary has kept the body in the station or sent it on. The waiter will be in presently with a piece of information for me, and he will know.'

Toppin evidently wondered what could be the nature of this piece of information, but he did not ask. He was under the orders of his colleague, and the latter had apparently got to work on some tack or traces of his own.

'Are we looking for the murderer?' ventured Toppin impulsively, 'or these valuables—you and I, I mean?' He reddened, as if he felt he had said something foolish. 'Because,' he added, nettled at the expression of patient endurance with which the inspector received this query, 'the French police are very susceptible of interference. We may be quite in order on the subject of the diamond robbery; but the murder is their affair, not ours.'

'If we find the diamonds for ourselves, we may find the murderer for *them;* if they find the murderer for themselves, they may find the diamonds for *us !*'

The waiter returned at this instant with no doubt the piece of information of which mention had been made.

'The slip of paper was not discovered by the commissary, monsieur,' he said, addressing Inspector Byde. 'It was picked up by one of the employés of the railway before the commissary arrived, but was handed to him when he came to draw up his report. The employé found it near the door farthest away from the body of this unfortunate gentleman. Ah, messieurs, what a terrible event! What could have been the motive of such a dreadful crime? Don't you think it may have been a case of suicide? The commissary believes that the unfortunate gentleman has fallen a victim to a secret society, because none of the valuables about him were disturbed. Do you believe that he has been assassinated for political reasons, monsieur— assassinated by the members of some secret society? I can't think so myself; I never heard of any such cases in Battersea during the whole time I was there, and I fancy *I* know the English people !'

'Did you remember what I asked you to ascertain exactly? Did you ascertain exactly whereabouts in the compartment the slip of paper was found?'

'Why, yes, monsieur. I did not forget, being interested

in this terrible occurrence, and likewise in the painful possibility of the deceased being that relative of monsieur who
might have travelled by the train from Amiens, though, as
monsieur said, it was most unlikely, seeing that he had
business which prevented his leaving that town during the
whole of the present week; though one never knows what
may happen at any moment to change one's plans or habits:
witness the hatter in the same street as my brother-in-law,
who never went out on a foggy evening, and never would,
until one afternoon his uncle came from the Mauritius, and
they went to the theatre together—I forget the name of the
piece, but it was a theatre high up on the boulevard—and
the night being a foggy one, the hatter coughed so much
that he came home earlier than the uncle, through a short
cut, and was assassinated and robbed, though he had
nothing in his pockets but seven francs forty-five centimes,
and a silver watch that never marked the hour; whilst the
uncle from the Mauritius, who had amassed a fortune and
wore jewellery such as a prince might not have been
ashamed of, walked home three hours later, very gay, and
was unmolested. It could not have been the relative of
monsieur, because my *confrère*, Monsieur Aristide, the
second waiter at the restaurant farther along, heard the
commissary state to his subordinate on the platform of the
station that the ticket in the possession of the deceased was
right through from London to Paris, and had been booked
the night before, that is to say, for the mail-train itself. As
for the slip of paper which I spoke of to monsieur, it might
easily have escaped attention, for it lay partly under one of
the seats at the far end.'

'At the far end?—that is to say, at a distance from the
body of this passenger?'

'So I learnt, monsieur, from the employé, thanks to the
piece of money I remitted to him in obedience to the instructions of monsieur, whose anxiety I trust is now ap-
peased, the unfortunate passenger being manifestly, as his
railway-ticket proves, not the relative of monsieur who
resides at Amiens, and who might by chance have travelled
in the train, though all doubt could be set at rest by a tele-
graphic message despatched to Amiens, if monsieur does
not wish to go to the Morgue and view the body, where it
will be exposed this afternoon, the commissary having

stated that before the inquiry could make any progress the identification must have been disposed of. By this time, probably, the body has been delivered at the Morgue.'

'Did the porter, or whoever the railway servant was, describe the slip of paper to you?'

'Yes; it was a single sheet of white paper, like English note-paper, and it had been folded once—just doubled.'

'And this writing you speak of—where were the characters traced?'

'On the inside. The name and address had been written along the single sheet of paper, and it had then been folded in two—like that, the employé told me'—the waiter illustrated his meaning by folding up the ornate bill of fare.

'And the address—could he give you any idea of it?'

'Oh no, monsieur, except that there were two letters at the end of it. He knows that "London" means "Londres;" but it did not say "London." It said "S.W." The name he could read, because it is a name we have in France— "Adelaide."'

'Did the commissary make any remark when the slip of paper was handed to him?' inquired Toppin.

Before replying, the waiter looked at Toppin's colleague, as if for assurance as to the *locus standi* of the new-comer. The inspector nodded, and the waiter quoted the commissary of police to the effect that the slip of paper must have been dropped by some person sitting near the far door of the compartment—perhaps by the deceased himself before changing his seat, for there was nothing to prove that the deceased had occupied the same place in the compartment throughout the journey.

'Was there any stain upon the paper—any mark of blood, for instance?' inquired Inspector Byde.

'No;' the waiter had expressly put that question, because he was aware of the great importance of blood-stains on objects found near persons suspected to have been murdered. He had read of a most extraordinary instance, in fact, in a newspaper taken at the hotel—not in the 'events of the day,' but in a life-like story which had been running through its columns and had been collected by the chambermaid of the first floor in order to be bound—'The Fortune-teller's Prediction; or, the Posthumous Vengeance of the Murdered Heir.' The first thing he had asked the employé

was whether there had been blood-stains upon this piece of
paper, and he had felt exceedingly disappointed to learn
that there were no stains of any description upon it.
'Monsieur will pardon me the indiscretion,' pursued the
waiter after a pause—'but would monsieur be, by hazard,
connected at all with the English police?'

'I!' exclaimed the inspector, laughing heartily, 'connected with the police? Ask this gentleman! Where did
you get such an idea as that?'

'From the station, monsieur—only vaguely, vaguely—
monsieur will excuse me'—and the waiter joined heartily
in the laugh at the ridiculous nature of his own supposition.
'It seems that an agent of the English police obtained a
view of the compartment before M. le Commissaire himself,
and that he took some notes, which has greatly angered
M. le Commissaire, who says for all we know he may have
taken not only his notes but something else besides. And
since monsieur has no connection with the police I may be
permitted the liberty of explaining that no one of my family
has ever been able to endure that class, and that I should
have personally much regretted rendering monsieur the assistance I have sought to render him by interrogating the
employé of the railway. I thought, perhaps, from the interest exhibited in the unfortunate occurrence—but monsieur
is perhaps architect?' He glanced at the diagrams, with
letters of the alphabet here and there, traced upon the
margin of the table.

'Just imagine that he should have divined it!' ejaculated
the inspector, turning with open admiration towards his
colleague. 'What clever people they are, now, all these
foreigners, are they not? You haven't heard him speak
English yet; but he speaks it so well, in the purest accent
of London, that you and I, being from the country, might
not do ill to take a lesson or two. It was in Battersea that
his studies were industriously prosecuted—and he knows
the language—oh, he knows it!!'

'Oh, yes—very well—London,' assented the waiter, for
Mr. Toppin's benefit; 'I speak in Battersea always the
most pure.'

'And just to think that he should have guessed it—
architect! What clever people they all are to be sure!'
Mr. Byde directed the waiter to bring him the hotel police-

sheet, on which he had purposely deferred registering
particulars anent himself. He then inscribed upon that
precious record that Mr. Byde, architect, forty-five years of
age, had travelled to Paris from the town of Brighton,
in the department of Sussex; country, England. 'So that
you will know, if telegrams or letters are delivered here for a
Mr. Byde, that they are for me,' he added. 'What a help,
Toppin,' observed the inspector, as the waiter bore away the
police-book, 'if we had all these papers to work from in
England! How we could trace aliases, hey—how we
could pounce upon stolen property before it had been passed
along!'

'Yes,' replied Toppin, 'and people sometimes do fill them
up honestly by mistake.'

'Architect!—well, well!—simple enough, and yet who'd
have found it?' Mr. Byde effaced the diagrams drawn in
pencil on the marble table. 'And so we *are* architects: of
other people's fortunes—or fates.'

'That young man who has been to Battersea looks to me
as if he might be in the pay of the police himself,' said
Toppin. 'This is just the right spot for keeping an eye on
suspicious arrivals and departures, and he would not talk
openly like that about the police for nothing. He is just the
sort of simpleton the Prefecture would get for their money
—just the *naïf* with a mixture of cunning. What can you
expect? They can't get clever people for their terms.
They want agents everywhere, but they can't afford to pay
such a number well.'

'We must see that slip of paper, if possible, Toppin; we
must have that address, if it *should* be an address. You
can have heard of this affair by chance, and you know
nothing at all about Remington's identity. Can you manage
it before the afternoon?'

'I think I can; though it will only be because they know
me. It will be necessary to ascertain whether the commissary has kept the paper for his own report, or sent it on to
the Morgue with the body, or handed it over already to the
Juge d'Instruction; and that may occupy a little time.'

'Notice whether the address was in a feminine handwriting.'

'Is there a woman in this case?'

'The name Adelaide is a name I like,' said Mr. Byde.

He knocked the ashes out of the wooden bowl, and restored the smaller of the two pipes to its leathern case.

' Shall we walk down together ?' suggested Toppin.

' I want to put on my considering-cap,' said the inspector.

He opened the bulkier case in black leather, and from a nest as soft as eider-down extracted a pipe in massive meerschaum. While he filled and lighted it, and drew from its capacious bowl half a dozen preliminary puffs, the inspector imported into his face an expression of such deep thought that his colleague did not venture to break in with any queries, or for the moment to follow up their conversation. The case had evidently a feminine side : did the inspector aim at keeping this from him ?

' Coming on nicely, isn't it !' remarked the inspector, at length, taking the pipe from his mouth, and complacently surveying the tinged meerschaum. The bowl was carved into the semblance of a sphinx, and was capped with a small plate of silver. The base had been smoked into a rich amber tint, the forehead of the sphinx was sallow, a tawny blush was mantling in the cheeks.

' A fine bit of meerschaum,' answered Toppin, with suppressed irritation.

' A present,' pursued his colleague. ' That pipe was given to me by a poor man who would have gone away for five years' '' penal '' if it hadn't been for me. The evidence was all against him, you would have said , no jury would have hesitated. I brought the right man into the dock only just in time. When the other was set free, he would have given me everything that belonged to him, and the neighbours in the street he lives in—it was only last Michaelmas—began to subscribe for a testimonial to Inspector Byde. I let the man give me this pipe, and what it has done for me during the past three months is something wonderful. I don't have to smoke at it long. The very last case I was in, the case I had before they put me on to this one—the alleged mysterious disappearance in the north of London, which I dare say you read of in the papers—mightn't have been solved for ever so long if it hadn't been for this meerschaum pipe. I was smoking it when I hit upon the idea which gave us the key to that ingenious little arrangement. It's coming on nicely ; but I shall be sorry to see it coloured, all the same.'

' The slip of paper found in the compartment,' began

Toppin, again, ' need not have been dropped where it was found. Suppose it had been dropped near the other door, by the side of the victim, the draught from the window, if it was open, or a single gust of wind from that door, if it had been left open for a moment or two, might have easily drifted it along to the spot where it was discovered.'

' And so ?'

' And so I conclude that no matter how the assassin entered the compartment, and whether he was there two minutes or two hours, the address on that scrap of paper may lead us to him; although we know that in practice criminals don't generally carry about with them incrimina-tory morsels of paper ready to be dropped out of their pockets, at the right moment for the cause of justice. Still, there's no reason why it shouldn't happen—it's not impossible. Don't you think the address might lead us to the guilty person.'

' It might.'

' Then you agree with me that this piece of paper may have belonged to the person who was the thief and mur-derer ?'

' It may have belonged to him.'

' And fell from his pocket, we will say, as he was stooping over the victim—at any rate, was dropped by him accident-ally ?'

' No.'

' How then ?'

' It may have belonged to him—yes; it might indirectly lead us up to his identity—yes; but that a compromising half-sheet of note-paper, just doubled, as we have heard, should be carried by an intending criminal in any such place as an open pocket, from which it could easily fall, at exactly the wrong instant for him—no, Toppin ! We see that sort of thing sometimes, at the theatre, when we take our wives ; but you know as well as I do——'

' What's the alternative suggestion?'

' The address may possibly incriminate another person.'

' Well?'

' The slip of paper may have been very carefully placed by the assassin himself where it was found.'

' Is that your view?'

' No.'

'What do you say then, inspector?' demanded Toppin.

'I say that the half-sheet of paper, doubled, may have belonged to the deceased. I say that it may have been lying in the inner pocket of the vest, and that when that pocket was turned inside out, or when some other article was snatched from it, this piece of paper may have fallen out, and floated to the spot where it was found. Whether the assassin noticed the paper or not, would not matter. He would have no motive for taking it away—quite the contrary. He would be more likely to throw down anything which was not the particular object he came for. What was done was done in a hurry. He had no time to replace things—besides, why should he replace them?'

'Granting all that, what becomes of the use of the address to us? We know who the victim is—we want to find the assassin.'

'So would other people want to find the assassin, viz., the original thieves. We don't know who they are, but they must have had their plans laid, and this property will be worth their taking some trouble over. Certainly, if I am right, this address won't help us to the identity of the assassin; but it may help us to the mode of the theft, in the first place. We had better see this half-sheet of note-paper.'

The two colleagues relapsed into silence. Inspector Byde was finishing his pipe, and staring down the café into the street, when he abruptly started to his feet, bundled the sphinx into its velvet resting-place, and gave Toppin some hurried instructions for the afternoon. Toppin was to go on to the Morgue, after busying himself about the address, and was to watch the persons who might visit that building to view the body. At the Morgue he would be rejoined by his colleague. In another second the inspector was in the street.

The fact was that from his seat in the café he could see the entrance to the telegraph-office over the way, and that a figure just passing into that establishment had caught his attention. The passenger from Scotland Yard had recognised the temperance lecturer, Brother Neel. It was to 'put on his considering cap' that Mr. Byde had lingered at the Terminus Hotel; and he was reflecting, as he now hastened across the road, that what he owed to that piece

of valuable meerschaum was extraordinary—was really, the
more he thought of it, quite undeniable, and most extraordinary.

CHAPTER VIII.

BROTHER NEEL, in issuing from the Telegraph Office,
looked neither to the right nor to the left, but at a quick
pace returned upon his path, directing his steps towards
a by-street in the immediate vicinity of the Northern
Terminus.

The building into which he disappeared was one of the
second or third rate hotels that abound near all the large
railway-stations of Paris.   In plain black characters the
name Hôtel des Nations extended across the plaster façade.
Inspector Byde noted the pretentious title, and endeavoured
to discover the designation of the street.   He had just spelt
out ' Rue de Compiègne ' from the metal tablet on a corner
house, when the temperance lecturer reappeared in the
street, and set off on foot in the direction of the Rue
Lafayette.

Descending this long thoroughfare, with a pre-occupied
and earnest mien which testified to his absorption in the
humanitarian purposes of the I.O.T.A., Brother Neel abated
his speed only when he found himself approaching the rear
of the Grand Opera House.   He turned off to the right-
hand, and proceeded for a short distance along the Boulevard Haussmann.   It was clear that he was well acquainted
with the particular spot which formed the objective of
his journey, for, without pausing to regard any of the num-
bers, he presently turned into one of the entrances with
such abruptness that he ran against an individual just then
passing out.   Inspector Byde himself, taken rather unawares, pulled up more brusquely than he would have
considered creditable in a subordinate—Toppin, for instance
—had he been playing the part of a spectator merely, and
not one of the principal personages.   He loitered at the
uninteresting window of a paper-hanger's shop, and while
admiring fragmentary patterns of impossible flowers, endeavoured to keep an eye upon the doorway through which
Brother Neel had unexpectedly vanished.   He waited, and

waited; there was no sign whatever of Brother Neel. The inspector would have liked to examine the premises his friend was visiting; but suppose that, at the very moment he reached the door, he met him coming out again? That might prove slightly awkward for his operations in the future, and would be handicapping his chances prematurely. There was not much danger, nevertheless, of his being identified with the passenger from London who had worn the large blue spectacles and had been so heavily muffled up. Suppose the building had a double issue, and the temperance lecturer had dexterously led him up to one side of it in order to leave him there while he very promptly walked out at the other? For an instant the inspector felt quite nervous. Any such conduct as that would imply—no, it could hardly be!—and besides, he was quite certain that he had followed his man much too cleverly to be detected. And, then, did he not know the Hôtel des Nations, in the Rue de Compiègne? Ah! but—how could he say that that address had anything to do with Brother Neel? A pretty state of affairs if he and Toppin were both, in the same morning, to allow their quarry to slip away.

Inspector Byde moved warily up to the portals of the spacious vestibule into which the temperance lecturer had plunged. As he glanced along the handsome corridor he half-expected to find that it communicated directly with another thoroughfare. On the contrary, his gaze was arrested at the extremity by the high walls of a courtyard, relieved here and there by evergreen shrubs in large buckets. Two or three neat zinc plates, bearing the names of business firms, confronted the visitor from the lintel of the door. Upon one of these he read, ' International Organization of Total Abstainers (E. J. Bamber), 3e étage.'

Capital! Here was he—the great man sent from head-quarters on special duty—almost thrown for a moment into a condition of panic like the veriest novice, and the next moment, like the veriest novice, surprised to discover that a simple tale had been the true one. Out of sorts a little, perhaps—want of sleep? The inspector looked about him. Nearly opposite stood an establishment within which he could perceive both masculine and feminine heads regarding pleasantly in his direction. Their cheeks were tinted with a delicate rose; ' all day the same their postures were. And they said nothing all the day.' If the flowing whisker which the gentlemen exhibited had in each case the aspect of belonging to someone else, the tresses of the beauteous dames who arched their necks so proudly looked as though they never could have belonged to anyone in this world, into such imposing structures had they been built by the expert hands of a Parisian hairdresser. 'English spoken here.' This announcement in gilt letters apparently aided the inspector to arrive at a decision. He made the shortest of detours, traversed the boulevard, and strolled into the hairdresser's premises. By installing himself in a favourable place, and obstinately remaining in it, he could still command an uninterrupted view of the entrance to the offices across the road.

When his colleague had excused himself by asserting that if he had been thrown off the track that morning it must have been done 'as quick as lightning,' Inspector Byde had responded that to have been done as quick as lightning it must have been done because the men in question saw that they were followed. That implied a reflection upon the skill which Detective Toppin brought to the performance of his professional duties. It, of course, also implied that the men in question had some reason for concealing their movements.

Vine, *alias* Grainger, and Finch, *alias* Walker, were indubitably indicated by all the appearances of the case. Why on earth had he, Byde, planted himself in that barber's chair, with his eyes constantly levelled at the ground-floor entrance to the offices opposite? It was true that under any circumstances he must have been condemned to inaction for the next few hours. The two suspicious characters designated in the first place by the telegrams from Scotland Yard must be sought for on the regular methods, and upon these Mr. Toppin was now engaged. The fact was, however, that in the course of a long experience the inspector had acquired an almost morbid mistrust of the 'appearances' of any case which presented matter calling for an interposition by the 'Yard.' But there was another reason that guided him. He looked steadily across the road at the headquarters of the society of whose humanitarian campaign Brother Neel was one of the zealous pioneers; and perhaps his cogitations took a shape perfectly well known to his comrades of the Yard, and commonly ex-

pressed by those roguish persons in the simple formula,
' He don't like 'em !'

He did not like them—no, he ' could not cotton to ' (we are
quoting the inspector in his hours of ease) ' the fellows who
dressed themselves up in sham clerical clothes, wrote half
a dozen initials after their names, and called themselves
temperance missionaries or teetotal preachers !' It was his
only bias, but he could not conquer it. When laying down
rules of conduct for his son, he would occasionally remark,
inverting the old rhyme, that where the prejudice was strong
the judgment would be usually weak. Unlike a good many
people who are similarly addicted to the practice of genera-
lization, Mr. Byde always applied his dicta to himself, and
did not merely frame them for the rest of the world. And
consequently he was quite aware that this prejudice against
an entire order constituted a weak place in his own
character. But, although he did his best, he could not
overcome this odd antipathy. He did not like vain and
idle folk; and when he was safe at home would scornfully
dilate upon the idleness and vanity of these fellows who
dressed themselves up in sham clerical clothes—a line of
denunciation which was by no means justified by facts.
He did not like these gentlemen, however, and once upon
a time his dislike of them had led him into a dreadful mistake. The blunder was notorious, and the organ of the
I.O.T.A. in the press had made good capital out of it, con-
troversially, ever since.

The elegant and jewelled young man, pitted with the
small-pox, who was attending gracefully to the inspector's
needs, cut his hair very short, trimmed his beard to a point,
and curled the waxed ends of his moustache sardonically
upward. The inspector caught a glimpse in a mirror of the
metamorphosis thus wrought in him, and gazed at his new
head with some astonishment and respect.

' That youthfuls you,' observed the artist, noticing his
look. ' If you came to me all the days I would arrange
you with much taste. You are bettaire like that than
before. The ladies take you like that for cavalry officer.
In France the ladies like very much officers !'

Mr. Byde asked whether the customers of the establishment included any English people.

Why, yes ! great many, from the large hotels close by—

English people from Canada, America, London—all sorts; that was how he learned to speak the language.

Mr. Byde did not mean travellers. He meant residents, people living in the neighbourhood. Perhaps there were none living in the neighbourhood?

Oh, *pardon!* There was the English gentleman who kept the bar just down the street—*un bien charmant garçon:* the best dressed person of all his customers—and, *tenez!* there was Monsieur Bambaire, who resided opposite—Monsieur Bambaire, who was the agent of a great English society. The artist went to a drawer and produced from it a handbill, adding as he passed it to his questioner that here was a *circulaire* of Monsieur Bambaire.

The inspector gathered from the handbill that the large lecture-room, library, and conversation-rooms of the I.O.T.A. were now open at the address given below. All persons, irrespective of sex or nationality, were eligible for membership on payment of the small subscription collected in advance quarterly, half-yearly, or annually. Lectures three times a week. Conversaziones. Full advantages of membership set forth in the prospectuses, to be obtained from Brother E. J. Bamber, superintendent of Paris branch, Boulevard Haussmann. The site of the large lecture-room, library, conversation-rooms, etc., lay in the Rue Feydeau. A special appeal to English-speaking residents in Paris terminated the circular.

The artist addressed a question in his own turn. Monsieur would be able to enlighten him as to the nature of this association. He had been enrolled in it by Monsieur Bambaire, who had pointed to the lowness of the terms, and to the opportunities which would be afforded him of making the acquaintance of English heiresses, the facile prey of any fascinating Parisian. He had paid one visit to the new premises in the Rue Feydeau, but on that occasion there were no heiresses present. Was not the society, however, invested with some political character? had it not some secret object, either reactionary or revolutionary? He had entered it in order not to forfeit the goodwill of Monsieur Bambaire, long a regular client, but of course he had his own position to think of, and the political police of Paris kept their eyes wide open. Mr. Byde explained the philanthropic purposes of the I.O.T.A., but saw that his account of this and kindred bodies in England only excited utter incredulity. League yourselves together for no other reason than that it suited you to abstain from alcohol!—*ah, non, par example !—trop forte, celle-la !*—Did he not think, then, that the future of the I.O.T.A. was of a particularly promising description so far as Paris was concerned? No, he should rather imagine he didn't, on such a basis as had been described to him by monsieur. He had heard of something of the kind in France : a French temperance society whose members drank wine freely, but engaged themselves against the abuse of alcohol ; but total abstention ! ah, no —monsieur knew very well (and here the artist half-closed his eyes and tossed his head repeatedly, with an air of great significance) that to assign such a motive as that for the foundation of a society, with council, secretaries, agents, and all the rest of it, was not treating him seriously, as man to man.

Inspector Byde responded that he could not conjecture what other aims could actuate the society. To inform himself more fully upon the subject he would step across and seek an interview with Monsieur Bamber. When that gentleman made his next call upon the artist the latter might repeat their conversation, if he chose ; Monsieur Bamber would recollect his (the speaker's) visit, and might consider that he owed it to the artist's zeal and friendly offices.

On mounting to the third floor of the building opposite the inspector found the residence of Brother Bamber indicated by a small brass-plate, very brightly polished. His summons was quickly answered by a female domestic servant.

' Monsieur Bambaire ?' demanded the visitor.

'Engaged for the moment,' returned the domestic sharply.

' I will wait,' said the inspector, and he at once moved into the ante-chamber.

' What name shall I announce to monsieur ?'

' Oh, he won't know my name ; I am a stranger to him personally.'

' Is it on the business of the International ?'

' Yes, on the business of the International.'

' Monsieur has his card, no doubt ?'

The inspector took a blank card out of his pocket-book,

and wrote upon it in lead-pencil, ' Mr. Smithson—passing through Paris—ventures to address himself to Monsieur Bamber, of the I.O.T.A., for information as to progress accomplished by this interesting movement.' Watching him as he was thus occupied, the smartly-attired French maid-servant, whose tone and manner had been acidly impertinent, softened at the spectacle of his military moustache, and inhaled quite pleasurably the perfumes with which the inspector had just been inundated. She received the card with a coquettish smile, and tripped into one of the apartments communicating with the vestibule. There was an appreciative expression about the inspector's face, as he gazed after her. He had an eye for the sex when he was out of his own country.

Yes, his expression was most thoroughly appreciative. His instantaneous processes of induction had already led him far. This Brother Bamber——?

Inspector Byde brought his hand down heavily on the arm of the chair. Would he never subdue that mischievous prejudice? The dreadful blunder he had perpetrated—was it to teach him no lesson? Was he fated to repeat it, and would he be lured on to a second disastrous error by some illusively apparent possibility of redeeming the first?

The sprightly French maid returned with the message that Monsieur Bamber, being extremely busy, begged to be excused just then, but that madame could furnish the visitor with the information he desired, if Monsieur Smithson would be good enough to wait for some few minutes. Mr. Byde was perfectly willing to wait, he said ; and he directed a professional scrutiny at the damsel who delivered the message. The report he drew up mentally of this young person might have been of a less flattering nature than she seemed to suppose. She furtively smoothed her raven locks ; and, as she looked upward at her interlocutor pressed her chin down tightly against her chest in order that her large dark eyes should open widely and display their fullest lustre. Mr. Byde thanked her, and with a grim smile began to pace up and down the ante-chamber. He was familiar with all these feminine shows of artlessness. To encounter them in the ' vivacious French brunette ' appealed in a powerful degree to his rather cynical sense of humour.

It was an old friend of his, who had lived a good deal on

the Continent and in the foreign colonies of London, who
used to attack so vehemently the consecrated phrases,
'vivacious French brunette,' 'the exquisite politeness of old
French marquesses,' 'typically impassive French duellist,'
'fascination of the Parisian manner,' etc. He used to say
that all those phrases were false, that some of them the
French themselves would be the last to claim. It would
have been almost perilous to employ these stereotypes, understood to have been as a rule devised by lady writers, in conversation with the inspector's old friend on his bilious days ;
and it was assuredly a symptom of intellectual decline that
the ordinary illusions of ' piquant *Parisienne*,' 'bright and
cheerful French waiting-maid, so willing and so clean,'
' jolly little French girl—quite the *grisette*, don't you know,
out of the Latin Quarter,' could sometimes deprive him of
articulate speech, so misguided and inane they seemed to
him. Of course he must have been hypersensitive and
ultrabilious. At the same time, in such strange ways had
his life been cast that he knew all about the *dessous des
cartes*, that is to say, the 'wheels within wheels' of the
entire machinery. Anyone of the foregoing phrases, harmless as they were, would launch him into some anecdote or
narrative which, commonplace at the commencement, incredible at the end, would be drawn from the dark stores of
his own experience. The inspector had first met his old
friend years before, amid surroundings which they never
referred to afterwards, except when alone. He had a great
respect for his old friend's erudition, by the way.

The passenger from Scotland Yard suddenly laughed
outright. He was picturing this ' vivacious French brunette '
imported into the service of an honest middle-class English
family. She had brushed by him with short, quick, studied
steps, and with an air of unconsciousness that was delight-
fully artificial. How pleasant, he thought maliciously, she
would make herself towards the young ladies of the house—
how materfamilias would extol her prompt obedience ! And
then a day would come—well, well—whoever would have
guessed it ! The interposition of the ' Yard ' was not demanded always in these cases when they happened in
England ; but materfamilias, who had possibly missed one
or two of her most valuable trinkets as well, would resolve
that no further importation of the same article should ever

take place so far as her own household was concerned. The 'vivacious French brunette,' however, who has graduated in the Paris *faubourgs*, seldom strays into a northern clime unless under circumstances independent of her choice. People from the northern climes are far more ready to travel southwards.   The gay Lothario—

> 'That haughty, gallant, gay Lothario,
>   That dear perfidious !'

—who graduates at Hoxton or at Cambridge, at Oxford or at Rosherville, at Richmond, Houndsditch, or the Hay-market, will not infrequently extend his researches to the seats of learning endowed in 'Parry.' But he looks vainly for Calista in the *faubourgs*. He encounters the vivacious brunette instead of that tearful penitent, and he probably observes that in the *faubourien* soil the tree of knowledge flourishes in the rankest luxuriance. Overweighted by his *rôle*, and for the occasion resigning it, Lothario perhaps reflects with bitterness that the true Calista was a much more tolerable person than this make-believe, whose boundless lore he never, never would have suspected. What! This vivacious French brunette, this piquant *Parisienne*, this bright and willing French waiting-maid, this 'jolly little French girl, don't you know, quite the *grisette* out of the Latin Quarter,' has been passing her lifetime under the shadow of a knowledge-tree whose giant variety was not even mentioned in the text-books of his Alma Mater? Ah, Sir Lothario, yes! If a native-born *faubourienne*, she has learnt many secrets from the lush branches of that tree.

'Mr. Smithson?'

The speaker was a lady who had advanced from one of the apartments into the ante-chamber. She was a pale and prematurely-wrinkled blonde, of a gentle and sympathetic expression of face. Her violet silk-dress, which rustled at every instant, was all awry, as though it had been hastily donned for the meeting with the visitor; and with it had been assumed a mincing manner and an affected pronunciation, both sustained with difficulty, but well meant. The inspector, whose business took him everywhere, recognised the type of domestic martyr.

'My husband is unfortunately occupied at the present moment on important business of the society,' pursued the lady. 'If there is any information I can furnish I shall be most happy, I am sure. We are all enthusiasts in the good work.'

As a well-wisher to the cause, Mr. Byde held forth with great fluency on the general question, and followed these remarks up with professions of solicitude for the prospects of the International. It was a noble movement, he observed.

'A noble movement, indeed,' concurred his hostess; 'but we are still only at the outset of the good work. Funds are what we need most urgently, and all our friends should do their best to aid us in rendering our strenuous efforts fruitful. Are you a member, sir, of the I.O.T.A.?—I do not think we have the name of Smithson on our list. The most practical way of helping on the good work is by personal membership, and by donations. I could enrol you in the society at once. We need no proposers and seconders, nor do we care to prosecute inquiries as to our new members, preferring to trust to their own assurances, to rely upon their own representations—for what is more demoralising than mistrust? There is a nominal entrance-fee, and the subscription is payable in advance.'

Mr. Byde would certainly be proud indeed to link himself to a grand enterprise that might prove the common salvation and unification of vast communities, hitherto separated sternly from one another by history, by language, and by race. But he must be so well known, he believed, at the headquarters of the International in London that the directors there would take it ill of him if he entered the stream at any other point than at its fountain-head. A feeling of the deepest sympathy for the good work, together with an ardent wish to form the acquaintance of Brother Bamber, whose devotion to the temperance cause was famed throughout its ranks, had impelled him to venture these inquiries, profiting by a temporary visit to the French metropolis. He regretted to have presented himself at an inopportune moment; Brother Bamber would naturally be absorbed by his regular duties at this particular period of the day.

Oh dear no—not at all! Mr. Bamber's onerous duties engrossed his time all day long, from morning until late, very late, at night; but ordinarily he was accessible at any hour to well-wishers of the good work. The exceptional occurrence which demanded his attention at the present moment was the visit of a colleague from headquarters. One of the most industrious and eloquent lecturers of the society had arrived that morning in Paris, having travelled from London by the night-mail. He was the bearer of instructions and counsel from the board, and had of course at once sought an interview with her husband. If Mr. Smithson could wait a little longer, both Brother Neel—the eminent lecturer to whom she had referred—and Mr. Bamber would be exceedingly happy to receive him.

The conversation had continued in the drawing-room, which opened on to the vestibule. Mr. Byde could hear a murmur of voices in the apartment adjoining, and incidentally remarked upon the fact. The voices were perhaps those of Brother Bamber and his colleague? Yes, replied his hostess—the adjoining apartment served Mr. Bamber as his private office.

'And what may have been the progress of the last three months, should you say?' inquired the inspector most engagingly.

'Much good work has been done by the International in Paris during the three months just ended—thanks, I may say, to my husband's untiring zeal and energy. The enrolments show an increase over the previous quarter, and they are at length becoming of a decidedly international character. We find that we have only to make the idea known to ensure recruits. The French are always greatly impressed by the novelty of the idea and its humanitarian character, as well as by the practical methods of the organization. Other bodies of the same order have appealed too exclusively to the young. Our society recruits its members irrespective of age, and of course from amongst all nationalities. We meet with obstacles, and, singularly enough, they are not raised by the general public, or by classes whose vested interests might suffer through our success; our annoyances have occasionally sprung from the regularly-constituted authorities, who, it seems, misapprehend the nature of our association in the most extraordinary manner. My husband tells me that he has more than once been followed and watched by French detectives. We feel certain that there are members of both the criminal and political secret police who have enrolled themselves among us here! Odd, is it not?'

Mrs. Bamber recited this discourse like a lesson, and at its close laughed with a curiously shrill abruptness.

'There was a friend of mine named Bamber,' said Inspector Byde tentatively, but with quite a friendly warmth; 'a very dear friend of mine who came from Chicago, and whom I have not seen for two or three years. His name was Fitzpatrick Justin Bamber. Would it be the same—though I do not think he then had temperance leanings? Perhaps it is not my old friend?'

'Oh, no! Mr. Bamber's initials are "E. J."—Egan Jewel Bamber. He resided in America for some time, but never, I believe, at Chicago.'

'A moment's thought might have convinced me,' pursued the inspector, more cordially than ever; 'of course it could not be my old friend. A pleasant look out from this window, most pleasant!'

'Yes, is it not a pleasant look out?'

'Charming in summer, I should fancy?'

'Very agreeable in summer.'

'And that, I presume, would be the boulevard below—the Boulevard Haussmann?'

'Yes, that is the boulevard; a pleasant thoroughfare, and conveniently situated.'

'My old friend Bamber retired to Rome, I think; and that must have been at a date prior to the foundation of the I.O.T.A., with which, indeed, he could hardly have co-operated long. Political societies were the only organizations he understood or cared about.'

'Oh, dear me! There is a wide difference between anything of that sort and the I.O.T.A.'

'Why, naturally—naturally!' The inspector joined a few genial bass-notes to the shrill volley emitted by Brother Bamber's better half. He transferred his gaze from her false teeth to her glassy eyes, and added, 'My friend Fitzpatrick Justin was one of America's most glorious sons, although he shrank from fame. He led the new school of revolutionary heroes, and had done a great deal of good work with dynamite.'

Mr. Byde reiterated fragments of these two sentences as though gratified with their sound. The undisguised expression to be seen upon the countenance opposite his own was one of alarm at the revolutionary sympathies he appeared

to express.   Whatever might have been his views with reference to Brother Bamber, it was clear that this worthy
dame must be absolved from any complicity in secret propaganda such as he seemed to suspect.   Poor woman! in the
lines of her face he did not read happiness.   What he read
between the lines was meekness and a narrow intelligence;
the capacity of thinking in a limited rotation of ideas, and of
learning accurately by rote.

Inspector Byde was well aware of the advantages accru-
ing to conspiracies by the employment of women in the
more dangerous portions of their work.   If the errand of the
female emissary succeeded, the conspirators exulted over
their own superior cunning, or, with more modesty, reviled
the stupidity of their foes; whereas if the superior cunning
of their foes detected the little mission of their female
emissary, and obstructed its course ungallantly, there remained always the recourse to indignant championship of
weak women; the other side were cowardly and brutal, subjecting delicately-nurtured ladies—mothers devoted to their
sons, or, as the case might be, innocent young girls who had
nursed their brothers on the bed of sickness—to outrageous
insult.   But the physiognomy now before him, said Mr.
Byde inwardly, altogether vindicated the amiable Mrs.
Bamber.   Vindicated her?   Of what?   Here he stood once
more yielding to this terrible bias!   Why should there exist
any co-relation between the Fitzpatrick he had invented,
and the Egan who sat in the next room conferring upon the
business of the International?   The conference appeared to
be over.   He heard the two colleagues moving towards the
door.   If for the sake of his peace of mind alone, he fervently
hoped at that minute, as he regarded his hostess with con-
trition, that the physiognomy of Brother Bamber might
prove the fitting counterpart of hers.

The hostess advanced to meet her husband, and conveyed some intimation to him before he crossed the
threshold.

'Welcome, dear friend,' said Brother Bamber, as he
approached from the doorway with outstretched hands.

He was a man of slender build and fair complexion.
What hair he had was of so light a colour that he might
have been supposed entirely bald.   His eyelashes were of
the same hue as his hair; and not much deeper in their

shade were his eyebrows and long silky beard. He wore
gold-rimmed spectacles ; and, as he now smiled, fixedly,
the gold stoppings of his front teeth gleamed at Inspector
Byde.

'An esteemed colleague from London,' added Brother
Bamber, introducing Brother Neel. The latter came forward with a pompous demeanour and deliberate gait. It
was plain that he had no recollection of the passenger from
Scotland Yard. Mr. Byde again explained the deep interest
which, as a consistent upholder of the good work during
twenty-three years, he felt in its latest development, this
courageous enterprise ; and then a chorus of expletive
platitudes ensued. 'We were intending to step down to
the new mission-rooms of the league in the Rue Feydeau,'
concluded Brother Bamber.

Mr. Byde observed that he should be delighted to accompany them.

'Victorine !' called Brother Bamber.

The vivacious brunette tripped into the ante-chamber in
answer to the summons. Her master demanded his hat,
overcoat, etc., and she furnished him with those articles
with an air of effusive *naïveté* which perhaps only the inspector properly appreciated. A parcels delivery porter
presented himself at the apartment just as they were ready
to leave. Victorine received the package, and handed the
book to her master to sign with the most captivating jaunti-
ness imaginable. Inspector Byde could hardly suppress
that grim smile of his as he watched her. Brother Neel
watched her also ; and the better half of Brother Bamber,
as she stood aloof, likewise watched her. As for Brother
Bamber himself, he did not once direct a glance at Victorine.
He placed his signature in the book in a perfunctory manner,
and gave a brief direction about the package. It looked like
a stout wooden box, in shape like nothing so much as an
ordinary household gas-meter. From the inscription on the
red label of the *European Express*, the package seemed to
have been consigned to Paris from Boston, U.S.

CHAPTER IX.

ON their way to the Rue Feydeau, Brother Bamber favoured
'Mr. Smithson' with a batch of most interesting statistics,

proving that, soon or late, the crusade of the I.O.T.A. must inevitably prevail.   The statistics were drawn from his own past reports, and from those of his colleagues.   All they need do was to push the good work boldly forward ; adherents would ally themselves spontaneously with the cause. His personal experience enabled him to attest this as a certainty.   Why, even the retail wine-dealer, who supplied his household with mineral waters, had joined the I.O.T.A.; and the hairdresser opposite his private residence had called upon him on Sunday morning just as he was going to chapel, and of his own free will had taken out a two years' subscription, payable in advance.

Brother Neel supplemented his colleague's figures by an array of convincing arguments extracted from the professional repertory.   As the inspector listened to both voices he decided that at any rate Brother Bamber was in complete ignorance of the tragic event of that morning.   Brother Neel excited his admiration while he talked.   He had good tones, and used them skilfully.   The matter of his homily might be trite and shallow, but the organ was so musically persuasive !   And with what a beatific serenity he looked, and walked, and waited !   To bring the case home to a man like this, mused Inspector Byde, would atone thrice over for that great mistake.

Brother Bamber smiled with irritating frequency in conversation.   Brother Neel never smiled, or scarcely ever, but seemed continually upon the point of smiling—which perhaps excited in the spectator quite as keen an irritation. Of the two heads, that of Brother Neel would manifestly the better adorn a public platform or the head of a procession. He wore his oiled hair long, and without a parting ; combed carefully straight back, it left exposed to view the whole extent of a forehead which the most vulgar would have recognised as noble.   His dark locks, neatly smoothed behind his ears, and at the nape of his neck terminating in a fringe, gave him in some unaccountable way the air generic to the fifth-rate poet, the tenth-rate tragedian, the twelfth-rate family doctor, the foreign pianist, and the professor of legerdemain who lets himself out for evening parties.   His clean-shaven visage looked blue, and the sturdiness of his frame might have fitted him for missionary work among savages.

'You must find your labours excessively fatiguing,' remarked the inspector to Brother Neel—'as travelling
lecturer, I mean. When did you run over from England?'

'I arrived this morning only,' was the reply; 'I came by
the night-mail from London.'

'The journey not too wearisome?'

'Oh, I am accustomed to it by this time, and I am an
excellent traveller, I should tell you, dear friend. When we
have once made the crossing, I can generally sleep through
the remainder of the journey.'

'Especially at night, I suppose—like me?' hazarded the
inspector, geniality itself.

'Especially at night.'

'Then by the night-mail you would be due in Paris
by——'

'We arrived at six this morning, or thereabouts.'

The inspector followed these apparently aimless questions
by some others of no greater seeming importance, but perhaps tending remotely towards the same end. When he
had exercised his ingenuity to his heart's content, he was
obliged to acknowledge that he remained just as wise as at
the outset, and no wiser. One test, however, yet lay within
his reach. It was with a growing eagerness that he awaited
an opportunity for applying that test.

Brother Bamber showed them all the premises in the Rue
Feydeau: the meeting-hall, the committee-rooms, and the
space allotted to recreation, education, and conversation.
It was small, he acknowledged, as compared with the parent
undertakings in England, but as the movement expanded,
so they could increase the accommodation by the establishment of district-branches. Here stood the members' lend-
ing library. They had standard authors in both languages;
works on politics and history; a few French novels, and
fewer English scientific works; and, thanks to the muni-
ficence of private donors, a perfect storehouse of temperance
literature. The French novels and the English scientific
works were subjected to the most rigid scrutiny before being
admitted to their shelves. Rooms were specially set aside
for chess, draughts, and cards, which were permitted on
week-days, but not for money stakes.

Brother Bamber wound up an harangue on the glorious

future of the I.O.T.A. by correcting a well-known apothegm. Instead of cheaply pronouncing that '*Le cléricalisme, voilà l'ennemi,*' Gambetta should have thundered into the ears of his compatriots that the enemy to be combated was 'alcoholism,' or simply alcohol. '*L'alccol, voilà l'ennemi!*'—how would that do for their motto here? 'Very well indeed,' said Mr. Byde.

A French gentleman, in a threadbare tall hat and frayed linen, advanced mincingly towards the three visitors, and, with the obeisance which betrays the lively sense of favours to come, presented Brother Bamber with an account.

'One of our French agents,' explained Brother Bamber; 'a little bill for the outdoor propaganda. That gentleman waiting over there is one of his English colleagues charged with the management of our European correspondence.'

Mr. Byde noticed that in the brief communication which the English colleague had to make to Brother Bamber, he preferred to employ, or employed unwittingly, the Irish dialect of the English language as spoken in America.

Their tour of the premises completed, they descended into the street. As they moved in the direction of the Bourse, a hawker ran by them with his arms full of freshly-printed newspapers. He was shouting the contents of the journal, and appeared to be hurrying towards the main line of boulevards. Another hawker, folding his papers as he hastened along, followed at a little distance, and behind him they presently perceived one more, likewise calling out the sensational news.

'The first of the evening papers,' remarked Brother Bamber. 'What is that he is calling? Another murder?'

'Assassination of an Englishman—mysterious affair!' shouted the first hawker.

'Strange discovery in this morning's mail-train from London,' called the next, out of breath—'robbery not the object of the crime!'

'The murder of an Englishman this morning,' repeated a third—'the police on the track of the assassin!'

Brother Neel purchased a copy of the newspaper.

'Robbery not the motive of the crime!' commented Brother Bamber. 'What then?'

His colleague spread the paper open, and they halted to peruse the latest intelligence. It was not difficult to discover the item in question. Lines in large black characters announced—'*Assassinat d'un Anglais—Un drame intime !*'

'Bless me!' exclaimed Brother Neel, after a glance at the opening sentences. 'That must have been the train I travelled in myself.'

'The very train you journeyed by from London!' echoed his colleague. 'Really, now!'

'Robbery not the motive of the crime?' repeated the supposititious Mr. Smithson. 'What do they think, then? A secret society at work?'

Brother Bamber looked over his gold spectacles at the speaker.

'Secret societies among Englishmen?' said he, smiling fixedly.

'No,' returned Mr. Smithson—'not among them: against them.'

'In France?'

'Perhaps. In France—but not French.'

'Surely you don't mean—you don't mean the old revolutionists, the American dynamiters?'

'Oh, personally, I don't mean anybody, or anything! Let us see what the paper says.'

'But the old revolutionists who worked from Paris,' persisted Brother Bamber, who, with his head erect, was regarding the other full through his glasses—'every man of them has long been known to the police, and none of them could stir without detection, I understood.'

'Indeed? And so they are all known, and watched— the centres, the head-centres, and the rest of the veterans here?'

'That is the general impression in what I may call the official British colony, which is the source of my own information. And a very necessary precaution—a most reassuring state of affairs. In that way they are absolutely compelled to remain inactive.'

'Of course they are. The veterans can do nothing while they are watched by the police; which, from what I have heard, accounts for their inaction while their younger confederates, who are not in the least known to the police, go on with the campaign.'

There was not the faintest tinge of irony in the speaker's tone.

'Why, I had understood that the association was on the point of collapse—the association of American dynamiters?'

'So had I,' responded Mr. Smithson, the picture of stupidity for the moment.

Brother Neel handed the newspaper to his colleague of the I.O.T.A. The latter translated the paragraph, and read it aloud. After setting forth the circumstances of the discovery, the paragraph proceeded as follows:

'We are enabled to state that the few papers which have been found in the possession of the deceased are not of a nature to establish his identity. The crime has manifestly not been committed for the sake of plunder. The pockets contained loose money amounting to a considerable sum, and the jewellery worn by the deceased has been left untouched. Either of the ordinary hypotheses becomes, therefore, at once disposed of, the idea of suicide being entirely precluded. Must we seek for the clue to this crime in some story of private feud, in some family *vendetta*, some tale of heartless betrayal or malignant jealousy? From time to time, indeed, the hypocrisy of English social life is brought home to all those of us who have suffered ourselves to be imposed upon by Pharisaical airs of superior virtue. Scandals of incredible magnitude, dragged from time to time into the light of day, remind us opportunely that beneath the apparent fastidiousness of our starched neighbours we may discover a corruption of manners to which the most licentious period of ancient Rome affords the only fitting parallel. Happily, we French—*nous autres Français*—are not like our Britannic neighbours. We may possess our faults—who can say that he is impeccable?—but our candour redeems them. The characteristic of France is generosity of thought, word, and action; that of England, an egotistical hypocrisy. The French are valiant, impulsive, and trusting; the English are calculating, cold, and braggart. *Ah, pudique Albion*—down with the mask! Our good police of Paris is already unmuzzled, and we may confidently expect a prompt unravelling of this latest mystery. One thing we may promise to British society, with its pyramid of *cannt*—this term has been invented by the English themselves, to express their own hypocrisy—we can safely promise that whatever may be the tale of scandalous vice connected with the tragedy of this morning's mail, the Paris press will be no party to its concealment. For our part wo shall give the most ample details. Our own relations with the Prefecture of Police have been too often turned to the advantage of our readers for any doubt whatever to exist as to our ability to place before the public any matters which may come to the knowledge of the authorities. We shall keep our readers closely informed of every development in this mysterious affair. The sources of information at our own disposal, independently of the Prefecture, are both varied and trustworthy. We will not say that we are not, even at this early juncture, in the possession of facts that might in a material degree influence the conduct of the inquiry. But to the police, who profess to have discovered something in the nature of an indication, we will do no more than offer the proverbial, but eternally true, counsel, " *Cherchez la femme !*" The body has been transported to the Morgue for identification.'

' My train seems to have been selected by criminals,' observed Brother Neel. ' We had an arrest at Dover—a sensational diamond robbery case, we were told.'

' If you could recognise the deceased as a fellow-traveller,' said Mr. Smithson, 'it might be possible for you to help tho authorities here in the matter of identification.'

' I do not think there could have been anybody in the train who was personally known to me,' replied the other.

' We might make a visit to the Morgue, if it is not too far from here,' continued Mr. Smithson ; ' we might just look in and see the body.'

' A somewhat ghastly spectacle,' objected Brother Bamber.

' People connected with the police are so peculiar,' went on Mr. Smithson, ' that if it were ascertained that our dear friend here had travelled by this very train, and in such a case as this had shown no curiosity as to the person murdered—a person whom he might possibly have noticed in conversation with suspicious individuals—they might subject our dear friend to all kinds of inconvenience.'

' That is true,' said Brother Neel—' and, for the sake of the I.O.T.A., anything of that kind must be carefully avoided. If the deceased should be some one whom I happened to notice in the society of other persons there will

be no harm in my volunteering the statement to the authorities.   My evidence might prove useful in the future—who
knows?—in corroboration of other testimony.   And if the
deceased should be some passenger whom I am certain I
have never seen, why then there would be no reason for my
coming forward.   I should say nothing whatever about my
presence in the mail-train, and there, so far as I am concerned, the matter would terminate.'

'As you like,' acquiesced his colleague.

They bent their steps in the direction of Notre Dame.
Traversing one of the bridges, they arrived on the island
which at this point divides the Seine.   In a few minutes
they were at the towers of Notre Dame.

Passing to the rear of the cathedral, and skirting the little
gardens which there lie, the inspector and his companions
saw that groups of idlers had already congregated in front
of the Morgue.   Persons were also approaching from the
bridges on both sides, and others were ascending the two or
three steps at the entrance to the building.   Visitors who
had satisfied their curiosity lounged through the doorway,
and down the steps, and augmented the knots of debaters
scattered along the pavement.   Some of the women and
children were cracking nuts and eating sweetmeats, purchased from itinerant vendors who had stationed their
barrows at the side of the road.   One hawker was endeavouring to sell bootlaces; another was enumerating the
titles of the comic songs which he exhibited in cheap leaflets, strung together on a wooden frame.

'And so this is the Morgue!' exclaimed Mr. Smithson,
gaping at the long, plain structure opposite the gardens.

Anyone would have affirmed most positively that Mr.
Smithson had never visited the spot before.   As they
mounted the stone steps, Brother Neel stopped short, and
Mr. Smithson, who had followed close upon his heels,
stumbled against him.   He turned back for an instant, but
only to make a small purchase at one of the barrows.

The air, the aspect, the associations of the sinister place
might have affected momentarily the stoutest heart.   It
was not that the atmosphere could have been condemned
by any sanitary inspector; nor that the naked walls, with
curt official notices to the public painted in plain capitals
here and there, recalled the infected charnel house, or fright·

ful images of corruption which at some time or another we have most of us received into our minds, and which we carry about with us buried to the utmost depth, out of view and apparently forgotten, but capable of brusquely rising from their dark recess under a single lurid ray. It was not that the living who were issuing from these portals had drawn into their lungs unconsciously the icy, stagnant air poisoned by the dead. The Morgue was a peep-show, not a reception-room.

The groups now issuing from its portals had been staring through beautiful panes of plate-glass. A handrail hindered them from approaching near enough to dim the crystal with their breath, to flatten their noses at its surface, or to shatter the entire frame in their ingenuous eagerness to feast their eyes upon the corpses. To hinder the ladies and gentlemen who flocked hither on a 'good' day from scratching their names, or Scriptural texts, or possibly a humorous—even a ribald—couplet upon the windows of the Morgue, a safeguard more effectual was at hand. Officers of the establishment kept a keen watch on the company, an excellent precaution for more reasons than one. And where stood these officers? Oh, who could say? That was the dress—the semi-livery worn by the old campaigner yonder who was certainly just now chewing tobacco. There were others who wore no livery of any kind, and who on 'good' days would get into conversation with likely strangers. Were these really dead persons? they would perhaps ask —these figures extended upon sloping couches, and to all appearance gazing intelligently at the spectator—were they actually dead human beings, or imitations of the same, in wax? The murderer who has swaggered into the presence of his victim, out of bravado, or whom the fascination of his crime attracts and rivets to this spot, must, like his accomplice who has mingled with the crowd for purposes of information, beware of such lynx-eyed, casual neighbours, with their simple questions and their homely garb.

No; if the air on this side of the enormous glass panes could be condemned by any sanitary inspector, its noxious germs must have been given forth by the living who thus thronged the temporary habitation of the dead. Men, women, and children pushed forward indiscriminately to the great peep-show. You could see the bodies here for

nothing, whilst at the waxworks in the fairs there were
always a few sous to pay at the doors, to say nothing of the
extras for the models of anatomical curiosities, and the
catalogue ; there might be a good many more varieties of
death exhibited in the waxworks at the fairs, but the figures
were not, as a rule, well finished off like these, and that one
over there had just been brought in—murdered only that
morning, and the assassin had escaped. He was a foreigner,
the paper said—a German. *Non, madame, pardon*—an
Englishman ! Well, was it not the same thing—English--
German—was not all that just the same ? Not at all,
madame, if you will permit me—two quite different peoples.
I don't say that the Americans and the Germans might not
be near together, but the Germans and the English belong
to different countries, although the English can speak
American. Well—English, American, German—all that
was the same thing so far as the French were concerned.
Why could they not stay in their own countries ? They all
hated France. *Ah non, madame, je vous demande pardon*—
in matters of that sort—— 'In matters of that sort !' Was
it not well known that every one of these foreign countries
hated France because France had conquered them all in the
past, and they were afraid that she would get strong enough
to conquer them all again ? And for that reason they sent
spies into France. There were some people about who professed to know everything, and always wanted to correct
the rest of the world. She was only a poor widow who
supported herself, an invalid sister, and two children, by hard
work ; but she had not seen the *coup d'état*, the fall of the
empire, the siege, and the Commune without becoming
qualified to say something about politics—*tiens!* That might
be very true, *madame*, but all the same the body over there
which they would perceive presently, when their turns
came, was that of an Englishman. 'I want to see the
body of the Englishman who was murdered ! Take me up,
papa ! I want to see,' etc. 'Yes, yes, yes, papa will show
to his little Louis the body of the,' etc. 'No, I want to see
it now ! I *will* see it now ! That gentleman is treading
on me, they are crushing my new hat ! No, I don't want
any more cakes : I want to see the body of the Englishman
who was murdered ! Take me up and show me,' etc.,
etc.

Housekeepers returning from market, with their baskets
of provisions on their arms; nursemaids dragging their
little charges along by the hand after them; work-girls
chattering to be overheard, and giggling with the superan-
nuated *coureurs* who had remarked them in the next street
but one, or who had been struck by their piquant carriage
as they flirted through the garden opposite—' *Est-elle gen-
tille !*' ' *Hé—la blondinette !*'—a sprinkling of blue blouses ;
bank messengers ; a priest or two ; barristers from the law
courts hard by; an occasional apparition in fur, lace, and
velvet, of which the masculine sense retained a vague impression of the thick veil, a hat, and a muff, together with
the faintest odour of white rose : to this restless and changing
throng came Brothers Neel and Bamber, accompanied by
' Mr. Smithson.' Brother Neel had stopped a second time ;
but merely to glance over the frames of photographs nailed
against the wall. Of that ghastly collection the originals
had tenanted the Morgue, nameless; and nameless they
had been lifted from their couches, on the other side of the
plate-glass windows, when . . .

It was surely most improbable that Brother Neel could
have known the originals of any portraits exhibited within
these precincts. They were all neatly numbered, and they
thus awaited, with the last look which death imprinted upon
their faces, either the chance recognition of some passer-by,
or their ultimate consignment to complete oblivion. Poor,
disfigured features, durable enough on the photographer's
film of paper, but too transitory in the mould which nature
gave them : who could say what tragic story they had not
provoked or witnessed—who could divine the occasion of
that cast of terror, the humour of this lingering smile, the
anger of that lowering brow, the secret of those disconcert-
ing, sightless orbs ? Several of the heads bore wounds that
had been strapped up after death—merciless gashes, some
of them; others, swollen and bloated, wore the sullen,
almost animal, look to be observed among the drowned
whose bodies have lain long immersed ; a few revealed the
sharp contractions of despair and anguish marking the
victim who, in the French phrase, 'sees himself die,' and
rebels against his fate,

PREFECTURE DE POLICE.

NOTICE.

The public are invited to make a declaration of the name of any individual whom they may recognise, to the Registrar's office, at the Morgue.

This declaration involves no expense either to strangers or to friends and relatives of the deceased. *Elle est toute gratuite.*

Inspector Byde loitered behind with Brother Neel. While they both paused, a gentleman in later middle life mounted the steps from the street and moved unconcernedly into the building. The new-comer was attired almost as scrupulously as an old beau, but there was something about his physiognomy which might have been considered less typical of the old beau than of his coachman. He had a pear-shaped red face, with a short white whisker at each side. He gave you the impression at first sight of being uncomfortably hot; but you were soon led to the conclusion that the glow which overspread his countenance would be more properly attributable to the generous vintage produced by the sun, soil, and science of Oporto. Quite a small nosegay of winter flowers adorned the button-hole of his stylish overcoat; and his new kid gloves were bright enough to be reflected in his polished hat. No one would have imagined that his night's rest had been interrupted; although we know that at six o'clock, a.m., he attended at the Gare du Nord to meet the mail from London. It was grandpa.

Brother Neel saw no faces he could recognise, that was clear. It was Inspector Byde who recognised one of the faces that he saw.

The recognition, indeed, was mutual. Grandpa nodded to Inspector Byde with an air of pleased surprise, and the inspector nodded back. Their salutations took place unperceived by the two colleagues in the service of the I.O.T.A. Brothers Neel and Bamber had penetrated into the crowd, and Mr. 'Smithson' immediately rejoined them. There was another person whom grandpa recognised, but to whom nevertheless he sent no salute, a figure posted near a recess,

away from the mass of spectators, and devoting a good deal
more attention to the latter themselves than to the object of
their curiosity. It was the manly form of Mr. Toppin, who,
stationed like a sentinel, resolved to ' bid any man stand in
the prince's name,' no doubt fancied he was acquitting himself of his duty with no less discretion than zeal. Mr.
' Smithson ' possibly dreaded at that moment an untimely
greeting from his vigilant subordinate.

Edging their way through the rows of gossiping spectators,
the three companions at length caught a glimpse of the
'Englishman who was murdered.' A minute more and
they were face to face with the corpse. The detective had
watched his neighbour, Brother Neel, most narrowly, and
by placing himself a little in his rear, contrived to maintain
his scrutiny unobserved. Brother Neel betrayed the sensibility, transient but perfectly undissembled, which under
the circumstances would be altogether natural. The communicative Mr. Remington lay before him. At not much
more than arm's length he saw, supported by the sloping
couch, on the other side of the plate-glass window, his
fellow-passenger of the previous night—the obliging narrator
of the Wilmot case, the sceptic in young Mr. Sinclair's innocence—dead. The life-like appearance of the body might
well have startled him, as it startled persons who had never
until now set eyes on the deceased. Beyond, apparently,
the shock of noting the few signs which had been described
concisely by the inspector in his report that morning to
Scotland Yard, Brother Neel evinced no species of emotion.
A consumptive lady, borne down by ponderous gold earrings
remarked to her daughter on the dim expression of astonishment and alarm which the features still retained; would
not anybody say that the deceased, as he reposed upon his
couch, was about to open his lips and call for help? The
daughter—a dark-eyed maid, with a woman's torso but an
infant's face—read inquiry, also, she commented, in the blue
and bloodshot eyes of the deceased. Sometimes the dead
bodies at the Morgue, continued mademoiselle, had a look
of meditation, or an air of listening; this one seemed as
though he were searching for some one in the crowd, or as
if he meant to question them, if they would wait.

' Do you think that the assassin could come here, and
stand in front of this, unmoved?' asked the young lady, who

appeared to interest herself in criminal exploits and physical decay.

'I can't imagine how he could,' replied her mother. '*I* couldn't.'

'I dare say he might, though, all the same,' continued the daughter. 'It seems to me that if I had courage enough to commit a murder, I should not in the least mind seeing the body afterwards. You know they are dead: what does it matter?'

'Ah, but the guilty quail before their lifeless victims; that is well known,' responded the elder lady, glancing round for corroboration.

'Not necessarily, madame,' put in a neighbour, who forthwith enforced his view of the matter by citations from the popular records of criminal jurisprudence.

'A profitable discussion, truly!' sneered Brother Bamber to his colleague.

'Well, my dear friend, I agree rather with the elder lady,' said Brother Neel. 'I believe in the resonant and mighty voice of truth. Were the assassin, now, of this unfortunate man at present here, gazing or about to gaze upon the victim of his impious deed, I think his conscience must betray him.' He, too, cast a glance around him as he concluded. It seemed as though he half-expected to encounter some such mute avowal of guilt. The regard which met his own was that of Inspector Byde.

'Do you identify the dead man?' asked Mr. Smithson.

'No,' replied Brother Neel.

'You have no recollection of his face at all? I should fancy it would help on the authorities materially if someone could identify this person. You do not remember observing him among your fellow-passengers?'

'I have no recollection of ever having seen that man.'

'Then we need not remain here any longer,' suggested Brother Bamber, less at ease in the crowd than in the offices of the I.O.T.A. They turned to depart. The inspector told his two companions that he would join them presently outside the Morgue. He wished, no doubt, to exchange a word with the praiseworthy Mr. Toppin; and grandpa was hovering persistently in his neighbourhood, remarked Mr. Byde.

But he had a different reason for remaining in his place a

moment more. Two female figures, advancing through the crowd with difficulty, and manifestly shrinking from the contact of this mixed assemblage, had caught his attention as they made their way towards the window. It was easy to distinguish them as English ladies. They were both veiled. The toilette of the elder, rich but in good taste, had a decidedly Parisian stamp. The appearance of the younger lady, who was attired in a semi-travelling costume, was more characteristically English. Mr. Byde noted that the younger of the two leaned upon her companion for support. As they approached the window, he stationed himself behind them.

' I dare not look,—I dare not—oh, I dare not!' murmured the younger lady, in agitated accents. ' If it should be——'

' My dear child,—come—come ! There,—I told you these fears were groundless.'

' Heavens !—what can it mean ?' The young lady raised her veil, and, as the colour came back to her cheeks, gazed with astonishment at the lineaments of the dead man.

' Why,—do you recognise him ?'

' Yes,—oh yes ! What can have happened ?—oh,—let us go from this horrible place !'

Mr. Inspector Byde signalled to his colleague, Toppin.

CHAPTER X.

In the course of the evening Mr. Toppin presented himself at his colleague's hotel. He had been not a little astonished at the arrival of the inspector at the Morgue in company with two clerically-attired gentlemen, with whom he appeared to be on easy terms. To observe the inspector salute a third acquaintance, in the shape of an elderly party who looked like a real old swell, rather ' horsey' in his style, perhaps—a Jockey Club Crœsus, no doubt : English race-horse owner established in France : too solidly British, or not quite over-dressy enough, to be a vecomte, or a marky, or a dook—had added to his astonishment. Anybody would have imagined that this Byde was lounging about his own metropolis, which lay upon the other side of the English Channel !

Detective Toppin was directed upstairs to a private sitting-

room retained by the inspector. He found the latter seated
in an armchair at the mahogany table, and busily engaged
with inkstand, blotting-pad, pen, and writing-paper.

'Don't wind up your report until you have heard what I
have done,' said Toppin, in good spirits.

'All right,' replied the other; 'I was waiting for you.'

Toppin approached the table, and perceived that what
engrossed the attention of his esteemed superior was something apparently quite different from a report to 'the Yard.'
Mr. Byde had covered pages of his note-paper with pro-
positions 9, 10 and 11. He had bisected a given rectilineal
angle; he had bisected a given finite straight line; and he
had drawn a straight line at right angles to a given straight
line from a given point in the same. He was just killing
time, don't you see—he explained to his subordinate.

'We shall have them to-morrow or the next day,'
announced Mr. Toppin, ' as safe as houses !'

'We shall have them to-morrow or the next day, shall
we?' answered the inspector cheerily. 'That's all right,
then.' He put down his pen, and, as he closed the small
volume at his left hand, murmured, 'Wherefore two straight
lines cannot have a common segment.'

'To begin with, here is a fac-simile of the morsel of paper
found on the floor of the compartment.'

The inspector took the slip of paper proffered him, and
read upon it, ' Adelaide, X. Y.,' with an address, ' to be left
till called for,' at a post-office in Knightsbridge. 'Did you
wire to the Yard?' he asked.

'I wired at once to have the post-office watched. Parties
applying for anything addressed to " Adelaide, X. Y.," were
to be followed.'

'Yes?'

'And—in case they should overlook it—that a hint to the
postmaster might be advisable. For all we know, a letter
might never be claimed, and yet might disappear. For all
we know, a post-office clerk may be in this.'

'Good.'

'I'd lay ten to one it's a confederate in the original
robbery—a man !'

'I should not be surprised if it's a woman,' remarked the
inspector.

'Well, whatever they may think proper to do at the Yard,

I know what *I* should do. I'd have application made, by a plain-clothes man, for anything to that address; and I'd have it opened, whatever it was!'

'Opened?'

'That is what would be done here, as a matter of course.'

'I have a good mind to return to-morrow,' observed the inspector jocosely. 'What could be clearer than the case, as it now stands, at this end? The two suspic.ous characters who travelled by the same train as the deceased, who hastened away immediately the train arrived at its destination, and who obviously applied themselves to elude pursuit, are safe to be pounced on by the French police to-morrow or the next day, wherever they may be hiding. It's not much use for me to stay here. *You* can act with the French authorities and get credit for the capture, at the Yard—which you deserve, friend Toppin.'

'Oh, but——' exclaimed Toppin eagerly, 'this is *your* case!'

'If you can finish it off, it shall be yours.'

'Mr. Byde, sir, it's a real privilege to work with a colleague like yourself. If others at the Yard that I could name would only show the same consideration for the younger men, and those who've never had their chance, things would go on much better, sir, all round. We should all work together, sir, more harmoniously, and the public interests would greatly benefit, and the Yard would find that it possessed the confidence of the entire community in a fuller degree. Young and talented members of the force would see that their abilities were to be allowed free play, instead of feeling that their best efforts only profited their superiors. I am a young member of the force myself, sir, and I think I may say, without any boasting, that with the opportunity I could prove that I am not one of the least able. I feel confident of my capacity to conduct the present case to a speedy and satisfactory termination, and should I be so fortunate as to receive your commendation, I know that it would carry great weight with the Department. Mr. Byde, sir, I am deeply sensible of your kindness.'

'All right, Toppin, all right. But is it so sure that we shall have these men to-morrow or the next day?'

'How can they get clear, with myself and the French police after them? Wherever they go in this country they are conspicuous as foreigners. If they leave Paris for the provinces they can be traced with comparative facility, and can be stopped by telegraph. Their only chance is to keep inside Paris. Now what means of concealment are available to them inside Paris? They are hidden in the residence of an accomplice, we will say. Then every morning and every evening the newspapers render it more and more hazardous for the accomplice himself to keep any parties of the nationality specified in the public press hidden away upon his premises, or in any manner apparently avoiding observation. As a party to the crime, he will very soon have had enough of it, and will either hand them over, to get out of it, or leave them to themselves. The *concierge*, the servants, or the neighbours—there is always someone here to start the gossip—notice that the new arrivals do not leave the house, or leave it, we'll say, only in the evening. They wonder why, and even if no crime has been publicly announced, they are more likely than not to regard these new arrivals with suspicion. If, on the other hand, these parties should decide to go in and out of the house quite freely, in order to save appearances, they are continually running the risk of identification by some person or persons who travelled with them between London and Paris. Suppose they disguise themselves: they are still foreigners, not natives of the country; and they might be followed—*filés*—on "spec," at any minute. Anybody may be in the pay of the police here—the cabman, the vendor of a newspaper, the postman, the *concierge*—who knows? They are not all stupid; and they are all officious and inquisitive. Suppose, however, that they put up, like ordinary visitors, at an hotel—a small private establishment, or one of the largest and most fashionable. Suppose that no suspicions arise in the hotel itself with regard to the coincidence of their arrival and the date of the crime. Every hotel, lodging-house, and boarding-house, having to furnish a police return of the persons arriving at their premises for even a single night, the returns do usually afford the police some sort of indication. The kind of handwriting, whether disguised or not—the kind of names chosen by parties who enter themselves falsely—the people at the Caserne de la Cité (our Scotland Yard, you may say) can of course turn all these things to account, especially in a case like this, with me to help them. But, there!—I am telling you what you know already. And *you* are not the man, Mr. Inspector, whom your own false entry on your own hotel-sheet would have misled, if you had been looking for yourself !'

'Well done,' said Mr. Toppin's colleague, with a smile. 'When do the returns for the day get into the hands of the police?'

'The next morning, as a rule. I have been to the Caserne de la Cité, and by to-morrow, all the hotel returns ought to have been examined and the questionable cases noted. The premises queried can be visited at the first convenient moment. Now, as strangers here, these two men are most likely together in some out-of-the-way hotel, under assumed names, and with false addresses. I should expect them to have described themselves as Americans. They tell me at the Caserne de la Cité that the bullet which caused the death has not yet come into their possession; but if a revolver or a pistol should be discovered at the premises tenanted by the two men it will of course be something, even though the bullet should never be found.'

'And now—with regard to the two ladies I indicated to you, at the Morgue?

'With regard to the two ladies,' continued Mr. Toppin, 'this is what I have ascertained. The elder is a Mrs. Bertram, who resides in the Avenue Marceau; the other is a Miss Knollys. On quitting the Morgue they walked along the Quai de l'Archeveché, until they came to a cab which seemed to be in waiting for them. They stepped into the vehicle and gave a direction to the driver. I took another cab and followed them. The driver pulled up at a telegraph-office, and both ladies alighted. I went into the office a moment after them, and saw that they were filling up a telegraph form. The younger lady was writing the message, but was consulting the other about every word of it, I should say. I went to the same desk for a telegraph-form and a pen, and was able to glance at their message. I had no time to read the contents nor to secure the precise address, but the place to which it was to be despatched was London, and the name of the person to whom it was being sent was—Sinclair.'

'Sinclair!'

'Yes.' The inspector gathered up his diagrams and put

them on one side, under the small volume of the 'Elements.'
His colleague added, after a pause—'Yes, I was astonished
myself!'

'Someone who expected him by the night-mail, has not
heard of his arrest, has been alarmed by the story of an
Englishman found murdered, on the arrival of the train
here, and has attended at the Morgue, in the fear that the
dead man might be Sinclair,' summed up Inspector Byde.
'Someone who knew the deceased also, but did *not* expect
him. What have you learned about this Miss Knollys?'

'She is a visitor, staying with Mrs. Bertram. She arrived
quite recently from England. Mrs. Bertram is a widow, the
concierge told me. She lives in good style, and from what I
can make out, possesses a considerable fortune. While they
remained in the telegraph-office, Miss Knollys appeared
extremely agitated; the other seemed to be consoling her,
but did not show any emotion herself. From the office, they
drove to the Avenue Marceau, and it was then that I gleaned
the particulars I have related to you.'

'Would it be possible, through the *concierge,* to see all
the post-marks of the correspondence this young lady
receives?'

'Possible!' Toppin drew his hands out of his pockets,
and spun a twenty-franc gold piece upon the table. 'We
can even procure a little delay in the delivery—and something more, still. It depends upon how many of these we
can set spinning at the same time!'

'Well, then, see to that. Before my arrival at the
Morgue, did you notice anyone else of English nationality?'

'A cartful of tourists came, led by a guide. There was
nothing about the behaviour of any of them that attracted
my attention. You arrived soon afterwards, with the two
clerical-looking gentlemen.' Toppin evidently wished for a
hint on the subject of Inspector Byde's companions. The
inspector did not gratify his wish, however. A minute later,
a knock was heard at the door. In answer to the inspector's
demand, the handle was turned, and the door was discreetly
opened.

'An inopportune moment, perhaps?' inquired a voice
apologetically.

Toppin twisted his chair round, and faced the visitor, as
the latter politely comprehended him in his salute. It was

the elderly party who had nodded to his colleague at the
Morgue—the real old swell, ' a little horsey in the cut of his
figure-head,' thought Toppin.
' Not at all, not at all!' responded their host, rising. ' We
are old acquaintances,' he explained to his subordinate.
' Haven't met for years. Came across each other by chance
this afternoon, and just had time to ask my old friend to
step up and see me.'
Toppin listened with a deferential bearing.
'But if I disturb you——' pursued the new-comer.
' By no means!' exclaimed the inspector; ' on the
contrary—we were just talking over my return to London.
If you had deferred your visit, we might have lost the
opportunity of discussing those private matters in which we
are both interested. Besides, I suggested this evening, if you
remember. And so the family are in good health?—Yes,
yes—quite so—the family are in good health——'
Toppin understood that he was not wanted. All the
better if his chief had other occupations while he stayed.
It would leave his own hands for a larger share of the work
on which they were engaged together. He made an appointment for the following day, and took his leave.
' Well, Byers,' said the inspector, as soon as he found
himself alone with the elderly party whom Toppin had
connected with wealth and fashion. ' You and I know each
other, of course, but I did not suppose that you and my
friend might be acquainted?'
' Never had the pleasure of meeting the gentleman,'
replied Mr. Byers, seated in the chair which Toppin had
just vacated. He held his polished hat in his left hand, and
with the other was gently balancing a slender silk umbrella
that seemed hardly heavier than a lady's fan.
' A young friend of mine, and a fellow after your own
heart; but there's no reason why we should tell him our
little secrets.'
' That's like you, Mr. Byde—always considerate for others;
always considerate, when it doesn't interfere with your duty.
Not that I have any secrets to tell, but I can always listen
to the secrets of other people, without going to sleep—and
keep them.'
' Or sell them, hey, Benny?—Ha! ha! ha!'
' Ah, no!—Those days are gone.'

'Now—what shall I order?' The inspector prepared to ring.

'Oh, nothing for me!—nothing whatever, I pray.'

'Renounced it?'

'Not altogether; but I'm thinking of doing so. The evils resulting from the consumption of intoxicating beverages are patent to the merest observer. Alcohol is the scourge of modern society, and it behoves us all to set the right example. There is an excellent society here which I shall doubtless join one of these days for the sake of its laudable purposes—an English movement—the International Organization of Total Abstainers. You must be aware of its existence, by the way. If I mistake not, one of your companions this afternoon was the active and single-hearted president of the Paris branch, Brother Bamber?'

'Ah! you know friend Bamber?'

'In the very slightest way.'

'Charming fellow, is he not?'

'A worthy, dear, good man. And so your young friend who was here just now has run over with you for a day or two?'

'Oh dear no!' said Mr. Byde. 'He's established here in business.'

'Like myself, then!'

'More or less, I dare say. What may be your line of business, Benjamin!'

'Insurance—yes, old friend, the insurance business; and pleased you will be to hear, I think, that I am prospering exceedingly. I have my office in the Rue des Petits Champs —quite a business quarter—and none but the most respectable firms are among my clients.'

'Some of my colleagues would be interested to hear that, Benjamin—though they won't hear it from *me*. We thought you went out to Australia; and I dare say that by this time some of them at the Yard think you are dead. Personally, I fancied that New York was more like it; and I never expected to tumble across my old chum Byers—Ben Byers —in the Morgue at Paris.'

'You all used to love me at the Yard, didn't you?'

'We admired your talents, Benjamin. You have given us more trouble at the Yard, I should say, than any other single individual of your time. And all for nothing! It's past and gone now, and we can talk it over without feeling. We never got well hold of you, but I can tell you that we meant having you some day or other.'

'*I* knew you meant having me,' said Mr. Byers complacently. 'But there was only one man of the whole lot clever enough to put *me* away, and that was Byde.'

'Come, that won't do to-day, Byers,' protested the other with a laugh. 'What a character he is, my old chum, Benjamin! There's not the smallest need for it, but habit's too strong for him! Can't help soft-soaping you, although there's nothing to be got by it. Pearson was a better man than I, and so was Baird. And there are still Fullerton and Pilch who know more than I do at the game.'

'Fullerton! The man who muffed that forgery case! I read about it in the newspapers. And as for Pilch, I remember him well enough at the Yard. There's nobody can teach Pilch his business in any department of it, that I *will* say; but he's not in it with you, Byde—and for this reason. Pilch is an obstinate man. Now, in your line of business, obstinacy doesn't do. If Pilch takes up an idea, he wants to bring everything round to it; and that affects his judgment. He wants to pick and choose his facts to suit himself if he once takes up an idea, whereas *your* mode of going to work is never shaped by any preconceived idea, obstinately adhered to. *I* know that, the way you persecuted me in days gone by! No, no; I don't say it to flatter you—what motive could I have for flattering you?—but *you* are the man I fancy, Mr. Byde; that is to say, the man I should not like if *I* were a criminal to have upon my track. You have no prejudices.'

'Yes, I have,' returned Mr. Byde slowly; 'I have a prejudice, and I know it. I have a prejudice which got me into trouble once, and will again some day, if I don't look out.'

'Ah, that temperance case,' responded the visitor after a pause. 'Well, as I said, I am not here to flatter you; and certainly you came down over that!' His tone enhanced the bluntness, real or assumed, of his words; and he added, 'You don't seem to bear the brethren any malice, though?'

'How? What do you mean?'

'Beware of Brother Bamber!' Mr. Byers said this jocularly. 'He is a great hand at conversions.'

' If they convert *you*, Benjamin, they ought to show you on their platforms, like their converted members of Parliament and chimney-sweeps.'

' I made the acquaintance of your other companion this afternoon—the lecturer from London, Brother Neel.   You had been gone some time when I called at the Boulevard Haussmann.   It was about insurance business that I had placed myself in communication with Brother Bamber, and I resolved to look in this afternoon for a personal introduction.   He presented me to his esteemed colleague—a man of great eloquence, it seems, and zeal.'

' You did not refer to me as connected with the Yard, I hope ?' demanded the inspector seriously.

' Well, hardly,' said Mr. Byers, with a bland smile ; ' I supposed you were on business, and I refrained from mentioning you at all, though I should scarcely imagine that you are likely to disturb our dear friends of the I.O.T.A. And yet if you could wipe that case out, as an old chum of yours and a warm admirer, Byde, *I* should be glad for one. I believe in the temperance cause, whether I practise it myself or not ; but there are black sheep in every flock, and let them be punished, I say, wherever they may be found.' Mr. Byers paused, and cast a sharp glance at the inspector. As the latter offered no response, he continued, ' So far, however, as these two gentlemen are concerned, I should be the last to suggest that they are anything but ornaments to the cause they serve.   It is true that I know nothing of the lecturer who has just arrived from headquarters in London ; but the Paris agent of the I.O.T.A. is a man of the loftiest probity, from all I hear.   I shall very likely be entrusted with Brother Bamber's insurances, his own life and perhaps that of Mrs. Bamber, in one company, and the property of the I.O.T.A. in another.   With regard to Brother Neel, after all, I am not qualified to speak.   By-the-bye, it appears that Neel came over in last night's mail from London—the train in which this murder was committed.   I suppose you know that, however ?   He does not recognise the victim, he says.   Rather curious that, isn't it ?   The papers say there were not many passengers by the train. And yet, of course, you can't be expected to notice every passenger who travels by the train you may happen to come by, although there may be few of them.   Still, in anybody

with a black mark against him in the police records of either
London or Paris, oversight of that sort would be looked at
twice. Yes, there's the world! Just the difference between a
fustian jacket, or a bit of Scotch tweed, and a shiny black
coat with a sham clerical cut to it and a starched white
cravat at the top of a high waistcoat.'

'I know he travelled by the mail last night,' said Mr.
Byde; 'they told me so. But I don't suppose he noticed
anybody from the time he left London to the moment he
arrived here. These trading teetotal spouters are always
thinking over their platform effects. I dare say he passes
the whole of his time tampering with statistics, or inventing
"fatal instances of alcoholic excess which, my dear friends,
have fallen within my own personal observation."'

Mr. Byers laughed, and laughter suited him. His clear
eyes twinkled merrily, his florid visage deepened in its glow;
and at the temples and the corners of the mouth the lines
lay so disposed as to lure into responsive mirth the least
sympathetic of spectators, whether frigid or stupid, or merely
artificially reserved. Even the passenger from Scotland Yard,
who knew the laugh of old, yielded to it.

'Like old times,' sighed Mr. Byers presently, 'to see you
sitting there, and hear you talk like that. Ah, those old
times! None of you would let me rest. And yet you could
never show any ground for your suspicions! Ha! ha! ha!
ha!'

'No, we could never prove anything,' replied the inspector.
'You were always too sharp for us, Benjamin.'

'I was always unjustly accused, you mean!'

'Ah, yes, that was it! I remember now, "Innocent
Ben," we used to call you at the Yard : "Old Ben Byers,
the receiver—Innocent Ben." It looked bad for you, though,
in that fraudulent pretences case ; and now I think of it,
that must have been your last appearance in public over
there?'

'Quite right ; that was the last. And an abominable
miscarriage of justice that case threatened to be !' said Mr.
Byers, in a complaining tone. 'I was as nearly falling a
victim to appearances, in that case, as ever an innocent
man was in this world. My counsel brought me off, but a
pretty sum it cost me! I thought it best to leave the
country after that. The Yard was too eager. You would

have driven me into a conviction or a lunatic asylum, if I had stayed. No, I got out of it. I took my little savings to America, and as there's no chance for an honest man in the United States, came over here at the first opportunity, and set up. But it was hard to be persecuted in one's native country, and to be driven abroad!'

'Never mind, Benjamin,' returned Mr. Byde good-humouredly. 'That's all over now, and you've had a fresh start—and it seems to agree with you. Of course you have too much sense to mix up with compromising people for the future. What led you to the Morgue this afternoon?'

'What led me to the Morgue? I'm sure I don't know: curiosity, I suppose. What led other people to the Morgue? I read of this mysterious occurrence in a special edition of a morning paper, and, as I happened to be passing, just looked in. Did anyone ever meet with persons like these gentlemen from Scotland Yard! What led me to the Morgue! Come, now, Mr. Byde, that's very unkind of you—it is indeed!'

'Well, don't be angry! I'm bound to ask questions, you know.'

'What led me to the Morgue? Now, I am really very much hurt, Mr. Byde—I am indeed—very much hurt, by the way you put that question. It's most unkind. What led your I.O.T.A. friends to the Morgue?'

'*I* led them there.'

'That may be satisfactory enough,' retorted the visitor, profoundly wounded by the abrupt demand. 'But, at any rate, *I* was not a passenger by the night-mail!'

Grandpa blew his nose with vehemence, and was visibly affected. His host endeavoured to appease him, and grandpa at length recovered his cheerfulness. He no longer spoke, however, in the sanctimonious tone which had been noticeable at the outset of their interview.

'As to that murder,' said he, 'I rather wonder what the motive could have been.'

'Find out the motive,' replied the inspector, 'and you find out the man.'

'Is that your maxim?'

'One of them.'

'And you rely upon it?'

'Not I! The man in my business who relies upon

maxims will either go wrong or make no progress at all. My maxims are as good as the rest of them—that is to say, useless truisms, or only half true. " *Cherchez la femme,*" they say here. That may do in France, but it won't hold water in an Anglo-Saxon community. And I should think that here, too, the criminal must often be delighted to see the police hunting desperately for some feminine intrigue as the commencement of their clue. What are all these maxims worth? " If there were no receivers, there would be no thieves," says a prisoner to me the other day in the cell. " If there were no thieves," I told him, "there would be no receivers." '

' Good !' commented grandpa.

Inspector Byde hauled his two pipe-cases out of his pocket, and began, as was his custom, to weigh inwardly their respective claims.

' I must be going,' said grandpa ; ' on my way home I have a call to make.' The inspector stirred the fire, and pulled at the bell-rope. ' But now that I know where to find you,' continued his guest, rising, ' I shall call in passing, and take my chance. You don't go back yet, of course ?'

' Can't say.'

' Well, to-morrow, if you are in the neighbourhood of the Rue des Petits Champs—here's my card—ah! by the way, the name is Bingham, as you see, not Byers. Byers is defunct. Obliged to do it, sir ! Hard lines, but obliged to do it. Driven out of your native country, and forced to take up another name ! Cruel, sir, cruel ! Ah ! the law can make terrible mistakes.'

' When were you last in England ?'

' Long, long ago. Ah, dear old England ! " With all her faults," you know, etc. Well, well ! Occasionally I receive a visitor from the old country—business, pure business— insurance agency, and that sort of thing, you know !'

' Keep clear of compromising characters, Benjamin.'

' Oh, my dear Mr. Byde—come, come !—I suppose further details of that murder case will be out by this time. Strange thing that man Neel never noticed his fellow-passenger. Ten hours' journey—two changes—long stoppage at Calais —travellers not numerous : strange thing !'

When the door had closed behind his visitor, and the

waiter had brought up his tumbler of hot grog, the inspector resumed his survey of the two pipes, and eventually decided for the ' considering-cap.' He reopened the blotting-pad, and selected a sheet of note-paper on which no diagrams had been traced. Then, each sentence punctuated with a puff of smoke, and with the Sphinx looking down serenely on his labours, he indited by easy stages the subjoined paragraphs :

' If A (Byers) is known to B (from Scotland Yard) as confirmed suspicious character, is not B justified in regarding C (Bamber) and D (Neel), acquaintances or possible associates of A, as hypothetically suspicious characters ?

' But if A were involved in any illicit transactions with C, would he not carefully avoid all mention to B of his acquaintance with C, especially under the peculiar circumstances of B's former relations with A ?

' If A, conversing with B, repeatedly introduces the name of D, in direct connection with a certain mysterious affair, is not B justified in suspecting A of a desire to compromise D in the judgment of B ?

' Now, if A wishes B to suspect D, might it not be in order to divert the attention of B from A himself, or from A's associate E (unknown) ?

' A has, therefore, presumably, no illicit transactions with D. And A either suspects D in connection with mysterious affair, or, having himself (A) or E to shield, wishes D to be suspected by B. Whence,

' To watch both A and D ; and to find E.'

To find E, the unknown person or persons. Persons ? The very men who came from London by the night-mail, he would lay his life upon it ! And Toppin had missed them ! Well, they would now see what the value of it might prove —this famous registration system of the Paris police. Toppin had declared that they would have these men in a couple of days. But suppose A, through E, we would say, had certain special reasons, bonâ-fide, for suspecting D ? Phew ! what a stroke of luck ! The inspector put his pipe down with a look of gratitude at the Sphinx. The good ideas he owned to that pipe !—it was amazing !

At that moment, A and D were chatting together quite pleasantly in the Hôtel des Nations, Rue de Compiègne.

The temperance question, from the actuarial point of view, formed the subject of their colloquy. Mr. Bingham, *né* Byers, had called upon the lecturer of the I.O.T.A., Brother Neel, as he had offered to do in the afternoon; and in No. 21, the comfortable chamber tenanted by Brother Neel, the 'confirmed suspicious character' was expatiating on the superiority of 'teetotal lives.' He congratulated Brother Neel upon his excellent quarters—not too high up, and wonderfully tranquil for the vicinity of the station. Mr. Bingham walked round the spacious room with the experienced air of the Paris resident. No noisy neighbours, he hoped? Ah, true; the room was at the extremity of the corridor—that he had perceived on his arrival. The party-wall of the building would, of course, lie on that side, quite so; and from that direction consequently there could be no disturbance. Still, a very little might disturb us sometimes when we were engaged on difficult work, actuarial calculations for instance, or the details of the I.O.T.A. The neighbour on the other side might, perhaps—what, no neighbour? Unoccupied for the present—the bedroom adjoining? Most fortunate for Brother Neel, if he had work to do; so much the better in the interests of his tranquillity. Would look in to-morrow on the matter of the proposed policy. Goodnight!—And so No. 19 was untenanted!

CHAPTER XI.

MR. BINGHAM did look in on the following morning, but at a strangely unseasonable hour. No one was stirring, when he presented himself next day, but the earliest of the hotel servants. He had brought with him an invalid friend who had travelled all night from the South of France, he remarked to the porter, an Alsatian peasant, who had a surly and half-imbecile air. The apartment for his companion was already taken, he had engaged it himself on the previous night. The room was No. 19, on the second floor, almost at the extremity of the corridor.

His invalid friend had been a great sufferer, added Mr. Bingham, when they had assisted the new-comer to an arm-chair in the hall. Urgent business was recalling him to England, but the state of his health required that he should break the journey for a day or two, and for a day or two, therefore, he should remain in Paris. Was the room No. 19 ready for its occupant? Everything quite in order? Capital. Then we would have the fire lighted at once, and we would support No. 19 upstairs to his apartment. Oh, he had grown stronger on the breezes of the Mediterranean, but there was still much to be desired. Just now, the fatigues of a long journey, and sleeplessness, were telling upon him; but with repose and quiet he would soon recuperate. An undermining sort of malady, though. What malady? Well, something constitutional—debilitated frame —took after his parents. Mr. Bingham had known his young friend's father well, and it was exactly the same kind of physique—*ainsi, voyez!* Oh, but he was not always prostrated like this. The vigour he would exhibit sometimes would even astonish his medical advisers—and they were of the best. Repose he needed, and tranquillity—tranquillity and judicious nursing. Luckily, he could pay well. The invalid understood little of these explanations, it seemed. He lay back languidly, enveloped in his rugs, and hardly for a single moment unclosed his eyes.

'How pale he looks, the poor young gentleman; and how drawn his features are!'

'Ah, you may well say so—yes, indeed;' acquiesced Mr. Bingham, who had seen to that matter before he started with his young friend for the Hôtel des Nations, and who stood for a minute or two critically studying his own handiwork.

The early servants were beginning to sweep the corridors, as the new arrivals passed along. On the second-floor, a citizen of the Republic who had unmistakably the scowl of him who nourishes in secret dreams of an anarchical Utopia, was collecting, with a moody resignation, pairs of boots thrown outside the bedroom doors. He treated the boots less roughly than, perhaps, could he have had his way, he would have treated their unconscious owners. And yet, as they proceeded slowly down the corridor towards No. 19, the visitors observed him kick one or two pairs savagely, as though their elegance offended him. He spat, indeed, on some : they had blue silk linings, high heels, and innumerable buttons; and, as the visitors moved by, he turned and stared insolently at them, with undisguised contempt and hatred. The spectacle of the invalid brought to his face a sneer of gratification and of the bitterest malignity.

' A subscriber to the *Lanterne ?*' asked Mr. Bingham.

' Oh, worse than that !' replied their conductor smilingly, and still turning over in his pocket the piece of gold given him by this affable old gentleman. ' Grégoire is our black-flag politician. If you could hear him talk downstairs, in the kitchen, about the next rising of the people ! I'm advanced, myself; I want the Commune, but I don't go so far as Grégoire, in the means. He'd begin by a massacre of all the persons staying in the hotel—all except the foreigners, that is ; and then all the servants who refused to join his revolutionary group should be marched into the street, in front there, and shot. He wants to see all the well-to-do classes exterminated, and then to have everybody do every description of work by turns. All that I fear, monsieur, is one thing: that Grégoire may some day lose his patience and change his doctrine. And that is why I have ventured to trouble monsieur with such long details after monsieur's generosity, and monsieur being a foreigner —indeed, an English, who are not cruel to the working man. Grégoire might be driven one day by his hatred to put his theory into execution ; justifying theft, as we call it, Grégoire might one day commit theft. And that—ah, but that would change our sentiments towards our *confrère !* Just imagine, for one minute, how we should all be compromised ! I say nothing against advanced views— monsieur is perhaps conservative in his own country ? No? —but I don't see that all the rest of us should possibly incur suspicion because we have a *confrère* whose political school denies the rights of property. No, monsieur ! I have a young nephew who would like to take his place, and who seeks to enter a good establishment. Anything, therefore, that monsieur might miss from his room should be mentioned. Monsieur will pardon me?—and this is in confidence. But of course in these observations I study alone the interest of monsieur and of the establishment.'

Left to themselves at last, in No. 19, Mr. Bingham and his invalid companion alike underwent a marked alteration of demeanour. The invalid pitched his hat across the room, stretched his arms, and gaped. His elderly friend drew his chair up to the recently-lighted fire.

'What was he talking about all that time, grandpa?' inquired the invalid.

'Oh, it's too long to repeat. But there's something in it that might turn out useful.' Mr. Bingham hummed a little tune and stared into the fireplace.

'Lucky we had that snack before we started, grandpa. But I shall soon be hungry again—and I'm thirsty, now, I give you the tip. Ain't you?'

'Now, Bat, you just listen to me,' said the other, without paying any attention to this hint. 'I'm paying most of the expenses of this little affair, and I expect you to do the best you can for me. You've got to do your best, to-day. It's for your own good as well as mine.'

'All right, grandpa; don't you be uneasy. If it's in my line, I'll do it. Is it here I'm to go to work?'

'On one of those two doors; and in the meantime you must not be heard. On the other side of one of these doors you're going to find the Wilmot diamonds.'

'What—— ?'

'——Just so! I brought you away this morning for no other reason.'

'Grandpa, old Clements ain't in it with you!—no, nor Byde from Scotland Yard. And as for me and Sir John—well, there! Bar accidents, and I shall do it, if it's to be done at all. But if I'm to go to work in here with any confidence I must know that you're outside on duty!' The speaker had adopted now as low a tone as his compani n. He threw open his roomy ulster, and unwound his woollen scarf; and the weazen face and slight proportions were those of Finch, *alias* Walker. He locked the door by which they had entered.

Some time elapsed before they heard their neighbours move in either of the rooms adjoining. The chamber they were occupying belonged properly to a complete suite; but, as often happens in the Paris hotels, the several apartments had been let off singly; inter-communication being arrested by the locked doors, which are usually hidden by tapestry, curtains, or a massive wardrobe. The suite can be restored at will, either wholly or in part. A convenient device for the hotel-keeper, the system proves less agreeable for his tenants. One is often an involuntary auditor; one is often unwittingly overheard. Eaves-droppers are well housed in these hotels.

'Which is it?' murmured Mr. Finch, indicating the opposite doors, to the right and to the left of the windows.

His companion nodded in the direction of a mahogany toilette-table, to the right. It had been placed against the door communicating with No. 21, which was the spacious chamber at the end of the corridor, to the left hand, allotted to Brother Neel.

'Key in the lock on the other side?' demanded Mr. Finch. His companion rose, and moved silently towards the toilette-table. A curtain nailed above the door and descending to the ground concealed the lock from their view, and in the dull light of the morning Mr. Bingham, as he held the curtain away, could not satisfy himself on the point. 'Strike a match,' whispered Mr. Finch. Grandpa shook his head; their neighbour might be awake at this moment, and might hear them. It was just as well that Brother Neel should still suppose the adjoining room unoccupied. 'Hear!' muttered Mr. Finch; 'he won't hear this, I'll lay a thousand!'

In another instant he held a small flame in the hollow of his hand. Noiseless matches formed part of Mr. Finch's stock-in-trade.

'Door locked, and the key not on the other side,' whispered Finch, *alias* Walker, after an extremely knowing examination. He helped to move the toilette-table slightly, produced a second little flame, and passed it up and down the edge of the door. 'No lower bolt on the other side,' he pronounced; 'and let's hope there's no higher one. Door opens this way.'

They replaced the piece of furniture against the curtain. Presently a stir in the far room announced the awakening of, at any rate, one of their two neighbours. He appeared to be a French gentleman with a retentive memory for the refrains of Paris concert halls. ' *Thérèse, Thérèse* '—he threw off encouragingly at intervals, as he clattered about his apartment—' *Mets toi donc à ton aise !* '—adding the exhortation, now and then—

> 'Ne fais pas de façons !—
> C'est bientôt Char-en-ton !'

'What does he say?' murmured Mr. Finch suspiciously. Mr. Bingham was too intent upon the enterprise before them to respond. The Gaul in the next room varied his references to Charenton, and his counsels to Thérèse, by a verse or two from sentimental ditties, which he intoned in a vibrating falsetto, and for which he would occasionally 'encore' himself with great enthusiasm. 'He wouldn't sing like that if I had him on the Dials,' growled Mr. Finch. '*Tu m'as promis un baiser ce soir !*' quavered the vocalist, imitating the applause of the gallery immediately afterwards, and vociferating, '*Bis !*' They heard a crash of broken glass, and the vocalist subsided into a species of prose which brought a fleeting smile to grandpa's countenance. 'Put his elbow through the looking-glass, I dare say,' commented Mr. Finch.

The voice of some person apparently declaiming met their ears, however, from the opposite direction. The two occupants of No. 19 exchanged glances. They had nothing to do but wait in patience.

Yes, it was the eloquent lecturer of the I.O.T.A. exercising in his platform style. He kept his voice at a subdued pitch, but most of its rehearsed modulations they could follow with ease. Now he assailed with impetuous ire the demon tempter lurking in every nook, beneath myriad disguises. The alluring shape and the deceptive blush— Alcohol! The honeyed accents of the faithless lover— Alcohol! Betrayals of the husband's trust—desertions of the faultless wife—unnatural neglect by parents, barbarous abandonment by ungrateful offspring—fraud, insolvency, ruin—Alcohol!—'yes, my friends; in every physical and social ill, in all deformities of mind and body, in sickness and in woe, under the mask of pleasure and in every lineament of vice—we can detect and stamp out, if we choose, the serpent form and the envenomed sting of Alcohol!'

Brother Neel repeated the various clauses of the foregoing denunciation with different inflections of the voice, and at differing speed. He tried the sentence in a sustained high key; then in a measured, awe-stricken bass; and finally he mixed both manners in about equal proportions. He seemed a little undecided about the construction of the final clause. Should it not run, ' detect the serpent form, and stamp out the envenomed sting,' or, say, ' detect the envenomed sting, and stamp out the serpent form '—or, stay : would not ' serpent shape ' go better, because of the alliteration,—' serpen-

tine shape,' rather?—no, not 'shape,' because we had had
'alluring shape' at the commencement; 'serpent form,'
then, or 'coils:' yes?—' serpent coils' was good, was it not?
Brother Neel disposed of this point, and proceeded to re-
hearse the vein of anecdote.

'Why, my dear friends, the other day a poor man came
to me, and he said—he was a poor miner, my dear friends,
and he had been a miner from his youth upward, and his
father was a miner, and he said—and his face was careworn
and his limbs were weary, and he had waited at our temperance hall until the hour came for our evening conference,
when we meet together for our mutual comfort and our
mutual inspiration—for who amongst us is there that can
say he never flagged and never faltered in the arduous on-
ward march?—and this poor man came to me, and he said,
" Guv'nor," he said, " I want to leave off drink." Oh, my
dear friends, what welcome words were those! " I want
to leave off drink, guv'nor," he said. And he stood with his
grimy face and his horny hands, and he looked at me so
wistfully, and he said to me so simply and so earnestly,
" Guv'nor, it's a 'ard life, working in the pits!" And I
gazed into his grimy face, and I grasped his horny hand,
and I said to this poor man, I said, " And it's drink that
makes it hard." And, oh, my dear friends, if you had seen
that honest face light up with relief and joy and hope!—
and my heart bounded and throbbed within me—and he
said, " Guv'nor, I want to leave off working in the pits."
And I said, " It's the alcohol you loathe and abhor, my dear
friend, is it not?" And he said, " Yes, guv'nor; and the
pits." And I said, " Can you leave off alcohol, and be like
me? Am I not happy without alcohol?" And he replied,
" Guv'nor, that's what I've come about. I want to leave
off alkeroil, and be like you. It's a 'ard life working in the
pits. I want to be happy like you; and if you'd take me
in and learn me to preach to people, guv'nor, I'd leave off
alkeroil. And so would my missus, and so would my son."
And that poor man has been rescued, my dear friends—
rescued from the curse of drink; and his son and his wife
have been rescued also; and now they are missionaries of
the I.O.T.A., well clad, comfortably housed, and content,
and receiving three times their former wages. And such is
the value of a good example that we have since had innu-

merable applications from that poor man's district, for similar places in the I.O.T.A. Ah, yes, the cause is prospering, my friends——' etc., etc.

'That's him, sure enough,' remarked Mr. Finch, whose frown had disappeared. 'He's preaching to himself.'

'Do you think you can do it, with what I have here?' asked his companion in a cautious undertone. 'They're not what you have been used to; they're of French make, you know.'

'Let's have a look at them, to see how they make 'em in this country.' Mr. Bingham produced a bunch of skeleton keys, upon which articles his young friend bent an intelligent scrutiny. 'French make, are they?' he continued. 'Well, then, give me Clerkenwell!'

'Can't you work with them?'

'Oh, I'll undertake to do it. I'd do it with three hairpins, grandpa, if you could spare them out of your chignon!'

'Well, the first chance we find we'll lose no time about it. If this is the man who's got the property, to-night would be too late. If the Wilmot diamonds are in his possession at all—and I'd stake my life upon it—he can only leave them in his portmanteau in that room under lock-and-key, or else carry them about with him. There is one other place where they might be; but though they might be there to-morrow, or to-night, I do not think they can be there already. When he goes out of his room presently, we shall see whether they are stored away in his portmanteau. If they are not in his portmanteau, he is carrying them about with him. If he is carrying them about with him——'

'I object to violence, grandpa, as you know. I told old Clements I wouldn't have anything to do with violence.'

'You can't object to it more than I do!' ejaculated grandpa, with virtuous emphasis, but still speaking in low tones. 'I always have set my face against violence. But we can't stand in Sir John's way, if he fancies a short cut rather than a long way round. And if our man in the next room should persist in carrying stolen property about with him in the streets of Paris, why Jack may as well have a try for it as any of the garrotters here. You haven't come all this distance for nothing, I should hope? I haven't gone into this spec—and spent my money on it when times are bad, and given my energies to it—for nothing, I can tell you! That man in the next room is a thief. He is a thief on as big a scale as ever I saw; and he's something else, too, if we put the dots upon the "i's." However, we don't concern ourselves about anything but the property. We don't care how he came by it; we believe he's got it, and we mean to take it from him. Now, if he chooses to carry the valuables about with him, he'll have to reckon with Sir John.'

'Well, you know what Sir John is. He'll very likely follow his old tack: hit this man on the head, put him out, and manage to throw all the appearances on to us, grandpa.'

'Not while *I* am in the neighbourhood, Bartholomew, will he manage to throw appearances on to us. But I don't believe our man would carry the stones about with him. It's all against that. Why? He knows very well that if he did happen to be suspected by the French police—how can we say that he was not seen by some other passenger, a Frenchman, perhaps, and that they may not be making their preparations, now, to come down upon him?—and that's why we must lose no time—if he did happen to be suspected, the people from the Prefecture would take him just as they'd take any rough out of the streets, and they'd search him without any ceremony. What do they understand about Brother this and Brother that; and what do they care? We are not in England. Now, suppose that diamonds of extraordinary value are found upon his person, what answer can he give? But if a fortune in diamonds should be found concealed in his trunk at the hotel he could always reply, however preposterous it would seem, that "some malicious person must have placed them there"—the real thief, perhaps. And that is what he *would* say, in a minute, and in England it would go down with a lot of people. The I.O.T.A. would back him up in England, and most probably present him with a testimonial. No; he'll leave the property hidden somewhere in his portmanteau. And to convey the impression that there's nothing of any value in his room to tempt the servants, it's odds he leaves his door unfastened when he goes downstairs to the *table-d'hôte* breakfast! You think these instruments will do? The lock of the door you can deal with, I know; but what about the portmanteau? A portmanteau was the only luggage he had that I could see.'

'Don't you trouble about that, grandpa. I was educated by parents that did their duty by their Bartholomew, the eldest of seven. I'll unlock any portmanteau in this house with these instruments,' said Mr. Finch, adding, as he spread out his delicate fingers, ' and these !'

'Bat, you're a smart boy! What a pity you live in London: there's a fortune to be made here by an artist like you! Why don't you come and set up? I'd run you.'

'Not me! Leave London for this place? Why, they tell me there are never any fogs here; I should be out of work half the time. Leave London? Leave Soho, where I was born—and Regent Street, Piccadilly, and Oxford Street, where I've earned my living since I could use my hands— not me, Mr. Wilkins—no, sir !'

'I could put you in a good line, Bartholomew. It would pay you well.'

'Thank you, grandpa—but I'd rather stay in London, on a little. All my relations live in Saint Giles's parish; except Uncle Simon, who went to Birmingham to set up, and was committed a fortnight ago to take his trial at Warwick Assizes. Give me the West-end on a foggy night !'

'Your parents must be proud of you, Bartholomew.'

'Oh, I'm a good mechanic. That I *will* say; but you should see my second brother ! There's one thing I can *not* undertake to do, grandpa, and I dare say you've thought of it. I'll unlock this door, and I'll unlock that portmanteau, but I'm—— if I can undertake to lock them again, after-wards !'

'That's a little matter we can risk. Our man will make no fuss, when he finds it out. At the worst, there is some-body in this building we can throw suspicion upon.'

'Suppose we get it, what are you going to do with Sir John ?'

'Leave him where he is till we're out of danger. We can't have him hampering us, while there's any danger; he'll get his share all in good time.'

'But you said that the police here would be safe to pounce upon him in two or three days, if he stays in the same hotel ?'

'And I say so still. What of that? It gives us time to get clear, and to negotiate the stones. They couldn't prove anything against him, and they'd be bound to let him go. If we had him with us in this room he'd spoil everything— with his rage against the man next door for besting him in the train. This man got there first, there's no doubt about it, and Jack would be at him, if he had to cut through that wall. When Mr. Toppin and the French police have had a look at the hotel registers for yesterday morning, they're certain to turn up at Jack's address. Let them take him. A week or so in the Dépôt won't do him any harm !'

'The Dépôt? What's that—quod?'

'Yes; and not so nicely furnished as the House of Detention.'

'Grandpa, look here ! It's all square between us three, isn't it? We're not going to sell old Jack, are we, grandpa?'

'Sell him? Of course not ! He'll be all right. He's come over on a trip—that's his story. He's going on to Nice and Cannes, and broke the journey at Paris, to enjoy himself. If they identify him, he took a false name because he knew the other might get him stopped, and he wanted change of air and a little amusement. When I paid your bill this morning, I told them you were going on first. Let Mr. Toppin have him put *au secret*, and let the police search him for a week, if they like. They won't find anything, as Jack himself says, now that he has removed those blood-stains. Awkward, those stains ; but he had no luck. While they are engaged with friend Jack, you and I will be in Amsterdam.'

'It must be all square between us three, grandpa; or else I don't go to work.'

'Sell Sir John ? I wouldn't think of such a thing. When he came out, he'd swing for the man who sold him !' There was a pause. 'It might perhaps be disagreeable for Sir John if they found a firearm in his possession. What weapons does he carry?'

'I thought of that,' replied Mr. Finch, 'and last night I did what I could to set my mind at rest. I never saw him with any weapon but the dagger in that cane he carries.'

'Would you like to get through this without me, since it has taken a different turn?—come, now ! I've put you on

the right track, but I'll pull up at this instant if I'm objected
to in this affair. For all I know, if I chose I could manage
it by myself, for myself; and even if *you* got the diamonds
you might lose them again ; and somebody *I* know, and *you*
don't know, and Clements never heard of in his life, might
be the party who would find them.'

' *Me* lose them, to anyone *here* / I'll lay a thousand no
one here can give *me* any lessons.'

' Suppose you went to sleep for a few hours, hey?
Suppose you were not in the least sleepy, and you suddenly
went to sleep—very soundly to sleep ? Oh, I have a good
many strings to *my* bow, and I know your name is Walker !'

' I'd lay a thousand no one——'

' Well, well, we'll drop that side of it. But if you get this
property, how can you liquidate it ? You can't without the
aid of Benjamin Byers, deceased. Can either you or Sir
John put any of these diamonds on the market, even the
small ones, if there are any small ones ? How many can
Clements, a known receiver, dispose of ? But *I* can do it in
half an hour among my clients in Amsterdam ! *I* can pass
every one of them through the market—yes, and at fair
terms ! But if you'd like to see me out of this, if you'd like
to go on by yourself—say so !'

' *Me ?* Such a thought has never come into my head, I'm
sure. Why, what a state you're in about it, grandpa !
You shall hold the property yourself. I'm not afraid of the
confidence-trick being done on *me* / Go on without you,
grandpa? not me ! No, sir—not me, Mr. Wilkins !'

A waiter knocked at the door, and, on Mr. Bingham's
unfastening it, inquired whether the invalid young gentleman
would not wish to have a slight repast served in his apartment instead of descending. Most decidedly, was Mr.
Bingham's answer. His young friend would take all his
meals in his own room. And breakfast could be brought up
to them as soon as it was ready. The repast need not
necessarily be a slight one. He had a prodigious appetite
himself, and he should remain to keep his young friend
company. The waiter stood upon the threshold and peered
inquisitively into the room. He could not see the invalid
at all, and Mr. Bingham made way for him to enter.
' Monsieur slumbers?' asked the waiter, in a whisper. Mr.
Bingham could not say, and he moved on tiptoe to the bed

and gently pulled the curtain on one side. He shrugged his shoulders, with a gesture of uncertainty, but whispered that the breakfast might, all the same, be served as soon as it was ready. Mr. Finch, who had taken a flying leap through the bed-curtains when the knock came at the door, was breathing in a laboured manner, and occasionally he uttered plaintive moans.

They had finished their repast subsequently—and a prodigious appetite had certainly had full play, although it was not grandpa's—when a bell sounded for several moments in the court-yard.

' The table-d'hôte !' said Mr. Bingham ; ' get ready.'

The invalid rose with alacrity, and followed his considerate attendant to the corner of the room. Mr. Bingham moved quite as noiselessly as Finch, *alias* Walker, and the latter was in his stockinged feet. They lifted the toilette-table from its place. The French gentleman, droning his concert-hall refrains, had gone down some time before. They now heard their neighbour on the other side preparing to descend. There was the click of a lock, and the jingle of a bunch of keys. Brother Neel marched with a heavy step to his door, opened it, closed it after him, locked it, and passed along the corridor.

' He has locked his portmanteau, and he has locked the door of his room, too,' commented Mr. Bingham. ' Good sign !'

They waited. Other doors communicating with the corridor opened and closed ; footsteps resounded for an instant, and died away ; and then they seemed to be alone in that corner of the building, beyond the possibility of disturbance. Mr. Bingham produced an odd-looking handful of twisted wires, some of which were no coarser than thread. He handed them to Mr. Finch. The invalid, who had his wristbands turned up, immediately bent down to the lock of the door communicating with No. 21.

Mr. Bingham stepped out of No. 19 into the corridor, and shut the door carefully behind him. There was no one to be seen. He walked up and down outside the entrances to those two chambers situated at the far end of the corridor, and then by degrees extended the limits of his patrol. You would have said that Mr. Bingham had given a rendezvous to somebody who tenanted a room along that corridor, and that he was impatient about his non-arrival.

When Brother Neel, the Chrysostom of the I.O.T.A., re-mounted the staircase, a golden toothpick protruding from his lips, he was bringing with him a roll of stout brown paper and a stick of sealing-wax. The elderly gentleman, with the inch or two of white whiskers and the florid pear-shaped face, had evidently grown tired of waiting for the absentee, for he was no longer to be observed pacing back-wards and forwards in the corridor. Brother Neel pro-ceeded towards No. 21, and re-entered his apartment. It was just as he had left it—altogether as he had left it. His portmanteau stood upon one of the chairs, and on the port-manteau lay his newspapers and a bundle of printed docu-ments tied together with broad red tape. Just as he had quitted it he found the room.

Brother Neel began to hum—'I charge thee, halt ! Say —friend or foe !' He went to a table and spread out the roll of brown paper. Upon this he placed a newspaper doubled. He then lighted one of the candles on the mantel-piece, and deposited near it the sealing-wax ready for use. He transferred the printed documents, and the half-dozen journals underneath, to a chair close by, and drew from his pocket a small bunch of keys. One of these keys he inserted into the lock of the portmanteau. . . . What could be wrong with the key? . . . The portmanteau was already unlocked !

How was this? Had he really omitted to secure the lock, in spite of his precaution, before quitting the room ? Brother Neel threw open the portmanteau, tore away the uppermost articles, and plunged his hand into a recess, con-trived, no doubt, specially for the reception of jewellery or valuables of similarly moderate bulk. The keen anxiety of his expression, however, disappeared almost at once. From the recess he drew an oblong package in white tissue-paper. The paper was tarnished here and there with an irregular stain ; at the contact of one of these insignificant patches, Brother Neel let the little parcel drop from his hands and stood for a moment staring at his fingers. It was not terror that his countenance now betrayed ; it was not surprise, nor was it horror. It was aversion simply that his countenance betrayed ; and a second longer look at these few barely noticeable maculations revealed them to be, not blots of dark red ink, but splashes most probably of blood.

He took up the oblong package again, and partly unfolded the outer sheet of tissue-paper in which it had been wrapped. At this moment he abruptly looked behind him, penetrating every corner and alcove cf his apartment with a quick, alarmed, suspicious glance. And yet he could have heard no sound in either direction, and he had certainly double-locked his door.

The object enveloped in the folds of tissue-paper had the form of a pocket-book. But it was not in leather nor prunello; it was a sort of pocket-book in black velvet, though from its external aspect its contents could not be the correspondence of the I.O.T.A. The black velvet case was neatly bound up with thin bands of green silk. It bulged here and there in a curious manner; perhaps Brother Neel kept his signet-rings in this case—or articles of jewellery which, in recognition of his merit, might have been presented to him by grateful converts, grudging colleagues, or admiring friends. He pressed the velvet with the fingers of both hands, and then, as the protuberances which met his touch satisfied him, replaced the neatly-bound velvet case in the first sheet of tissue-paper, and so made up the little package as before. The blotches that resembled blood-stains might have been consumed in a single minute in the flame of that one candle. Far from destroying them, Brother Neel apparently took pains to expose them precisely as at first, although he still avoided touching the marks themselves. Mr. Bingham, or Inspector Byde, with their experience of the world and their trained insight into criminal motive, would have assigned an identical reason for this measure, and, with the impartiality of experts, might have commended it as an act of the most wideawake sagacity.

Brother Neel surrounded the package with a heap of pamphlets and written documents, which he procured from his portmanteau. Amidst half-yearly reports, tabular statements, popular leaflets, etc., it soon became entirely lost to view. The papers so accumulated he deposited with great care in one of the journals spread out on the table. The parcel thus made up he enclosed in another newspaper, and then he enveloped the whole in the stouter sheets which he had obtained from below. The last layer but one he knotted securely with cord, and on every knot he placed a seal. The final enclosure he paid less attention to ostensibly. He sealed it only in a single place, and he attached the cord in such a fashion that his precious parcel looked like the most ordinary parcel in the world. What he next did was to inscribe the name of the society upon the covering. With the rusty pen of the inkstand on his mantelpiece, he printed in large capitals along the brown-paper covering—' I.O.T.A., Personal Notes, Reports, etc.'

Later in the day, when discussing business with Brother Bamber, at the offices in the Boulevard Haussmann, Brother Neel desired him to take temporary charge of documents which he should most likely need in the course of his labours. They would be more conveniently lodged at that spot than at his hotel, so far from the quarters of the I.O.T.A. as well as from the National Library, where he should be prosecuting his researches. Brother Bamber placed the parcel in the large safe of the I.O.T.A.

Brother Neel had not, however, made his journey unobserved. The gentleman who had ambled along at a safe distance in his rear, from the Rue de Compiègne to the Boulevard Haussmann, had stationed himself at a point from which he could easily perceive the eloquent lecturer, as he issued from the offices again. It was Mr. Bingham who thus awaited him; and Mr. Bingham noted that the precious parcel had undoubtedly been left in Brother Bamber's keeping, at the premises of the I.O.T.A.

CHAPTER XII.

A SECOND visit to the Avenue Marceau had provided matter for notes which covered page after page of Mr. Toppin's memorandum-book. He did not mean to communicate all his information to his London colleague, but the one or two facts which he did intend to report relating to the point more immediately before them would, he reckoned, rather show the inspector that he knew how to conduct an inquiry with despatch. About the time that Mr. Bingham and his young friend, Mr. Finch, the native of St. Giles's parish, were the concealed auditors of Brother Neel's rehearsed harangue, Detective Toppin was insidiously plying questions in the Avenue Marceau.

Fact No. 1: Miss Knollys had received a letter from abroad by the last post on the previous evening. The postmark was 'Dover.'

Fact No. 2: Miss Knollys had been suddenly taken ill; and Mrs. Bertram, who usually visited a great deal, and whose very day of reception this day happened to be, had at once given instructions that, in consequence of a family bereavement, she was not at home to any callers.

And so the two ladies were connected by family ties? Well, perhaps they were, and perhaps they were not—how could she tell?—the *concierge* had responded. The family bereavement was very likely no bereavement at all; the servants had mentioned the orders transmitted to them, but they all believed that the sudden indisposition of Mdlle. Knollys was the sole 'bereavement' which afflicted Madame Bertram. Bad news, most probably, from England—a death? A death!—but missives containing intelligence of that kind generally had a mourning border, and nothing with a mourning border had arrived through the post for either lady. Telegram? Well, but no telegrams had been delivered at the address for a week or a fortnight. *Tenez!* —the last telegram that ever came to Madame Bertram's address was prior to the arrival of Mdlle. Knollys. It was a message from the latter,—announcing her departure for Paris, had stated Madame Bertram's maid, when gossiping in the *concierge's* lodge the same afternooon. And, indeed, the young lady had arrived that evening with her own maid —an Engleesh!

Ah—Miss Knollys had an English maid? What sort of a person—pleasant-like and sociable? Sociable! Ha! If she had a tongue in her head it must be only because it was the fashion to have one! Could not exchange a word with anybody as she stalked in and out of the house, and never even looked in the direction of the lodge. A pretty piece of assurance, she should think, for an ill-dressed awkward grenadier like that to take a place as lady's-maid, when she didn't know how to hang her own clothes on her angles! But who ever found an Engleesh, mistress or maid, who had the slightest notion of elegance in dress, until they learnt, like Madame Bertram, by residence in Paris? Yes; ladies'-maids like that—there were plenty of them, working in the beetroot-fields, in France! And as to being 'pleasant,' she seemed about as pleasant as the dentists at the free hospital, down town. ' But you can judge for yourself,' added the *concierge;* ' there she goes, out for a little walk before breakfast. *Drôle de pays, votre Angleterre !* a country where the women get up early in the morning to take walks in the cold, for the benefit of their health, as they pretend, when it's so much easier to remain in bed !' Mr. Toppin assured the virago whom he had bribed into this flow of language that the hygienic practice she alluded to was not by any means absurdly prevalent among his countrywomen.

The *concierge* had glanced through the window which commanded from her lodge a view of the lobby. From his own position, as he stood conversing with her, Toppin could not catch any glimpse of the derided ' Engleesh.' He heard the glass-door of the marble lobby opened and closed, however. Then, as Miss Knollys's maid stepped on to the stone pavement leading past the lodge-entrance to the main gateway of the building, he saw her, and was struck with astonishment.

The maid held an envelope in her hand, and, as she approached, it seemed that she was intending, on this occasion at any rate, to address herself for guidance to the inimical portress. At the lodge door she perceived Mr. Toppin. Her hesitation was quite momentary, and might easily have escaped notice. She resumed her course, and in another instant had passed through the archway into the Avenue Marceau.

' I do believe she had it in her mind to ask me a question,' exclaimed the *concierge*—' a question with regard to some errand, no doubt, on which she has been sent ; a direction, perhaps, written on that envelope. Ah, she would have been well received ! You would have seen how I should have received her ! I should have said, " Mademoiselle, I am the portress ;" I should have said, " I am the portress, mademoiselle—not the commissionaire of the next comer, nor the General Post-Office !" Aha !—she would have been well received. I think I know how to put people in their places ! Airs like that ! Would not anyone fancy she was the mistress ? Except that the mistress is as gentle and unpretending, and refined, from what I have seen of her, as the best-born lady of the true high-world : whereas, this— that ! That can't speak to honest persons in its own station, and gives itself airs because it has a complexion and a figure!'

Toppin gazed at the empty archway. The imperial shape had vanished, but—oh, poor Toppin!—it had crossed his path. On heedless ears fell the harsh monotone of his informant. He could still see a clear pale face, black hair and eyebrows, and large dark eyes that looked full at him for a moment—large eyes of the darkest blue.

'Airs like that! I think I'd show some taste in toilette before I went about posing for a princess. What a costume, and what a hat!'

Mr. Toppin remembered no detail whatever of the hat, and of the costume he remembered only that it fitted the wearer tightly, and was plain. One fleeting attitude, statuesque and unstudied, defined itself again before his view, as he stared blankly through the glass doors of the lodge; and he half thought he saw again, as the imperial shape continued onwards to the archway, the self-conscious movement of the handsome woman who knows that she is watched admiringly. He had not observed any angles, he presently declared; nor had it occurred to him to guess at any.

What did the male sex know about the artifices of the toilette! It was always easy to deceive them—always—unless they happened to be man-milliners. But certainly monsieur had been impressed by Mdlle Lydia — that was the new maid's name—what, not impressed? Oh, there could be no denying the fact; monsieur was undoubtedly impressed. Well, she had a figure and a complexion, but as for any taste, grace, or refinement of the wardrobe, why, the commonest little street girl of Paris, lazy, thoughtless, and slovenly, and loitering on her way to school to play at marbles with the telegraph boys, could choose her colours or put on a piece of imitation lace with more discernment than this professed Engleesh lady's-maid. Still, if the striding life-guard who had just gone out responded to the notion which monsieur had 'formed of feminine attractiveness, why did he not offer to escort her? This Mdlle. Lydia was his compatriot—*pas?* At all events, the *concierge* added, she herself really must now turn her attention to her regular duties.

The temptation to offer his assistance to his superb fellow-countrywoman, who, after all, if strange to Paris, might have been grateful for the aid, had already presented itself, in fact, to Mr. Toppin's mind. What restrained him was a sentiment rather unusual with this gentleman—an odd feeling of inferiority. If it had been the mistress who was masquerading in the maid's attire, the habitual gallantry of Mr. Toppin, when he found himself among his social equals, could not have been more suddenly frozen. Just as well that he had shown her no civility, thought Toppin; it might have involved him in attentions which would have distracted him from the inquiry. Ah, it would not do to allow his mind to be distracted; it would not do to let this chance of distinguishing himself professionally slip through his fingers! He meant to show Inspector Byde that there was one at least of the younger men who understood his business. Detective Toppin resumed his interrogation of the portress, and by that sagacious female was introduced in an off-hand way to one or two domestics of the establishment. The process necessitated a disbursement of the fee admitted in forensic circles under the designation of the 'refresher.' The coachman and the *valet de chambre* construed 'refreshment' in a sense more literal. They adjourned with Mr. Toppin to the first turning on the left. Here they were welcomed with smiles by the tavern-keeper's wife, who called them by their Christian names. The tavern-keeper asked them how they felt after their libations of the previous night, and placed small glasses of a dark crimson fluid before them, without waiting for their order. Mr. Toppin lingered in the hope of snapping up some unconsidered trifle of the conversation. But although they all talked freely upon the inevitable topic among domestics, 'the masters and the mistresses,' nothing rewarded his patience but the customary sarcasms of the servants' hall. He learnt as much about Mrs. Bertram as he could have wished to learn, and probably more than was authentic. He failed, however, to elicit any substantial information with respect to her visitor, Miss Knollys. The character of the majestic Mdlle. Lydia could not be expected to escape review from acrimonious fellow-servants. She was cold and silent, mysterious and disdainful,—'but with all her prudishness, no better than the rest of us, *allez !*' Toppin heard these animadversions with annoyance. He did his best to change

the subject, and succeeded ; for the actions of that handsome
Mdlle. Lydia, pronounced Mr. Toppin mentally, could not
by any possibility be ' material to the inquiry.'

Toppin was wrong. His colleague, the inspector, would
have been shocked at the mistake, so gross it was, and
palpable. In a very different manner would Mr. Byde have
acted had he been placed in Toppin's situation ; but Byde
himself, in delegating an important branch of the inquiry to
a subordinate, proved that, as grandpa had observed to his
friends from London, he was not necessarily infallible,
although eminent and respected, and ' one of the best.'

Hastening from the Avenue Marceau, Mdlle. Lydia had
directed her steps towards a cab-rank in the immediate
vicinity. There she had shown to a cabman the lower part
of the address upon the envelope ; and in another minute
the vehicle containing her was being driven rapidly enough
in the direction of the Tuileries Gardens.

The cab stopped at the temporary premises of the General
Post-Office. The tall figure clad in the plain tight-fitting
costume alighted quickly from the vehicle, and passed
through the swinging doors in front of which a sentryman
was posted. Once inside the building Mdlle. Lydia proceeded more leisurely about her errand. It was with the
poste restante that her business lay. The clerk who sat idle
at the desk forced her to repeat her application, as he sent
an insolent stare into her dark and brilliant eyes ; and
while she wrote her name upon a slip of paper for his better
comprehension, he coughed in a significant manner to attract the notice of his comrades. There were no letters
waiting at the *poste restante* for a Miss Murdoch—Lydia
Murdoch—he replied, after a studiously deliberate search.

The applicant then drew forth the envelope we have
already seen. It was addressed in a feminine handwriting
to ' Grenville Montague Vyne, Esq.,' and in the charge of the
poste restante employé it was forthwith deposited by Miss
Knollys's maid. The latter made her way back to the
swinging doors unconscious of the pleasantries exchanged
behind her. To do them full justice, these dilapidated
clerks of the French Post-Office refrained from raising their
voices to an unmannerly and compromising pitch ; and
their comments were either in ' half-words ' intelligible to
themselves alone, or in broken phrases which, if challenged,

could be indignantly repudiated with the most convincing invocations of personal honour—as usual.

By the time Miss Murdoch had returned to the Avenue Marceau, Toppin was well on his way to the Detective Department of the Paris Police, Ile de la Cité. The functionary upon whom he made his call kept him kicking his heels in an outer office for a longer period than Mr. Toppin thought respectful.

'*Eh bien, Monsieur Toppeen ?*' demanded the functionary in question, in a patronising tone, when he at length admitted his visitor to an audience. ' What's the news—*quoi de neuf ?*'

' Anything fresh?' asked Mr. Toppin, insinuating a compliment, and stringing his interlocutor's titles together with tolerable fluency.

' Fresh? Well, as you see, the Ministry are good for another six weeks. They came through the vote yesterday in excellent style.'

' I mean about the night-mail affair—the mysterious occurrence in the night-mail from London?'

' Oh—*bien, bien !* That little business of the Englishman —quite so—perfectly ! Well ?'

' Whenever you need my help, you know, in the difficult process of establishing identities, you know—of course, I am not aware how far you may have gone—I am at your disposal, Monsieur Hy — quite at your disposal, you know.'

' Yes, yes—identities—at our disposal, Monsieur Toppin— identities—yes, yes ! Well, we shall not have to trouble you just yet, for the assistance thus amiably offered—not just yet—no, *mon cher confrère*, not yet.'

' Then, up to the present, your men have lighted upon no traces ?'

' No traces? *Tiens, tiens !*—how fast he goes, our excellent and admirable Toppin—how fast, how fast ! No traces? On the contrary, *mon brave*—on the contrary, *nom d'un chien*—yes, *nom d'un p'tit bonhomme !* On the contrary, *que diable !*'

' I thought it would be singular, Monsieur Hy, with your talents and experience to direct the men.'

' Oh, oh, oh !—*ça !*—We do what we can—we just do what we can ! And the health, how goes the health of the respectable and valiant *confrère*, the ingenious, active, and invaluable Toppin—the little health, how goes it?'

'Not too badly,' answered Toppin, endeavouring to bear up.

'That's right—that's capital—that's very well. *La p'tite santé va bien!*—"oh yes! vayry good," as you say in English.'

'Well, you know—when you want my services for the identities, you know, or any other portion of the inquiry——'

'Identities—yes, yes—identities. *Eh bien*, Toppeen—looking over what we fancy we have ascertained, I do not think, I really do not think, we shall need to call upon you, or to disturb you in the least.'

'Indeed! A clue?'

'A little clue—a little, little, quite a little clue! But still'—Monsieur Hy closed his eyes, raised his eyebrows as far as they could go, and imitated the sound of an effervescent beverage escaping from a bottle—'sufficient!'

'What!—you have picked out the murderer?'

'Oho—oho! A rather brutal statement of the proposition, that—*mon ami Toppeen*. Too hurried, too hurried! Affairs like this are not easily decided. You are not going to tell me that you get along with such rapidity in London. Why, the crime was only committed yesterday morning, before daybreak!'

'Just so,' acknowledged Toppin.

'Well, then!'

'But—come, come, Monsieur Hy! With all respect for your authority, *I'm* not a novice either. Permit me to tell you that if you hold a clue it can be only to one of two men, and that if you want a speedy identification of them *I* am the only person who can do it.'

'Two men? Ah, perfectly!—the two men you reported here yesterday: yes, yes—I have their descriptions by me somewhere. The local returns have not yet come in, and so far as those individuals are concerned the matter stands where it did. No doubt a good many travellers arrived in Paris during yesterday and took up their quarters at hotels —no doubt, no doubt! That is one side of the inquiry, and we shall explore it as a matter of course. To go through all the returns, however, selecting the likely cases, and then to attend upon the spot for the final inquiries, will require some time. The precaution will not be neglected, but we need not distress ourselves. A day or two more or less, *voyons!*'

The speaker shrugged his shoulders and smiled compassionately upon Toppin.

' You will pardon me, Monsieur Hy, but don't you think we shall be giving these two men the opportunity to change their quarters and get away?'

'Oh, they shall not get away! They are foreigners, and we have good descriptions of them, through you, *mon cher Toppeen*. But to be plain with you, excellent friend, and fully recognising your commendable vigilance, we have looked for the guilty person elsewhere.'

Mr. Toppin offered no response. He knew the capacity of the French police for the achievement of astonishing discoveries as well as for the perpetration of amazing blunders.

' Yes, we have looked elsewhere,' resumed Monsieur Hy— ' we have looked in another direction, and we have found— firstly, a certain person whom you are acquainted with yourself, Toppeen, with whom you have been in communication, and whom I should advise you, in a friendly spirit, just to keep your eye on.'

' *Qui ça ?*'

' A gentleman who came from London by the night-mail, described himself as an English detective officer when the train reach Paris, viewed the corpse before the arrival of the station commissary, took hasty notes in a suspicious manner, and gave a different description of himself entirely when he filled up the police-sheet at his hotel opposite. A gentleman who wrote down on the police-sheet of the hotel that he was a traveller from Brighton, in the department of Sussex, and an architect by occupation.'

Byde !

' A gentleman who has since received '—Monsieur Hy opened a desk and glanced at a memorandum—' it was this very morning, early, to be exact—a telegram, of which I need not say we know the contents, and the sender's name. A gentleman who knew from the commencement that suspicion would descend upon certain other persons—viz., the two men our laudable Toppeen can identify ; and a gentleman who care-

fully refrains from acting in concert with the Prefecture,
but watches our investigations through the loyal, honest
confrère always welcome with us, Toppeen !'

Byde ?   Inspector Byde ?   No ; this was too much !
Toppin laughed, loud and long.

'*Hein, hein,*' continued the gratified functionary, his face
beaming with approval—'have I hit it, *hein ?*   Laugh on—
that's nervous, that laugh !   I comprehend that it should
surprise you ; but have I hit it ?'

'Of course you see what the supposition implies ?'

'Of course I do.'

'And do you think it probable for a single instant ?   Come
now, Monsieur Hy, from colleague to colleague, do you mean
to tell me that you think it probable that a well-known police-
officer—and I may as well say at once that Byde is one of
the most respected men in Scotland Yard, the English
Sûreté—would take advantage of accidental circumstances
to commit a robbery, and not only so, but commit a murder
for the sake of robbery ?'

'And do you mean to tell me that you think it improbable ?   Well, well, Toppeen, *mon bon ami*, from colleague to
colleague—we are alone, here—can you look at me fixedly
in the two eyes and say, knowing what you know, that the
supposition is extravagant ?'

'On the English side of the Channel—yes ; altogether
extravagant.'

'Whereas, on this side ?'

'Oh, I won't permit myself to pass judgment on your
compatriots, Monsieur Hy !   The man we are speaking of is
a compatriot of my own.'

'Well, then, I *will* permit myself to pass judgment, Monsieur Toppeen.   I know my own compatriots, and I know
human nature, too, I rather flatter myself—and I flatter
myself that I don't flatter myself unduly.   Given the temptation, and human nature always yields.   But do I say that
the temptation always arrays itself in the same guise ?   Not
in the least, not in the least.   You have to find the *moment
juste,* I don't deny it; but for every—mark me, every—type
and specimen of human nature there exists some form or
other of temptation which is irresistible.   Why are your
country-people to be considered as of superior morality to
my own ?   Do your newspapers prove that they are so ?

Not exactly! Why should this Monsieur Byde of necessity escape suspicion?'

'Then that is your precious clue? You are really aiming at Inspector Byde? who, I don't mind adding for your information, came over precisely to watch the movements of the deceased.'

'Ah, indeed! He came over precisely to watch the movements of the deceased? A fact to be noted in the *dossier.*'

Monsieur Hy opened the desk again. He propped up the lid, put his head inside the desk, and noted his new fact upon a sheet of white foolscap, ruled with water lines. Toppin reddened with vexation.

'But I haven't enlightened you upon our " secondly," ' resumed Monsieur Hy; 'and our " secondly" is serious. For, of course, our "firstly" was but academical conjecture—ha, ha, ha!—a case for my volume ; my volume—bah ! a little work I am preparing for the use of the police in every country with a civilization—a manual, *oui, monsieur,* a manual on " The Theory of Surmise in Undetected Crime." '

'So you have a " secondly "?'

' *Oui, mon bon!* and a substantial " secondly"! otherwise —no, don't look at me like that !—otherwise our worthy Toppeen would be legitimately suspected—oh, I justify it in the " Theory "!—of connivance in the crime by reason of his communications with the suspected criminal. Ha, ha, ha ! our worthy, zealous, and patriotic Toppeen, so anxious that the Sûreté shall discover the two men hiding away in Paris, taken into custody himself, cast into the felon's cell, rigidly cross-questioned by a *juge d'instruction* who—we'll take it for granted—doesn't like the English, and eventually brought up at the Assizes, with his respected *confrère,* who was a passenger from Scotland Yard. Ha, ha, ha ! that solemn face would make the joke assassinatingly, too exquisitely piercing. What a scene !—oh, oh, oh !— with that solemn face !—no, keep that solemn face—don't smile ! *Ah, mon Dieu !* I thank thee for the joy of this. What a rapturous tableau — what a deobstruent ! *Eh, va donc, vieux farceur !'*

Monsieur Hy snatched up a long flat ruler, and mirthfully poked Toppin in the ribs with it. Mr. Toppin acknowledged the fun with a lugubrious smile.

'What a pity we can't realize such a scene!' continued Monsieur Hy, changing to a mournful tone. 'What a pity, what a pity! It would make an artistic situation, and would ravish the gallery. Officers of the English Sûreté, on the track of criminals, tracked themselves, and finally convicted by their colleagues of the French Sûreté! The man who could do that would be made. *I* could do that. It would be a fine illustration of my "Theory," part 2, section 8. What an advertisement! Edition upon edition of "The Theory of Surmise in Undetected Crime;" and the Legion of Honour for its author, Michel Auguste Hy. Ah! what a pity we can't manage it!'

'Can't you manage it, indeed?' asked Toppin sarcastically; for he was nettled.

'Well, you see, there's our "secondly," which is serious. We looked at all the possible hypotheses, I should think, and the one we have selected seems to be pretty well borne out by the researches. What were the main hypotheses? Our journals talk of a *drame intime;* they are always eager to insinuate *drames intimes*—a family scandal or a vengeance. Now, to affirm a family scandal, we must know something more about the identity of a victim than we can ascertain by means of linen marked with only two initials. Then, as to the category of vengeances, you have principally those which are inspired by women, and those which women carry out. We might have spent a great deal of time over matters of this sort, had not circumstances helped us to a simpler explanation. We say that the present story is the common one of murder for the sake of gain. And the assassin? We have him—the assassin.'

Monsieur Hy reached across the desk for a newspaper.

'You have him—in custody?' stammered Toppin.

'We have him,' repeated Monsieur Hy, turning to the money article, and apparently perusing it with keen interest. 'When I say the assassin, of course I don't mean to say that he has been brought up before the Seine Assize Court, and found guilty by a jury of his fellow-citizens— Three per Cent. Perpetuals, rise of fifteen centimes; Unified, stationary; Portuguese, going up — nor do I mean to say that he has yet made his confession. We haven't seriously questioned him; we're waiting—waiting till he gets sober.'

Toppin only partially succeeded in dissembling his bewilderment.

'Banque de Paris, 770; stood at 745 day before yesterday. Crédit Foncier—good; Crédit Lyonnais—— When he gets sober we shall question him. Guess who it is! Can't? Why, the guard of the train, *mon brave !*'

'What, the English through-guard?'

'No; the French guard from Calais.'

'Ah, the French guard from Calais!'

'Yes. You wouldn't have thought of that?'

'No; considering that the rings and other valuables worn by the victim were not disturbed, and that there was a fairly good sum of money in his pocket.'

'Money in his pocket, yes; but how much he had about him before he was murdered we don't know. One or two of the railway servants fancy they have noticed this man at the Gare du Nord as an occasional traveller. His appearance is that of an ordinary business man, and what sums of money he might travel with we can't tell at present. We find that the guard has been long enough on the service between Calais and Paris to know some of the periodical passengers. These railway affairs are becoming scientific, *nom d'un chien !* The valuables and money are of course left as a blind.'

'A case of purely theoretical suspicion, then?'

'No, because we have the weapon used.'

'Found on the prisoner?'

'No. If we had found the weapon in his possession we might have entertained grave doubts as to his guilt. Assuming that the crime was committed after the last stoppage, viz., Creil, we ordered the line to be searched along both sides. The regular guard, being familiar with the country, would in all likelihood select a favourable spot for ridding himself of the compromising weapon. We therefore had the search conducted more particularly among the trees which border the line so densely on this and the other side of Chantilly.'

'And the weapon has been found already? Quick work! But why connect it specially with the guard of the train?'

'We, therefore, in this manner reconstruct the crime: The French guard has passed along the footboard of the entire train once or twice in the earlier portion of the

journey to examine the tickets. That forms part of his
duty, but nothing exists to hinder him from passing backwards and forwards as often and as deliberately as he
chooses. Very well. In the night he is quite invisible for
the passengers, but he can plainly see, from his post outside,
the whole of the interior of every compartment which may
not have every one of its blinds closely drawn down. The
guard notices this passenger alone in the compartment.
The passenger is asleep, or has his eyes closed. *Bon !* The
guard has the right of asking for the traveller's ticket again,
and this right not ouly accounts for his re-appearance at the
window while the train is running at full speed, but excuses
his entry into the carriage itself, if the traveller should suddenly discover him. *Nom d'une pipe !*—what happens?
He shoots him at his ease, and picks his pockets with celerity but discrimination.'

'I don't think,' objected Toppin, 'that with premedi-
tation such as that a man would choose a firearm for the
business.'

'Sure, and clean !' said Monsieur Hy impatiently.

'And the report?'

'Covered by the din and rattle of the train. And then
the guard, who knows the line, knows where the railway bridges cross it ; and at those points the noise
redoubles.'

'And what is your explanation of the scrap of folded
paper found on the floor—the paper with the address on it :
Adelaide, care of a London post-office ?'

'Pulled out of the breast-pocket hurriedly, with whatever else was taken from it—pulled out unperceived, and
dropped.'

Byde's explanation exactly, remembered Toppin. But
Byde had the best of reasons for his opinion ; he believed
that the breast-pocket had been supposed by the thief to
contain the Wilmot diamonds. How would the didactic
Hy, who must be ignorant of the Wilmot case, explain the
rifling of the inner-pocket, whilst everything else had apparently been left untouched ? He put the question.

Why, said Monsieur Hy, it was simplicity itself. Either
the guard had some especial knowledge of this periodical
voyager by the Northern Railway, in which event they need
look no farther ; or the guard acted upon the general pro-

position that most travellers carry their most valuable property in places concealed from common observation. What
did they perceive in the present case? A coat and waistcoat unbuttoned. A pocket in the lining of the waistcoat.
To shorten the explorations of an experienced thief, nothing
could have been better designed than this capacious pocket
in the waistcoat-lining. The first thing he looked for, naturally! The stolen property consisted either of bank-notes or
precious stones, Monsieur Hy concluded; and the amount
must have been considerable for all those good rings to have
been left upon the fingers.

'Yes, but how do you connect this firearm with the guard
of the train?' demanded Toppin aggressively.

'Because it was not found along the line between Creil
and Paris, but elsewhere. The search along the line is still
going on, as a matter of routine. But——'

There was a knock at the door. Monsieur Hy interrupted
his exposition to growl '*Entrez!*' which, not being heard,
he had to repeat, and which he did more loudly repeat,
appending a sonorous epithet. A subordinate officer entered
and saluted.

'—— But in the first place we can go back a long way
in the guard's antecedents, and they are bad.—What is it,
Duval?'

The new-comer advanced three steps, handed a note to
his superior, saluted, and fell back three steps again.

'And, in the second place, the revolver, recently discharged, was found hidden away in the prisoner's dwelling.
Then comes the question——'

Monsieur Hy had broken the seal of the envelope, and
was perusing the missive.

'Then comes the question, in the third place, whether
——but you can read this for yourself.'

He folded down the upper part of the communication,
and passed the note across the desk. Toppin glanced at
the passage indicated. The style was that of a succinct
report. He read it through twice, and with a sigh passed
it back to Monsieur Hy. He had there read that the bullet
which caused the death of the Englishman lying at the
Morgue had been found to correspond exactly with the
chambers of the firearm hidden on the premises of the man
now in custody—the French guard of the train.

CHAPTER XIII.

THE telegram to which Monsieur Hy had referred in his conversation with Toppin was, as a matter of fact, a message to Inspector Byde from the Criminal Investigation Department, Scotland Yard. It apprised the inspector of an important proceeding on the part of the Mr. Sinclair who was arrested at Dover. Sinclair had affirmed and re-affirmed his innocence, had demanded that writing materials should be furnished to him without delay, and had then curtly refused altogether to reply. He had no explanations to make, he had said; he had already reiterated the declaration of his innocence ; and he ' should not stoop to make any further responses.' He had immediately availed himself of the writing materials, however, remarking that he wished particularly to catch the next mail from Dover to the Continent. The letter which he had handed over to the local authorities for transmission by the post bore a Paris address. It had been duly forwarded, and in the ordinary course of things should have been delivered in Paris the same evening. The direction was to the Avenue Marceau, No. 95, *Aux Soins de Madame Bertram.* The recipient was a Miss Knollys. Would the inspector see to this ? concluded the telegram.

Thus it happened that not long after the departure of Detective Toppin from the Avenue Marceau, Mr. Inspector Byde presented himself at the residence of Mrs. Bertram, No. 95. Madame Bertram was not at home, answered the *concierge*—at least she believed not. Monsieur could ascertain for himself, if he chose to take the trouble to mount two flights of stairs. The suite tenanted by Madame Bertram was ' on the second.' There was a lift ; monsieur knew how to manage it without doubt ? Mdlle. Knollys? oh, yes--a young English lady visiting Madame Bertram— recently arrived from London. Mdlle. Knollys was not at home either, believed the *concierge*. She had been taken with an indisposition on the previous evening, and would not be at home to anybody.

The inspector had arranged his programme before leaving the hotel, and this answer, which he had extracted from the portress by the disbursement of a five-franc piece, placed him in readiness for his reception 'on the second,' at the private apartments of Madame Bertram.

'I should recommend you to make quite sure that Mdlle. Knollys is not at home at this moment,' said he in his *panaché* French, with its three dialects. 'Take my card, and remember that it is Mdlle. Knollys, not Madame Bertram, whom I wish to see. I am in no hurry, and can wait whilst you are prosecuting your inquiries in the household.'

The footman was the free-and-easy individual who had been imbibing with the coachman an hour or two earlier at Mr. Toppin's expense. He had since then had time to don his morning livery, and to tone down his complexion, and to arch his eyebrows as a well-paid and well-nourished footman, who has served in good establishments, and entertains respect for his employers, ought to learn to arch them permanently. He measured Mr. Byde with the disdainful sweep of the regard which only footmen, fashionable beauties, and illiterate millionnaires can practise to perfection. The look should have withered the inspector, but unfortunately for its success that gentleman habitually took no notice of such manifestations as the superb attitude, the haughty stare, the frigid manner, and the crushing retort. It is true that he was not at all a diffident, sensitive, or feeble person. Although a man of worth, he was perhaps but a superior sort of peremptory sergeant, a very shrewd policeman with the policial disregard of any weapon that might not be positively lethal. And nevertheless there are men of worth, and women, too, strange to say, whom the direct menace of the lethal weapon will affect less keenly than any footman's jeer or any courtesan's insult, the triumphal march of any illiterate millionnaire, or the cold scorn of any handsome woman who, in her lounge through flowery meads of life, has not yet chanced to encounter the variola.

Inspector Byde enclosed his card within an envelope. The latter would easily open, being freshly gummed, he observed to the domestic; at the same time he would strongly advise him not to open it in the kitchen before delivering it to his mistress, for Miss Knollys. Measuring his interlocutor with another proud look, a look which a false Continental marquess standing on his dignity might have envied, the domestic vouchsafed a few contemptuous syllables to the effect that the strange visitor had apparently mistaken his whereabouts.

'*Allons donc!*' interrupted the inspector, a little brutally. 'Do you think I don't know the servant's hall?'

The astonished footman looked twice at the cut of the inspector's clothes.

'It's a foreigner, Marotte,' said he to the cook when he reached the kitchen; 'but where he comes from I can't make out. Sometimes he speaks like a Marseillais, sometimes like a Swiss. The *concierge* must have told him that our people are at home, for he insists. What's to be done with this card? Madame will be angry if I say the person is waiting while I take it in.'

'You should not have allowed the person to wait. You had your orders, had you not?'

'Well, I don't know how it happened, but he had a manner! Not a person of the best world, I should say; but still he had a manner——!'

Marotte suggested that he should refer to the English maid, who had returned from her walk some time ago. Lydia Murdoch betrayed some surprise at the sight of the superscription. It was impossible, however, for her to express any opinion, she commented. She could not say whom the visitor might be. Thereupon the simple process familiar to the servant's hall, as well as to the *cabinet noir* of certain Governments, was neatly and expeditiously performed.

It was his professional card that the inspector had enclosed within the envelope. The lines engraved upon it might have been Chaldaic writings for the eyes that now glanced over them,—except for the eyes of Lydia Murdoch. For Lydia Murdoch they were assuredly full of significance.

'You had better convey the card to mademoiselle,' she said briefly.

Inspector Byde waited with the utmost patience, the delay convincing him that the 'not at home' was no more than the conveniently untrue formula of ordinary usage. If after this delay, he pondered, the 'not at home' should be persisted in, despite the announcement of his visit in professional capacity, there would be not a bad ground for assuming, just inferentially, that the original supposition was being confirmed.

The original supposition had been, had it not? that young Mr. Sinclair, formerly Mr. Wilmot's private secretary, and suddenly dismissed a few months ago, was the actual thief in this matter of the diamonds, and that he had acted with some party, then unknown, whose office in the undertaking was to receive the property from him and to realize it. A vague suspicion had fallen upon Remington, the circumstances of whose death might possibly be held to justify that suspicion. But it had also been on the cards that the abstracted property, notwithstanding its exceptional value, had been despatched like a common parcel by Sinclair himself, or by some confederate, unknown, to an address in Paris, where it would be subsequently recovered. Now, he had learnt through the wire that Sinclair had been searched at Dover, and that the property had not been found upon him. Putting on one side for the moment the murder of Mr. Remington in the night-mail and the rifling of the breast-pocket—and the misdeed might, after all, have been fruitlessly committed—suppose that the original conjecture were the accurate one, and that the parcel had been forwarded in the simplest manner to the Miss Knollys, of No. 95, Avenue Marceau, to whom it had been Sinclair's first thought, after his arrest, to write? Improbable— because the superscription upon his letter gave the police the clue? Not in the least improbable! It was important for him to communicate with the Avenue Marceau: was he not expected to arrive in Paris by the night-mail? A prompt telegram from him to the Paris address would of course attract attention; a letter might just possibly escape notice. The letter might be couched in perfectly common-place terms, and yet might convey to its recipient both a warning and instructions. Or—it need not have been actually to this address that the parcel was consigned; it would be quite sufficient, for the theory, that the address to which the parcel had been consigned was known to some one here. But had this place the air of a receiver's premises?

Judging by the apartment into which he had been ushered, the lady of the house must be in the enjoyment of considerable opulence. The vestibule, encumbered with evergreen plants and the few hardy blossoms of the season, had had the aspect of a carpeted conservatory as he passed through.

The lofty apartment in which he was now seated reminded him of an antiquary's cabinet as much as of anything else. Across the walls here and there hung portions of old Flanders tapestry, the adventures of Ixion which they had once depicted in tones warm and rich having since become problematical, owing to the ravages of moths, and to the decolourizations of time. A curious old cabinet, with little columns of lapis-lazuli, stood at one end of the room ; and a large Venetian mirror, with a frame of quaint carving, formed another conspicuous ornament. The chairs were Louis Treize ; and half a hundred smaller articles completed the main effect. With dry logs blazing cheerfully on almost a bare hearth, it seemed a pity that the mantelpiece should mark the last quarter of the nineteenth century.

From his contemplation of this interior Mr. Inspector Byde was roused by the reappearance of the servant who had first answered his summons. Mdlle. Knollys had been slightly indisposed since the previous evening, but would receive the gentleman whose card had been enclosed to her. The next minute Mr. Byde was shown into a luxurious drawing-room, and, as he entered, two ladies rose to their feet. Yes! they were the ladies who had visited the Morgue.

' Miss Knollys ?' said the inspector inquiringly.

' Any communication you may have to make to me may be freely made in the presence of this lady, Mrs. Bertram, my friend,' replied the younger of the two, in a low voice.

' My business relates to a matter which concerns yourself intimately,' hazarded the inspector. ' I have received the fullest information from London on the subject, but have deemed it only proper to place myself in direct communication with you, Miss Knollys. I am aware that I have no right to intrude upon you here; I am here only by your courtesy. As you have been good enough to receive me, however, let me beg you, in your own interests, to facilitate, as far as you can do so, the inquiry I am engaged upon for Scotland Yard. My business relates to your acquaintance with Austin Wortley Sinclair, now " wanted " by the police on a charge of diamond robbery.'

' Mr. Sinclair must be the victim of an absurd mistake !' exclaimed the young lady. ' The whole occurrence is inconceivable ! Mr. Sinclair is either the victim of a perfectly

ridiculous blunder—a stupid, idiotic piece of misunderstand-
ing, or else——,' she stopped, and twisted her handkerchief
nervously, ' or else of heartless malice—the most cruel,
cruel, vindictive malice !'

She burst into tears.

' Oh, Adela !—my poor child !' murmured the elder lady
moving to her side.

Adela ?

Mr. Inspector Byde repeated the syllables mentally two
or three times, in the hope of lighting upon the diapason.
The name seemed to set some chord of his memory in
vibration, but for the moment he could not single it out.
' Adelaide ' had been the name scrawled on the slip of paper
found on the floor of the compartment occupied by the
murdered man. That fact, however, had remained quite
prominently before the inspector's mind, and it did not at
all correspond to the faint reminiscence now abruptly evoked.
Miss Adela Knollys—Adela—Adela ? A pretty state of
things, thought the inspector with a twinge of real alarm, if
the very best of his professional instruments, his memory,
should be beginning to fail him ! His countenance betrayed
so acute an inward trouble that the lady of the house
softened as she turned to speak to him, and her tone was
milder than perhaps she had intended.

' Is it absolutely necessary that you should put any
questions to Miss Knollys ? She is not at all well, as you
can see ; is it absolutely necessary that you should torture
her with questions ?'

' I shall be sorry to cause the young lady any pain, and,
if she wishes, the conversation can be deferred. I am
entirely at your disposal ; but—it might be better, it might
be really better——'

' You must call again,' said Mrs. Bertram ; ' I cannot see
the poor child persecuted in this way. At any rate, she
shall not be persecuted in this gratuitous manner while she
remains in my house, under my care. I don't know how
my address came into your possession ; and I am not at all
sure that we are acting wisely in receiving you.'

' As you think best, madam,' returned the inspector, very
politely, and rising from the chair to which he had been
motioned. A pause ensued. The hostess bent over the
figure of the young girl, who was weeping silently, and

whispered some soothing words to her. The sincerity of this emotion and the charm of this feminine sympathy went to a soft place in the inspector's heart. He drew back a step or two, and then hesitated. 'When may I wait upon you again?' he asked in a sepulchral voice, which, to tell the truth, was rather unsteady, and needed his short, dry cough at the close.

'Oh, let this gentleman remain!' said the young girl, speaking with her face averted, and with her handkerchief still pressed to her eyes. 'How weak of me to give way!'

'Do you think you can bear it, dear?'

'Yes—oh yes! And he will tell me of—— Oh, it is wicked of them—wicked, wicked!'

'It must be a mistake,' said Mrs. Bertram gently.

She glanced towards the visitor, and smiled. The inspector moved back to his chair, coughed again somewhat huskily, and sat down.

'Tell me about Mr. Sinclair!' exclaimed the young girl impulsively, dropping her handkerchief, and turning to face the gentleman from Scotland Yard.

'He is "wanted,"' said Mr. Byde.

'What does that mean?'

'"Wanted" by the police, on the charge I told you of.'

'Why, he wrote to us that he was in prison! He wrote to us from Dover. The police arrested him at the Dover railway-station. Did you not know that?'

'Oh, really—they have found him, have they? My information is from London, and deals more particularly with the circumstances of the robbery. Ah, they have found him?' The professional habit of laying traps had been too much for Inspector Byde, and he had yielded to it, in spite of his sensibility of the minute before. However, he need not anticipate concealment in this instance, it seemed. There were no wiles to be combated.

'Found him!' both ladies had the air of indignantly repeating. 'Mr. Sinclair could have had no notion whatever that his whereabouts were being sought for,' replied Mrs. Bertram; 'he was the last man to evade search or inquiry—the very last!'

'Yes, indeed!' concurred Miss Knollys warmly.

'We received a letter from him last night. He wrote from Dover to say that on his way here by the night-mail

he had been arrested on an absurd charge of diamond robbery, and that, without wishing to alarm us, he was afraid
from what he had been able to ascertain that appearances
were somehow or other very strong against him, and might
place him in an extremely serious position. If we felt quite
free to communicate some family matters to you, Mr.
Byde, you would at once understand the situation of great
delicacy which an event of this kind creates for Miss
Knollys.'

'Dear Mrs. Bertram!' exclaimed the young girl, em-
bracing her friend enthusiastically, ' we know that we may
count on you, and I am ungrateful to forget how much I
myself owe to your kind aid. But I feel that my own
position is nothing compared to the dreadful one into which
poor Austin has been thrown—just at this moment, too !
It must be very much more grave than we can imagine, for
him to have acknowledged to us that the affair was in the
least degree serious. Poor fellow ! what a humiliation for
him, and what a misfortune—and just at this moment !
Poor Austin !'

A tear still sparkled upon the long eye-lashes. The inspector noted that the young lady began to twist her lace
handkerchief again. He transferred his gaze to the nearest
oil-painting on the walls, and studied with great intentness
a blurred rainbow in the ' Passing Shower,' treated uncon-
ventionally. When he ventured to look back, the symptoms
had disappeared and the compressed lips were relaxing. It
was ill taste in him, reflected the inspector, to stare at Miss
Knollys so persistently. But as she sat there facing him,
he did not think he could have seen in all his life a prettier
picture than this fair-haired English girl, with her flushed
cheeks, her frank and clear gray eyes, her dark, decided
eyebrows, the chaste and sweet expression of her mouth.
Trifles—trifles !—the inspector's even judgment suddenly
reminded his indulgent sense. Well, not exactly trifles, if
you liked, but accidents of nature, not implying merit in
the individual, and quite unconnected with considerations
as to complicity in an indictable offence. Mrs. Byde had
never been half so good-looking as this young lady ; but he
would defy you to discover a truer haart and kinder nature,
the whole world through, than Mrs. Byde's. And then as to
looks—

> ' Where's the sense, direct and moral,
> That teeth are pearl, or lips are coral ?'

Mr. Byde, who loved to improve himself, had committed to memory this and other couplets out of ' The Progress of the Mind.' ' Come, come ! Let us get back to the Wilmot case,' urged Mr. Byde mentally.

' Pray excuse me, ladies,' he resumed, ' but my duty obliges me to address a direct question or two which you may look upon, at first sight, as unwarranted by the circumstances of my presence here. I have to ask Miss Knollys, to begin with, what is the nature of her acquaintance with Mr. Sinclair ?'

The two ladies exchanged glances.

' Can I answer that, do you think?' demanded Miss Knollys, a little timidly, of her friend.

' *I* should not answer it, my dear,' was the response. ' It cannot possibly concern this gentleman, or this gentleman's employers.'

' What did you understand to be the object of Mr. Sinclair's journey to the Continent ?' proceeded the visitor.

' He was coming here to enter upon an appointment as secretary which I had procured for him through private channels,' replied Mrs. Bertram.

' And can you account for his haunting the Park Lane residence of Mr. Stanislas Wilmot for several nights previous to the robbery ; for his disappearance immediately after the robbery ; and for his attempt to get away to the Continent unnoticed by the night-mail ?'

The ladies again exchanged glances, and a slight blush deepened the rose upon Miss Adela's cheeks.

' I can perhaps account for Mr. Sinclair's being frequently in the neighbourhood of Mr. Wilmot's house,' she said, after some embarrassment and with the suggestion of a shy smile ; ' but if he " disappeared," as you state, it was most likely before the robbery, not afterwards. I cannot imagine that he could have the least appearance of desiring to leave England unperceived ; and the train he travelled by had been selected, not by himself, but by me.'

' I must now ask whether you are acquainted in any way with the owner of the stolen property, Mr. Stanislas Wilmot ?'

'Mr. Wilmot is my relative, and my guardian,' replied the young lady.

Adela! Of course! He found the chord now, though not the full diapason. The dead man, Remington, had pronounced the name when relating to his fellow-passengers certain details in the mysterious diamond robbery at the Park Lane house. Remington had told them that old Stanislas Wilmot lived there with his niece, Miss Adela. How was he, Byde, to know of any difference in the surnames? Sergeant Bell had omitted to furnish him with this point either when he, Byde, hurriedly took up the case, or through the post since. Such negligence was perfectly disgusting. How could he make progress if the whole of the facts were not reported to him? And suppose he had drifted into a blunder? It was ever so. You did your best, and half the time you were hampered by others. You were at the mercy of some careless or conceited subordinate, who either had not the faculty for picking up little points or else discriminated for himself very sagely amongst the details, and left out whatever it might please him to consider unimportant—as if in their business there were any such things as unimportant details! Who could say upon what ostensibly insignificant item an investigation might not turn! The door and the doorway might be in the same material; might be more or less massive, and might be in contact or out of it; but they were separate objects, requiring for their absolute co-relation, you might say, the hinge; and the hinge was nearly always in a different substance, of bulk insignificant as compared with the two objects it connected. What might be the other valueless matters, he wondered, which Sergeant Bell had omitted to report to him?

It was in this way that the best of officers might be sent off on wrong tacks, and possibly forfeit their reputations. Had it been his own fault in the great Temperance scandal that—— Well, well! we should see! And they should see, also, those Temperance people, who since that affair had never been able to let him alone in their snarling and canting newspaper. *He* knew well enough certain members of the flock whose goings on——well, well! time would show. For the present the inspector's thoughts reverted grimly to the case of Brother Neel.

'Miss Knollys has usually been spoken of as the niece of

Mr. Wilmot,' remarked the hostess. ' That is not their relationship. Nor was she a poor relation of his wife's, as he appears to have given out. He was a cousin of her mother's, and had always managed her mother's investments. Mr. Wilmot is a very clever man; and her mother named him in her will as Adela's guardian, and left everything in his hands. So like her, that was!' added Mrs. Bertram, with a deprecating little smile to Miss Knollys, ' so like your poor mother, my dear. She trusted everyone, and was utterly thoughtless in all her own money matters. I don't believe she had the slightest notion as to the extent of her means when your father's fatal accident left her so suddenly a widow. Stanislas Wilmot offered his assistance—most generously, she said : a little too eagerly, I thought myself— and in the end she allowed him to dispose of everything. It always struck me that he had contrived the quarrel between your poor mother and her husband's family, although, to be sure, they were a disagreeable, tuft-hunting set. Her own brother showed the very greatest promise, but he died, as you know, in India, when you were a very little girl. As for her two elder sisters, your aunts Eglantine and Amelia, they have always been the most frivolous creatures in the world, and the last time I saw them—you will forgive me for saying so, my dear—I really thought that they were the silliest women of their age I had ever, ever met.'

' They are certainly very helpless,' acquiesced Miss Knollys ; ' and I am afraid it is no more than the truth to add that they are rather selfish and unkind. It was hard to think that I could not look to them for aid in my difficult position.'

' So that Mr. Wilmot has been able to dispose of the money-matters exactly as he liked. And I always thought, you know, Adela, that he intended to dispose of *you* likewise !'

Miss Knollys made no answer.

' Well, heaven knows what may be the condition of your affairs—whether you have a farthing or a fortune !'

' Oh, I have felt so glad, so delighted, to be away from him that I would have relinquished all I may be entitled to, if there is anything, for the mere sake of never seeing him again, and never hearing from him. Austin would not like me to accept anything either—I know he would not.'

'That is all nonsense, dear! You are entitled to what is your own, and in the spring, when you come of age, your guardian will have to give it up. Whether he likes it or not, he will be bound to make a full restitution of what belongs to you.'

'But suppose he has spent it?' asked the young girl innocently.

'Oh, well, if he has spent it—I don't know—of course he cannot restore to you what he hasn't got of yours—if he has spent it—I don't know—of course——'

'Prosecute him for misappropriation of trust funds,' put in the inspector, deeply interested.

'Yes, evidently that would be the proper course to follow,' assented Mrs. Bertram; 'you would prosecute him for misappropriation of trust funds. Take proceedings against him. He deserves it!'

'Oh no!—oh no! Let him rest, if he is satisfied with his dishonesty. There may be nothing after all, and if he says there is nothing, let us drop the matter and never mention his name again. I am too thankful to have escaped —for I call it an escape. But we are wearying Mr. Byde with all this?'

'On the contrary,' protested that gentleman, 'these matters are all pertinent to the inquiry. Allow me to demonstrate. Suppose that A. B., trustee of the estate of C. D., a minor, has misapplied the moneys of the said C. D. You follow me?'

'Oh, quite!' said Mrs. Bertram, frowning with her mental effort to pursue the abstract relations of A. B. and C. D.—'Perfectly!'

'And suppose that A. B., on the approach of C. D.'s majority, fears that, on C. D.'s behalf, it may be demanded of him to render an account of C. D.'s estate, and that in anticipation he pretends to make exceptional, honest, but unfortunate, investments of certain of the moneys. You follow me?'

'Entirely,' said Mrs. Bertram.

'And suppose that A. B., speculating in precious stones, makes a plunge on diamonds, in the ostensible interests of C. D.'s estate, to the extent of £20,000. Suppose these diamonds, purchased for the estate of C. D., are abstracted from his custody and never traced. C. D. may subsequently

render the position of A. B. somewhat unpleasant, if so
minded; but A. B. may be judged to have acted in good
faith, and C. D. may for various reasons let the matter
drop. Now, then, we have only to suppose that A. B.
never did lay out the moneys of C. D. in diamonds to the
extent of £20,000, and it would result——I beg pardon, but
—you follow me?'

'Quite well,' said Mrs. Bertram.

'It would result—that the diamonds never were stolen
at all. If we suppose A. B. to be Stanislas Wilmot, Esq.,
and C. D. to be Miss Adela Knollys, his ward, we then
arrive at the conclusion that the Wilmot (Park Lane) case,
with regard to which I have ventured to present myself,
ladies, and upon which I have been specially commissioned
from Scotland Yard, is neither more nor less than—non-
existent.'

'Then you will tell them to set free Mr. Sinclair at
once?' demanded the younger lady, with great promptti-
tude.

'There might be a case for letting him out on bail,' replied the inspector; 'his own and other recognisances, to
a substantial amount. But I can't say what they may
have gathered, in the way of corroborative testimony, at the
other end.'

'Oh, how unjust the law is!' exclaimed Miss Knollys.
'I would not be a lawyer for anything, if I were a man!'

'Well, you see——' began the inspector.

'Unjust and stupid, the law is!' reiterated Miss Knollys,
her colour heightening again.

'Why should Mr. Sinclair have been indicated to the
police? We were bound to take notice of the information
laid with us.'

'And who laid the information?' inquired Mrs. Bertram.

'Stanislas Wilmot, Esq.,' replied the visitor.

'Just as I thought!' exclaimed Miss Knollys to the elder
lady. 'Did I not tell you so? Malice—wicked, vindictive,
designing malice!'

'May I question you as to the occasion of Mr. Sinclair's
departure from the employment of your guardian three
months ago?' asked Mr. Byde.

Miss Knollys consulted her friend with a regard. The
hostess answered with an expression which seemed to

convey—' Well, do as you like, my dear, but I should not tell this strange man all my personal affairs.' The signals, believed to be imperceptible, continued.

Divining, as men of the world usually do divine, the code in that feminine telegraphy by which the fair operators fondly imagine they conceal their interchange of impressions from the other sex, Mr. Byde went on to say that the position of Austin Wortley Sinclair ' might be injuriously affected by circumstances attendant upon his dismissal a few months before.' If he had been suspected of mal-practices, for instance, or detected in suspicious company : indeed, worse than that might have happened.

' You see,' pursued Mr. Byde, ' the case for Mr. Wilmot is that the property was abstracted from his strong room during the night, and that the locks must have been opened with duplicate keys. His keys had not been out of his possession for some time previously, and certainly not while this property was lying in the strong room of the Park Lane residence ; but he did once mislay them while Mr. Sinclair was in his employment as private secretary. Now, if Mr. Sinclair is accused of taking away certain keys in order to have patterns made of them, that will form an awkward accusation to rebut. When we know why he quitted Mr. Sinclair's employment——'

' He went away because of unwarrantable freedom on the part of Mr. Wilmot,' interrupted the young girl haughtily. ' Oh, you shall hear the story !'

' Adela !'

' On second thoughts, no, not the entire edifying story; but you shall learn what you wish to know. Mr. Sinclair was taunted by my guardian with endeavouring to involve me in an engagement to him, for the purpose of obtaining the control of my fortune—an imaginary fortune, he added, in his gracious manner. In the same breath he said he should dismiss him at once ; but that was of course need-less, for Mr. Sinclair would not have remained another moment in his house. The entire rupture did not occupy more than a few minutes. Mr. Sinclair had no opportunity of communicating with me, and from that day I became, without guessing it, almost Mr. Wilmot's prisoner. Mr. Sinclair would not descend to anything clandestine, and the letters which it seems he sent through the post to me were intercepted. His sudden departure was misrepresented, and I was condemned to listen to calumny upon calumny. Mr. Wilmot had other views for me, I understood later—other views!' She blushed once more—partly with anger, perhaps.

'You eventually met Mr. Sinclair again?'

'Mr. Sinclair guessed the reason of my silence, and at length made a call at our house. He timed his visit expressly for an hour when my guardian was usually at home. Mr. Wilmot refused to receive him, and forbade me to enter into any communication with him. Any such prohibition being tyrannical nonsense, I declined utterly to observe it. It has been due to myself that Austin Wortley Sinclair, as you think fit to speak of him, thenceforward occasionally "haunted" the Park Lane residence of Mr. Stanislas Wilmot—poor fellow! The concealment we were obliged to observe formed an additional humiliation for him. He had been already insulted; he was in poverty and without prospects for the time; and if I had not assured him I should never change, I think he would have gone away for ever. What gave him courage, however, was the statement by my guardian that I was absolutely penniless.'

Mr. Byde stared at the young lady with a surprise that was largely mingled with admiration.

'And it is owing to you, dear, dear Mrs. Bertram,' continued the young lady, with a grateful outburst 'that we should have been extricated from our embarrassments, if this horrible affair had not occurred. Austin will be set at liberty very soon—that is one consolation—but think how he will feel the stigma!'

'Mr. Sinclair's appointment here'—asked the visitor—'will he lose it through this case, in the event of his innocence being proved?'

'His prospects shall not suffer,' replied Mrs. Bertram drily; 'I have sufficient influence to ensure that. Are there any further questions you would wish to ask?'

'One—does Miss Knollys identify the man whose corpse lies at the Morgue?'

It was the young lady's turn to exhibit surprise.

'Yes,' she answered slowly, with a slight tremor; 'I recognise the dead man. It is Mr. Remington, one of the business people employed by my guardian. You saw us, perhaps, at the Morgue yesterday afternoon? We had read the news of that murder in the night-mail from London, and in the absence of any message up to that moment from Mr. Sinclair, whom we had expected by the same train, I feared that the victim might be he. Mr. Remington made periodical journeys to Paris for the purposes of his business, and had occasionally brought us a trifling souvenir. He was well acquainted with the arrangements of our house, and might have been of the greatest usefulness to Mr. Sinclair just now. It was very shocking to find that the victim was the Mr. Remington whom we were accustomed to see so often at home. Poor Mr. Remington!—to die in that manner—murdered!'

'I preferred that Miss Knollys, residing in my house,' observed Mrs. Bertram, 'should leave others to formally declare the identity of this unfortunate man. No doubt, in a day or two, all that will have been settled.'

Mr. Inspector Byde rose to depart. 'Another word, if I may be permitted,' he said; 'Miss Knollys expressed the conviction that Mr. Sinclair's sudden disappearance from the vicinity of the Park Lane house must have been prior to the robbery if there was a robbery, not afterwards. That might lead up to a good *alibi*. Was the opinion based upon any fact within her own cognisance?'

'It was based upon this fact,' replied Mrs. Bertram, 'that she herself disappeared from Mr. Wilmot's house prior to the date of the alleged robbery. There was no other attraction for Mr. Sinclair in the Park Lane establishment. Miss Knollys had found that any longer residence with her guardian would be unbearable, and I have been happy to place my own house at her disposition for any length of time. We desire particularly that her whereabouts may not be known to Mr. Wilmot for the present. He was well aware that Mr. Sinclair was proceeding to some Continental appointment, and, when he found that his ward had escaped from him, may have conjectured that she had intended to join him abroad. There are ridiculous provisions in her poor, weak mother's last will which place him in a position of quite arbitrary control, so long as his ward remains a minor —that is to say, unless she chooses to abandon the greater part of whatever may be her fortune. Now, I insist upon her sacrificing nothing. Who would benefit by it, to begin with ? Stanislas Wilmot, who most probably had the will drawn up. I feel persuaded that the property left by her mother was very considerable. I dare say Mr. Stanislas Wilmot had his own private reasons for causing the apprehension, and, if possible, for securing the imprisonment of his ward's *fiancé* ; for he must have discovered or suspected that they were affianced. But my solicitor shall take charge of Miss Knollys's interests.'

'This Mr. Wilmot seems to be quite the "wicked uncle,"' observed Mr. Byde facetiously, as he dandled his hat preparatory to taking his leave. ' We shall have to ask him for an exact description of the diamonds, and for some particulars as to their purchase ; the name of the firm, whether British or foreign, from which they passed into his hands. With stones of great value, such as these, every precaution must have been taken in the trade. Perhaps there was a diamond robbery, perhaps not. But before we could convict any man upon a circumstantial case, we should want strong evidence about the identity of the stones. I will wire the Yard to look the point up without delay.'

' Mr. Wilmot is a very clever man,' repeated the hostess, re-conducting her visitor.

' He is well known in the City,' said Miss Knollys, with some awe.

' He goes behind the scenes,' added the hostess.

' He knows Lord Alfred Edgbaston very well, and Major Chase, the equerry-in-waiting,' remarked Miss Knollys. ' They go to Richmond together, and sometimes Prince Egbert Rudolph goes with them, *incognito.*'

' To look at the sunset from the hill, no doubt !' commented Mrs. Bertram sarcastically.

' Yes, you get a beautiful view of the sunset from the hill,' observed the young girl. ' But I thought that no one went to Richmond, now ; and yet they go constantly ! Lord Henry Exbore, who is another of Mr. Wilmot's friends, and owes him a great deal of money, goes there too, sometimes —to study the industrial English-American excursionists, he told me one evening, when he dined at our house. What a charming view you get of the sunset from the hill, do you not, Mr. Byde ?' She spoke quite cheerfully now, and beamed upon the inspector with gratitude : a sentiment which a satirist has not ill-defined.

'A very nice view,' said the inspector, with his countenance curiously puckered. Had he not come across old
Exbore there himself—old Exbore with his dyed moustache
and vinous mirth—studying the industrial English-American
excursionists with one eye, and with the other (his lordship
squinted) contemplating in mute ecstasy the gorgeous
sunset? Did he not remember what the manageress of the
Purple Peacock (a fine woman) told him as to that
Hexbore lot as come down of a week-day and bribed the
waiters to inform them Yankees, quite accidental-like, as
how their lordships was present, and which they was? The
manageress didn't half like to have their lordships using her
house; it got her a bad name. She objected to see her
well-trimmed gardens and her spacious dining-hall turned
into a sort of show-ground for broken-down swells who ran
up long accounts. If that old Edgbaston and that young
Claude Beechamtre broke any more chairs she should call in
the police, the manageress had said. Let them go somewhere else and fish with their titles for these wealthy
Transatlantic prowlers—the artless widow and the 'hartful
young American miss.' The last time the inspector had
seen old Exbore at his Richmond post his lordship was
entertaining a sporting journalist, a circus clown (at that
time out of an engagement), and a pugilist who had just
won a fight at catch-weight for £100 a side. His lordship's
other guests seemed very charming girls, with a great flow
of spirits when the waiters were out of the room. Two or
three of them, who had been gaily singing snatches of their
choruses in the new burlesque, had unfortunately to leave
for the theatre at an early hour. As they passed him on
their way downstairs the inspector had seen their sweet and
carmined lips curled with disparagement of their entertainer;
and the language in which they summed up his lordship's
peculiarities, both moral and physical, included the oppro-
brious epithets which, known in the highest as well as the
lowest society, and not always whispered, have never yet—
the gods be praised!—infected the vocabulary of printers or
their devils, and are uniformly conveyed to the sagacious
reader, therefore, by the symbol '——.' Lord Henry
Exbore had received his rents that week, and was merry.
He had once been discovered by the inspector in an

inavowable sphere, and had since then cultivated the
inspector's friendship anxiously. On the last occasion of
their meeting Lord Henry had called to the inspector from
the balcony of the Purple Peacock, to insist upon his
joining the party. He had then privately announced to
Mr. Byde his approaching union with a colossal New York
fortune—grains, and cotton—of Seven-Hundred-and-Ninety-
First Avenue ; the lovely Miss Virginia Wattle, presented at
Court in the previous month. When the inspector sat down
with his fellow-guests, to a nip of chartreuse and a grand
cigar, their noble entertainer had assured the beauteous
vision in white muslin skirts and black, tight-fitting velvet
bodice, who occupied the place next to his own, that,
bewitching as she had showed herself in the Christmas panto-
mime, and deeply as he should always adore her, he
respected the new-comer far more highly, and to oblige him
would go farther out of his way. ' I don't believe you, that
I don't !' had playfully responded the vision, tapping his
lordship's wrinkled knuckles with her fan, and ogling the
circus artiste. The inspector believed his lordship, though!
As he was now being slowly escorted by Mrs. Bertram and
Miss Knollys, the whole scene flashed vividly through his
mind. And what good features that young circus clown
had, he remembered ; and what an athletic young fellow he
was ; and how cleverly he performed in the arena with his
educated pig !

If fellows like Exbore, and Edgbaston, and Chase —
' Euchre ' Chase, as he was called in Jermyn Street—were
Wilmot's associates, the inspector fancied he could class him
easily. The description of the missing valuables would have
to be exact, indeed ; and there must be full particulars
provided as to the circumstances of their purchase.

' We shall be very glad to see you whenever you like to
call,' said the hostess.

' You will do your best, will you not ?' added the younger
lady, with an imploring voice and an appealing smile. ' Do
your very best, Mr. Byde ! . . . Our happiness depends
upon you.'

The visitor gone, Mrs. Bertram chid her companion for
the indifference she had displayed with respect to her real
and personal estate. ' Well,' replied the young lady, ' the
fact is, Austin would not like me to have money. You will

say I am credulous, perhaps—but I know him so well! He
would think that it humiliated him.'

'You are a couple of children, if you talk like that,'
pronounced the woman of the world. 'And pray why
should you consent to occupy the position of a burden? Do
you think that would be dignified? Especially when he
would be labouring hard to keep up appearances, and to
make both ends meet!'

'That is true,' answered Miss Knollys pensively, after a
pause. 'It would not be fair that I should bring him nothing!'

So that the inspector, on the whole not discontented with
the outcome of his visit, was departing from the Avenue
Marceau without having once perceived the lady's-maid,
Lydia Murdoch. Had he encountered that imperial creature,
had his regard touched for but a second the pale face and the
wondrous eyes which had arrested, not invited, the gallant
advances of the not ordinarily repressible Toppin, the
inspector must assuredly have recognised Miss Murdoch.
It was Inspector Byde who had reported upon the stranger
aspects of the great scandal in Mayfair; the ' scandal in high
life' which had ended so disastrously for a valetudinarian
hidalgo. Do we not remember the sensational divorce case
—the letters that were read—the verses that were produced,
copied upon vellum, stamped with a coat-of-arms, and signed
'Montmorency Vane'? Do we not remember that the
respondent had been a Miss Estelle Evelin Oakum, the
'belle' of Boston, who, to espouse the noble Spaniard, had
thrown over the Presbyterian auctioneer that afterwards
committed suicide? And had not Montmorency Vane
turned out to be Vine, *alias* Grainger? The respondent in
the Mayfair divorce case had discovered too late that her
own maid formed the veritable attraction for the patrician
Vane, and that, so far as she herself was concerned, ' her
purse, not her person,' had been the object of his siege. The
maid was Lydia Murdoch, now in her second place since the
sensational divorce suit. Inspector Byde would have
recognised her immediately; and if he had known that she
had left a letter at the *poste restante* that morning for one
Grenville Montague Vyne, he would no doubt have been led
to the conclusion that Miss Murdoch still kept up secret
correspondence with one Vine, *alias* Grainger, hiding at the
present time in Paris—and ' wanted.'

CHAPTER XIV.

From the Avenue Marceau the inspector bent his steps in the direction of Mr. Bingham's office. The card which had been left with him by that gentleman, when the latter requested the inspector to give him a call, contained the remarkable information that the Vicomte de Bingham, of the Rue des Petits Champs, No. 4 bis, was an ' *Agent pour les Assurances*,' and an ' *Acheteur de créances a l'Étranger.*' Amazing! commented the inspector, as he again consulted the card.

At the numb r indicated in the Rue des Petits Champs, he found that his old friend Byers, the receiver, was in excellent repute in the *concierge's* lodge, not only as a man of business with extensive dealings abroad, but as an English noble of illustrious lineage if unfortunate career. What a wonderful fellow he was, old Ben Byers, mused the inspector—what a wonderful old boy! It was a deuced suspicious circumstance that he should have referred so pointedly to Brother Neel.

' Well, he has picked out a business quarter for his operations, whatever they may be,' thought the inspector—' and, by George, he's quite capable of entering into business, *bonâ-fide*, and of making money at it !' On the ground-floor stood the show-rooms of an ostrich-feather importer, and the counting-house of an agent for the ' Delectable ' sewing-machines, extremely cheap, and made in Germany. At the end of the wide passage—the door opposite the staircase—you perceived the entrance to the workshop of the new platinum piano; whilst across the yard, around a window well lighted by reflectors, a bevy of young girls employed in Madame Truffière's artificial-flower factory could be seen, pallid and laborious, bending over the foci of irritant poisons which necessarily permeated the air they breathed. Upstairs, on the first floor, the inspector found himself confronted by a dentist's showcase. To the left lay the dentist's rooms. To the right lay the offices of ' M. de Bingham, *Agent pour les Assurances*,' etc. On the second, third, and fourth floors were other business premises. A cane-seated bench, much out of repair, and very dusty, stood against the wall.

It was the unpretentious aspect of the Vicomte's quarters

that impressed Inspector Byde.   He would be hanged if the
whole thing didn't look *boná-fide*, repeated Mr. Bingham's
old acquaintance.   ' Insurance and General Foreign Agent,'
he read in English on the door facing the bright silver plate
and regal bell-rope of M. Melliflu, Dentiste Lyonnais.   But
the Vicomte formed a suspicious feature.   And yet the
commercial methods of all countries did not run upon
identical lines.   Half the routine of a business man consists
of asking for some one thing or another, thought Mr. Byde;
and in a Republic it was quite natural that advantages
should flow rather towards the solicitant armed with the
symbcls or the semblances of rank.

He pushed at Mr. Bingham's office-door.   It appeared to
have been hung in such a way as to swing easily upon its
hinges; but it would not open.   He pushed again.   This
time he heard again the faintest tremor possible of an electric
bell—a sound which was gone before he could say he had
seized it—a tiny vibration which, as a full-blooded man, Mr.
Byde might have put down to a ' singing in the ears '—a
warning signal which at first he had not been quite sure that
he detected.

He waited, but the door did not open.   The inspector then
observed a square ivory button in a small recess at the side
of Mr. Bingham's door.   A neat brass plate invited callers
to ' Turn the button, s.v.p.'   The inspector twisted the
ivory button, and quite a loud, honest, reassuring bell-like
note at once rang out.   What could it have been that thereupon brought a smile to the inspector's countenance?

Mr. Bingham's office-door unlatched with an abrupt jerk.
The visitor stepped across the threshold, but a high partition
shut off his view of the interior.   He had just entered in
time to catch the dull bang of—apparently—a mahogany
drawer, sharply closed.   Footsteps resounded on a polished
floor, and the pink, pear-shaped visage of grandpa, with the
short strip of white whisker on each cheek, then appeared
round the edge of the partition.

' I beg pardon, sir,' said the inspector, assuming an air of
innocent inquiry—' the Vicomte de Bingham—might he
happen to be about?'

' Sir,' replied Mr. Bingham, in a corresponding vein, ' that
good old man is not—and I regret the circumstance—at this
present moment in the immediate neighbourhood.   The

Vicomte, sir, has been summoned by the ruler of a friendly Power, the admirer at a distance of his talents (not to say genius), and of his numerous (not to say innumerable) philanthropic, solemn, and valuable (not to say invaluable) sacrifices, enterprises, and achievements, to resign himself to that which in the case of any other personage, it mattereth not how eminent, would constitute a dignity, favour, or recompense—to undergo, *videlicet*, the form and ceremonial of a State investiture with the most ancient Order of Merit a the disposal of his most gracious and alien Majesty. The Vicomte is an aged man—but rare, sir, most rare!'

'I have come a long way to see the Vicomte. I'll step inside and wait for his return.'

'Pray, sir, step in! Step in, sir, and make yourself at home! I am his little boy.'

'What!—Benjamin?'

'The same, sir; Benjamin, Joseph's brother, whom Jacob sent not with his brethren; for he said, "Lest peradventure mischief befall him,"—strangely resembling one who had been sometimes called Old Ben Byers——'

'"Innocent Ben," gentlemen of the jury; never convicted hitherto, but always guilty!'

'"As your lordship pleases!"' Mr. Bingham shut the door and affably escorted his visitor to the other side of the partition.

'A d——d strange move this,—Benny, old boy! What's the meaning of it all?' The inspector surveyed the business premises of Mr. Bingham, and made clucking noises with his tongue.

'"The meaning of it?" Ha! Scotland Yard spoke there. It means, grave and reverend Byde, that this is the hive of the bee—the honey-stored hive of the busy, busy bee! Sit down, my boy; glad to see you! Take that arm-chair; and if you care for a good cigar—there's something contraband.' He pushed a box over the table.

Mr. Byde sank into the seat indicated. He found that it placed him in the full light of the window, and with his back to the door. Mr. Bingham took the seat opposite. The table which separated them was a sort of half-bureau, in mahogany. On the right and left hand of Mr. Bingham, who appeared to have installed himself in his habitual place, rows of drawers extended from the level of the table downwards to the ground. 'Ah, we work hard,' proceeded the host. 'The insurance business is about half developed in this country. But we do our best to teach them. We try to rescue the public from the perils of their own thriftlessness. Within these walls we indite the flowing phrase; within these walls we bid the quarterly commission a hearty welcome!'

'We?'

'Myself, and sleeping partner. Clerks? Oh yes, we keep a staff of clerks—two; and their desks are in that inner room. One, however, I have just dismissed. The rascal was robbing me. The other is a very gentlemanly youth—out just now—confided to me with a premium by his widowed mother, who desired to have her son instructed in English ways of business and in the English language. Touching—these maternal ambitions and this trust. Lucky the good lady fell into my hands! There are scoundrels about who would have fleeced her without mercy; and the premium came in just at a convenient moment. Pretty good premium—and paid down on the nail. The young man writes my letters for me, and helps me with the French clients. I have sent him off with a fire-policy, to the other side of Paris. He likes going out, I notice; and I'm sure *I* haven't the least objection. He needn't come back at all, unless he likes. One or two more of them, with even bigger premiums, would not do the business any harm!'

'Nothing in that, I suppose?' remarked the inspector, nodding in the direction of a massive safe.

'Nothing whatever,' acquiesced his host. 'Obliged to keep it there, though. Looks well: gives people confidence. Oh, we bank all our money at once! Wouldn't do to keep it on the premises. Risk too great. Lot of rogues about. D——d strange thing that you can't trust your fellow-creatures!'

'And so you have other little irons in the fire besides insurance?'

'Yes, yes—yes, yes!—take a glass of malaga?'

The visitor objected that it was too early in the afternoon. While Mr. Bingham helped himself from a buffet that looked like a bookcase, and chatted about reviving trade, the inspector took further mental notes of the spacious interior. His eye appraised the elegantly upholstered chairs, fauteuils, and couch, the pictures on the walls, the buffet—every article of furniture. On one of the ebony fluted columns rested a marble bust of the First Napoleon; on another, a bronze figure of Gambetta. Some common vases on the mantelpiece were filled with fresh flowers; brackets in the angles of the room, and a handsome *étagère*, supported ornaments more suitable to a private residence than to business offices. The room had no distinctive character; the large safe, however, seemed out of place in it. The gilt-framed mirror which rose from the black marble mantelpiece to the cornice reflected the wheels and pendulum of the clock, seen through the sheet of glass fitted into its rear. Likewise reflected in the mirror were a pair of goldsmith's scales, which had been pushed behind a small equestrian figure in oxidised iron. The inspector's roving eye took in this detail, and then transferred its scrutiny to the closed doors which apparently communicated with apartments beyond.

'The London evening papers of last night had telegrams about this murder of an Englishman,' said Mr. Byde. 'I saw one this morning at the hotel. Their correspondents here would wire the news, I suppose?'

'Something of the sort,' replied his host. 'Wonderful thing the press!—pioneer of progress—bulwark of freedom—Argus, of the Hundred Eyes—Rumour, painted with many tongues—wonderful thing! Try a glass of madeira. No? Marvellous institution, sir, the modern newspaper press! The trumpet of the law, the sentinel of order, the sleuth-hound auxiliary of retributive justice!'

'Ah, that's more in the old vein, Benjamin,' remarked the inspector tranquilly. 'Thought you had lost it, when you came to see me. Lord, how we used to love to hear you conducting your own case! You ought to have done better things, Benjamin, with the education you've had. I recollect a swell witness telling us once that he was a pupil with you at a private college, and that you carried away all the prizes when you liked to try. He told us you began life as a master in a cathedral town grammar-school. You were a better criminal lawyer than a great many of the managing clerks, and, as we know, the managing clerks are often better posted in their law than the principals. You could always make a fine speech to the jury, cross-examine a

witness, or argue on a point. And as for writing an indignant letter to the newspapers, I never did see your equal,
Benjamin! And, what? All your early advantages have
been wasted. I recollect that witness telling us—he was a
J.P. of his county, too!—that you knew more Greek than
anyone at the college, not excepting any of the masters,
and that you could write an essay better than the examiners.'

'Ha! ha!—Not very difficult, that—friend Byde! The
essays of school examiners—ha! ha! ha!'

'And mathematics!—you must have got very much
farther on in them than my boy! Well, what have you
done with it all? A man of your abilities, Benjamin, and
with the education you started with, might have taken to
writing for the press—and by this time—who knows?
—with industry, good health, sobriety, providence, and
luck——'

'The press!' Mr. Bingham, who was refilling his own
glass, spilt the wine upon the table, as he stared at his
visitor with astonishment. 'I'll tell you where—or, rather,
what—I should be now, Byde, if I had been deluded by
the dream which led away the only friend I ever had, and
that was in my youth. These trifles you have just referred
to come to my ears now with a strange sound. I studiously
forgot them long ago. *But* if you speak of journalism, I'll
tell you what I should be at this present time of day if I
had had your own abilities as well as mine, together with
the abilities of half a dozen schoolmasters, and the capacity
of two Secretaries of State. I should be a broken-spirited,
feebly struggling, despised, old palsied figure-head, grudging
the few sous necessary every week to read in libraries and
newsrooms the kind of books, articles, and perhaps speeches
which at one time I wrote better myself. To read them?
Yes, if I could still see. It sounds well, the press. You
and your colleagues who only come in contact with a single
class of pressmen find that *they* are often cleverer than you
are at your own business! And when you get a glimpse of
the higher ranks of journalism you find that the anonymous
writer—ill-paid, unspared, used by everyone, served by nobody—must almost show that he could qualify for a score
of absolutely different callings. The actor, the vocalist, the
painter, preacher, barrister, or demagogue can be known for

what he does. But the pressman? Society uses the working pressman, exhausts him, and then throws him on one side, without even having asked his name. The pressman in harness is the ladder by which others—able men as well as charlatans—mount upward to prosperity. How many self-styled statesmen and so-called orators owe their brilliant fortunes to the silent band of drudging journalists! How many grievances are aired, how many wrongs redressed! Tell me of a charitable movement which could have stood without the Fourth Estate, as they say. And the drudging pressman who has passed his days calling attention to the woes of others, what has he to look for in the hour of need, or when his health and strength shall fail? He, who has found asylums for the distressed in all other sections of society, can confidently look in front of him to the complete oblivion of everyone whom he has served.'

The inspector seemed so pleased at having stung his old acquaintance into this tirade, that he took a glass of wine with him.

'Look at me!' proceeded Mr. Bingham bitterly; 'I may be compelled to pocket the offensive pleasantries of a policeman—oh, you needn't interrupt! We know each other, Byde; I believe you sincerely wish me well, and in return for the service I once rendered you, you will permit me just for once to speak a little plainly—I may be a *déclassé*, virtually outlawed in my native country; I may have been driven by destitution to—what you will—in early years, and I may have more or less incurred suspicion since—but look at me! I am in perfect health, and my own master. The poor friend I had, years ago, went blind at journalism. I remember the receptions I met with, when I applied for some assistance for him, to wealthy people, some of whom had been made public men—ha! ha! public men, *parole d'honneur!* public men—by the labours of himself and of his colleagues. He died, poor fellow! He died—and I consider that his blindness and his death saved my own eyesight, and my own life. It was then that I made my choice of a career in earnest. With my gift of the gab I might have gone into professional philanthropy; with a little capital I might have made a fortune in quack medicines. I did better.'

'What was it, Benjamin?'

' More honest, all things considered.'

' I wonder what it could have been. We never found it out.' Mr. Bingham did not answer. ' Not the insurance agency line, I'm sure ; though it does seem a profitable line here, when you are a vicomte ?'

' A worker on the press !' exclaimed Mr. Bingham, with a final explosion—' I could buy a newspaper next week—but not out of money earned by serving the public in that sort of way !'

' I wish to goodness you'd buy that temperance rag that pitches into me,' returned the inspector.

They sat looking at each other for a few moments.

' I'm an old fool,' said Mr. Bingham, at length, composedly.

' Come, come !' expostulated the inspector. ' You've told me nothing.'

' You're pretty clever at the Yard, some of you,' continued Mr. Bingham ; ' and you're one of the best yourself. But I tell you what it is : you don't owe more than fifty per cent. of your successes to cleverness on your own part. Half the time it's the stupidity of the other people that enables you to bring it off.'

' True for you, Benny,' said the visitor. ' When they're not stupid they can get away—if they only knew it. Not in this country, though. By the way, I didn't explain that they have mixed me up with this Gare du Nord case. We shall soon put our fingers on the two London men who are suspected of the murder and robbery in the night-mail.'

He looked at his host steadily as he pronounced these words.

' Aha ! A case of suspicion ?'

Mr. Bingham did not flinch. It was not very likely that a man ' of his years and experience,' as he had observed to Vine, *alias* Granger, would be taken off his guard by sudden home-thrusts. His gaze became quite as steady as his visitor's.

Inspector Byde recounted the barest circumstances of the *primâ-facie* case against the two suspicious characters from London.

' We shall have them,' he repeated—' to-morrow or the next day. One of our men here is working with the French police, and I'm assured that the thing is safe for the day after to-morrow. What should *you* think, knowing Paris ?'

Each still met the other's regard quite steadily, and each wore a smile of easy unconcern. Grandpa made a show of turning the question over in his mind.

' Well,' he said eventually, ' upon what you say I should think these men are booked. Who are they ?'

' A man named Vine, who has a dozen *aliases*, and a West-end pickpocket named Finch. Yes, I fancy we shall find them. And, from what I hear, we shall also find a man who met them by the train—clearly a confederate—perhaps the man who is hiding them away.'

For the life of him, the speaker could not keep his eyes from wandering to those closed doors, which apparently communicated with other apartments. That side-glance enlightened Mr. Bingham.

' Why, what have *you* to do with a case of murder committed on French soil—in the French metropolis, you may almost say ?'

' To tell you the truth, Benjamin, I'm looking for valuable property supposed to have been stolen in England. My instructions are that the murdered man was in illegal possession of this property ; and, as it had not been found upon him, the presumption is that the property was abstracted from his person by the murderer or murderers. The two men I spoke of know that the Yard is after them. Consequently, they can do nothing in the way of liquidating the valuables, which, I may as well add, are diamonds. To get the stones upon the market, they must of course make use of the Paris confederate, the third man. Now, as one man of business to another—suppose you were in my place (determined to recover the property, but not at all obliged to trouble about the murder), and suppose the third man was an old friend, who had done you a good turn, and whom you did not wish to injure, what would you do ?'

Tr-r-r-r-r-r !

Before Mr. Bingham could reply, the electric bell resounded faintly behind his chair. At the same instant footsteps were heard outside.

' A caller—and somebody strange to the premises,' thought Mr. Byde, remembering his own experience.

Whoever the caller might be, he was either in great haste or in a violent temper. He appeared to be shaking the door, as well as he was able; he delivered a hearty kick presently upon the lower panel. The small metallic vibration resounded in a spasmodic manner behind Mr. Bingham's chair.

' Someone in a hurry to insure his life,' said the inspector. ' Don't keep him waiting, Benjamin !'

Mr. Bingham reached behind him and detached the communication.

' *Vous permettez ?*' he demanded, rising with a very grand air indeed.

' *Je vous en prie,*' responded the inspector graciously, not to be outdone.

Mr. Bingham moved towards the partition, and disappeared on the other side of it as a fresh blow was delivered against the panel. The inspector heard the snap of the lock as the door jerked open. An exclamation in English met his ears, and then a smothered reply by his host. The door banged ; the two voices now evidently proceeded from the outside.

Alone in the office, Mr. Byde promptly changed his place for the one which had been occupied by his host. He tried the drawers conveniently accessible at his right hand, but all were locked. On his left hand, however, the top drawer opened at once. The inspector cast a rapid glance at the two closed doors which had already attracted his attention —at a structural recess here and there in the spacious room —and at a dark nook formed by the position of the disproportionately high safe. Alone ? Yes, he was alone ; but free from scrutiny ?

The office-door had shut to violently. By accident? If he had not heard the murmur of voices outside he might have imagined that the loudly closed door was an artifice devised for his own benefit. ' There were no voices to be distinguished at this moment. Who might not be watching him from the other side of that partition ?

Suppose his wily old acquaintance had not passed over the threshold at all ? Suppose he had a partner with him on the other side of that partition, and they had a little plan concerted for securing his sequestration temporarily ? For all he knew, thought the inspector rapidly, they had 'got it up for him.' On some pretext or other he might be handed over to the French police, and before he could regain his freedom—he, the only man whom Byers was afraid of, and the only man after all who could satisfactorily identify the two men ' wanted ' — everything would have been settled. Vine and Finch would be out of the country ; all traces of the property would have been lost ; and Byers would come and offer him the fullest excuses, and would remind him privately that what had befallen him he only deserved, his own intention in visiting the premises having been simply to entrap an old friend.

It would be legitimate warfare, calculated Mr. Byde, and Benjamin was quite deep enough to resort to the manœuvre. A frightful experience for him—to be told off on Continental duty, and to get put into gaol himself. They would never leave off laughing at the Yard ! And that Temperance paper, with its headings—' Inspector Byde Again,' or ' The Latest Exploit of Inspector Byde !'

He listened, and could hear nothing but the rattle of the traffic in the thoroughfare below. It might be wiser, perhaps, to run no risks. And yet he would have given a good deal to be able to search these premises.

What if he actually found the property here—the Wilmot diamonds reported to the Yard as having been stolen from Park Lane ? Old Wilmot might have come to them with a true story—why not ? Suppose the property were actually in this room, and he found it ? Why, then he might be thrown into the hands of the French police, with a *primá-facie* case against him of having had the property secreted about him for an indefinite period. Remington once identi- fied with the Wilmot diamond robbery, he, Byde, having journeyed by the night-mail, would be at once connected with the murder itself. Amateur detective people, and any- one who nourished grievances against the police, would immediately declare that the temptation had been too great for his resistance, and that he had yielded all the more readily because he knew that suspicion would most naturally descend upon the two men from London.

Bah ! How he ran on ! Was it in the least degree pro- bable, now, that he should come across the stolen property here ? Was old Ben Byers, even if he really had the present custody of the diamonds, the man to leave those sort of things about—to leave then for a couple of minutes only, accessible to a fellow from Scotland Yard? No, no! Too old a soldier—Byers! It was hardly worth while profiting by his absence, if he really had gone out of the room. Oddly built, these older French houses. You could easily be hidden in that alcove over there. At night, a burglar or an assassin——! Bad light, this afternoon! The opposite houses were so high that you could not even see the leaden, wintry clouds.

The inspector pulled the topmost drawer wide open with his left hand.

'Who knows,' said he, 'what I may light upon? A spoilt envelope, an address card, an empty phial, the Soho post-mark, the name of Clements and Company, a revolver —*the* revolver, perhaps, by Jove?'

He pulled the mahogany drawer wide open, and glanced at the few articles it contained. It was almost too shallow to be used as a receptacle for revolvers. What were these odds and ends? Postage stamps, sealing-wax, twine, a pair of scissors. A bystander who could have divined the conflict just now raging in the inspector's breast might have pointed at him with derision. But the inspector has often remarked that in his business there are no such things as trifles. He did not touch the scissors, twine, or sealing-wax. He slipped the lid off a small, square, white cardboard box, from one side of which a fringe of white cotton-wool peeped out. A glittering object reposed within a little nest of snowy cotton-wool.

Mr. Byde unhesitatingly extracted the glittering object from its immaculate nest, and transferred it expeditiously to his own waistcoat-pocket; an act which no doubt he knew as well as anybody constituted an offence against the *droit commun* of France not less than against the common law of Albion, his native land. That done, however, he replaced the square cardboard lid, and left the spotless fringe escaping from one side exactly as before. Noiselessly he closed the drawer. Now, then, had he been watched?

Inspector Byde marched up to the deep alcove. In its dark shadow, no one. He strode towards the partition, but was arrested by a scraping sound—that of a key against a lock, evidently. It must be the Vicomte de Bingham letting himself in. Mr. Byde would have wished most earnestly to

explore the communications of the other two doors, but
it was impossible this afternoon. A pity! For all he
knew——

The office-door unlatched with its customary jerk. Mr.
Bingham banged it after him, and emerged from behind that
most conveniently-placed partition. There were no signs of
flurry in his manner, but he seemed less genial than it was
his wont to be. His eyes looked very bright. A frown
lingered vaguely about his brow.

'What is that equestrian statue I can just see at the end
of the street?' inquired the inspector, with his hands in his
pockets and his forehead against the window-pane.

'Louis XIV.'

'Who made our ancestor a vicomte?'

'You've been prying, I can see, my boy—you've been
prying about! Oh, there's no rural innocence here! Take
your hands out of your pockets and come away from that
window. It won't do.'

'Benjamin, you are ruffled.'

'So long as I didn't leave the safe unlocked!' Mr. Bingham
moved over to the massive safe, and tried the handle.
'That's all right,' said he coolly; 'I breathe again.'

'I dare say there's valuable property, now, in that
safe,' rejoined his visitor contemplatively—'a good deal of
valuable property, I shouldn't wonder—property of all
sorts?'

'The petty cash, and the De Bingham patents of nobility,
and one or two marketable commodities which belong to
clients.'

'Ah! Just think of it. The De Bingham patents of
nobility. The Yard would love to see those things. We'd
like a copy of them, Benny, for the museum. Couldn't you
let us have a copy of your title-deeds on vellum?' Mr. Byde
facetiously pronounced the word 'vealum.'

'What has this man been prying into, I should like to
know,' continued Mr. Bingham, substituting, with equal
playfulness, divers uncomplimentary designations for the
noun 'man,' as he repeated the phrase two or three times.
He glanced over the table, and tested each of the mahogany
drawers at his right hand, as he took his seat. 'No,' he
observed, 'I think I left no bank-notes and no documents
about.' The visitor pretended to be vastly entertained by

this undisguised mistrust, and joked on the subject, as he still stood with his forehead against the window-pane.

The lower of the mahogany drawers at the Vicomte's left hand were locked. He drew out the upper drawers carelessly, turned over a few papers which one of them contained, and that was all. The odds and ends thrown into the topmost drawer barely engaged his attention at all. Had it escaped the old gentleman's mind that in the shallow topmost drawer he had placed that little square box in white cardboard edged with gilt?

'What was it you were saying just now?' demanded Mr. Bingham, suddenly noticing his visitor's persistent stay at the window.

'Just now?'

'Before we were interrupted.'

'Don't remember.'

'An infernal fool, that fellow, by the way! A noisy brute who couldn't find the *sonnette*. A client. A few more clients of that description, and the firm would be discredited. Idiot! Here, take a cigar, Byde.'

'Thanks, no.'

'I dare say you thought it a deuced strange way for a client to call in at a business office on an afternoon?'

'I thought he might be in a hurry to insure his life,' the inspector answered without turning his head.

'D——d idiotic fashion to turn up at a respectable office,' repeated Mr. Bingham, a growing uneasiness visible in his manner. 'See what it is to have a large Royalist connection in the provinces. Ignorant clods, half of them, who want their money back as soon as they've entrusted it to you for prompt investment in profitable foreign securities!'

'Fools!' assented Mr. Byde.

'Cast your eye over our circulars. That will give you some notion of our agency business, and the extent of it.'

'I'll take your word for it, Benny.' Mr. Byde's forehead seemed positively glued to the window-pane.

'Something interesting you down there?' hazarded the Vicomte boldly.

'Oh dear no,' replied the inspector, turning from the window, and repressing a yawn. 'There's nothing very interesting in your street, Monsieur de Bingham—except the people who occasionally come there, hey?'

' Yourself, for instance, man of modesty ?'

' Just so—what I was thinking of.'

The inspector had been thinking of an entirely different personage. It was of the excited visitor, who, though a client, had not been able to remember the whereabouts of the bell at that respectable office-door, that he had been thinking. And sure enough he had finished by perceiving from the window the face of a man who appeared to be awaiting someone, as he loitered at the corner—sometimes within the view on this side, sometimes lost to sight on the other—across the street. It was a face he recognised very positively, this time. It was Vine, *alias* Grainger, who was loitering at the corner, over the way.

' Come,' expostulated Mr. Bingham gently, ' you don't expect that that will wash with me, I hope ? You were not thinking of any swell from Scotland Yard ; you were thrashing your brains about the swell who was here in a panic just now. Come—weren't you?'

' Benny, I was,' returned the inspector.

' Well, have you made your mind up ?'

' Benny, I have.'

' Well, isn't my word as good as another man's word—isn't it—you suspicious old villain you ?'

'It is, Benny, it is—quite as good as another man's.'

'Then don't begin on old Ben Byers again. Poor old, worthy old, ill-treated Benjamin Byers ! He was as honest an old gentleman as ever paid Queen's taxes and local rates. And yet they wouldn't let him go on peacefully. The Yard were always beginning on him. They hunted him until he was obliged to pack up and go. Poor old unfortunate Byers! They hunted him out of his native country—they drove him forth from his dear native land !'

' Don't cry, Benjamin !'

' No, Mr. Inspector, sir—I don't mean to cry. It was a dev'lish good thing for Benjamin, as it turned out, that they drove him forth. He ended his days in honour and in opulence : on a foreign soil, amid plenitude and at peace, he breathed his last. One Bingham rose up in his place——'

' *De* Bingham, Benny——'

' Who was as like him as two peas are like. But not so amiable ; with more money of his own, and more money at his back ; and with a few things up his sleeve that might make it a dangerous undertaking to begin on him. A dev'lish ugly customer, this Bingham ——!'

'*De* Bingham, Benny ——'

'And *I* should say that the man who thought he could begin on him was mad. And I should further say that the man who tried to hunt him would meet with accidents. He would be—down at the first obstacle, he would—and—very likely break his neck!'

'Threats, Benny?'

'No; entreaties.'

'Advice, you mean. Risky advice. But you always were audacious'—*ow*dacious, pronounced the inspector, in his facetious way. 'We'll have a glass of wine together. I must get back to the hotel.'

They exchanged actionable epithets with the greatest serenity and good humour; and then, in a glass of that excellent malaga, drank to each other's eternal confusion.

'I know my way out—don't rise!' urged the inspector politely, as he put on his hat and moved towards the counter and partition. 'I leave you to the clients.'

'Yes, I have an hour's work here,' responded Mr. Bingham. He touched the communication which unlatched the office-door, and in another moment the visitor had gone. Inspector Byde walked habitually with a heavy tread, and the sound of his retreating footsteps could be heard from within.

The inspector did not go downstairs, however. He ascended the staircase to a higher floor, and there he waited on the landing.

CHAPTER XV.

THE inspector stationed himself at an angle of the balustrade from which he could easily command a view of the two stories below. A few persons passed up and down the staircase; an office-door on either side of him would be opened and closed to allow of egress or admittance to some visitor or an employé; and from time to time a junior clerk who, as the inspector made his appearance, was just finishing a cigarette upon the landing, would put his head out of a doorway and examine the new-comer's back with marked inquisitiveness. Mr. Byde could on occasion see

all round him simultaneously—or at least could make you
think he had that gift ; the fact has been already remarked
elsewhere.   When it suited him to do so, therefore, he
detected the young gentleman in one of these examinations,
and, with a half-salute to him and half a phrase, conveyed
politely that his presence on that spot had no reference to
the young gentleman's firm.   The junior clerk, with the
true courtesy of his nation—in flute-like tones, and with a
gesture full of grace—invited the inspector to avail himself
of the bench placed there gratuitously for the general
use ; and, returning amongst his colleagues, told them
that the loutish imbecile who looked like a foreigner was
still hanging about the *palier*, outside, in a suspicious
manner.

At length Mr. Byde's patience met with its reward.   The
Vicomte de Bingham, personally, issued from the Bureau for
the ' *achat des créances à l'étranger*,' downstairs, and descended towards the street.   No one had an eye upon the
inspector at this moment.   He accordingly lost no time in
pulling a large silk scarf out of an inner coat pocket, and in
adjusting it to form a kind of not ineffectual disguise.   He
bound his face up with the scarf, and tied the ends in a
knot at the crown of his head.   This done, he pushed his
handkerchief inside the scarf at one side of his face, pulled
his hat down firmly, and turned up the high collar of his
overcoat.   On his way down he necessarily repassed the
dentist's showcase on the first floor.   M. Melliflu himself
had just shown a lacerated patient to the top of the stairs,
and as he caught sight of the inspector's bent shoulders
and bound-up head, that odontalgic expert—thought the
inspector—'looked extractions at him.'

The stylish black Inverness cape by which it would not
be difficult to identify the retreating form of Mr. Bingham
proved at first undiscernible, when the inspector cautiously
stepped out into the street.   On neither hand was it to be
seen.   His view of the corner, over the way, at which he
had perceived, restlessly pacing to and fro, Vine, *alias*
Grainger, *alias* Sir John, was intercepted for the moment
by the lines of vehicular traffic.   The same fact, however,
sheltered his own person from observation.   Presently he
detected the black Inverness cape hastening away from the
Rue des Petits Champs by the street which traversed that

thoroughfare. At Mr. Bingham's side strode the erect figure of Sir John.

It didn't surprise him in the least, reflected Mr. Byde—no, not in the least, upon his word and honour. The very clever people who made so many mistakes would have guessed at it right off, certainly. Toppin would have jumped at the conclusion without the shadow of a query, if Toppin had but known what *he* knew as to old Ben Byers. But, at the best of times, guesses were hazardous; and they might all have gone extremely wrong upon their obvious guesses. Now—what had led him strongly to connect the personality of Benjamin with this matter? What had brought him down to Benjamin's office? What had placed within his reach that piece of ostensibly indirect evidence which he now carried in his waistcoat-pocket—what had put him actually upon the path of one of the suspicious characters urgently 'wanted'? What? Why—remembered the inspector, as he warily dogged the footsteps of the companions in front of him—what but a process of pure logical induction?

He did his best to reconstruct his written argument of the previous night. As he had expressed them, the relations of A to B and C led up inexorably, the inspector flattered himself, to the hypothetical functions of X and Y 'to find, etc.' And, having applied his reasoning in a rigidly practical manner, having proceeded logically from A himself, here we were already trotting at the heels of some-one whom we might rationally infer to be either X or Y. How they cleared the mind, these formulas and symbols, meditated Mr. Byde. He would not deny that his colleagues who never used a single symbol, or any formula, could not have arrived at exactly the same result with a lapse of time precisely commensurate. But their methods were impressionist, not scientific. Any incident or fact of evidence which conflicted with their irrational treatment of inquiries could not positively be measured, and tested at once, and at once accepted or discarded; no, they must be always noting, always keeping matters in suspension, always multiplying side-issues, always losing themselves in the trite assumptions of officialism. Half their time they spent in dangling after false clues. How could it be otherwise, on a procedure by 'rule of thumb'? They succeeded—yes, they succeeded!

But they also failed. Give them something to do outside
the common run of criminal cases! Give them a problem
to solve in regions of pure reason—['regions of pure reason
—regions of pure reason,' muttered the inspector, with great
gusto—' one of the boy's phrases, I think ; ah, if I had had
the education which that boy has had !']—take them out of
the routine where their experience of the criminal classes
was backed up by the 'from information I received,' and
how many successes would be scored by the majority of his
colleagues? Acting solely in pursuance of his impressions,
a sharp colleague might have landed upon Vine, *alias*
Grainger, through the involuntary agency of Bingham—yes,
he would not affirm the contrary. But it would be guess-
work, mere empirics, you might say. Could that colleague
convince another mind, as he had convinced his own? Ha!
It was not enough to feel sure that you were right ; you had
to convince third persons that you were right. And on the
impressionist method how could you do this? Impressionism
was individual. Your own impressions might be accurate ;
but the persons who in the end were called on to decide (and
who might incidentally pronounce upon your conduct)—they
might be constitutionally unfitted to receive the same species
of impressions. Whereas a scientific method cleared the
head and shaped the judgment ; imparted confidence to the
inquirer, and wrung acquiescence from the most unwilling
of lookers-on ; climbing to an irrefragable conclusion through
irrefutable steps.

The foregoing is the inspector's language, and the reader
will anticipate us in a smile at the 'irrefragable conclusion'
which is attained by climbing ' through irrefutable steps.'
These were elegances of diction and proprieties of metaphor
due in great part to the evening class on rhetoric at the
institute in Camberwell. The inspector had interested
himself in numerous branches of the institute's curriculum.
Some of the hebdomadal classes he had followed for thirteen
consecutive weeks! Those who enjoy the privilege of his
acquaintance will admit that Mr. Byde is a man of undoubted
natural parts. At the same time it has been urged by certain
of his private friends, among themselves, that the art of
rhetoric, the palæozoic period, the Aryan race, elementary
physics, and Barbara, Celarent, Darii, Ferioque, turned up
too often in his familiar conversation. Topics of that sort,

have commented certain of his private friends, would be more suitably gone into with his son, who understands them. And, indeed, the inspector will sometimes talk so learnedly upon subjects taught, in the evening, at the institute at the corner of the Terrace, that we should despair altogether of transcribing his occasional utterances. Extremely fortunate must it be esteemed that in narrating the part he played in the Wilmot inquiry (Park Lane) there should be no necessity of toiling after him up any acclivity more precipitous than the rising ground of Book I. of ' Euclid's Elements.'

' Q.E.D.' was the inspector's rather premature comment as he observed Monsieur de Bingham pull up at a café and suddenly cast a searching look around and behind him. In the dusk it had been difficult, remaining at a safe distance in their rear, to keep the two figures ahead always in view. Mr. Byde could see, however, that their intention was to enter the café. That preliminary glance by grandpa, thought Mr. Byde, spoke volumes. It was that glance which had elicited from him the triumphant ' Q.E.D.,' although nothing whatever was yet proved—scientifically. In construing that glance into an avowal of clandestinity, Inspector Byde was plunging into rank impressionism.

The two confederates passed into the café by the main entrance. The man who was following them might have approached at once, for they moved towards the quietest portion of the establishment without lingering an instant near the door. Mr. Bingham evidently knew the premises well. It was he who guided his companion to their places, and the other accompanied him without offering a word. The café had three entrances, all communicating directly with the street. The dispositions of the interior corresponded with the respective entrances, the area forming three sections, which were marked off by columns, replacing what had apparently been, once upon a time, party-walls. In short, the café had the look of having been extended and enlarged on each of its sides. Where the columns indicated the boundaries, the rows of seats were ranked back to back. The bases of the columns formed a substantial barrier between the rows of seats, and upon their projecting angles lay directories, time-tables, newspapers, and other objects belonging to the establishment. It would be possible for the persons who might be seated upon one side of the columns to overhear the conversation of the neighbours with whom they were back to back. By the simplest of precautions neither need continue long unaware of the other's vicinity; but in the absence of any such precautions neither would be easily discoverable by the other. To one of these rows of seats Mr. Bingham conducted his visitor. They sat down with their backs to the columns, and to all appearances were secure from close observation. Vine, *alias* Grainger, leant against the padded bench with a sigh of relief, qualified by a singularly unpleasant scowl. Mr. Bingham abruptly remarked to him that here they might converse undisturbed.

A moment or two afterwards the inspector entered the café from the farther door. The establishment was not well lighted, and a thin cloud of tobacco-smoke, which seemed to penetrate to every corner, somewhat obscured the view. Inspector Byde threaded his way slowly among the tables, as though he were seeking out a suitable place. When he had made his choice, he might have been discovered reposing on the comfortable bench which stood back to back with the seats occupied by the two personages he had followed. Grandpa might have assured himself, by rising to his feet and looking over, whether or not on the other side of the barrier there were eavesdroppers. He did not do so; he did not even turn his head. Had he devoted some attention to the point, he might or might not have recognised Inspector Byde. His companion threw a glance at the seats immediately behind him, and dimly perceived a solitary form at the café-table on the other side of the barrier— the form of a man who, with his head bound up, appeared to be wrapped in profound slumber. Mr. Bingham's negligence on the subject might have been deemed incomprehensible. At this moment the café contained few customers. It was not yet the normal hour of *absinthe.* Their arrival coincided with the lull which usually precedes that dietary rite.

'Don't you talk to me about being compromised!' said Mr. Bingham's companion savagely. If you want your share in this, you must take your risk. Where's Bat?'

'I'll take my risk with anyone, if there's occasion for it, in a lawful way,' said Mr. Bingham, in distinct tones.

' As for anything unlawful, I will not be in it ; and once
more let me tell you, I will not be compromised !'

' What *is* this —— game ! what is it ?' demanded Sir John.

' It's my misfortune if I'm known to you,' continued the
other—' and I suppose that to some extent I am at your
mercy. But there's a limit, and I won't be compromised !
The position I occupy here in the commercial world is an
honourable one, and I can't permit anyone to damage it.
I forbade you strictly to come near my office, and I cannot
imagine what reason you could have had for coming to me
at all. If it happens again—mark my words !—if you take
a liberty like that with me again, I'll let out what I unfortunately know—I'll put the police on to you. As for what
you say about " shares," I really don't understand you,
John ; I should think you have been imbibing.'

' Look here, Byers ! Whom do you think you have got
to deal with ?'

' Now, I brought you in here for a moment for the sake
of being quiet. We can talk this matter over quickly here,
and we'll talk it over once for all. It's no use making any
disturbance about this. I told you originally that I would
have nothing to do with it ; and I tell you so again. That's
all I have to say ; and let this be our last meeting.'

' Then   you   have—managed—to—put—your—hands—
upon—the—property?' said Vine, *alias* Grainger, placing
an emphasis upon each word, and steadily regarding his
interlocutor. ' Then you have settled it with Mr. Bat, and
I am to be left out—*I*, who, if you must be told so, put the
Soho firm up to the whole affair ? Who would have known
anything about the Wilmot diamonds if it hadn't been for
my private sources of information ?'

' That is nonsense, and you know it. What have I to do
with Bat, or anyone else you may be mixed up with ? Come,
let us drop this sort of conversation. Why did you come to
my office ?'

' Oh, indeed ! oh, indeed ! Dear me, what a virtuous old
gentleman we are, and what nice weather we're having.
Without my private sources of information, who could have
put the firm on to Remington ? Where's Bat ?'

' The sooner we put an end to this the better. I have
nothing to do with either your movements or his. Now, I
haven't much time to spare, and——'

'Just as you please,' replied Sir John, with a certain ferocious tranquillity. 'Put an end to this at once if you like, so far as conversation goes. But when you go out of this café, I go too; and where you go, I go too; and whoever meets you, meets me too. And that's what I came down to the office to tell you, Byers; with this addition, that you may have been too clever for them at Scotland Yard in the past, but that the day you try on any double-cross business with *me*, your time has come!'

'Did I hear you rightly, John?' inquired the Vicomte de Bingham blandly—'my time, did you say, has come?'

'That's what I said,' returned the other, in an unchanged tone. 'My motto has always been "no violence," but I shouldn't stand upon ceremony with you. Don't you try any double-cross business on with me; because it's a thousand to one I get it back.'

'John—there's a good case of suspicion against you. Suppose I hand you over to the French police before you leave the street we are in? There's a fair circumstantial case of murder against you, John. Not that I believe it for an instant; but others might. How would you like that?'

'The wind has shifted, then, has it? What about the positive opinion grandpa had, so early in the morning, that it was Brother Neel, whoever Brother Neel may turn out to have been? It was Brother Neel who got there first, said grandpa; Brother Neel who settled the deceased first, and who dished Clements and Company afterwards.'

'Yes, I gave you that opinion in a disinterested way—it's true. But with that I washed my hands of the entire affair. And I tell you plainly that if you drag me into the nefarious scheme which you appear to have been personally involved in——'

'Drop this, Byers! There's nothing to incriminate *me*, and that you know. Besides, you haven't looked at the evening paper yet. They were reading it at the hotel, my disinterested, venerable Bingham. The French police don't want any clues that *you* can give them to the—the—murderer. They have their clue. They have the French guard of the train; and if they hold the murderer, they hold the Wilmot diamonds—come!'

The announcement should have formed an overwhelming

surprise for Mr. Bingham, but he did not betray more than the astonishment of convention.

'The guard of the train—the French guard, now!' he ejaculated mildly. 'The scoundrel!'

'Don't you think they're wrong, Grandpa Byers?' pursued Vine, *alias* Grainger, with a diabolical sneer. 'Don't you think—in a quite disinterested way—that if they clapped their hands on Brother Neel's shoulder they would be a very great deal nearer the mark?'

'I should have really believed so, John, from what you confided to me—much against my will.'

'Ah, what a victimised old gentleman is Grandpa Byers! And to think that he has very likely by this time got the very best evidence of the murder stowed away in his "office" at the place just down the street—loose diamonds, that is to say, to the value of £20,000, the property of Stanilas Wilmot, of Park Lane: having induced the said Neel to part with the said diamonds, or a proportion of them, or having taken them from him without directing the said Neel's attention to the occurrence!—Where's Bat?'

'I decline to listen to your insinuations any longer. They are monstrous, perfectly monstrous and incoherent! The property has doubtless passed out of Neel's possession, and if you want to know where it is to be found, I think I could indicate the place to you. He called this morning at the premises of his Temperance League, in the Boulevard Haussmann. I happened to be there on general business. When he arrived at the offices of the society, he had a parcel with him. When he came away, he had apparently left the parcel at those offices. It might be any parcel, you may say. Yes; but would Neel be disposed to keep property of that sort, under the circumstances, at his hotel apartment? And if not, where else could he place it? Besides, I know something about the I.O.T.A. Therefore, still in the most disinterested manner, I would suggest that you should turn to the Boulevard Haussmann with as little delay as may be possible, John. I won't deny that I may be wrong, you know; but I rather fancy that I may be right.' Mr. Bingham paused to note the effect of his statement, and then added, with a great deal of dignity—'In any event, remember, please, that I wash my hands absolutely of the transaction.'

Sir John appeared to be debating inwardly whether the news he had just been favoured with was to be relied upon. Supposing the information to be accurate, however, he did not see what useful purpose would be served by his repairing to the quarter specified. Bingham's attitude in the affair had become altogether puzzling. It would doubtless be better, all things considered, to adhere to his resolve; Mr. Bingham should not quit his sight. They lapsed into a silence which Sir John was the first to break.

'Where's Finch?' he again demanded.

Before replying, M. de Bingham threw a careless glance at the adjacent tables.

'We were lucky to secure this quiet corner,' said he.

The places in front of them, and on each side, were still unoccupied; and when he turned to survey the tables in their rear, he found that the scene in that direction also remained virtually unaltered. There was one change, however that should have struck him. The man who had been seated on the bench just on the other side of the barrier— the man who had his head bound up, and seemed to have fallen asleep—was no longer to be seen. Mr. Bingham's visage had borne a set and stern expression twice or thrice during the debate with his companion, but it now relaxed into wrinkles denoting an inward satisfaction, if not strong symptoms towards hilarity. It has been before observed that merriment suited Mr. Bingham's countenance. He began to look quite the rubicund, genial, freehanded old gentleman who willingly chucks bashful fifteen under the chin, and distributes halfpence among the little brothers. The widow and the orphan might have been pardoned for trusting their all to Mr. Bingham (*né* Byers), thus transfigured. The widow, in particular, could hardly have resisted such a dear old gentleman, with his good-humoured face and twinkling eye, with his easy-going simplicity, and his probable tendency towards apoplectic seizure, which might carry him off suddenly any day. Something or other was amusing him, that was sure. He sustained the suspicious, searching regard of Vine, *alias* Grainger, without in the least departing from his air of guileless content. On the contrary, had Sir John himself approached him with the orphan's piteous tale upon his lips, you would have felt exceedingly disappointed if this benevolent grandpa, as-

suredly meant by nature for a trustee, had not, in the fulness
of his heart, administered relief unto the forlorn applicant
out of the fulness of positively his own pocket.

'You are putting up something, Byers,' exclaimed his
companion, in a tone of suppressed exasperation. 'If it's
at my expense, by ——, mind what you're about!'

Sir John had a decidedly evil aspect as he uttered this
menace. His gray eyes were half closed, and he gazed sideways from under his eyebrows in a very peculiar and 'un-
comfortable' manner indeed. With his head bowed, he
was pulling restlessly at his moustache and twisting its long
ends mechanically and ceaselessly round his fingers. He
had his lips tightly compressed, and the corners of his mouth
curved malevolently upwards. His Roman nose looked just
now more than ever Roman.

What could there be about this man which always van-
quished, whenever he wished to vanquish them, not merely
the most beauteous members of the opposite sex, but those
who had ever passed for being the wittiest and the most
wise? What was it? He possessed neither the extreme
ugliness nor the remarkable beauty which have been the
most frequent causes, perhaps, of immedicable infatuations
among the fair. Sir John was slightly over the middle
height; he had a manly figure; and he had, likewise, the
habit of conquest. So far as his features went, the cultivated
physiognomist would have read there resolution, desperate
recklessness, and possibly a vice or two. There were a few
other attributes which neither Lavater himself nor the most
orthodox of his disciples might have dreamt of predicating, in
their summary of Sir John. He owed a great deal to his
marvellous faculty of dissimulation. It was most likely to
this valuable adjunct, aided by invincible assurance, and tact
in the use of flattery, together with a freedom from the
smallest scruple, that his prompt successes with the fair in
general were to be ascribed. Men would occasionally divine
him, and he knew well enough when he was divined. Only
on the part of his own associates, however, could any such
discovery or denunciation place him ill at ease. With all
this, he never indulged in scoundrelism that was unnecessary.
The widow and the orphan who addressed themselves for
succour to Sir John would have gone both unassisted and
unharmed away. Quite celestially interesting they might

have been, and either—for the mere sake of argument we assume this case—might have exerted, Niobe-like, or unlike Niobe, the full force of her captivations: Ernest Vine, *alias* Grainger, would have turned from them to peruse the police reports of the newspapers. The parish register of St. Botolph, Aldgate, proves that he was born and baptized in the Christian faith; but he was a Christian in whom the worship of shekels always dominated other descriptions of faith and sentiment.

'I have paid my little bill at that hotel you carefully lodged me in,' he resumed, 'and now I don't leave you, Byers. Where's Finch?'

'Pretty well, thank you, John; how are *you ?*' returned Mr. Bingham, still in keen enjoyment of some mental picture. 'I think we may now venture upon the step of rejoining the young gentleman. *Garçon!*'

'*V'la, v'la, m'sieur ?*'

'*Payez-vous.*'

'When you came to the hotel for Finch,' continued Sir John, picking up the small black leather bag he had brought with him from London, 'I thought you said he was to go to work upon this Neel, at once, and that if the story we told you about the journey was the right one, the thing was as safe as houses? And now you say that Neel has got away from you, and left the property at some place here—the offices of that society—where it's most likely locked up in some safe. What have you been about, you and Bat? What have you been doing with your time? You let this man slip through your fingers, and then you come and tell me where he has deposited the property, as if you fancied I should run off to the address, and go and ask the people who live there to 'hand it over to me, if you please!' We've lost the property, and you're the man to blame. You're a —— old idiot, Byers, a —— —— idiot! I was against your coming into this, from the first. I told the firm we didn't want you in it, but I never thought you'd actually spoil us when there was a chance of transacting the business. They can say what they like, but this was business which I and nobody else brought into the firm; and I ought to have insisted upon having my own way. If I hadn't been straightforward and honourable with Clements, nobody need have known anything about it. I could have done it all myself. Why should I have brought the firm in?'

'That's a matter between you and the firm. I suppose that if you didn't take business to them, you couldn't expect them to keep you in employment?'

'Well, but why the —— should Clements bring *you* into it, and put you down for a share? What could *you* do? You could only do what you have done—spoil us!' The speaker, pale with rage, uttered another imprecation.

'Clements brought me in because he had need of me—that's all. You couldn't make anything out of the transaction until you floated the property, and you couldn't float the property without *me*. Nonsense? Could *you* float it? Could Clements himself, or anyone else in the firm? You know you couldn't. You know how long you've had to hold other property, and what you've had to lose on it. At one time there was hardly a living to be made at the game for all of you, with the rents you have to pay, and the commissions, and the appearances you have to keep up. You know as well as I do that you've got a roomful of good stuff that you can't pass on. Clements told me himself that what you hold in red [gold] alone is worth a fortune: only you can't put it through—you daren't part with it. Scotland Yard would be waiting on the doorstep before you got home. Well, I've had enough of this. Go to the devil John—go to the devil!'

'We'll all go there together,' exclaimed Sir John fiercely. 'I'll go there for *you*, Byers, if you've sold me!'

They prepared to move out of the café. Mr. Bingham found it impossible to restrain his mirth, and after shaking for a few moments in silence, at length chuckled audibly until the tears came into his eyes.

'I declare,' said he, 'that poor old Grandpa Byers can give them all a good start and a beating. Are you a sprint-runner, John?'

Vine, *alias* Grainger, had extracted a letter from one of his pockets, and was re-examining its contents.

'Listen, John. Suppose that by chance this Wilmot property passed very soon into the custody of Inspector Byde?'

The other folded up the sheet of note-paper he had been perusing, and did not immediately respond to the cue.

' We'll pick up Finch as soon as you like,' he remarked
sullenly ; ' but first of all I have a visit to make to the
Avenue Marceau, No.——' He referred again to the
missive for the precise address—' No. 95.'

' Avenue Marceau, here, in Paris ?' Mr. Bingham did
undoubtedly exhibit surprise. ' Do *you* know anybody
there ?'

' A somebody happens to be there who knows Grenville
Montague Vyne, Esquire,' returned Vine, *alias* Grainger,
holding out the envelope. It was a letter bearing the name
he repeated, and directed to the Poste Restante, Paris. As
we were present while the superscription was being placed
upon that identical envelope, we may acknowledge without
any fuss or ceremony that the handwriting was Miss
Murdoch's. ' Ah,' went on the enviable recipient of her
note, cruelly inappreciative of his good fortune, but thawing
before the astonishment betrayed by Mr. Bingham, ' you
don't know everything, old Grandpa Byers! You don't know,
for instance, how I learnt that there would be diamonds to
be dug out in Park Lane, and that before the firm could
deal with the case it had been put up by the man Remington and another. No,—you don't know that ?'

' If I had, I'd have turned my knowledge to better account
than you have done, my fine fellow. Why, even now, you
can't put two and two together !'

' Oh, well, after a little calculation I shall arrive at it,'
replied Vine, *alias* Grainger, turning his half-closed gray
eye upon Monsieur de Bingham, with an exceedingly sinister
expression. ' We put Mr. Inspector Byde upon the proper
track for the recovery of the Wilmot parcel, and the efforts
of that distinguished gentleman from Scotland Yard become
thereupon crowned with success. Then Mr. Inspector Byde
gets hurt.'

' I don't say that it mightn't come to that,' acquiesced the
Vicomte airily. They had now gained the street. Summon-
ing a cab, they told the coachman to drive them to the
Avenue Marceau.

The feeling which asserted itself in the bosom of the
inspector, as he also had driven away from the café, was one
of thankfulness that, after all, the case entrusted to him did
shape into a tangible form. ' If it hadn't been for my

private sources of information,' had said Vine, *alias* Grainger, 'who would have known anything about the Wilmot diamonds?' By 'who' he meant, of course, what member of the Clements combination. Consequently, this man had known of the actual existence and actual whereabouts of the missing valuables, and with regard to their abstraction must have been able to place convincing evidence before his associates. Stanislas Wilmot, the guardian of Miss Adela Knollys, had therefore made no false statement when he came to the Department with that tale of a mysterious robbery from his strong room in Park Lane. The Wilmot diamonds were not fictitious; and they had been stolen. The inquiry became tangible once more.

Without his own private sources of information, the man Vine had proceeded, 'who could have put the firm on to Remington?'—the deceased. That brought them back to the case of vague suspicion with which they had started, pondered the inspector. As to the situation of Mr. Sinclair, he would have been heartily glad to see his way clear to the exculpation of that young gentleman. They were charming ladies, Mrs. Bertram and Miss Knollys—charming, charming ladies, he repeated, thinking solely, however, of Miss Knollys. For their sakes he would be glad if Mr. Sinclair could establish his innocence; and—yes, he would—he'd be willing to go out of his way if he could help the young man to that end. At the same time, the story told him by the ladies in the Avenue Marceau proved, for one thing, that the young man had been in pressing need of funds at the period of the robbery. To himself, Mr. Sinclair was unknown. Mr. Sinclair might be a young man capable of arguing that as an abettor in the despoilment of this mysteriously dishonest guardian, he would be merely recovering for Miss Knollys a portion of her withheld property.

So much for the original theft. Now, with respect to the present position of the inquiry—we should see what the organ of the I.O.T.A. in the press would have to say!

In accordance with instructions, Detective Toppin was awaiting his chief at the latter's hotel.

'Heard the news?' demanded Toppin.

'The French guard of the train?'

'Oh, better than that! Look here.'

Toppin unfolded an evening newspaper, fresh from the

printing-office. Amongst the '*Dernières Nouvelles*' appeared
an article headed 'The Assassination of an Englishman on
the Northern Railway.—A Hint for the Police.' Premising
with a laugh that a journalistic hint to the political police
of Paris might be counted upon to carry as much weight as
a sworn affidavit, Toppin translated the last paragraph of
the article in question :

'We should imagine that the indications we have quoted
will be generally acknowledged to be beyond dispute.
There can be no doubt that the leaders of the extraordinary
movement to which we have referred made Paris their
headquarters in the early part of the year now coming to
an end. A passage in our correspondence from Vienna on
March 23rd touched upon this subject in significant terms,
and uttered a public warning which no Government in
Europe should have found it possible to pass over. Unfortunately bureaucratic indolence and scepticism once more
prevailed. The warning of our correspondent was completely ignored, although it had nowhere been denied that
secret conferences of the federation had been held simultaneously in all the capitals of Europe two months before.
That the headquarters should have been transferred to
Paris is a matter of the gravest import. We suppose that
in a country like our own, possessing a fuller measure of
freedom than that which can be boasted of by any other
nation in the whole world, some abuse of our ungrudging
hospitality must be expected. But to say so much is to
say also that we should hold ourselves on our guard against
the abuses of our generous hospitality which are possible.
The revolutionaries of the world may have welded themselves together, with the organization and the programme
shadowed forth above, and may have conferred, as we
maintain, upon this metropolis the unenviable distinction of
selecting it as the heart and centre of their colossal system ;
they may do this, and we and others who are not revolutionaries may remain powerless so long as none but legal
methods are openly employed. When, however, they resort
to means infringing the law of the land, even as slightly as
in the few examples we have cited, we urge that the question
becomes one for diplomatic negotiation in view of common
action by all the Governments. And how much more neces-

sary does this course appear when assassination begins to take its place amongst the methods of the vast conspiracy we have been the first to denounce? The Nihilists of Russia; the Native Separatists of British India; the advanced Socialists of Spain and Germany; the German secret societies which spread like a network throughout the United States: all these, equally with our own Anarchist desperadoes, derive their inspiration henceforth from a common source, a single fount—the luminous orb of the world's intelligence, Paris. Those who are responsible for the preservation of order know full well that we are indulging in no exaggerations. We do not profess to teach them anything new, so far as we are dealing with the general state of affairs: but we can enlighten them as to one or two points which are not without a practical interest. The 'Maëlstrom'—for such is the portentous designation under which all these far-reaching agencies of trouble are affiliated—pursues its audacious *propagande* before their very eyes in the metropolis. If our suggestions are followed out we shall perhaps be told eventually that we have advanced allegations impossible to substantiate—that, unsupported by the smallest data, we are casting odium upon a foolish band of fussy but harmless zealots. *Vraiment?* And the Englishman who has been assassinated between Creil and Paris? And the valuables which were *not* abstracted by the assassin? And the visit made to the Morgue by certain individuals who were apparently known to one another, but affected to hold no communications one with another? We have indicated the Boulevard Haussmann to the police. We go no farther than that. It is not our business to denounce criminals to justice. The police must now search for themselves. A copy of the directory for the current year should amply suffice to guide them to the premises where important seizures of documents, plans, or ciphers may be operated. We happen to be in a position to inform our readers that a functionary of that same foolish band of harmless zealots formed one of the "certain individuals" to whom we have just referred. Monsieur Hy is possibly unaware of the fact. But our ediles of the Municipal Council will have to vote a great deal more money to the Prefecture if they are to outbid the reporters of the Paris press in their relations with the guardians of public order. Monsieur Hy, who is understood to be directing the present inquiry, may likewise be astonished to hear that the functionary in question—whose tactics appear to consist of placing himself *en évidence* as a means of disarming suspicion; he has become quite a familiar figure in the Rue Feydeau (*Proh pudor!*)—was accompanied at the Morgue by a stranger, also connected with the Boulevard Haussmann premises. We can state, for our own part, that the *Foreing Resident*, which is the principal organ of the English-speaking colonies in Paris, gives the name of the stranger in its column of "Arrivals and Departures." One of our *rédacteurs* calls attention to a striking coincidence, just as we are going to press. We suppress the name for obvious reasons; but we should like to ask the *rédacteur-en-chef* of the *Foreing Resident* at what time he received the note with regard to the arrival of Monsieur —— in Paris. Did he, *par hasard*, travel by the night-mail from England—the train in which this apparently inexplicable murder was committed—an outrage which we persist in regarding as a vengeance ordered by the "Maëlstrom"?'

'That's the news!' said Toppin, laughing, when he had finished the article. 'What do you think of it?'

'As to their "Maëlstrom," I won't pronounce,' replied the inspector thoughtfully. 'But I have my own reasons for looking after the gentleman they hint at, and we must be beforehand with them. Suppose we want to enter upon premises and operate a search, what authority do we require?'

'A *perquisition;* and that takes more than five minutes to get, I can tell you.'

'No other way? We will assume that what is wanted is a particular box—not large—or a particular bundle of papers, recently deposited on the premises. The parcel might have been lodged in some place of safety.'

'Bribe the servants, if you can wait a few hours. Bribe them well, and they will steal the keys—perhaps let you in at night, when you can have a look round for yourself. Are there any servants?'

The inspector mentioned the 'vivacious French brunette.' He did not doubt the potency of a fair bribe with that damsel, but the negotiations might require more time than he could spare,

'Not at all,' Toppin assured him—'just the most rapid at a bargain, that sort! Doesn't want to stay in service, that sort! Wants a wardrobe better than the *patronne's*, and jewellery. I'll undertake to have the search made by to-morrow morning.'

'Well—no,' said the inspector—'the case is ripe enough now, I think. We can go straight to the point now, I think. Come round with me to the Rue de Compiègne, Hôtel des Nations. That's where he has been staying, this Monsieur ——, otherwise Brother Neel.'

CHAPTER XVI.

'THE Mysterious Affair of the Gare du Nord—Important Arrest! *Demandez le " Journal du Soir "!*' '*Demandez " L'Echotier "!*—The Crime on the Northern Railway—Curious Indications—A Strange Story!—"*L'Echotier*"! *Vient de paraître !!*'

These were the cries which Inspector Byde and Detective Toppin encountered as they crossed the Rue Lafayette on their way to the Rue de Compiègne. The rival hawkers thrust their evening papers before the faces of the two colleagues, but Toppin flourished in return the journal from which he had translated the article printed in the Latest News. It was the *Echotier*, containing the ' *indices curieux* ' that we have just seen.

'That important arrest—what is it?' asked his superior officer—' the French guard?'

'Yes,' said Toppin, ' and they'll let him out to-morrow. There's nothing in it. Before coming on to you, I looked in again on Monsieur Hy, and—oh, he's too clever, he's much too clever for a world like this!—he wants to make out that they are letting the guard go in order to pick him up again next week, with an accomplice and the stolen property, all complete. These papers don't know that yet. The *Journal du Soir* has only got as far as the arrest, which I heard all about at the Prefecture this morning.'

He then repeated for the inspector's information certain passages in the earlier interview with Monsieur Hy, of which an account has been placed before the reader. With regard to the second interview, during the afternoon, it was

all very well for Monsieur Hy to play the excessively *malin*,
but the fact must be, added Mr. Toppin, that the case
against the French guard had completely broken down. It
seemed that when he had brought the night-mail into Paris,
and cleared the train, this man was entitled to a day off duty.
On the present occasion he had obtained leave of absence
for a couple of days by arrangement with a fellow-employé,
who was to replace him. Well, he had celebrated his holiday by a heavy drinking bout, as appeared to be his custom.
The police had found him helplessly intoxicated in a cabaret
near his lodging. He had been home to take off his uniform,
and the police had discovered a revolver hidden amongst his
clothes.

‘ “ Hidden !” ’ commented the inspector. ‘ The worst
species of impressionism !’

‘ I beg pardon ?’ queried Mr. Toppin, gaping at his
superior officer.

‘ Why can’t they say they “ discovered a revolver amongst
his clothes ?” That’s all they’re entitled to say—and see
how it tones it down !’

‘ Then the bullet fitted into the chambers of the revolver.’

‘ Ah, they’re not rare, friend Toppin—coincidences like
that. And who has decided that the bullet fits into the
chambers of the revolver ? Because I remember a case
once—it was all circumstantial—when a bullet was reported
to us as fitting into a particular fire-arm, and it was nobody’s
business for a few days to make the test. The bullet certainly would go into the barrel and come out again—oh,
there was no mistake about that !—only the bullet was more
than a shade too small to have been used with any weapon
of that calibre. I remember another circumstantial case in
which the ball had been flattened by the obstacle it had encountered, and the fact had not been properly allowed for.
Has this prisoner offered any statement ?’

‘ They told me this afternoon that he professes to be able
to account for the whole of his time—rather difficult, I
should fancy, for the guard of a train. They have lighted
upon nothing which points to any theft in the search they
have carried out on this fellow’s premises, etc.; but of
course he would have had time to get compromising objects
out of the way. What sort of an explanation he can furnish
I must say I don’t understand : unless he means to prove

that from Creil to Paris he was in the company of the other guard, or something of that kind.'

'Instead of letting this man out to-morrow,' observed the inspector jocularly, 'they ought to put the other guard in with him. Why, they'll be apprehending *us* next, Toppin—they'll be laying their hands on you and me!'

'Quite capable of it,' answered Toppin, with a queer glance at his chief.

The tall, angular dame presiding at the bureau of the Hôtel des Nations, Rue de Compiègne, replied to their inquiry for Mr. Neel that he had not yet come in. This was nevertheless his usual hour—in fact, a little past his usual hour.

'Does he not dine here, at the *table d'hôte*, every evening?' asked the inspector, looking at his watch.

'Oh, yes,' responded the angular dame, who, like all her compatriots in the hotel bureaus near the great termini, spoke English perfectly, and another language or two, perhaps, quite as well—'he dine all evenings.'

'Half-past five,' murmured the inspector, mechanically consulting his watch once more—'and your *table d'hôte*—at what time do you hold it?'

'There is two: the fierced at six-dirty, and the others at sayven.'

The speaker pointed to a framed announcement of these facts, and, behind the inspector's shoulder, threw killing regards at Toppin, who was really a fine figure of a young man, though inaccessible, it seemed, to the blandishments of maturity.

'Half-past five,' muttered Mr. Byde, again—'if he comes in after six, I can hardly manage it.'

'Excuse me, inspector,' said his colleague in an undertone, as they stood on one side—'but I suppose that when you travel you are always armed?'

'What should *you* think?' answered Mr. Byde, staring at the young man.

'The usual, I suppose?'

'And so they'd be capable of putting their hands on *me*, friend Toppin?'

'Well, the police here are no respecters of persons, you know—when they're dealing with foreigners. I thought I'd just mention it.'

The inspector was about to respond, but checked himself. Brother Neel entered from the street. Had nothing arrived for him, inquired the new-comer, addressing the lady president of the bureau—no telegram?

' No, sair, if you please, not ! *mais*——'

' *Mais ?*'

' There is come those gentlymen—there.'

Brother Neel turned in the direction indicated, and for the moment did not recognise the burly middle-aged man who, stationed with a companion in the obscure recess of the dining-room side-door, appeared to be scrutinising him very narrowly indeed. After a slight hesitation, however, he recollected Mr. Smithson, and advanced, repeating :

' Oh, my dear friend, pardon me !—Mr. Smithson, of course. A thousand pardons—a thousand, thousand pardons. Pre-occupied, dear friend. An inconceivable affair ! So kind of you to call, so very kind of you to call !'

' A minute—can you spare me a minute ?' asked the inspector.

' Certainly, my dear friend, Mr. Smithson, certainly. Come upstairs, my dear friend. *Have* you seen this abominable attack upon the " Iota " ? *Have* you read that unscrupulous evening newspaper ? *Can* you imagine that such reckless firebrands, or such foolish, credulous alarmists could be so,' etc., etc.

Inspector Byde and Mr. Toppin both evinced as keen an interest in the structural surroundings through which they followed Brother Neel, as in the temperance lecturer's cumulative denunciations of the odium wrongfully cast upon the I.O.T.A. Mr. Toppin's mental notes might have been open to the objection of being too obviously, too manifestly, taken down. Not a single means of egress could have escaped that searching eye. He glared at a bricked-up doorway ; tapped at a worm-eaten wainscoting ; peeped through the hinge of a partly-open door, upon the other side of which a handsome gentleman who had tied a white cravat to his perfect satisfaction was smiling at himself in a mirror, and making poses. On their way along the corridor to the apartment occupied by Brother Neel, they met the Anarchist ' boots,' reluctantly bearing on his shoulders the substantial luggage of a *bourgeois.* He scowled at Toppin, as the latter, more sturdily built than he, and with the advantage of a

head at least in height, swung by—a scowl so unprovoked
and so malignant, that Toppin—who did not know of his
Anarchist hatred for every species of superiority; for the
superiority of mere physique as well as for that of intellect,
or wealth, or rank—pulled up for an instant and took a note
of him, mentally, that ought to have proved ineradicable.

Arrived at the extremity of the corridor, Brother Neel let
himself into his apartment and proceeded to light the wax
candles on the mantelpiece.

'Won't our dear friend step in, too?' said he, as Mr.
Toppin loitered on the mat outside, and shuffled his feet.
Toppin obeyed the suggestion, closed the door, and posted
himself on the mat inside, as though he were a sentinel on
duty.

The inspector borrowed a candlestick from his host and
made a tour round the large room. Espying the door of
communication to the left on entering, he demanded in a
low tone 'what might be on the other side of it?'

Brother Neel, astonished at his question and his movements, stopped in placing chairs for his guests, and replied
in a low tone, likewise, that he was sure he could not say,
but that no doubt it could be easily ascertained. The door
most likely would communicate with some other hotel apartment, similar to his own. When he had taken up his
quarters here the neighbouring apartment was unoccupied,
but he had heard someone stirring to-day, he thought, and
by this time he most probably had been furnished with a
neighbour—unless, indeed, the persons moving about the
room had been employés of the establishment.

'We don't need to be overheard,' remarked Mr. Byde, still
lowering his voice, ' and before we go on, I think it might be
well to be assured upon the point.'

The imminent smile quite died away. Brother Neel ran
his fingers through the plastered locks of hair which he wore
so vigorously brushed back from his forehead and behind
his ears, and which terminated in an oily fringe at the nape
of his neck. He ran his fingers twice through his hair in a
somewhat nervous manner.

'Why, this is very singular!' said he. 'Precautions?—
Precautions against listeners? In whose interest are they
adopted—why adopt them?'

'We'll come to that,' answered the inspector, his voice

sunk to little more than a whisper. 'Personally, I hate being overheard, whenever or wherever it may chance to be —and so does my friend here. It's a little weakness which we are both subject to. We only approve of listeners when we've reasons for particularly wishing to be overheard. At present there are no such reasons. You don't know my friend, I think?'

Brother Neel responded with a gesture meant no doubt to assure the sentinel at the door that the privilege of forming his acquaintance, though at the eleventh hour, was one which he, Brother Neel, should always prize. The smile did not dawn, however, nor did the eloquent lecturer of the I.O.T.A. find his resonant voice. Mr. Toppin returned the gesture with a virile dignity, sniffed, and fastened his eyes upon his superior officer. Mr. Byde moved a step nearer his host, and added :

'Detective Toppin, of Scotland Yard.'

'Scotland Yard!'

The exchange of whispers, the immobility of the three figures, the uncertain shadows in the flickering light, lent to the scene a sudden dramatic impressiveness.

'Detective Toppin, acting with myself in this inquiry. And my name is not Smithson. I am Inspector George Byde, of the V Division.'

Brother Neel remained standing sideways at the hearth —his elbow on the mantelpiece, his head supported by his hand, and part of his features illumined with distinctness.

'Have you any questions to ask?' continued the inspector monotonously.

'No.'

'Any observations to make?' ·

'No.'

'Any statement to offer?'

Brother Neel paused before replying to the third query.

'No,' he repeated, at length.

'Then you will allow us to go on with our inquiry in your presence?'

'I have no desire to stop you in the performance of any duty you may have to discharge,' said the temperance lecturer slowly—'neither any desire nor any motive. I shall be glad to know, however, in what way *I* can be connected with investigations in Paris by gentlemen from Scotland Yard?'

'You shall know in one moment. First of all—excuse me ——' the inspector moved towards the bell-rope, and rang. 'In one moment you shall hear.'

They waited in silence for an answer to the summons. Presently footsteps were heard in the corridor, and a knock followed.

'*Entrez !*' called Brother Neel; and Mr. Toppin opened the door.

The Anarchist appeared upon the threshold, his arms laden with faggots for the fire.

'This man does not understand English,' premised Brother Neel.

'I'll interrogate him for you, guardedly, on the points you mentioned, if you like,' observed Toppin to his colleague; adding to the Anarchist in the latter's language—'Put those things down for a minute. We want to ask you a question or two.'

'I am not here to answer questions,' was the sullen response. 'I am here to clean your boots, to carry your luggage, and to light your fires.'

'Ah, you must be just the man we would prefer to talk to. —You are for the *prochaine*, are you not?' demanded Toppin shrewdly. 'Well, in our own country so are we!'

'You!' muttered the man, with a sneer, as his glance wandered from Mr. Toppin to the figure at the mantelpiece.

'*Vive la prochaine! Vive la révolution sociale !*' exclaimed Toppin. 'Will you say as much?'

'*Viva la révolution sociale !*' responded the other fiercely.

'Among *compagnons*, no humbug—no standing upon ceremony!' Toppin produced a small gold coin, and tendered it in off-hand fashion.

'*Pardon—excuse*—I cannot !' The scowl began to gather again.

'For the cause !'

'For the cause !' The speaker gazed at his interlocutor with an expression of mingled scorn and incredulity. 'What species of revolutionist can *you* be, *compagnon* self-styled? The true revolutionist does not employ: he only serves— until the joyful coming of the *prochaine !*'

'*Des chansons—des chansons !* In our country the com-

pagnon both serves the cause and employs the *bourgeoisie.*
Come—accept the obole of more fortunate comrades—it's
your duty to the cause—the revolutionary obole!'

'Ah! the revolutionary obole, then——' he placed his
burden on the floor, and took the piece of money. With the
door once more closed, and after a fresh reminder as to
possible listeners, Inspector Byde, through his subordinate,
put a few questions to the Anarchist which very considerably
astonished Brother Bamber's London colleague. One or
two of the questions were answered in the affirmative.

'Now, then,' proceeded Mr. Byde, 'I want to engage the
next room for to-night.'

That would be impossible, intimated the Anarchist, sullen
from force of habit, but won over by the batch of questions
which had astonished Brother Bamber's colleague; it would
be impossible, because the English *bourgeois* who had arrived
in ill-health early that morning had taken that very room,
and was occupying it still. Was there a pampered English
bourgeois at that present moment in the adjoining room?
Of course, he was at that present moment in the adjoining
room—seeing that the whole day long he had not quitted it,
being—as his elderly accomplice in the exploitation of the
working-man, another *bourgeois; mais un vrai type de
l'exploiteur, celui-là!* had stated—by the physician's order
confined to his bed—*eh, qu'il crève, donc! Un fainéant de
moins—quel malheur!*

'I may have to beg your hospitality for to-night,' observed
Mr. Byde to Brother Neel, 'unless you will favour me by
accepting my own. We shall see.'

'From what I understand,' was the reply, 'your business
tallies with that monstrous invention of the evening journal?
What—as men of the world you can believe that story for t
single moment, or any story like it? The I.O.T.A. implicated in dynamite plots! But you shall do as you think well,
and I am at your service. There is one preliminary which
you will be good enough to fulfil. You gentlemen are doubtless what you represent yourselves to be; but I have not
yet seen your credentials.'

'Dismiss that man, Toppin,' said the inspector.

Mr. Toppin asked for news of their Anarchist's lodge,
'The Iron Hand,' and promised to attend one of the Sunday
conferences. He then helped him up with the bundle of

faggots, solemnly exchanged the salutation, and showed him out.

'My colleague here is a Paris agent of the Criminal Investigation Department,' resumed the inspector, 'and is well known at the Prefecture. With regard to myself, you are probably not unacquainted with my name, Mr. Neel.' He handed one of his official cards to the travelling lecturer of the I.O.T.A.

'Oh, I have read about Inspector Byde,' said Brother Neel maliciously. 'I should have thought he would have been satisfied with one blunder. It was a blunder of sufficient magnitude, one might have fancied!'

'Very well. Listen. You deposited a parcel at the offices of the International Organization of Total Abstainers, Boulevard Haussmann, in the course of this morning?' Brother Neel turned abruptly away from the flickering candles. His arms fell by his side. 'Did you not?'

'I did,' he replied, with an effort,—'what then?'

'I have to request that you will enable me to examine the contents of that parcel.'

'The contents? Draft reports and returns relating to the business of the I.O.T.A.; statistics, pamphlets—reprints of a speech by Sir Wilful Jawson in the House of Commons. What can there be in matters of that description, pray, to concern Inspector Byde?'

'My request is to receive the parcel, intact, for the purpose of personally examining its contents.'

Brother Neel hesitated again. His manner betrayed so evident a calculation of chances that Detective Toppin made another hasty survey of the apartment, as if he suspected the existence of concealed means of escape.

'You are an adroit member of your profession, Mr. Byde,' resumed their host,—'I don't deny your adroitness But, believe me, you are on a mistaken course. The thing is absurd altogether. There is absolutely nothing of a political character in the parcel which you say you want to examine.'

'There is nothing of a political character about the objects which I expect to find.'

Mr. Toppin opened his eyes very widely. What on earth could his superior officer be driving at? And what was the matter with the temperance gentleman, all at once?

' We are pressed for time,' added the inspector, still in that hushed monotone.

' I am innocent,' whispered Brother Neel, sinking into a chair.

' Of what?' asked the inspector. ' Stay where you are, Toppin !'

' As you say,' returned their host firmly, raising his head and looking his questioner in the face : ' As you say—of what ?—You shall see the contents of the parcel, gentlemen.'

' That's right !—at once, then. We'll proceed immediately to the premises in the Boulevard Haussmann.'

' Promise me one thing, gentlemen—promise that you will not place me under arrest ?'

' That's as may be,' said the inspector—' that will depend.'

' I implore you to think of my position—think of the cause, I implore you !'

' We shall do nothing that the circumstances may not warrant. We shall of course avoid subjecting you to unnecessary inconvenience. Be good enough to step downstairs, Mr. Toppin, and send for a cab.' Mr. Toppin obeyed. ' In the meantime,' continued Mr. Byde, ' it is my duty to caution you against making any statements which might be used against you as evidence. Any explanations, however, which you may desire to furnish, we are of course bound to listen to.'

Brother Neel had retained his overcoat throughout the interview. He now crossed the room to take up his hat and walking-stick.

' Never mind your walking-stick,' observed the inspector, who had undemonstratively placed himself between his host and the door, ' you may as well leave that here. And——
I don't wish to search you, but——there are no weapons about you, I suppose ?'

' Weapons ? Oh dear no !'

' Button up your coat then, sir, if you please.'

Mr. Toppin was soon heard hastening back. They quitted the room in silence, and in silence returned along the corridor and down the stairs. Mr. Toppin led the way, the inspector bringing up the rear.

When they arrived at the bureau on the ground-floor, Brother Neel stepped aside to inquire again whether any missive or message had been delivered for him—whether there was no telegram. Nothing had been delivered for him, replied the lady president of the bureau snappishly. They had interrupted her in an operation of the toilette. Saffron, alas, were the once rose-fair cheeks, now wrinkled superciliously, and brick-red was the Grecian nose; and this proud organ she had been patting and stroking in front of a hand-glass with the anemone of the boudoir, a white and fluffy growth, choked with *poudre de riz.* Should they reckon upon Monsieur Nill for dinner, she asked, launching at the irresistible Toppin the brightest of an ex-beauty's languishing regards.

Before responding, Brother Neel glanced at Mr. Byde.

'Tell her yes,' the latter answered; 'at seven o'clock, yourself and perhaps a friend or two. If you can get back in time for it, Toppin and I may like to join you at the *table d'hôte.*'

'*Demandez le " Bulletin !"*—The body at the Morgue !' '*Demandez le " Journal du Soir !"*—The Drama of the Gare du Nord !' '*" L'Echotier !" Vient de paraître !*—The Conspirators of the Boulevard Haussmann!—*Demandez "L'Echotier" !*'

At frequent points upon their route newsvendors met them with these cries. As their cab turned out of the Rue Lafayette into the Boulevard Haussmann, a man ran by the side of the vehicle, shouting the contents of an evening paper, and thrusting a folded copy of the sheet through the window:

'*Deux sous, " L'Echotier "—deux sous !*—The New *Internationale !*—Foreign Revolutionists in the Boulevard Haussmann !—*Deux sous, " L'Echotier "*—just out !—*Lisez l'Echotier—deux sous !*'

'My God !' burst forth Brother Neel, 'what a fearful affair !'

'Tell me,' demanded the inspector, as their cab drew up before the offices of the I.O.T.A., in the more tranquil portion of the thoroughfare, some distance farther along, 'does the gentleman whose name appears on this plate— Mr. Bamber—does that gentleman know the precise contents of the parcel you left here ?'

'He does not.'

'Weigh your words before replying; does anyone but yourself know of the precise contents ?'

The other was on the point of answering, but suddenly stopped. A new idea seemed to strike him.

' Why,' he exclaimed vehemently, ' your information must have come from Mr. Bamber !'

' No.'

' No ? Then I have told you all I have to say, sir !'

' Excuse me. If we find this parcel as you left it, no one but yourself can have been acquainted with the contents ?'

' I have nothing to add.'

' Very well. Toppin, tell the man to wait; we shall want him to take us back. Come upstairs with us. I may want your evidence, hereafter.'

On reaching the third floor, where the highly-polished brass plate of the I.O.T.A. shone radiantly under the gas, Mr. Byde informed the temperance lecturer that he as well as Mr. Toppin would assume the *rôle* of simple spectator during their brief stay on these premises. There was no intention of discrediting Brother Neel unnecessarily. It would therefore be for Brother Bamber's colleague to recover the parcel without loss of time, to assure himself that it had not been tampered with, and to at once return with his companions. This rapidly stated, the inspector rang at the front door.

To their summons came no response. The inspector rang again, and still there was no answer. Mr. Toppin, whom the proceedings of the last half-hour had somewhat bewildered, began to exhibit symptoms of disquietude. A third time the inspector rang.

It was the ' vivacious French brunette' who at length opened the door.

' Monsieur Bambaire ?' demanded that functionary's colleague.

Yes, monsieur was at home ; in his bureau she believed. Would these gentlemen give themselves the trouble to step in and seat themselves ? Very busy, Monsieur Bambaire! She hardly ventured to disturb him ; but—— affairs of importance, without doubt ?

Brother Neel handed the young woman his card, in order that there should be no mistake. She had shot a look of recognition at Mr. Byde, and had commenced the smile which she knew called up a pair of dimples. During the production of the card, however, she had had time to survey the form and features of the bemused Toppin. It was for the latter's benefit, not for Mr. Byde, that she continued and sustained that widely arch and dimpling smile. She shut her chin down tightly on her chest as usual, opened and closed her eyes with the incessant motion which we know to be an unerring sign of artlessness in members of the dominant sex in many parts of the civilized world, and in mistresses as well as maids—perhaps in the mistresses more commonly than in their maids; and she tripped away with the short and studied steps that in males we often call a strut, and in females dainty grace.

'Ah, dear friends—come in! Come in, dear friends!' Brother Bamber, with a pen in one hand and some sheets of foolscap in the other, emerged from his private office by the doorway communicating with the vestibule. 'Hard at work—you see me hard at work! Our dear brother there understands what labour it involves—the maintenance and furtherance of an organization, with its multitudinous detail and its multifarious claims. Ahem! Pray come in, dear friends. A recruit, our dear young friend here? Welcome, welcome!'

Brother Bamber enveloped Mr. Toppin with his fixed, fraternal smile.

To explain their errand proved the simplest of tasks for Brother Neel. He had found that the papers which he had left in his colleague's care would be indispensable to him that evening. These gentlemen had kindly accompanied him to the premises of the I.O.T.A. He regretted infinitely to be breaking in upon the grave preoccupations of his colleague, unsparing as he was of himself, and indefatigable in the interests of the cause; but there were documents in the parcel he had left with him which he should absolutely need to consult. So sorry—so very sorry! But the cause before everything—was it not so?

The self-possession of the speaker, as he proceeded with various observations in his platform voice, impressed Mr. Byde as particularly admirable. He listened with an almost æsthetic gusto to the lecturer's fine tones, and the beatitude of this platform physiognomy filled him with a serene bliss, a secular exultation. If he could bring the case home to a man like Brother Neel!——

What a triumph for him at the Yard! What a capture! What a prisoner he'd make—a fellow like this, with a voice like that, and, as grandpa had put it, the ' gift of the gab!' Lord—how the trial would be reported, to be sure! Great big lines on the contents-bills of the London evening papers, all the evidence reported the next morning fully, his own examination-in-chief and cross-examination—ah, he'd like to see the counsel on the other side who'd shake him. Counsel? Yes, he know well enough whom they'd give the brief to, on the other side, to lead—Shoddy, Q.C., who frightened them all, when he rose up to smash a witness. They should see how Shoddy would get on with him, George Byde, of the V Division! That Q.C. had had the best of it, when they last met, in the great temperance prosecution, which had broken down. On that occasion he, Byde, had been misinformed ; and Shoddy had upset him altogether, with his minute system of cross-examination. But this time there would be no error. He'd have the case in a nut-shell; and he'd just show them at the Yard how Shoddy, Q.C., was to be discomfited! And what was more, he'd wake up some of the knowing ones at the Yard! He'd read them a lesson on impressionism and rule-of-thumb. None of them appeared to divine that in their business lay vast possibilities of scientific method. It was his misfortune to be incapable, educationally, of exploring, defining, and expounding those methods proper to the domain of pure reason, as his son would say; but at any rate the concep-tion was his own—the conception of a scientifically-trained detective force applying mathematics to their regular work, reasoning on infallible processes, with symbols and by formulas. *He* might be incapable of realizing the concep-tion, but there was his son Edgar!

They had all three followed Brother Bamber into his bureau. Their host had looked about for his keys, and had then gone to unlock a small safe which stood in one corner. He drew the brown-paper parcel from the lower shelf of the safe, and handed it to his colleague. The latter received it without pausing in his observations upon the progress of the cause. It was a pure and lofty cause, he said. It stimu-lated moral qualities which too generally, etc., etc. ; and it tended with certainty, if by slow degrees, to kill and elimi-nate all those germs of social morbidity which, etc., etc.

Is that your package, then '—asked the inspector, with what appeared to be merely formal concern—' is that what you wished to bring away ?'

' That is the bundle of papers, yes,' replied Brother Neel, glancing at the unbroken seal and at the tightly knotted cord.

' It has been in secure keeping,' remarked the inspector jocularly, indicating the safe. ' Robbers would not get at your papers locked up in there !'

' Well, I just lodged the parcel there, by the side of other documents,' said Brother Bamber, with his fraternal expansion.

The gold stoppings of his front teeth gleamed again, and he pushed his gold-rimmed spectacles close up to his sandy eyelashes and silky eyebrows.

Brother Neel would have been pleased to pay his respects to Mrs. Bamber ; but that lady was not at home just now, her husband stated. She had not yet returned from the lecture-room, nor would she be back for perhaps three-quarters of an hour. A true helpmate, Mrs. Bamber ; yes, were it not for Mrs. Bamber, dear friends, the routine work alone of the Paris branch—the daily routine work, dear friends—would be crushing, overwhelming, *tute-à-fay accablant*, as the French said !

None of the visitors had yet spoken of the sensational news served up that evening by the *Echotier.*

Had Brother Bamber seen to-night's papers, now demanded his colleague, stopping at the threshold of the offices, and bending upon the Paris agent of the I.O.T.A. a look in which Inspector Byde clearly distinguished mis· trust. As yet he had not seen a single evening journal, responded Brother Bamber—not one, not one ! Too busy. Organization. Multitudinous detail. Multifarious claims. Enormous responsibility, the Paris branch. Great cause, the I.O.T.A.—noble enterprise ! He gleamed at them fraternally, and adjusted his gold-rimmed spectacles.

Brother Neel relinquished his copy of the *Echotier,* for his colleague to peruse when he found a little leisure.

They drove back in the direction of the Gare du Nord. It was not, however, to the Rue de Compiègne that the inspector proceeded. The address he gave was that of his own hotel.

Arrived at his destination, the inspector conducted his companions in silence to his private apartment. He had taken the parcel into his own charge, and, as soon as they were secure from intrusion, he prepared to sever the cords which bound up the I.O.T.A. papers. Brother Neel stayed him with an impulsive gesture.

'Be careful—I warn you to be careful in whatever course you may be going to adopt!' urged the temperance lecturer, with his hand on the inspector's arm.

It might be anger that had paled his cheeks—it might be anger that shook his voice and palsied his hands : anger equally with apprehension—conscious innocence equally with conscious guilt.

'If you have any statement to make,' returned Mr. Toppin's superior officer, in a business-like tone, 'we can hear it. Only be quick, please !'

He paused for the other to continue.

'The society I represent possesses friends in high quarters. Be careful! We are a powerful organization !'

Mr. Byde waited. Mr. Toppin flushed with the anticipation of triumph. At the same time Mr. Toppin could not altogether make it out.

'If the great cause I represent, with all the influential interests that are engaged in it, should be damaged in my person, remember——'

'Come, come, sir,' replied Inspector Byde, 'you have nothing to complain of. You are not in custody. Is that all ?'

Brother Neel transferred his trembling fingers from the inspector's arm to the sealed cover of the parcel itself.

'I know you by repute, Inspector Byde,' he went on, 'and I expect no mercy at your hands. But you are wrong. You are on the brink of another great mistake. Can you not give me the respite of a day—one day?'

The inspector pursed up his lips, raised his eyebrows, and very slowly shook his head.

'I tell you, you are *wrong*—WRONG !' thundered Brother Neel, with a sudden maniacal rage. 'I—TELL YOU SO—DO YOU HEAR !'

Mr. Toppin took his hands out of his pockets, and stood with his arms loosely hung ready for a spring.

'There is only one thing I understand,' said the inspector, still calmly, bending over the table, ' and that's evidence !'

' Evidence ! — ha ! — *evidence !* — Listen, you obtuse clown——'

' Enough of this,' interrupted the inspector quietly; ' another man in my place might have passed you on to the authorities here for your attempts at intimidation alone. We must go on. I am responsible to my superiors.'

' And some of your superiors are at our head !'

' And if they were found with stolen property in their possession, under circumstances they were unable to explain, they would be treated just as you will be treated, sir—neither more nor less. For shame, sir—for shame !'

Brother Neel flung his arm up with an air of recklessness. His eyes sparkling and his forehead heavily knitted, he began to pace up and down the inspector's private sitting-room. Every now and then he would toss his long, dark, oily locks back from his forehead and behind his ears. It was an effective gesture for any public scene. In this limited space, with only two spectators in the gallery, and both of them in their ways of thought exceedingly matter-of-fact, this leonine carriage of the head, this ample, commanding action of the arm, seemed unnecessary and ridiculous. Brother Neel, of the International Organization of Total Abstainers, looked every inch a charlatan.

Detective Toppin had stepped round to the door-mat as before.

' That's the article I want to look at,' said the inspector, as the packet in white tissue-paper slipped out from the midst of the printed and manuscript documents he had spread along on either side, on breaking the inner seals. The white tissue-paper bore stains and blotches which, even in the imperfect light of the candles, Toppin could perceive from the door.

With great care the inspector stripped off the white tissue covering, and unfastened the green silk binding together the sides of the bulky pocket-book, or letter-case, as it appeared to Toppin.

Almost as soon as the silk thread had been removed from this letter-case or pocket-book, a little heap of glittering crystals tumbled from both its sides on to the table.

' *'Cré nom de noms !'* ejaculated Toppin. ' Diamonds !'

' Yes,' answered Brother Neel sneeringly, his head thrown back, and his arms folded on his chest— ' diamonds !'

Really?

The inspector uttered an exclamation of ungovernable surprise, and, picking up half a dozen of the objects in question, held them for examination close to the flame of the candle.

CHAPTER XVII.

I<small>T</small> was undoubtedly an exclamation of surprise—the exclamation that had burst from the inspector as his eye fell on the heap of brilliants which had poured from the twin sides of the small portfolio. Toppin could not see the brilliants from his position at the door. Around them like a rampart lay the documents belonging to the I.O.T.A.

' Yes, diamonds !' reiterated Brother Neel, with a sneer of still greater intensity, at once mocking and defiant—' yes, diamonds !'

' *'Cré nom de noms de noms !'*

In his excitement Mr. Toppin swore with triple force in French. It dawned upon him now that these were the Wilmot diamonds, value £20,000.

The half-dozen stones picked up at random by Inspector Byde were promptly replaced, and with the rest put back into the folding velvet case. The inspector was not by any means a bad judge of precious stones.

' Are these your property ?' said he, leaning forward, with both hands on the table; retaining his hold, however, on the small portfolio.

' No, they are not,' replied Brother Neel.

' Can you account for their being in your possession ?'

' I can.'

' At once, then, please !'

' I can give the clearest account of their being in my temporary possession—those diamonds,' returned Brother Neel deliberately. ' In twenty-four hours I shall be able to furnish you with the fullest explanation, I think.'

' Twenty-four hours !'

' Yes, sir—that's what I said : twenty-four hours. Perhaps less ; not more, I should hope.'

' I should hope not, too. Try and make it less, Mr. Neel—in your own interest, try and make it a good deal less. They don't allow us little vacations of that sort at Scotland Yard.'

' For the moment I am not my own master.'

' Come, come, sir—a detail or two. How did these valuables pass into your possession ?'

' I desire to postpone my answer, which will be complete and authoritative when I give it.'

' *When* did they pass into your possession ?'

' I must ask you to consider that as bound up with the other question.'

' Oh, no mysteries, please ! You are speaking to police-officers. Realize the situation, sir.'

' For the moment I can say no more. Do as you choose. I realize the situation—oh, don't be alarmed, I realize it ! In a parcel of which I admit the ownership, amidst the documents of the society employing me, and virtually responsible for my character, you find extremely valuable property secreted—for that is what it amounts to, does it not, Mr. Inspector Byde ?—secreted. The inference is that I have stolen this property, or that I am the confederate of the actual thieves. Very well, sir. Do as you think proper. I cautioned you at the outset ; I tell you now that all can be explained to you in, say, twenty-four hours. If you cannot wait, you cannot wait ! Take the risk. Appearances are with you, although if you trust to them you will rue it. I don't know that I need dread the consequences of your hasty action, either for myself or for my cause. Do as you wish, Mr. Byde. Place me under arrest. I shall be delighted to see you perpetrate another blunder.'

Without being aware of it, Brother Neel had hit the inspector on a weak spot. Mr. Byde's morbid mistrust of ' appearances ' has been alluded to before. He took refuge in a curt platitude, hoping that the other's fury might prevent him from remaining passive.

' Besides,' resumed the temperance lecturer roughly, ' you are in a foreign country, please to recollect. Ha ! Place me under arrest ? You will be careful to keep your hands

off me, both of you. Where is your warrant to take me
into custody? I was weak—by the Lord Harry, now I
think of it, I was incredibly weak!—to yield in the first
place to your meddling with my personal affairs. Arrest
me at your peril!'

'Toppin can do it in a few minutes, if you'd like to see
how it's to be done,' observed the inspector. 'I'm afraid
you don't quite grasp the situation yet. A man believed to
have had stolen property in his possession was found murdered in the mail-train which arrived in Paris from London
early in the morning. The property in question was missing. You, who were a traveller by the same train, are now
found, on the second evening after the murder, to have the
missing property in your possession : I won't say "secreted."
Now, the French police—with whom Mr. Toppin has official
relations—are very actively occupied in seeking out traces
of the crime ; and if you were indicated to them you may
depend upon it that without waiting twenty-four minutes,
to say nothing of twenty-four hours, they would have you
under arrest as——'

'What!—As a murderer?'

'As the individual implicated by the circumstances of the
case.'

'What!—*I* should be suspected of the murder of that
man?'

'That is what would happen if Mr. Toppin, my colleague,
called them in. That is what *will* happen, I am afraid ;
for, upon this evidence, unexplained'—the inspector touched
the small portfolio—'we shall be bound to call upon our
French colleagues.'

'But as we drove along just now, the evening newspapers
were announcing the arrest of the assassin.'

'Yes?'

'Well, then—how——' Brother Neel was about to put
an obvious question, but suddenly changed his tone. 'That
could not be'—he recoiled, as he gazed from Inspector Byde
to Detective Toppin, and from Detective Toppin to Inspector
Byde.

'Oh, no,' interposed Toppin impetuously—'a mistake,
that case!'

'This is hard to bear!' exclaimed Brother Neel, striking
his forehead with one hand, and clenching the other.

'Yes; and we can't waste any more time over it,' said the inspector peremptorily. 'Now, I will go farther with you than my duty requires me to go. You arrived in Paris yesterday morning by the night-mail from London, due here at 5.50. Not long after your arrival you returned to the post-office at the railway-station—come : you see we know more than you imagined! Make your explanation now, and have done with it. Otherwise——'

'I went back to the station post-office,' answered Brother Neel readily enough—'because I had an urgent telegram to send off, and a letter. The letter was addressed to the council of the I.O.T.A., and the telegram to the secretary of the I.O.T.A., informing him that the letter was on its way, and begging him to call the members of the Council together for business of the most important nature. This business is the same with regard to which you have demanded explanations. The reply from the Council may arrive to-morrow morning, or at any time I may receive a telegram. My object, however, in requesting the delay of twenty-four hours, was that I should be enabled to wire to the secretary at once, urging him to send me back by the very first post my own letter to the Council, with my own envelope bearing the stamps, post-mark, etc. He would, of course, do as I requested, and I should receive them back by to-morrow evening—that is to say, in twenty-four hours' time.'

'What would that prove ?' inquired Inspector Byde.

'Prove ? It would prove——' The speaker stopped short as though he measured his own situation for the first time with independent eyes. 'Well, it would prove my good faith,' he went on, with some embarrassment—'and yet I suppose that—I suppose that you would not admit it to prove anything!' He took a hasty turn or two about the room. 'So far as that goes there would be nothing in the contents of my letter to the Council which you could not learn from me now, if——' He went abruptly to the mantelpiece, poured out a glass of water, and drank it nervously. 'I am not my own master in this. The I.O.T.A. must not be compromised, and I ought not to move until I hear from them. If they are compromised by me—if the cause in general suffers through my instrumentality—why, my prospects would be entirely ruined ! In one moment I

should forfeit my position, I should lose my means of livelihood. My name is known on temperance platforms from
one end of England to the other; I should be a marked
man, and cast out. What would become of me? At my
age begin life again——how? How? Would you have
me sink into crime or into genteel mendicancy? What
work could I offer to perform—what work could I—I
—tamely sit down to and drudge at after so many years
of——'

'Ah, things are made very pleasant for you "brethren"
of the temperance bands,' observed Mr. Byde irrelevantly,
and with a sternness in which his idiosyncrasy asserted itself.
'You lay down the law to other people quite old enough to
decide for themselves; you take their money and spend it
on yourselves; and you are answerable to nobody but yourselves. I don't wonder that your lazy, prating, selfish life
unfits you for useful work.'

'I see that I must expect no mercy from you, Inspector
Byde,' was the reply. 'I see that I must take my risk; I
see that if I refuse to speak until I receive the sanction I
have asked for—asked for, loyally—in the very interests of
the people I serve, and with no other motive—I see that my
struggle with the circumstances of the moment will be of no
avail. You will do your duty—you *must* do your duty. In
the absence of explanation from me, you will have to cause
my arrest. The harm which I am seeking to stave off will
be done irremediably. Perhaps I shall serve them best by
speaking at once.' He refilled the glass, and moistened his
lips. 'If you could await my letter, you would acknowledge
that I have acted in good faith—in apparent good faith I
mean, of course: oh, I comprehend your bias! If I had
any doubts whatever upon the subject, the extraordinary
observations you permitted yourself just now would extinguish them. I don't know, by the way, whether it forms
part of your duty, Mr. Inspector Byde, to lecture your
prisoners'—the inspector waved his hand in deprecation,
and, yes, a slight flush mounted to his cheeks—'for that is
what my position here amounts to!—to lecture your
prisoners on their choice of a vocation: but allow me to say
that an attitude of that kind constitutes a gross abuse of
your advantage. You will not believe my story, I suppose.
But you shall hear it!'

'As briefly as possible,' said the inspector, in a gentler tone.

Brother Neel threw himself into a fauteuil.

'I was a passenger from London with the man whose body lies at the Morgue. I know his name; he told it me in conversation. He gave me some idea, ostensibly, of his business position, too. Between London and Dover——'

'We are acquainted with your movements during the first part of your journey; and only one thing concerns us —how did this property pass into your possession?'

'You may ask me why I have not come forward to identify this man, knowing what I know from his own lips? That is one point upon which I preferred to consult the Council of my society. The deceased and myself were fellow-passengers from Calais to Boulogne. There were individuals travelling with us whose looks neither of us liked, and whose society we both endeavoured to avoid. From a curious incident on the journey I half suspected that the deceased was a member of your own calling, instead of being, as he had related for the benefit of us all, a Mr. Remington, residing in the Park Lane neighbourhood. He changed compartments, and I must say that I followed him, preferring his society, at any rate, to that of the two individuals with whom he would have left me. The deceased had the appearance of a man who had been drinking continuously. Towards the latter portion of the journey he became extremely drowsy, and could scarcely keep awake. I thought he wanted a compartment to himself in order to be able to sleep, and when he changed once more I did not move from my own compartment, where, indeed, I was alone, and comfortably installed. From your own information you will be aware of the fact, I dare say, that very few passengers had travelled by the train. I now come to the first material fact.'

Inspector Byde had been meditatively sharpening a long lead pencil. Out of his capacious pocket he now extracted a note-book of ominously official aspect, and, opening it, sat ready to jot down what he might consider of importance in the narrative.

Toppin heaved a fluttering sigh.

'We had touched for an instant at Creil, which was the last of our stoppages before reaching Paris, and about fifteen

minutes had elapsed—fifteen or twenty minutes—since we
had run out of the Creil station. I was leaning back in the
corner of the compartment, with my face to the engine,
when, even above the great noise made by the train as it
rushed along at full speed, I fancied I heard a detonation,
close to my ear. The travelling cap I wore enabled me to
rest my head against the wooden partition, and I suppose
that that acted as a sort of sounding-board. One report
only was what I heard, if indeed it were a report at all.
Had we been travelling in the daytime I might have concluded that the sound was caused by a pebble thrown at the
passing train and striking one of the windows, or that as we
dashed under a bridge a stone or other missile had been
dropped on to perhaps the metal frame of the carriage-lamp.
It was barely five, however, on a December morning, and
pitch dark. The detonation, although not distinct, had
seemed close to my ear, and as I reflected I felt convinced
it was a pistol-shot that I had heard. The French guard
of the train had once or twice startled me, during the
earlier part of the journey, by suddenly entering the compartment from the footboard for the purpose of examining
tickets. I don't know what it was—why I should have
thought of any such thing—but a suspicion of foul play
forced itself upon my mind. The occurrences of the journey
had been peculiar—the story told by the deceased about the
Wilmot diamonds—the night arrest at Dover—that young
man's calm protestation of innocence—the persistency of
the two individuals whom we repeatedly met, but who never
spoke to us—and then the abrupt appearance of the French
guard while we were hurrying through the storm in the
dark—all these things influenced me, I suppose. I jumped
up and went to the far window. Letting down the glass
and looking out, I could just detect the door of, not the
next, but the second compartment in my rear, swinging
open. If the door had swung towards me I could not have
perceived it. But it opened in the contrary direction to my
own, and what enabled me to see it was the faint gleam
from the lamp on the inner surface of the door, which was
painted in a light colour. The lamp had apparently burnt low,
as in my own compartment. Nothing but this glimmer of
faint light as the door swayed slightly with the rapid
motion of the train was distinguishable in the utter gloom.

In my place, Mr. Inspector Byde, what would you have done ?'

'Let us get on, sir,' said the inspector, fidgeting with the lead pencil.

Mr. Toppin expanded his chest, and sniffed with remarkable significance.

'Rung the alarm bell, and stopped the train? On what ground? What had I to show as justification? A sound— which, after all, was I certain I had heard?—and an open door? My own alarm was personal to myself, arose from the condition of my own mind, might be due to mere physical fatigue, at that moment in the twenty-four hours when the vitality is lowest. Had I really, as a matter of fact, heard the detonation I imagined I had heard? Had I not been asleep? The open door? The door might have been carelessly closed, and left unfastened. However, I resolved to see!'

The inspector flattened out his note-book, and prepared to write.

'Yes! In the interests of my own safety, I resolved to see. For on the other hand, if it were some deed of violence, a sinister plot by the very servants of the railway, *my* turn might arrive next: did I know? I opened the far door of my own compartment, and stepped on to the footboard. It was an easy proceeding to pass along outside. The supports available for the ticket examiner, as he swung himself from carriage to carriage throughout the entire length of the train, were available to me also in the few steps I had to make. The carriages rocked and jolted once or twice, and I had to grope my way; but I kept my footing without any difficulty. The whole affair occupied a few seconds, I should say. Well, what did I find? The compartment immediately behind my own was empty. The curtains had been drawn down, and had been left drawn, but through the window of the door I could see that there was no one in the compartment. Arrived at the compartment next it, farther along, I found the curtain drawn there too—but, peering round the edge of the doorway, to my amazement, I saw——'

Brother Neel broke off abruptly. The scene he conjured up appeared to overwhelm him ; or was it that the delicacy of his own position now struck him with a paralysing force?

' You saw ?' demanded the inspector in a passionless voice, as the lead pencil came to a standstill.

' I saw the figures of two men—and blood,' continued the narrator, his hushed and slower accents betraying, perhaps awe, perhaps horror, perhaps consternation. 'One of the two men had his face turned away from me ; and he was stooping across the body of the other. He had his back towards the doorway of the compartment, and I could see that he was searching in the pockets, in the lining even, of the other's garments. The other lay motionless along the seat. The light was dim, but not too dim for me to fail in recognising the features of that other. It was the man whose body has been transported to the Morgue—the man who had been my own travelling companion up to, it seemed, but a few minutes previously—the man with whom I had been talking, hour after hour, until weariness overcame us both. In spite of the dim light, I could discern the look upon his features, as without intercepting my view of them, the figure between us bent still lower in the search. On his countenance I saw the look which it has ever since retained, the look which you may study at the Morgue, if studies of the murdered leave but a transitory impress on your mind, my good sir—" Mr. Smithson "—but the look which I need no visit to the Morgue to call up ; for I see it plainly—I can see it now !' Brother Neel flung out his arm, and started to his feet. ' The eyes were open, and they glistened in the dull, yellow light from the lamp above. Blood was oozing from a wound in the temple.'

' Blood was oozing from a wound in the temple,' repeated the inspector, in the same passionless tone, as he wrote down the words. ' The right temple—or the left ?' The question and the glance were like a couple of electric rapier thrusts.

' Why—the left, of course,' answered Brother Neel, with the natural hesitation of the man who refers to a fixed mental image. ' The deceased was in a recumbent position, on his right side, with his back to the engine. My impulse was to enter the carriage and seize the man who was leaning over, away from me, almost within arm's length. The consequences, however, flashed through my mind. It seemed improbable that the man before me was without confederates. A confederate might be watching at that instant : I myself in one moment more might—— Just then, the man appeared to have' extracted some object from the breast-pocket of the deceased. He held the object away from him, in his left hand. As he extended his arm, the object came within my reach. I snatched it from him. The object I speak of was the package in white tissue-paper which you have discovered among the documents of the society.'

' What happened then ?'

' The individual in front of me, instead of at once turning, made a dash through the carriage to the opposite door, through which I imagine he escaped—but on that point I know nothing. All that I can tell you is that I never saw his face. I don't profess to be a hero. So far as bodily encounters are concerned, I should hear myself called a coward with perfect equanimity. My youth and early manhood were passed among Quakers, and what the world might choose to term poltroonery, I could vindicate by the precept or the example of prominent members of that faith, one or two even illustrious. I immediately swung myself back, and retreated along the footboard to my own compartment. The incident had thoroughly unnerved me, although it was not at the time, but afterwards, that I underwent its full effect. With great difficulty I retained my footing and my hold on making my way back. At first it seemed inevitable that I should be pursued. I remained for several minutes on the alert, ready to ring the alarm-bell on the slightest appearance of danger. But no single incident arose to excite suspicion or misgiving. The night-mail thundered onwards through the raw air of the black winter's morning. A traveller had been murdered in his sleep, but no one knew it—no one but the murderer and myself!'

Brother Neel's vocal organ once more aroused the inspector's disinterested admiration. The subdued tones thrilled you quite deliciously. It was hard upon the temperance lecturer that though he no doubt spoke the truth, the whole truth, and nothing but the truth, as often as most other people, his native oratorical gifts gave you constantly the impression that he was addicted to the opposite practice, reinforcing the less likely of his fictions by the rhetorician's graces, the elocutionist's art.

' Had you no means whatever of identifying the assassin ?'
' None.'

' You could not say whether he wore a guard's uniform or not ?'

' It was impossible to distinguish anything of the sort.'

' Could you say whether he wore a cap or hat ?'

' Yes; I can positively state that he was bare-headed. That I noticed as he rose from his stooping posture, when I snatched the small package from his hand. What light there was fell directly on his head.'

' Then you can tell us something about this ghostly gentleman after all : whether he wore his hair in long ringlets, or in curl papers, whether cropped short, or in a chignon, or whether he was bald ?'

' He had short, dark hair, like a few millions of other men—that is all I can say,' coldly responded Brother Neel.

' When did you examine the contents of the packet?'

' Not until I reached my hotel, Rue de Compiègne.'

' And what did you find ?'

' What you have just found.'

' Never mind about me, if you please. My question is, what did you find ? and be particularly careful about your answer, because it may be necessary for evidence.'

' I found that the case contained loose diamonds of considerable size. I did not count them; but there were, comparatively speaking, a large number of them. I replaced them——'

' All ?' Rapid thrusts in *carte* and in *tierce*.

' All ?' echoed Brother Neel ; ' yes—all !'

The iteration and the manner were equivalent to a ' *Touché !*' The inspector's lead pencil laboured across the page. ' I replaced all the diamonds in the case, but did not count them,' he repeated aloud, reading from his notes ; and he added a private memorandum in the margin—' Has probably kept some back.'

' You made no declaration, I believe, to the authorities here. May I ask whether you have spoken of this to any person whatever until now ?'

' To no person whatever. But what I did, without a moment's loss of time, was to telegraph, as I have said, to the secretary of our great society, advising him of the communication which would follow by post. That communication I duly forwarded, as you are aware. It simply related the occurrences I have just described, and requested a suggestion or instruction from the Council. Until the Council directed me as to my course of action, I pledged myself to divulge to no one the part I had involuntarily played in this mysterious crime. You can understand plainly that for the I.O.T.A. to be mixed up, through one of its accredited agents, in an affair of this kind, just at the moment when its roots were striking deeper into foreign soil, became a matter of the greatest gravity. Misapprehension so easily arises ; motives can be so easily misconstrued abroad. What may prove the answer of the Council I know not. If they had ordered me to preserve an absolute silence—resolving to transmit those valuables anonymously to the police—I should have obeyed them. Such may still prove their answer, for all I can affirm. But we have not reckoned with Scotland Yard. Ah, what a terrible disaster ! these two affairs happening simultaneously—the stupid calumnies of that sensational paper, and then this ! What a catastrophe, great heavens !' Brother Neel wrung his hands. He had introduced an effective quaver into his notes on the lower register.

'It's a pity you neglected to count the stones,' observed the inspector, collecting himself for a decisive lunge—' and it's a pity you restored them all—all, every one of them—to the case ; a great pity, really, sir !'

The other kept an unmoved countenance, as he listened.

'Because,' resumed Mr. Byde, brusquely fixing him with a look,—' these diamonds are false !'

There was a dead silence.

'Floored,' wrote the inspector as a purely private memorandum ; 'has kept some of them back.'

''Crè nom !' muttered Toppin.

The temperance lecturer began an undefined melody in a toneless whistle and sank back into his arm-chair.

'Just come and look at these articles, Mr. Toppin, will you ?' said the inspector.

Mr. Toppin advanced with alacrity to the table, and took up a few of the scintillating crystals pushed towards him by his superior officer.

'Well, it's not a good light for the purpose,' he remarked, after an examination by the flame of the candle, ' but you're right, inspector, they're not the real thing.'

'The real thing !' was the emphatic reply ; ' they're paste !'

' The best I ever saw, though,' said Toppin.

' Yes,' concurred the inspector ; ' good, and no mistake, but paste. It must be a new process.'

' Well, then, gentlemen,' exclaimed Brother Neel, springing briskly to his feet—' how do we stand ?'

' Why, there's a *primâ facie* case against you, sir,' returned Mr. Byde. ' And what makes it worse is that you demanded twenty-four hours' grace. These are imitation stones, are they not ? Well, an ignorant policeman might conjecture that the genuine ones were in the hands of a confederate. The confederate could skip across the frontier on a twenty-four hours' notice, or, if already in Amsterdam, could throw the diamonds into the market at a slight loss of value but no loss of time. Oh, dear me !—what a pity you did not keep one or two of them back—just one or two —as specimens !'

' I regret the omission,' said Brother Neel, reddening. ' You are not going to accuse me, I presume, of being engaged in a dishonest transaction, such as that, with a confederate ? The mere suggestion is disgraceful. Whether they are spurious or genuine, the stones you have there are the stones I found in the case that lies before you. The parcel has been out of my own custody, that is true. But the seals were intact when it came into my hands again, and I do not see how it could have been tampered with, or why —even admitting a possibility of such conduct on the part of my colleague, Mr. Bamber, which I do not admit.'

' Of course you can see what those facts involve—with regard to the perpetration of the crime you have narrated ?'

' That a murder was committed to obtain possession of paste diamonds? Yes, that must be the inference, I suppose. The murderer knew of some such objects as these being in the possession of the deceased, I suppose, and erroneously believed them to be genuine diamonds.'

' Ah, but we are advised that the deceased was most probably in unlawful possession, likewise. Had he, also, been deceived ? The merchandise is good, I don't deny it, but not so good as all that—come ! And the fact is undeniable that the Wilmot diamonds, represented by these things, are missing—under circumstances that connect the deceased with their abstraction.'

' Well, those are matters for yourselves, gentlemen. They

don't concern me. I can't engage in the detection of crime,
with you. The articles before you are compromising articles;
that I understood from the outset. You have asked me how
they came into my possession, and why I wanted to defer
my explanation; I have told you. Now, Mr. Byde, sir—
pray what does your duty require you to do?'

'Just see if you can recollect whether, between your
acquisition of this package and the moment at which you
lodged it with your colleague, it did not pass out of your
control? My duty doesn't require me to put this to you;
and you needn't answer unless you like.'

His recollection was clear enough on the subject, said
Brother Neel. So long as the property remained in his
personal keeping he was in danger; that he had very
speedily realized. And until he should receive the instructions of the council of the I.O.T.A. he stood absolutely at
his own devices. He had therefore with great care
examined the chances of his own situation. It had seemed
to him that if he carried about with him such valuable
property as this property had appeared to be, he would be
exposing himself needlessly to risks of an extraneous
character. A street accident — anything — might unexpectedly bring to light the nature of the package; whilst if
he had been identified as a passenger by the night-mail, and
if he had been temporarily detained and searched, the
discovery of the supposed diamonds would have inculpated
him tremendously. He had concluded that it would be
safer, of the two courses, to leave the package in his
portmanteau, locked, at the hotel. This he had done,
arguing—to be quite frank with Inspector Byde—that the
presence of the property in his luggage did not necessarily
inculpate him. It might have been placed there, somehow,
by someone else, who—having kept back a portion of the
supposititious valuables — sought to definitively exclude
himself from the scope of possible suspicion by directly
implicating some third person. Why should not the guards
of the train, or one of them, have done this? His luggage
had been registered through, and from London to Paris he
had not once set eyes on it. Not a bad story, that!
concluded Brother Neel cynically.

'Not at all,' approved Inspector Byde.

It had afterwards occurred to him that a more secure

depository would be desirable than a locked portmanteau in a room at an hotel. He did not know that the lock of his own portmanteau was a particularly difficult one; and the servants of the hotel——

'The servants?' burst forth Toppin, his countenance illumining—'the servants?—that's it!' In two strides he was at the inspector's elbow. 'That Anarchist fellow,' he whispered, almost inaudibly to the inspector himself, although he bent down close to the latter's ear and walled in his words with his hand. 'That Anarchist!'

'Well?' growled Mr. Byde, in real anger at his colleague's exclamation.

'Picked the lock and stole the genuine. Put the paste in, *pour donner le change.*'

'Pooh! Nonsense!' returned the inspector loudly. 'Nonsense!' he repeated, as if endeavouring to undo the effect of Mr. Toppin's outburst. 'A great pity you replaced the property intact, sir,' he continued in a bluff and jovial manner; 'a great pity you did not put by one or two, say, just as specimens! Did you ever find your portmanteau unlocked, on returning to your room?'

'Yes—once. It was just before I made up that parcel in order to leave it at the offices of the I.O.T.A., Boulevard Haussmann, in a place of safety.' Brother Neel related the circumstance with which the reader is acquainted. He had simply gone down to breakfast at the *table d'hôte*, after having, as he thought, secured his portmanteau as usual. When he got back into the room he discovered that he must have failed to turn the key in the lock, after all; because the portmanteau was unfastened. He had had a momentary misgiving, but the package was all right, and so were its contents. It was then that he hastened to convey it to a place of greater safety. With regard to the observation by the inspector's colleague, just now, of course the hotel servants had access to his apartment. The servant who answered his bell, as a rule, was the man they had both seen that evening. The man who did not speak English—the Anarchist.

'One word more, if you please. Was it part of your system, Mr. Neel, to deny, categorically, at the Morgue, that you preserved the slightest recollection of the deceased?'

'Just so. A lie, was it not? But it appears to have been

a part of your own system to present yourself as a Mr. Smithson, strongly interested in the welfare of the I.O.T.A.: a lie, also, was it not?'

'Well, yes,' responded the inspector, making his preparations to depart, 'and my conscience is black with lies of that description, I'm afraid. " 'Tis my vocation, Hal," as Byron says. I hope that in the business which you follow, sir, you are under no similar obligation of lying frequently, and with a plausible face.'

They were all ready to accompany the inspector whither he listed. Mr. Byde regretted that the hour for the second *table d'hôte* was past. Possibly they might secure some dinner all the same, at the Hôtel des Nations; for that was the spot to which they must now repair. For the present he and Mr. Toppin would be under the necessity of imposing their society upon Brother Neel.

'There will be no scandal, I trust,' urged the temperance lecturer. 'You Scotland Yard men——'

'At Scotland Yard, sir, we are men of business—and gentlemen. It is not *we* who make scandals.'

'Because, you know, I warn you! The I.O.T.A. will suffer in my person; and we have powerful influences—people you would not dream of, perhaps—with us in the I.O.T.A. Our Grand Worthy Master——'

'Oh, say no more about that body, I beg!' The inspector led the way to the door. 'The I.O.T.A., sir, and its Grand Worthy Masters!' he retorted, stopping with his fingers on the handle; 'I don't recognise their existence, sir, I don't know them. Brother Neel may be concerned in this case, and that's all I can report about. As for I.O.T.A.'s, they've no more to do with this affair than—than'—the inspector hesitated, at a loss for his parallel—'than the *pons asinorum*, sir! Unless, indeed, this particular I.O.T.A. should turn out to be organized receivers of stolen property: in which case we shall require to have before us a very great deal with respect to the extent of their powerful influences!'

'*'Cré nom!*' ejaculated Toppin.

CHAPTER XVIII.

MR. BYDE was met, as he descended with his companions into the vestibule of the Terminus Hotel, by the travelled waiter who had moved in the patrician spheres of Battersea.

'A lettaire,' said that accomplished linguist, 'a lettaire for Mistaire Bydee which have been leave.' The superscription on the note he handed to the inspector was in a feminine handwriting.

'Why,' exclaimed Toppin jocularly, 'this is our friend who can't stand the police!—never could stand them—no one in the family has ever been able to endure them. Hates the police, and everything connected with them!'

'*Ah, vous savez,*' answered the student of the English social system, as he beamed and raised his eyebrows, and brought one shoulder up under his ear, in a shrug of gratified protest—'*vous savez*—there are those little weaknesses that run in the blood! It's that, or it's this: like a predisposition to a malady—*tiens?* Some people will inherit the germs of scrofula; others abhor blackbeetles and rats. *Moi*—I—it's policemen: *je ne peux pas les voir en peinture!* That is how I am—*c'est plus fort que moi!*'

'A nice old cup of tea *you* are!' Mr. Toppin spoke with the disgusting familiarity in which at times he would permit himself to indulge, and he pinched the waiter's frail forearm between his finger and thumb. 'How are they getting along at the Prefecture?'

'I beck parton?' Relapsing into the English language, the speaker threw an alarmed look behind him; but there was no one to overhear. 'The lady have wait in her carriage reply,' he hastened to inform Inspector Byde.

'Come here,' proceeded Mr. Toppin, with insular brutality, 'whom do you think you've been getting at? The next time you go down to the Prefecture, you tell Monsieur Hy that you've made my acquaintance—that is to say, the acquaintance of Mr. Detective Thomas Toppin, of the English Sûreté—Yes! And don't you talk so much about the police. Your overdoing it, young fellur!'

Mr. Toppin was superb, just now. If anything, he was the junior of the two; but he had the assurance which accompanies mediocrity. When he said a thing, he not only looked as if he meant it, every word of it, but as if he meant a good deal more than, out of consideration for his hearer, he would wish to put into words. He did not, as a rule, however, mean very much more than he actually expressed, to do him justice. He was a remarkably fine young man, with—by nature—a portentous cast of countenance ; and he always imposed upon other mediocrities, and sometimes upon quite superior persons.

The recipient of the missive hurried through the vestibule, and crossed the pavement outside. A private carriage stood waiting nearly opposite the hotel entrance.

'I'm so sorry to trouble you, Mr. Byde,' said Mrs. Bertram, as she approached the window—'but you must lay the blame on this wilful young lady here. She *would* insist upon our calling to see if you had any news, and we have come expressly. There !—now justify yourself, Adela !'

' Oh, *have* you any news, Mr. Byde?' exclaimed Miss Knollys, her profile suddenly emerging from the deep shadow. ' You haven't any bad news, have you ?' In the young lady's accent the inspector distinguished that he was implored *not* to have bad news to communicate. ' I feel sure there ought to be no bad news—but the suspense is terrible.' The full rays of the carriage lamps fell on the inspector's face, as he listened, but the obscurity of the interior shrouded both occupants from his own view. The figure of Miss Knollys appeared the vaguest of out-lines to him. When she had impulsively bent forward, the bright eyes which he had seen filled with tears glistened clearly through the gloom ; and, now, as a little half-nervous, half-apologetic laugh ended her appeal, the dark shadow seemed to be touched by one transient ray from a star.

Yes, he would certainly do whatever he could—whatever he could—for a charming young lady like this, thought Mr. Byde : a charming young lady, so——Eh ? Why, what on earth—— ! Two or three of his favourite couplets rose up simultaneously to rebuke him. And indeed a pretty frame of mind for the systematic opponent of impressionism ! What if young people *were* blessed with good looks—where was the sense—

> ' Where's the sense, direct and moral,
>   That teeth are pearl, or lips are coral ?'

What had *he* to do with the charms of young ladies personally interested in the results of his investigations—with their charms and with their woes? Very unfortunate for this Mr. Sinclair, if he found he could not prove that——

'Ah—you *have* bad news—that was what I feared—and I was right to come! Something has happened! I knew —I knew—that something must have happened. Tell me what it is: I have a right to know!—or let us telegraph, dear Mrs. Bertram—let us telegraph to Austin that we know he has been concealing something from us, and that we want to hear the worst!'

'Ladies, I assure you——'began the inspector.

My dear, I see no reason why you should imagine that Mr. Sinclair has kept back the worst from you. On the contrary, his letter was exceedingly frank—not only frank, but sensible and businesslike. He told you plainly the position which the arrest placed him in, as far as he could ascertain it, at the moment; and to-day he telegraphs, repeating that he can soon dispose of the entire ridiculous charge.'

'Yes, but I know he has done that out of thoughtfulness!' persisted Miss Adela Knollys.

Well, it was abominable, reflected the inspector, if this young gentleman, Mr. Sinclair, were being detained in custody without sufficient cause. To stop a man on suspicion when he was leaving the country might be one thing, but to keep him like that when they had had plenty of time to examine the circumstances against him was quite another, especially looking to the exhaustive character of his (Byde's) own reports, and the hints he had therein furnished. Another case of 'appearances,' he supposed. 'Appearances!' He detested the term. They could be so easily invented, fabricated, or maliciously combined — appearances! Yes, he would certainly do whatever he could to wind this case up sharp, and to help that young gentleman in bringing forward his proofs. It was no fault of his (Byde's) that the young lady before him was attractive.

'Mr. Byde——' implored the young lady.

He would help him. And if the arrest had been an error —another good blow at the impressionists!

'You *will* be candid with me, won't you, Mr. Byde?'

Thus beset, the inspector unscrupulously took refuge in

the fluent phrases of the hopeful friend. So far as positive information went, he really did not know that for the moment he had anything to impart which could in the slightest degree affect Mr. Austin Sinclair prejudicially; he might go further, and say that certain researches upon which he, together with an extremely able colleague—Detective Toppin, stationed permanently in Paris by Scotland Yard—was at this very minute actively engaged, might not impossibly procure the unconditional release of Mr. Sinclair before the expiration of another fortnight—or, perhaps, ten days—perhaps less. A long time? Yes, it did seem long, no doubt; but we must not be impatient. We must be patient. Things were seldom done well which were done over-quickly. And then at any instant fresh intelligence might reach him from London. For all he knew Mr. Sinclair was triumphantly establishing his utter ignorance of the Park Lane diamond robbery while they—he, Mr. Byde, and the two ladies with whom he cordially sympathised—were now conversing on that very spot. Of course the connection of Mr. Sinclair with the diamond robbery was absurd, preposterous, a totally untenable hypothesis—of course! How *could* it be? Why, it could not possibly be! Mr. Sinclair would soon be discharged, for want of evidence. The only conceivable witness against him was the man who had since been murdered: he asked pardon for putting the case in a rather hard, practical manner, but that was the way in which it would be put by the authorities over there, and it was best to look at the least favourable aspect of matters like this now, wasn't it? Why, yes. Therefore, we must be patient. We must repose our faith in justice, and trust to the right arm of the law. As for Mr. Stanislas Wilmot, who laid false informations with malice aforethought, and to compass private objects deliberately sent the Department astray, that gentleman might be called on for an explanation of his conduct, and for redress; and it might be worth while instituting some inquiries as to the history of the Hatton Garden firm, the nature of its transactions, and a good deal more. Diamond 'faking' had been managed pretty extensively for some time past. The Department had not yet hit upon the precise source of the larger 'faked' diamonds that had been passed off on buyers; but they were on the look-out for diamond merchants with laboratories attached

to their domiciles or business premises. These yellow Cape
stones, treated with chemicals so as to appear brilliants of
the purest water, had been turning up too often lately; and
Mr. Stanislas Wilmot might find occasion one of these days
to regret that he had drawn upon himself the notice of Scotland Yard.

Miss Knollys apparently deemed it not incompatible with
consistency to inveigh anew against her guardian, and, in
the same breath, to plead for him very earnestly with Inspector George Byde. Her interposition to the latter effect
completed the surrender of Detective Toppin's colleague.
He could only respond with a few more soothing aphorisms
and sanguine pledges.

Mrs. Bertram said that they had purposely deferred their
dinner-hour that evening in order to be able to make their
call at the inspector's address. Would Mr. Byde do her
the pleasure of returning to dine at the Avenue Marceau?
The inspector hastily excused himself, at once explaining
the urgency of the situation. It might be that he had
already lingered too long; but the anxiety of persons intimately concerned in the welfare of Mr. Austin Sinclair was
of course quite explicable, and it gratified him beyond measure to have gained the confidence of ladies who—of ladies
that—of ladies whom—ladies, in short, whom it was a real
pleasure to serve.

'Oh yes, we have the *greatest* confidence in you—the
very *greatest!*' came from the shadowy form in the Cim-
merian corner. Did he understand that Mr. Sinclair had
telegraphed during the afternoon—in good spirits? In
excellent spirits, replied the elder lady; it would be 'all
right,' he believed in a day or two: and that signified a
great deal, from what she knew of Mr. Sinclair. He was
not at all inclined to take either optimist or pessimist views
of events; he looked at a matter steadily, weighed everything on both sides, and then gave you just what he thought
about it; although it might be that in a case like this—yes,
she would not say it was impossible—he might have de-
parted from his custom, out of consideration for them both.
It might be that he had assumed this cheerfulness in order
to spare them the increased alarm which an exact statement of his position might excite in them.

'We'll prove an *alibi* for him,' cried the inspector gaily.

Could the speaker be George Byde, of the V Division !
Such frivolity as this in an allusion to a grave affair—such
an astounding indifference to principle ! A sad, a melan-
choly outlook, if scientific methods were to be employed to
serve impressionism !

' Whatever happens,' urged Mrs. Bertram, as the inspector
turned to see if Mr. Toppin and Brother Neel were still
waiting at the hotel entrance, ' you would not leave Paris
without paying us a visit, I trust?'

Mr. Byde promised to do his utmost, whatever happened,
to make a visit, though perhaps a brief one, at the Avenue
Marceau. But much would depend upon the occurrences
of the next twelve hours. He had unexpected indications
with respect to the present whereabouts of the missing
property itself, and he could not pronounce whether, at this
time on the following day, he should be on French soil at
all.

' Oh, *really !*' exclaimed both ladies in breathless admiration.

Might be across the frontier to-morrow : might be on the
other side of the Channel again. Mr. Byde began to fidget ;
he had stayed too long.

' Might have to leave at once for Amsterdam,' he added,
as he bade his visitors adieu — ' or by first train for
London.'

' Oh, how *clever* you *must* be !' said Mrs. Bertram.

' Thank you so much,' issued in a tremulous tone from
the corner beyond.

The profile suddenly re-emerged from the deep shadow,
and a gloved hand advanced towards the inspector. He
took the slender hand mechanically in his own broad palm,
and pressed the yielding fingers, whose warmth faintly
penetrated through their glove, just as he used to press the
wasted fingers of his own little daughter, May—when every
morning the poor child begged him to come back soon and
read some more of the story to her at her bedside : the bedside to which he had one day returned to burst into a flood
of tears.

The carriage rolled away, and the inspector, struck down
by a reminiscence, stood motionless at the edge of the pavement, staring vacantly before him. As there was no object
that could be discerned in the obscurity by Detective Toppin,

whose eyes were younger than those of his superior officer,
that zealous representative of the English police concluded
that his colleague was a gay old dog, and half made his
mind up to be facetious with him.

'Aha, inspector!—would you—would you!' he had a
good mind to say to him—'That's how you carry on when
you come over to Paris, inspector, is it? *I'll* tell Scotland
Yard about you! And a married man, too! Aha—aha!
Go along with you, you monster! Has ladies drive up in
their carriages to see him at his hotel, and gets that fetched
by them that he's struck all of a heap, he is!'

Mr. Toppin more than half resolved to step up to the
inspector and accost him in this friendly strain. Perhaps,
on the whole, he had better not, he reflected; the inspector
mightn't like it, all things considered. No, it would be
better to take no notice of the circumstance; he'd pretend
he hadn't been looking that way at all.

It was with an air of strictly professional deference that
Mr. Thomas Toppin greeted his colleague, when the latter,
shaking off that cruel arrow from the quiver of the past,
turned to resume the work of Inspector Byde. Brother
Neel had been fretting impatiently; which Mr. Toppin
regarded as but natural, being himself quite ready for his
dinner.

In silence they proceeded to the Rue de Compiègne,
Hôtel des Nations. As they halted at this establishment,
Detective Toppin reminded his superior officer that he might
count upon his, Toppin's, assistance in the task of cross-
examining the Anarchist. 'As safe as houses, it's the
Anarchist,' repeated Mr. Toppin.

'Just tell me the number of your apartment here,' said
Mr. Byde to their companion.

'My apartment is No. 21,' answered Brother Neel, somewhat loftily.

'We should like to glance over your register for the past
week,' observed the inspector to the lady-president of the
bureau. 'We have been expecting friends, and very likely
they have stopped here, on passing through.'

The book was duly placed before them by the fascinating
widowed Parisian spinster, whose nods and becks and
wreathed smiles diminished with abruptness at the spectacle
of Mr. Toppin's obduracy. The inspector ran his finger

down the names inscribed along the pages since the arrival
of Brother Neel.

' There's a handwriting that looks as if it were disguised,'
he remarked to his subordinate, indicating one of the more
recent entries.

' So it does,' concurred his subordinate.

Brother Neel, who chafed quite noticeably under the
restraint imposed upon him, was for adjourning to his
apartment ' to procure some I.O.T.A. documents,' while the
two gentlemen from Scotland Yard were searching the hotel
register.   He muttered that he would rejoin them in a
moment, with the documents in question, and in his impatience
had begun to ascend the staircase before the inspector could
arrest his progress.

Mr. Byde called him back in a peremptory manner, and,
speaking with greater sternness than he had hitherto
employed, told the temperance lecturer in an undertone that
if he did not wish to force them into disagreeable measures
he would do well to consider himself no longer free to act as
he might choose.   Although not formally in custody, for the
time being he was morally their prisoner.   Circumstances
might bring to a speedy termination the existing unpleasant
state of affairs ; but in the meantime Brother Neel must not
delude himself.   Until he might be requested by the
inspector, or by the colleague acting with him, to procure
from his apartment any documents relating to the I.O.T.A.,
he would be good enough to forget the I.O.T.A., so far as
the case at present occupying their close attention was
concerned.   It might or might not become necessary to
search Brother Neel's apartment, No. 21.   He would
doubtless aid them usefully in searching it.   He could not
be permitted, however, to make a visit to the apartment in
advance.

' But if you suspect that man—that Anarchist man,'
objected Brother Neel, with a slight trace of uneasiness.
' you don't suppose that he has chosen my room for the
concealment of anything ?'

' Oh, come, sir—pray don't argue our inquiry for us.   Do
as I beg of you, please !'

Brother Neel slowly retraced his steps.

The handwriting to which the inspector had referred,
undoubtedly, as Toppin now commented, bore the appear-

ance of having been laboriously disguised.   The characters
all leant backwards.   In the particulars which set forth that
the subject of the entry—a young gentleman of a by no
means unfamiliar patronymic—was of English nationality, and
was travelling northwards, from the Mediterranean, without
a passport, there were ' r's,' ' s's,' and ' t's,' in considerable
abundance.   From whatever cause—through inadvertence
or haste ; hardly by design—the 'r's' and ' t's' had been
formed in two different manners, whilst the ' s's ' looked
suspiciously elaborate, and the capital letters, also, seemed
either crude or florid to excess.

'Whenever you like, about that Anarchist,' said Mr.
Toppin.   ' I know enough to make out that it's on the
business of his lodge we want to see him.'

Mr. Byde politely addressed himself to the ex-'Parisienne.'
She had ensconced herself within the stifling boundaries of
her bureau, and was doing her best to show her contempt
for three booby foreigners who could not summon up
responsive glances for a still handsome woman—was she
not still handsome?   *Parbleu !* Handsome enough for
stupid English, whose wives and daughters had projecting
upper teeth, large feet, and not an inch of padding inside
their clothes where padding ought to be !   She bit her lips
as Mr. Byde respectfully pushed open the door of the
asphyxiating bureau ; bit them well to make them once
more ripely red—irresistible perdition, as her last admirer,
the Baron X., who absconded with her savings, used to
madly say—and she smiled upon the timorous intruder with
the winning grace, the encouraging tenderness, that resides
in wrinkles along a sheet of parchment.

Mr. Byde rather fancied, he began with a flattering show
of embarrassment, that this entry—or the other, just below
it—might refer to one of the friends whom they were
anxious to encounter during their passage through Paris.
The name in one case, at least, appeared to indicate the
fact — that name, there, in the curious handwriting, all
backward ; it was no uncommon name, to be sure, but at
the same time, if the gentleman was—how was he, now, in
point of age ?

Oh, that ? That was No. 19, believed the lady-president,
affably scanning the virile features of Inspector Byde.   In
one second, one little second only, she could make sure of
the fact by a reference to her own book.

Number 19? And Brother Neel's apartment was the adjoining chamber, No. 21!

Yes, it was as she had supposed, continued the quondam idol of the Baron X. The person in question occupied the No. 19. An invalid. Young. Had arrived in Paris by an early morning train, and was too feeble in health to quit his room. *Très comme-il-faut;* had behaved most generously in the matter of gratuities—at least the elderly gentleman, his friend, had behaved, on his behalf, very generously : because the elderly gentleman was relieving the shattered young invalid of all the trouble incident upon travelling, and had given in the first place all the necessary orders for him. Did monsieur think it might be his own acquaintance, this young gentleman who was ill?

Inspector Byde really shrank from again disturbing mademoiselle, but——

Comment donc, cher monsieur !—mais, comment donc ! Was she not there to answer the queries of visitors like monsieur? How she regretted that monsieur had not addressed himself earlier to the bureau for information! If she could have known, when monsieur called before, that he was seeking for some friends who had most likely stopped at the hotel—what an unfortunate oversight! It would have been so easy just to cast her eye through the register, and to save monsieur from unnecessary displacements— seeing that he had doubtless been engaged in inquiries for his acquaintance with the ordinary name; which would of course involve journeys and calls, though not outside the limits of the neighbourhood, if the acquaintance of monsieur were known to have determined to descend at some hotel in the vicinity of the Northern Terminus—it would have been so simple to have directed monsieur to this very No. 19, which was, *tenez*, just the next room to the large chamber tenanted by Monsieur Nill *là !*

The inspector resumed, in his very best composite French, that he was *désolé*—no, but, *désolé* positively—to intrude and thus monopolise the valuable time which mademoiselle——

' Ah, monsieur—too happy—— '

' Which, mademoiselle, *dont la gracieuseté*—— '

' Oh, monsieur !'

And *empressement* and kindly *égards*, joined to—might he say it—ahem !—charms of manner and——

——h—h—h !

A most superior man—oh, truly, a man of quite superior qualities ! He could not be an English, like the clod who stood in the vestibule out there, his companion. Now she looked at him, this one was certainly the better of the two ; and how could she have passed him over ? About the middle-age, this one, she should imagine : widower, from the softness of the sidelong glance: rich?

Why, there were even visitors at this actual moment in the No. 19, she responded to the question with which the inspector at length wound up—yes, visitors who had come to dinner with the young gentleman who was ill. There were—let us see how many—two, yes, two visitors to the occupant of No. 19; and they had been here some little time, seeing that covers for the three had been ordered for service in the apartment itself upstairs, at the time they were preparing to serve their *table d'hôte* downstairs, at 6.30. Would monsieur wish to send up a message to the No. 19, or possibly to go and see them? It would be so easy just to go and see : and even though they should not prove to be the acquaintances of monsieur—when you were compatriots, *n'est-ce pas ?* Perhaps, however, monsieur was not himself an English?

Mr. Byde answered rather absently that Britain was in fact his nation. Before his mental vision had loomed indistinctly the letters ' Q. E. F.' A choice of courses lay before him : which should he decide upon? ' Q. E. F.!' What magic in those characters ! He tasted his triumphs in advance ; in advance, he tasted his repose ; he saw himself already back in Camberwell ; already blissful, on a well-earned leave of absence; already lolling in his own arm-chair, with a long clay pipe in his left hand— oh, for a whiff at a sweet long clay ! and oh, for a draught of that brown old ale—whilst within prehensory distance of his right would lie the battered and discarded school - books of his boy. Mild was the effulgence of the inspector's eye. Picturing again those evening classes at the Institute (corner of the Terrace), dreamily he smiled.

The ex-beauty—alas ! she had never abdicated, she had been deposed, and it was long ago—resolved that for that smile, and for that look, the wealthy widower might be pardoned his nationality. He would undoubtedly ' ask her,' if he got into the way of coming to the hotel. She should say—yes. Well, why not? Had she not once had her apartment in the Avenue de Villiers; had she not once been the typical Parisienne (whose parents lived in the country), and had not one of the boulevard journals once rapturously described one of her midsummer toilettes, the description having been loyally paid for, notwithstanding the exorbitant tariff?

Which of the two courses ought he to follow? mused Mr. Byde, turning towards the glass partition, through which he could contemplate the physiognomy of Brother Neel.

Either a bachelor, or a widower, or divorced from his wife, that was unmistakable, argued the dowager Parisienne, ex-queen of so many emigrated subjects—some of whom had been quite respectable members of the aristocracy. Rich, also, he must no doubt be. All these *insulaires* were rich; and the richest were those who pretended to be poor. If he hadn't been unattached, he wouldn't have looked at her like that; because it was an earnest, serious look— from the heart, she thought: *bah*, why not?—the sort of look she had often slighted in the past; a very different sort of article from that other look she had likewise frequently encountered in the past, without frequently slighting it, the furtive, but, oh! quite comprehensible scintillation from the insurrectionary helot of the marriage vow. She should say —yes! Then she would find out the whereabouts of the Baron X. He had always adored her; and for his conduct there was every excuse—he had never been accustomed to be short of money. And if he had absconded with her savings, which had rolled up to a goodly sum—an unclean heap, like a huge miry snowball—had she not begun it? Had she not in the first place relieved him of the financial remnant left him by her predecessors—angels who by no happy lot could ever be entertained unawares, their enter- tainment involving riot and disorder, and their pampered appetites rejecting banquets of unleavened bread. She had plunged him into irredeemable debt, and after a time he had grown tired of living upon her mere bounty: or—no, it would be impossible that he should have eloped with some- one else! Wasn't there every excuse for him? And he was a real, real baron—no *rastaquouère !* When she had said 'Yes,' she would find him out; and how they would enjoy themselves with the money of this English—who, after all, did not seem to have more than six—*mettons* sixteen— words to say for himself! Stupid, after all, everyone of them, these insulars! All the better! She would have no difficulties to vanquish—and if he came back to the hotel for a few days! And even supposing he should be married already in his own land? Was a Parisienne to be with- stood? A little divorce case, with the wife as the petitioner, would end quite nicely for herself and for the Baron X. She bit her lower lip savagely, and smiled to show its redness off against her even teeth; forgetting that the path of time is everywhere.

What on earth could she be smiling at—this good lady? wondered the inspector.

He had decided upon his plan of action. Benjamin should be extricated from his compromising situation, if it could be done decently. The old boy might or might not have been mixed up actively in this affair; but he would try and bring him off, unless the old boy had gone too far. The inspector fancied there was not much room for doubt as to the identity of the three persons now carousing in the apartment No. 19. Ah, he should soon affix 'Q. E. F.' to the foot of the problem!

And it was in his most business-like manner—with an air which immediately took a story from the superstructure of the castle run up hastily in Spain—that the inspector ven- tured to request mademoiselle *dont l'amabilité*, etc., to send up to the No. 19 with a message. If one of the two visitors were a M. de Bingham, by hazard, there was a gentleman downstairs who desired to see him on insurance business, a gentleman from the Boulevard Haussmann.

While the commission was being executed, Mr. Byde and his two companions sought out quiet places in the dining- room. It was perhaps a proof of the inspector's absorption in his task that he allowed Mr. Thomas Toppin to direct their repast. Mr. Toppin had not borne the delay with the best grace in the world. How far could Byde have gone with this inquiry, he would like to know, if *he*, Toppin, had not been at his elbow? And here was Byde, in spite of his fine promises, keeping him down, as they all did with young fellows of promise, these men who had succeeded, when they found they had the young fellow of promise under their orders.

Byde meant to keep him out of it, now it came to the pinch, although the key to this unexpected puzzle in the affair had positively been supplied by Toppin himself.

'Let me know when I am to interrogate the Anarchist for you,' pronounced Toppin majestically.

'D——n the Anarchist,' said his superior officer.

'The Anarchist? D——n the Anarchist?'

'Yes, d——n the Anarchist; the Anarchist be d——d!' replied the inspector tranquilly; plagiarising from his miscellaneous reading a famous anathema once launched against the Queen of Carthage, daughter of Belus, King of Tyre.

'The Anarchist? Why, I thought——' Mr. Toppin's heart swelled in his bosom. No, it was not this case that would give him his chance—he should have to wait for another, he could clearly see. Another sensational robbery or murder, of direct interest to the British public? Ah, they were not so common, and he might wait a very long time before he could come across a case like this. It was hard. Young fellows of promise could get no chance. And the lack of enterprise about the criminal classes was enough to disgust you with your profession. A lot of idle, loafing vagabonds, the criminals of the present day! They had no enterprise, no energy. They wasted nearly all their time! Mr. Toppin served the soup in an extremely dismal fashion, and broke his bread as if it were a rope he was endeavouring to pull asunder.

The Vicomte de Bingham, *né* Byers, appeared at the portals of the dining-room, and looked about him for the gentleman who had called from the Boulevard Haussmann on insurance business. As he stood there, with his head back, an after-dinner satisfaction upon his cheery countenance, and with his left hand gently stroking his chin, he looked a very honest, comfortable, dignified grandpa, who liked a glass of good Burgundy, and who had just been discussing two or three.

'I love that old man,' commented the inspector, within himself. He signalled to Mr. Bingham, and grandpa approached. 'Not the movement of an eyelash, I'll take my oath,' continued the inspector mentally—'and yet to see the three of us together, he must guess the game's all up. What an artist! No I can't, I mustn't hurt him!'

Grandpa met the crisis like an artist, verily. Astonish-

ment—none ! Chagrin—none ! Alarm—demoralization ?
Not the minutest atom. He saluted with a tact in differentia-
tion that was really exquisite : cordial warmth, towards the
inspector ; towards Brother Neel, a meek urbanity ; for
Toppin, ceremonious recognition. They had all risen.

' Vicomte,' said the inspector, ' a word with you.'

He led the new-comer to a side table.

Detective Toppin could scarcely believe his ears. Vicomte !
How was it possible that this old swell should be mixed up
with the inquiry ! Vicomte ? He did not recognise him as
a secret agent of the French police !

Oh, Byde was going all wrong ! Well, let him go wrong,
then : he, Thomas Toppin, had had enough of trying to put
him right ! A pretty muddle Byde would land the case in.
He'd end by getting himself ' taken '—he would !—that's
how he'd end. That Hy, at the Prefecture, would have him
' taken,' *'cre nom!* The mirth with which this prospect
filled him, Toppin would have longed to share with Brother
Neel. They awaited silently the inspector's return ; Brother
Neel exhibiting a stony indifference to all that might be
done and said.

' Benjamin,' began Mr. Byde, as they sat out of earshot,
' get out of this while you've time.'

' Dear me ! what can you be alluding to, old friend ?'

Mr. Bingham gazed about him as though he had been
warned against an imminent conflagration—as though he
thought the flames might just be bursting through the walls.

' There's the Paris Directory just behind you ; reach
it over for me, there's a good fellow.' Mr. Bingham
obligingly complied with the request. ' You have not been
quite candid with me, Benny,' observed the inspector, as he
turned the leaves ; ' but of course we both know what
things are. Look here,' he proceeded, indicating the section
Courtiers en Bijouterie-Imitation—' under the B's of the
dealers in imitation diamonds, etc., I find the name of
Bingham, Rue des Petits Champs !'

' Yes, yes,' acquiesced grandpa, ' that's myself.'

' You didn't tell me that you combined that business with
your insurance agency.'

' Bless me—I believe that, now you mention it, I did
forget that portion of my business. Oh—a trifle, a mere
nothing ! Market not overgood.'

'The stuff you deal in isn't like the market, then.'
Inspector Byde took a small object out of his waistcoat-
pocket and handed it to Mr. Bingham. 'My compliments,
Benny. First-rate!'

Grandpa received the object imperturbably, and examined
it.

'Yes, those are my goods,' said he; 'pretty near the real
thing, hey? Cost of production low, too.'

'I borrowed it from your office when you went out in a
hurry to insure that life.'

'Ah, yes—yes! Strange thing if you hadn't put your
hand on something or other. Can't leave you Scotland
Yard gentlemen alone for half a minute; must go 'lifting'
something! Dare say you thought it was the real com-
modity?'

'I'm glad for your sake, Benny, it was *not*. We've got
to find the originals, you know—the *originals*—and I'm glad
for your sake that this was only a fair specimen of the
substituted gentlemen.'

'Good product, isn't it!' returned grandpa, closing one
eye as he again examined the imitation brilliant restored to
him. 'Sample of some new work.'

'Well, now—where are the originals, Benny?'

'My dear Byde, what on earth can you be talking about?'

'Well, I won't press you, Benjamin. I know what things
are. But satisfy me on this point: suppose we searched
you now—here—should we find a single genuine——'

'Not one,' responded Mr. Bingham with alacrity, 'not
one, even set in a ring. And you can either take my word
for it or make your search.'

'Very well. Now, if you take my advice you won't
rejoin your friends upstairs.'

'I think I should like just to step upstairs, and wish them
good evening—not to be uncivil, don't you know—little
business visit—take leave——'

'What *was* your business with them, Benny, in case of
very awkward questions, hereafter; what was your little
business?'

'Insurance—lives——'

'Bad lives; one, at any rate, if our information can be
relied upon. I think you had better not rejoin them,
Benny?'

The inspector's tone and manner were decidedly signifi-cant. Mr. Bingham hesitated, shot a keen glance at his old friend, began a response, and then checked himself. The look upon his pleasant visage was no longer cheery.

' Not ?' said he.

' I think not,' answered the inspector. ' I have got to go and see them.'

' Oh, well; if you think——! All right, then. I don't insist.'

' Come and talk to our friends, until I return,' suggested the inspector, ending the colloquy.

They went back to the dinner-table, and apparently wound up an important conference on the character of certain con-tinental banks. The inspector blamed his companions for awaiting him. He then filled a very small glass with brandy, swallowed the contents, and said he did not expect to be very long detained upstairs.

CHAPTER XIX.

The inspector had gone as far as the door, when he stopped, partially retraced his steps, and beckoned Mr. Toppin towards him. That zealous and active officer obeyed the summons with promptitude.

' Give me a quarter of an hour,' said the inspector to his subordinate. ' If I don't return by a quarter of an hour from now'—they both looked at the large clock over the mantelpiece—' come for me to No. 19—second floor.'

' Danger ?' asked Toppin, in better spirits.

' Shouldn't think so ; but in case——'

' What am I to do with this man, No. 21, the temperance swell ?'

' Either call in a policeman, show your credentials, and hand him over to the French authorities without any more fuss, or—yes, this will be the better course—tell my old friend there, the Vicomte, that it's my express wish that he should remain with Neel until one of us comes back. The Vicomte will understand it, and he'll never leave him. Yes, that will be the better course. We may as well keep the affair in our own hands. The French police can do what they like with the murder case ; but we don't want to have them meddling with the diamond robbery, which is strictly *our* business, Toppin.'

'Just so,' assented Toppin, in still better spirits; '*our* business entirely. I am quite of your opinion.'

'Then, in fifteen, or, say, twenty minutes from now.'

The inspector resumed his journey through the vestibule, to the foot of the staircase. As he slowly ascended the two flights of stairs, he summed up the eventual aspects of the Park Lane inquiry. There was absolutely no evidence against anyone. There were presumptions—oh, any number of presumptions, likelihoods, and contingent 'moral certitudes'—but when it came to finding the numerical values, as you might say, of these expressions, how the deuce were you to work them out? The inspector wished he could have brought his son Edgar with him, on this investigation. How that boy would have set to work upon his simultaneous equations of the first degree, with more than two unknown quantities!

Whether or not he succeeded presently, where was the case he could take into court? What connected the dead man, Remington, with the diamond robbery at old Stanislas Wilmot's residence in Park Lane? Young Mr. Sinclair, and the butler of the house, supposed to be the possible confederates of the deceased might be held to connect him with it. Yes; and young Mr. Sinclair would prove an *alibi*, very likely; and the butler, if apparently implicated, could get out of the position in a thousand ways, clearing the character of the deceased at the same time as he effected his own extrication. Suppose he, Byde, obtained possession of loose diamonds which would answer to the description of the property abstracted from the strong-room in Park Lane? Who was going to swear to them in court? Would Stanislas Wilmot, Esq., get into the witness-box and swear to the identity of the stones produced? Not exactly—to the satisfaction of the twelve good men and true. It reminded him of a trial he had once looked on at, in the Midlands. He must relate that story to his subordinate, when he rejoined him downstairs. With regard to the Wilmot diamond robbery, there was no mistake about it—he had no case.

It did not follow that, because he had no case, he had no prospect of recovering the actual Wilmot property. For he

certainly believed by this time that the property stolen
from the Park Lane house were genuine diamonds, of the
value represented. Any lingering doubt upon the subject
might perhaps be dispelled by careful search of Brother
Neel's luggage. He felt certain that the temperance lecturer had 'sweated' the contents of the black velvet
diamond case, that a brilliant or two—or three—or four—
might be discovered in some corner of that gentleman's
portmanteau, or in the lining of some garment, newly sewn.
It was just possible that he was on the right track of the
missing valuables; but he did not see a tangible case for a
jury, so far. When *he* took cases into court he got convic-
tions. It was his reputation for always clinching the
evidence, all round, that had made his failure in that great
temperance prosecution so terrible a blow. He could not
risk his credit this time on the flimsiest of circumstantial
claims. He'd get the property back, and ask no questions.

And Brother Neel, of the I.O.T.A.! Was he, Byde, to
lose this precious opportunity of wiping out that blunder
which these temperance people brought up on the least
occasion? He had hoped to hit them very hard indeed
through Brother Neel.

Would he not be justified in indicating Brother Neel to
the French police? Let him go and tell them such a tale as
he had told Inspector Byde that evening, in the presence of
Toppin! What would the Sûreté here think about it, and
what would be their practical response? Ha!—a pretty
narrative, would be their comment, to explain the possession
of an object which had avowedly been taken from the
murdered man! Well—did he, George Byde, of the V
Division, believe that narrative? To be quite frank upon
the matter—hang it, bias apart!—yes, he did.

Brother Neel had stated that he could furnish no detail
tending to identify the murderer; and it redounded to his
credit, thought the inspector, that he had committed himself
to nothing which might inculpate another individual,
although he must have entertained suspicions, however
slight, coinciding with those entertained by the inspector.
Besides, if he, George Byde, should one of these days find
it feasible to cancel that sign——with that +, he wished to
do it unassisted, with his own weapons, in a straightforward
way. He did not want his colleagues, anywhere, to strike

his retaliatory blow for him. It would be sweet to strike that blow, mused this vindictive inspector, of Division V— very sweet, afterwards, to quote Coriolanus to Aufidius, though not to die immediately thereupon.

Number 19. The inspector used no ceremony. There was the handle of the door; he turned the handle, pushed the door open, stepped across the threshold, and closed the door again behind him. The two occupants of the room were lounging in easy-chairs before the hearth; and from the cigars they held screwed into the corners of their mouths ascended thin blue wreaths of an exceeding fragrance.

'Well, who was your friend, Byers?' demanded Sir John, with a patronising drawl. Neither he nor his companion turned, or looked up, as the door closed.

'Grandpa's particular, that he's engaged to, I'll lay a thousand,' observed Mr. Finch—'oh, the forward young woman!'

'Now, my lads,' began the inspector briskly; and at the sound of his voice they both sprang from their seats—'I dare say you both know *me* !'

Sir John muttered an oath, pitched his cigar into the fire-place, and gathered himself together with an unmistakable air of menace. The violence of his movement had been such that the cigar scattered the white ashes along the side of the log-fire.

'Do *you* know the gentleman, Alfred?' inquired Mr. Finch innocently.

'Not I !' growled his companion with another oath.

'Blest if *I* do !' proceeded Mr. Finch. 'Made a mistake in the room, sir, ain't you?'

'Now what's this game, my lads?' went on the inspector. 'Come, out with it !—You, Vine, stay where you are ! Don't you advance another step. I've come prepared for *you* !'

'Be quiet, Alfred—stand back,' urged Mr. Finch mildly— 'I'm sure this gentleman isn't a robber.'

'To what do we owe the pleasure——' demanded Sir John, his face set, and his steady gray eyes shining very curiously.

'Ah, I see you know what I've come about,' said the inspector sternly. 'You, Bartholomew Finch, *alias* Walker, I've not had you through my hands yet; but be careful how

you behave. As for you, Ernest Vine, *alias* Grainger, I
remember you well enough, and you remember me. It
depends upon your conduct at this instant where you pass
the night. Now, then, be straightforward, and save me
trouble. If you are straightforward, I dare say we can
give you a fresh start. If you fence, you are in the
custody of the French police to-night, as sure as you're
alive.'

' Why, now I look at him it *is*—it's Mr. Byde ! Beg
pardon, Mr. Byde, sir, didn't recognise you.'

Mr. Finch uttered these words with the most convincing
air of pleased surprise.

' In the custody of the French police ? On what charge,
I should like to know ?'

' The charge of murder.'

' Murder !' echoed Sir John, with a defiant laugh, but his
voice faltering. ' Why, you are joking with us !'

' Yes, that's it,' said Mr. Finch cheerfully—' he's joking,
Mr. Byde is—ha ! ha ! A d——d queer joke, though,
Ernest.'

' And a —— dangerous joke, I give you the tip !' In Sir
John's extremity, the genteel veneer which ladies nearly
always took for good breeding disappeared. The ruffian
suddenly asserted himself. ' Murder—eh ?' said he with a
ferocious sneer. ' And where's the —— victim ?'

' The victim lies at the Morgue,' replied the inspector
rapidly. ' Once more, stay where you are, or I'll bring you
down !—You travelled in the night-mail from London with
him—and with me. You followed him from place to place
until you got to Amiens. Just after leaving Creil you
climbed along the footboard of the carriage until you came
to his compartment, and you shot him as he lay there
dozing, and before he could defend himself. Then you
took a packet from his breast-pocket. In that packet were
loose diamonds, which can be identified. It's for those
diamonds I've come to see you now, for I know they are in
this room !'

There was a pause.

' This is pretty hot,' observed Mr. Finch. ' It's not true,
Jack, is it ?'

' True ? Haven't I told you just what happened ! The
thing was done before I got there, and the pocket was

empty. You'll bring me down, will you, Mr. Inspector Byde? By —— I'll charge you with this murder myself! I'll swear I saw you do it, and Bat here will back me up.'

'Me?' protested Mr. Finch — 'me? No, sir — no perjury for Bartholomew! Not for Bartholomew, Mr. Wilkins!'

'No more of this nonsense,' pursued the inspector. 'I'm sure of my witness, Vine. I've got the man who interrupted you.' The speaker flashed the look at Sir John, which, during his interview with Brother Neel, the latter had twice or thrice encountered. 'That temperance fellow told us the truth, by the Lord Harry!' was Mr. Byde's mental pronouncement.

'That won't do,' returned Vine, *alias* Grainger, doggedly. 'Lock me up if you're sure of your witness; and we'll see what he'll prove. We'll charge your witness with it, that's how we'll reward your witness. Where's this property, then, you talk about? Have I ever had it: is your witness going to prove that it has ever been in my possession? Suppose we guessed at your witness; suppose we told you where to put your hands upon the packet you're looking for; suppose it was your witness who had put that packet in that place; what sort of a case would be left to you, Mr. Inspector Byde, with your witness who knows all about it? Ah?—what sort of a case?'

'That's it!' approved Mr. Finch, winking with a very astute expression, and wagging his head. 'You're on the wrong scent, Mr. Byde, take my word for it, sir. Not but that I will not say—that—if—we liked to speak out—hey, Jack——?'

'Yes—if we liked to speak out'—echoed Sir John slowly.

'We know what we *have* remarked, don't we, Jack? We *have* formed certain suspicions — as to — certain parties——'

'That travelled by the same train — a certain party——'

'As had a good deal to say to the deceased—on the way down—a d——d sight too much to say to be cocum, if you ask *me;* and, if my memory serves me'—it was an air of enrapturing guilelessness, the air with which Finch, *alias* Walker, consulted his memory—' yes, I did !—I made that observation to you at the moment, Ernest ?'

' You did,' acquiesced Sir John, watching the inspector.

' Give me the man that likes his two of gin,' proceeded Mr. Finch absently. ' These temperance Kaffirs ! Wouldn't trust the king of them all with change for a sovereign ! No, sir—not me ! That I wouldn't !'

' Pretty nearly done ?' asked the inspector sharply. ' Come to the point, my lads ; I've only got a few more minutes to give you. Out with that property. I don't want to know how you came by it ; I'll avoid putting any question, either now or hereafter, if you conduct yourselves like sensible lads ; but that property is in this room, and that property I must have. Now I know your school : you are boys from Tudor Street. Show yourselves worthy of your school—show yourselves lads of sense. You're licked to-day. Throw the sponge up !'

' Shall we stand this, Bat ?' growled Vine, *alias* Grainger.

' My goodness me,' murmured Mr. Finch—' I can't think what Mr. Byde's alludin' to !'

' For the last time '—went on the inspector very quietly —' put those —— diamonds on that table ! In another minute you will be too late. My colleague, with the French police at his back, will be knocking at this door in another minute. You know what that means. It means that you are both searched on the spot, the room ransacked, too, and that you are both locked up in a French prison for putting that man out, and robbing him of the diamonds which we know he had in his possession. It's the guillotine for both of you—or, at least, they'll send you both away for life.'

' What have I done, Mr. Byde, sir ?' protested Mr. Finch.

' What do I care ?' returned the inspector, with a sort of grim tranquillity. ' If, on the other hand, you behave sensibly, I give you my word I'll say no more about the matter. My business is to take that property back to England, and I intend to take it back. And that's all. You've been minding it for me, you understand. You were not the original thieves ; and what has happened upon French territory concerns the French.'

' Jack,' observed Mr. Finch to his companion, ' very likely

Mr. Byde is alludin' to that little parcel which we picked up in the street.'

There was no answer. Vine, *alias* Grainger, and Inspector Byde stood looking at each other for an instant or two in silence. The one was manifestly weighing the chances of a sudden onslaught; the other manifestly held himself prepared.

' It won't pay you this time,' said the inspector at length simply. ' Another day, Vine.'

' You know, Jack, that little parcel which we picked up while we were out walking on the bullyvards.'

' Byers, Bingham, or whatever he calls himself, has it,' replied Sir John sullenly.

' He's in detention downstairs in case we want to search him. But I know what I am about; and I begin with you. —Come !'

Vine, alias Grainger, brusquely plunged his hand into a ready pocket—the deep breast-pocket of a loose frock coat. For a moment, in that attitude he stood immovable. . . . The suspense—the gesture ? . . . On the countenances of the two spectators an identical thought called up oddly-contrasted expressions. It was Mr. Finch, however, who exhibited alarm.

' Jack !' he shouted, in a tone of warning.

Whether or not more than a single object lay within the dark recesses of that loose breast-pocket, the object which Sir John wrenched with an effort from its depths appeared to be not that which the two spectators had with differing sensations anticipated. His right hand grasped a canvas bag, tightly fastened, and he banged this ' little parcel ' on the table in front of him, as he had previously hurled into the log fire his unoffending, fragrant cigar. The contents emitted a slight rattle, like pebbles. Before an observation could be proffered, there was a knock at the door.

' My colleague,' announced the inspector ; ' you see I told you the truth. We need not let him into our affairs, and he can wait outside.'

He opened the door a little way; but it was not Mr. Toppin who had knocked.

' Well !' demanded the inspector gruffly, of the person outside.

A few French words ensued, of surly apology. Yes, re-turned the inspector, in his Bordeaux accent, the sick

gentleman of No. 19 certainly was at that juncture engaged
with visitors ; go away, and come back later ! The service
of the apartment? It could not be attended to just then,
the apartment : *allez-vous-en faire votre service ailleurs.*
' Oh, there you are, Toppin,' added the inspector, as his
colleague now approached along the corridor. ' Send this
Anarchist savage about his business, and guard the entrance. You needn't come in. I mustn't be disturbed for a
little while.'

Closing the door again behind him, he observed the precaution of turning the key in the lock inside.

' That's in your interest, my lads,' he remarked, tapping
the key. ' You've shown your sense in being straightforward, and I shall keep my word. It will be your own
fault if you make my colleague's acquaintance.'

Sir John moved back to the hearth, and sank into his
easy-chair again. As he sat there, restlessly pulling at his
moustache, and scowling at the pictures which his mind's
eye imagined in the flames that sprang out fitfully from the
half-charred logs, Inspector Byde advanced towards the
round table, and picked up the securely-tied canvas bag.
The inspector had to use his penknife, for the knots were
perfectly Gordian.

' A lucky thing we happened to be passing,' ventured Mr.
Finch ; ' a lucky thing we happened to notice it. There it
was, just lying on the pavement, the edge of the pavement ;
and you wouldn't have thought it was anything at all ! I
said to Jack, "Jack," I said, "what's that?" I said,
" Looks like a tobacco-pouch," I said ; and Jack said——'

The inspector poured forth the contents of the canvas
bag. Oh, marvellous, indeed ! A blazing prism lay before
him. One of the charred logs in the open fireplace gave
way under the weight of fresher fuel, and from the new logs,
hissing and crackling, a bright red flame shot up, broad,
steady, and ardent. The dazzling heap of pebbles which
the inspector had poured forth seemed to seize and intensify
that sudden red flame—to break it up into innumerable
sparks, vivid in their play of hue, and surely little short of
ignescent.

' The genuine article, and no mistake,' ran Mr. Byde's
mental comment ; ' what quality, and how they're cut !
Phew ! Not so big as to be identified easily, but, by the

Lord Harry, quite big enough to go to Portland for! And as to the value of the whole lot—under-estimated by forty per cent.! The old story. They do think that they are so clever, these people in the trade! They think it's clever, some of them, to under-state their loss, in any case like this—they fancy they can get the property restored on easier terms from the thieves. Yes, when you can get the thieves into negotiations—nice and confidential negotiations —through some third person's third friend's third wife.'

' And that's how it was we went and picked it up,' concluded Mr. Finch. 'Lucky we saw it. Somebody else might have come that way the very next minute, picked it up, and said nothing whatever about the discovery. Jack and I thought we'd advertise it. Best thing to do, wasn't it? We were talking about an advertisement in the newspapers just when you called in. Lucky you called, Mr. Byde—being acquainted with the rightful owners. Ah, it's a load off my mind! And it's quite upset poor old Jack, here!'

The inspector counted the stones, and replaced them in the canvas bag. Having secured the little package to his satisfaction, he deposited it in one of his own pockets protected with a row of buttons.

'Just come here a second, Finch,' he then remarked, ' I want you to hold this candle for me.'

Mr. Finch obeyed the request without any sign of wonder. Sir John, however, wheeled round in his chair, for an explanation of the words. The speaker had held one of the candlesticks above his head, and was now terminating a scrutiny of the entire apartment. He noted the three doorways, the alcove, and the windows; and oft and benignantly he nodded. And why? Behind him lay the entrance from the corridor. In front of him were the windows; to his immediate left stood the alcove and the hearth; and, to the right and left of the windows were apparently doorways communicating with apartments upon each side, beyond.

' Well, it was no guess-work—that I can truthfully say,' pronounced the inspector in a soft voice, and with a sigh of content; ' it was a scientific process of induction.'

' Ah,' ejaculated Mr. Finch, to show his politeness, in the brief pause that followed—' Ah, now?'

' Scientific induction did it!'

Mr. Finch wrinkled up his chin by effacing its angle, and turned to his confederate with a puzzled air.

'And if we would only learn to bring scientific induction into all this work,' mused the inspector aloud, 'not many cases would go wrong!'

Mr. Finch coughed deferentially.

'Excuse me, Mr. Byde, sir,' he insinuated, 'but if he's one of the officers at the Yard—one of the divisional inspectors—perhaps—if you didn't mind—we should like to know his name and his division, if I'm not taking a liberty, sir——'

'Eh?' responded the inspector, roused; '"he?"—who?'

'The party you was alludin' to, sir—the artful one—you'll excuse me, Mr. Byde; no offence, I hope?—the party that you'd like to bring into this work—Cy——'

'Oh, you mean my old friend Scientific Induction, Esquire,' exclaimed the inspector good-humouredly. 'No, Master Finch, I fear you'd put the Tudor Street school on to him, and block him!'

'Well, it's no use trying to put the double on with *you*, Mr. Byde, sir,' replied Mr. Finch, with a good-humour equal to the inspector's; 'and there's no mistake: we *should* have try.'

The inspector led the way to the closed and curtained door communicating with the chamber at his right hand, No. 21. He entrusted the candlestick to Mr. Finch, and proceeded to remove the light article of furniture which stood against the curtain, a plain sheet of chintz. This done, he called his neighbour's attention to the fact that the curtain ended at the space of a foot from the floor. Had not Mr. Finch found the room draughty? Not at all, Mr. Finch assured him. The inspector went down on his knees, and asked for a match.

'Don't think there's such a thing about the place,' declared Mr. Finch.

'Oh, I've some of my own,' replied the inspector, 'but I want one of the right sort—one of yours—the matches that last a devil of a time and don't make any noise when you strike 'em! It's odds you've got some on you!' he urged jocosely.

'Right you are,' said Mr. Finch, with equanimity, pro-

ducing half-a-dozen noiseless matches from his waistcoat
pocket.

'There's your boulevard,' resumed the inspector, passing
the flame of the match along the flooring, at the bottom of
the door; ' there's the edge of your pavement. You forgot
this line of dust, my lads. See how you disturbed it!
Anybody can see it's quite freshly disturbed.'

'Where?' protested Mr. Finch stoutly.

Sir John interposed, speaking from the other side of the
room.

'It's no use denying it,' said he calmly; ' Inspector Byde
has found the road out. All's well that ends well. This
ought to convince you, inspector, that we could have stood
out, if we had liked. I don't blame you for threatening us,
to force our hands and wind the affair up sharp, but still, to
threaten us with the charge of murder, and the guillotine,
was coming it strong, inspector, wasn't it.'

'A bit strong, perhaps,' concurred the inspector, rising
from his knees, and returning to the middle of the room.

Mr. Finch restored the candlestick to its place.

'Not to keep anything back,' pursued Sir John; ' we
recognised you in the train, before it started from London.
Even if we had come on business, was it likely that we
should have tried at anything, with a passenger from Scotland
Yard about us, especially when that passenger was *you* ?'

'Not very likely !' exclaimed Mr. Finch.

'But we *hadn't* come on business. We'd come for a little
holiday and change of air, and it's very unfortunate that
circumstances should have made appearances awkward for
us. But we know that *you're* not one of the gentlemen who
are misled by appearances ; and the fact is, we mean to cut
the Tudor Street school, and turn over a new leaf—don't
we, Bat ?'

'We do,' answered Mr. Finch.

'And, therefore, now you have found out how that
property came into our possession, and we've admitted that
you are right—and you have pledged your word, on consideration of our behaving in a straightforward manner—
that ends the whole matter, doesn't it? I mean that of
course it's quite clear we can't in any way be mixed up with
the case you threatened us with—the murder ?'

'Oh, that's not my business,' returned Inspector Byde; 'my mission ended with this'—he tapped the buttoned pocket containing the canvas bag. 'We shall have the identity of the victim established by a colleague of mine, and the body will then be removed from the Morgue, for burial here, or for transit to London. No doubt the friends of the deceased will pay the necessary charges, and have the coffin sent on from here. As for the murderer, the French police may either shelve the case as *classée*, or get hold of somebody or other who had nothing to do with it, and cut his head off; but against the real perpetrator of the crime there does not seem to me to be—and of course I know something, although its a French affair, and doesn't concern me personally—the smallest piece of evidence that could be put before a jury.'

'But the man next door, No. 21—the man we got this from?' demanded Sir John, rather eagerly.

'Ah! the temperance party, Mr. Byde, that had so much to say, and that had the property by him, afterwards?'

Mr. Finch appeared to be asking himself why the inspector could not immediately add two and two together, and, without any fuss at all about it, make the sum total at once four.

'Brother Neel, of the International Organization of Total Abstainers?' Inspector Byde uttered these words slowly, but with no undue emphasis. 'Whoever murdered that English traveller by the night-mail from London, I *know* that the man Neel could not have been the murderer.' He turned the key in the lock. 'A last word, my lads,' he added facetiously; if you'd like to go back to-morrow with me, say so, you know! Anything to oblige two boys who've shown so much good sense. What do *you* say, Finch—Bartholomew Finch, *alias* Walker? There's nothing against you just now, I believe; will you go back with me to-morrow?'

'You'll excuse me, Mr. Byde, but—no thank you! Go back with you, sir? No; not exactly—you'll excuse me. Why, what would people say if they saw Bat Finch a-travelling with Inspector Byde? It would be a disgrace for life; I'd lose my character. I never could get over it! Not me, Mr. Wilkins—no, sir!'

'And you, Vine?' asked the inspector pleasantly; 'will *you* keep me company to-morrow? The 8.20 a.m. train from the Gare du Nord, Calais and Dover, due Holborn Viaduct at 5.33 p.m., or in Victoria—which would be handier for you—at 5.30. It's the morning mail from Paris.'

'I would accompany you with very much pleasure, indeed,' replied Sir John, with his most elaborate drawl; 'but I am positively over for a holiday, and may run down to the South. Thanks all the same for your kind offer.'

He had overcome his rage and disappointment, there could hardly be a doubt about it; he had recovered his assurance and his superfine genteel veneer. This was no longer the foul-mouthed desperado of vile origin, whose aliases had been recorded in the Golden Square case of two years ago; this was the man whose criminal associates, and whose pariah female patrons, in their admiration, nick-named him The Honourable (with sometimes a strong aspirate) or Sir John.

Here he stood, liar and swindler—faithless, extortionate, and spendthrift—a good-looking fellow, well-built, well-dressed, and, when the pinch came, quite the last man to be called a coward: here he swaggered—the specious knave whom the most wise among the fair had always helped and liked; who never told them they were less than perfect; and who never sought them but for purposes of aggrandize-ment. When he passed a season at some fashionable resort, his surreptitious triumphs among the more exclusive sets became perfectly amazing from the moment the cold shoulder had been turned upon him by cousins, brothers, and lovers.

His most remarkable victory, though an unremunerative one, he grumbled, had been gained at Scarborough just before the Golden Square case. He had irretrievably com-promised a professional coquette (a failure on the stage, though honoured by the notice, and, as it was understood, by the personal favours of—well, go to, no matter for the dish—the least said soonest mended), who had upon that untoward incident vanished from the public scene, with —among other good deeds—a separation, two divorces, an attempt at suicide, and four great bankruptcies to her credit.

Sir John's gentility and splendid impudence had, on much worthier occasions, thrust aside plain merit or refinement. His social 'form' electrified the Tudor Street school, when they recognised their swell mobsman in the Row, at Epsom, at Ascot, or at Goodwood. It was a joke among themselves that now and then they journeyed by excursion trains to fashionable 'fixtures' out of town, for the object, and for that alone, of feasting their eyes upon the grandeur of Sir John. In immediate contact with them, he maintained his 'form' uneasily; and he certainly ought not to have indulged in it with any representative of Scotland Yard. Yet, with a swagger, he now stood drawling his responses to Inspector George Byde, of the V Division; surveying that experienced officer, by the Lord Harry, through an eyeglass!

'My lads,' concluded the inspector, on whom such manifestations were always lost — 'we start clear from this evening : keep out of my way.' In another instant, he was gone.

Mr. Toppin informed his colleague, as together they retraced their steps, that he had adopted the precaution of just speaking to a French plain-clothes man, in a friendly way, to watch the temperance gentleman downstairs, whilst he himself should happen to be absent. He had noticed the plain-clothes man hanging about at the end of the street, and fancied he would do well to enlist his temporary services ; seeing that the Vicomte, Mr. Byde's elderly friend—and here Mr. Toppin glanced at the inspector dubiously—had altogether failed to comprehend him when he, Mr. Toppin, tipped him the office, gave him the hint, and tendered him the cue. In fact, that old buck would not stay in their society at all.

'What, he's left you?' demanded the inspector, startled, notwithstanding his conviction that he had fully grasped the entire case, and that no issue remained over unaccounted for. Yes, he had left them, but he had promised to come back for a chat with Mr. Byde by the time the latter had dined. Before quitting the hotel he had appeared to be gossiping with the lady in the bureau. He, Mr. Toppin, should say that the old chap had created an impression in that quarter.

'You look pale, inspector,' added Mr. Toppin inquisitively.

The inspector said he felt he wanted an underdone beefsteak and a pint of good stout in a cool tankard.

'You can't get that here,' observed Mr. Toppin.

'No ; but this time to-morrow I'll be drinking your health, friend Toppin, in the finest stout in the borough of Westminster. And I'll be dining off a British beefsteak at the 'Silver Gridiron,' where there's a draught from every door and window, and sawdust on the ground.'

'To-morrow, inspector ! Then you go back——?'

'By the morning-mail, 8.20 from the Northern Terminus.'

'How's the case, then ?' asked Toppin anxiously.

'All over but shouting, my boy ! The genuine property goes back with me to-morrow, and within three days you'll get a letter of commendation from the Yard.'

'Shall I, inspector ? You'll report——?'

'I'll do the right thing by you, Toppin ; you'll have no cause to complain of my report. I don't forget how you've helped me through.'

'Mr. Byde, sir——' began his subordinate with emotion.

'That's all right,' continued the inspector, 'I see what it is ; you only want a little encouragement.'

'That's all, Mr. Byde, that's all, I assure you,' declared Toppin eagerly. 'A little encouragement—that's just it !'

At the foot of the staircase the inspector checked his companion.

'Now here's a minor part of the inquiry you can deal with by yourself,' said he. 'The Wilmot diamonds are now in my pocket—all of them, we'll suppose, except, perhaps, two or three or four. I rather imagine that those two or three or four may be met with in room No. 21, hidden away somewhere, under lock and key. Take the man Neel upstairs with you, and find them.'

Brother Neel barely deigned to move as they rejoined him. On being apprised of Mr. Toppin's errand, however, his perturbation became evident to at any rate one pair of penetrating eyes. Outraged virtue protested in his tone ;

the honour and dignity of the I.O.T.A. confronted a traducer, in his phrasing and his magnificent pose. How he did sublimely cast those long, unparted oily locks back from his noble brow—the platform gesture of a million oratorical mountebanks! Oh, the generous fire of that regard, and oh, the leonine head!

The inspector looked on like a very wicked old Grimalkin, whose mere aspect at this moment should have cured any unctuous, tub-thumping Grand Worthy Master or brother of the I.O.T.A. of any incipient tendency towards moral turpitude.

At length alone, the inspector set about his late meal in good earnest. His subordinate officer and Brother Neel remained longer absent than he had anticipated.

When Mr. Toppin reappeared, he was unaccompanied by the lecturer.

'Nothing!' he exclaimed excitedly; 'found the lock of his portmanteau forced when he got upstairs. "The Anarchist, for a thousand," said I. "Haven't the least cognizance of your meaning, my dear friend," said he. And here it is! he won't admit that the lock has been forced—d——d glad he is that it *has* been forced! Of course I searched, and of course there was nothing. But I'm after the Anarchist now! He's done his work and gone home it seems; and I'll be after him, if I take a streetfull of the police to get the stones for you by to-morrow morning—or perhaps to-night.'

'No, not to-night, Toppin—I want a good night's rest, and I shall turn in early. Before 8.20 to-morrow morning, at the Gare du Nord. And, by the way, I want you particularly to see me off. You had better come to my hotel first. I expect to be followed on the way back to London, and I want you to watch the station here.'

The inspector escorted Mr. Toppin to the vestibule. Grandpa had returned to the hotel bureau, and was gossiping more than affably with its lady-president. Grandpa's gallantry of manner grew with each compliment he rounded, and with each compliment more melting grew the widowed maid.

'Wonderful old boy,' murmured the inspector. 'They'd make a nice old couple, too!'

But the inspector here, at any rate, misread the manifestations. Grandpa was reflecting—

'Clever woman—knows the world—must look in soon and offer a commission—directly Byde's out of the way. Could put a lot of business into our hands, this wide-awake old rosebud here!'

'The lady was reflecting—

'*Mais il est charmant, ma chère—charmant—mais charmant, ce vieux monsieur! D'un galant! D'une distinction!* There are then Englishmen like this? What courtly grace, and what adorable simplicity! His foreign accent not too harsh —piquant, when you get accustomed to it—*oui, ma chère— et puis, un vicomte!* The usage of the best world! And so I should be *vicomtesse?* The Baron X. will be so glad to hear of this! And when he knows I'm rich and married he's certain to come to me again!'

'You think, then, you'll be followed back to-morrow?' inquired Toppin seriously. 'They'll have another try?'

'I hope so,' answered the inspector. 'I've laid the trap!'

CHAPTER XX.

INSPECTOR BYDE had noted down so many points for his brief conference with Toppin on the following day, prior to his own departure from Paris, that he had intended to rise somewhat early, in the hope that (Mr. Toppin being a young man who was never punctual to his appointments, but always vexatiously in advance) half an hour or so might be available for the discussion of some hitherto unattempted theorems. He did rise early—earlier than he had intended. An unexpected caller sent his card up at an untimely hour. The inspector was still wrapped in the refreshing sleep which no doubt blesses 'virtue's votary' quite as often as it recompenses vice, after the 'pleasures of a well-spent day,' when a discreet knocking at his chamber door roused him at 6.12. It was one of the hotel servants, who struggled out of his bed every morning to meet the arrivals by the English mail.

The gentleman who sent this card up to monsieur, explained the servant apologetically, would not wait a single instant. He was a gentleman in a hurry to see monsieur: a foreigner: had luggage with him: not much luggage, but——the candle? to bring in the candle? certainly, monsieur—the dawn not breaking at this season of the year until close upon —— was it that he was alone, the traveller? Apparently the traveller was alone: but peremptory—in a hurry to send his name up to monsieur.

' Mr. A. W. Sinclair,' read the inspector, by the light of the candle.

Yes, there were the characters—Mr. A. W. Sinclair. Information against him must have broken down, then? No case whatever, that was evident! In his heart of hearts the inspector could not repress a certain feeling of surprise that so much promptitude in releasing this innocent person should have been employed by, as he phrased it with habitual caution, the powers that be. It might have been found that not the slightest justification could be adduced for the information laid by old Stanislas Wilmot; the wrongful detention had been shown to be a glaring instance of wrong, etc., etc.; and notwithstanding all that—well, did he not understand the way they went along, too many of them?— and did he not know how easily the magistrates of police courts could be led into conceding unfair postponements and remands, prejudicially though these might affect the prisoner, and warranted only by impressionist conjecture, mere ' appearances?' He should say, whatever might be the resources Mr. Sinclair had controlled, that the young gentleman was to be congratulated on getting out of this Park Lane affair so soon. Strange, all the same, that he himself should have received no word by telegram of the release. Inspector Byde looked at his watch, gave the servant a direction, locked the door again, satisfied himself once more as to the safety of the packet in his temporary charge, and plunged his head into a basin of cold water.

The visitor, who was ushered upstairs after the short interval ordered by Mr. Byde, addressed the latter in a cheery voice, at once recalling to his mind the night of the arrest on Dover platform. A suspicion as to the genuineness of this card bearing the name of Mr. Sinclair had, to tell the truth, occurred to the inspector, and before admit-

ting his caller, he had gone back to the heavily-curtained
bedstead to possess himself of two small objects, reposing
well out of view, but well within the sleeper's reach, underneath the pillow.

He had never seen this Mr. Sinclair. The frank accents,
however, that now fell upon his ears were undoubtedly
those which had so firmly and distinctly replied to the condolences offered by the dead man Remington—the false
condolences of the very man who, at the moment of his
uttering them, had the stolen Wilmot diamonds in his own
possession.

'You will know me by name, I dare say, Mr. Byde,'
began the visitor, with no trace of either chagrin or resent-
ment—' at least, when I tell you that I am just in from Dover,
and that the supposed case against me altogether collapsed,
you will know where to place me in connection with your
present business here. They told me at Dover that I might
do well to give you a call immediately on arriving in Paris,
and that coincided with my own desire. They fancied, for
some reason or other, that you might be leaving for Amsterdam, or elsewhere, the very first thing this morning—if you
had not, in fact, already gone away. If I would be good
enough to do so, they said, I was to report myself to Mr.
Byde, Terminus Hotel—I was to report myself and my
release at once. And as I had heard by telegram of your very
great kindness to friends of mine here, I was particularly
anxious to intercept you.'

He added a few simple words of thanks, naming only Mrs.
Bertram in reference to his friends; and then expressed a
perfectly impartial hope for the inspector's early and complete success in the investigation.

It was too bad to intrude upon him at such an hour; but,
apart from the suggestion submitted to him with great
courtesy at Dover, Mr. Sinclair had wished to know without delay what news the inspector might be able to give
him of the friends he had spoken of—the friends residing in
the Avenue Marceau. Of course he could not present himself there yet awhile. He had wired to them, definitively,
last evening; and no doubt they were in expectation of his
arrival. Had the inspector heard at all from the Avenue
Marceau, late last night?

Packing his valise with the celerity of a practised campaigner, the inspector answered this and other tentative
queries in a manner which indicated to his guest that he
was substantially cognisant of the tie that bound Mr. Austin
Sinclair to Miss Knollys. Their mutual avoidance of the
young lady's name only brought into greater prominence her
passive share in the determination of Mr. Sinclair's recent
fortunes.

It was Mr. Sinclair himself who eventually pronounced
her name. He did so with an effort, as though shrinking
from an act equivalent to desecration; but, having once
broken silence with regard to her, he spoke of no one but
Miss Adela Knollys to the inspector.

Sincerely, how had she borne the news of his disgrace?
The inspector had visited at the Avenue Marceau, and had
seen both ladies since: how had Miss Knollys appeared to
view the frightful humiliation he had undergone—the
shame of a suspected criminality, the blemish of imprisonment?

'I am afraid—I am afraid,' continued this young fellow,
with a very honest blush, and his voice beginning to
tremble; 'I was confident and steady enough until it was
all over, but then—well, by Jove, inspector, I couldn't help
fearing for the moral consequences—you know—as a man
of the world——'

The inspector shut down the top of his valise, and stood
upright again.

'I tell you what it is, Mr. Sinclair,' said he, ' and having
been honoured by the confidence of that young lady, I may
perhaps have had fairly good opportunities for judging—you
are an extremely fortunate young gentleman, sir!'

The visitor sprang to his feet and grasped Inspector Byde
by the hand.

The inspector had been seeking for symptoms of the ' per-
emptoriness ' reported to him, but had sought for them in
vain. On a closer examination he fancied he could detect a
considerable store of the decision of character to which he
had heard Mrs. Bertram make allusion.

This was a fellow, thought the inspector, who would
grapple with difficulties, and no mistake; although this was
also a fellow in whom a great deal of sentiment, don't you

know, existed side by side with heaps of silent energy—not the commonest of co-ordinates. It was to be remarked that the inspector phrased it ' sentiment,' not ' sentimentality,' and that—a man of the world, as Mr. Sinclair had observed —he did not in the least appear to look upon sentiment as either effeminate, or ridiculous, or in any conceivable fashion · bad form.' He judged according to his humble lights, did he not? And what is more, as a man of the world, he might have been found excusing even sentimentality. In his professional explorations of human nature he had so often traversed arid, flat, unhorizoned, monotonous wastes.

A few words enlightened the inspector as to the circumstances of Mr. Sinclair's release. That gentleman had not merely proved his own *alibi*, he told Mr. Byde ; he had incidentally furnished clues to the actual perpetrators of the Park Lane diamond robbery.

On and about the date of the robbery, he was attending the last moments of an aged relative, by whom he had been hastily summoned from London. His relative lived at Chelmsford, and so far as the *alibi* was concerned, it was complete. With the knowledge which he, Mr. Sinclair, had of Stanislas Wilmot's personal disposition, as well as of his business enterprises, he had had no difficulty in at once comprehending the real bearings of his own case.

That being so, while quietly submitting to the arrest, he had lost no time in assailing Mr. Wilmot through a certain channel of private influences—irresistible influences, by Jove! Wilmot had rushed down post-haste to Scotland Yard to retract his information, inasmuch as it affected his former secretary. And there they had talked to him rather sternly.

The thing might be made exceedingly unpleasant for old Stanislas Wilmot if he, Mr. Sinclair, chose to go on with it. But any measures of retaliation would infallibly bring before the public gaze at least one other name than theirs, and to avoid such an eventuality as that, he would be willing to resign himself to much more than had actually been visited upon him. Wilmot had sent a special messenger to Dover with an apology that might have satisfied the most exacting of individuals.

Mr. Sinclair laughed cheerily as he said this. What did

it matter to him, he added tranquilly, if he had not fallen
in the esteem of the sole person whose esteem he cared
about ! The testamentary appointment of Stanislas Wilmot
as the guardian of Miss Knollys vested powers in that
gentleman which could be rendered little short of despotic
during the legal infancy of his ward.

He, Mr. Sinclair, had not wished to involve Miss Adela
Knollys in large financial losses by any precipitate action of
his own ; at the same time, he had very keenly felt the
possible reproach that he was ready enough to wait until
she could come into the possession of her independent
means. It might have been feasible to upset the will on
the ground of undue influence.

However, matters had turned out satisfactorily. Wilmot
had ventured too far. Having by degrees shut his ward off
from all society except that of a few queer City associates
and their showy wives—whom the young lady, obeying her
instinct, had ultimately refused to meet—he had ended by
making her virtually his prisoner. She had been obliged to
quit the Park Lane house almost by stealth.

'She preceded me here,' concluded Mr. Sinclair—' and
sent me word she had done so : and of course I came on—
when that little interruption took place at Dover. I talk
freely to you, inspector, because I can see you are a good
fellow, and because, in the matter of confidences, you gentlemen exercise sometimes the sort of rights exercised by the
medical man. Besides, you have been very kind to her—I
know that from a message. Well, by Jove, look here—I
am not worthy of that splendid girl !'

'Yes, you are,' thought the inspector, watching him ;
although, as the reader does not need to be reminded, he
had himself been subjugated by the charm ; in which state
of mind, whether the homage be ' paternal,' or in the
strictest sense the converse of Platonic, the vassal frequently
exhibits the fiercest scorn for any fellow-slave who would
approach too near.

'I had not seen my relative for some years,' continued
Mr. Sinclair. 'We quarrelled a long time ago. He was a
dictatorial old boy, and wanted me to go into the Church. I
refused, and he took up one of my cousins, an awfully loose
fish at college, but now a curate. Well, what do you think

this poor old boy did ? Had my movements followed, wherever I went, and always kept an eye upon me as I was struggling along. I almost feel angry with him, now that I know it, for never affording me an opportunity of showing him that I was not ungrateful. Poor old boy, he's dead now. He received me quite roughly when I appeared at his bedside, the other day ; and then—and then—by Jove, in his last few minutes, he whispered that he had provided for me. And so he has—handsomely ! An old brick, he was—a fine old Englishman ! If it could have given him back his health at all, I'd have gone into the Church, even now !'

The inspector folded his travelling-wrap over his valise, and sat down for a moment after his labours. ' You are relieved of one great anxiety, at any rate,' said he.

' Yes—thanks to him.'

' And so all is going to end up happily ? Why, that's as it should be !'

' As it should be—yes ; and as too often it isn't. I don't see, either, what I've done, myself, to deserve this good fortune ; but there are so many rogues in the world who are infinitely more prosperous upon nothing but misdeeds, that I may as well accept it without any scruple. You'll think it odd, perhaps, but I half feel I owe it to the old boy to go into the Church.'

' Go into the Wesleyan Church,' urged the inspector, who, to please Mrs. Byde, rented sittings in the Wesleyan temple of their own locality, but never had been able to get along with the successive ministers.

' Well,' objected Mr. Sinclair, ' my relative was very Church of England.'

' Ah—just so !' acquiesced the inspector.

Directing the conversation upon his personal part in the Wilmot inquiry, Inspector Byde recapitulated briefly such of the main facts as he deemed it advisable to communicate. The murder was, of course, already known to Mr. Sinclair. The latter would not need to appear in that affair ; and no doubt the excitement it had caused here would rapidly subside. Remington would be formally identified through a colleague of Mr. Byde's. As to the assassin, the French police possessed absolutely no clue, and they would most likely add the case soon to their catalogue of *affaires classées*, that is to say, unexplained. He, Mr. Byde, was on the track of the missing valuables. It was lucky Mr. Sinclair had looked in; he was leaving by the morning mail at 8. 20.

Mr. Sinclair replied, after a pause, that there could be no reason why he should disguise the fact that Remington was one of the two men whom his information, furnished at Dover to a Sergeant Bell, from Scotland Yard, directly implicated. The details must be in course of verification at the present moment, and by the time Inspector Byde returned to Scotland Yard, the story would have been completed for him. Not to prejudice the other man unduly, he would prefer just now to withhold the name which had been coupled with that of the deceased. The inspector would go fresh to his facts on reaching London. Mr. Sinclair had left Dover at ten o'clock on the previous evening. The train was the regular night-mail to the Continent; the train by which he had originally journeyed; it was just as if he had stepped out for a stay at Dover, with the object of profiting by the sea air, and as if, when he had had enough of it, he had merely stepped in again, to come along. Mr. Sinclair laughed cheerily once more. Life had opened out brightly for him.

The travelled waiter who knew his Battersea arrived at this instant with ' correspondence for Mistaire Bydee which have been delivered late last night, and have been overlook by the *confrère* then on duty.' One of the missives he brought was a note which had not passed through the post; the other was a telegram.

' Have you opened these?' asked the recipient.

Opened them? *Mais, monsieur!*—

' Have you opened these?'

But, certainly we did not permit ourselves to violate the correspondence of our clients; and we had our honour—and we had our probity—and——

' Come! come! Have the contents of these gone down to the Prefecture?'—But assuredly not!—Monsieur Hy being in relations with the colleague of Monsieur Bydee! At the Prefecture he had been told so. Aha! monsieur was no architect, then, after all. He (Mr. Byde and the waiter) turned out to be colleagues—only it would be just as well not to mention the Prefecture at the hotel, *hein?* As you said in English, ' Ma'am is the word !' Monsieur would be coming down to breakfast? Plenty of time. Mr. Byde's colleague vanished, smiling mysteriously, like a brother mason.

'They have most likely been opened,' pronounced the inspector. The telegram proved to be from Sergeant Bell, communicating the fact of Austin Wortley Sinclair's release, and preparing him for that young gentleman's early visit. The note proved to be two notes: Mrs. Bertram wrote in the third person to inform him ' in great haste ' that shortly after reaching home she received a second message from Mr. Sinclair, announcing his departure for Paris, inasmuch as all had been disposed of. The coachman would convey this *hurried scrawl* to Mr. Byde's address at once. Mrs. Bertram would feel *so pleased* if Inspector Byde would dine with them on Christmas Day—quite *en famille.*

'Christmas Day?' exclaimed the inspector—' Why, of course, to-morrow's Christmas Eve! Capital! I can spend my Christmas at home in Camberwell—that is,' he added, half to himself—' unless I meet with accidents.'

'And the other note?' hazarded Mr. Sinclair, without heeding the ominous qualification.

The inspector opened the enclosure, a small sheet of rough gray note-paper, folded fantastically.

'From Miss Knollys,' said he, after glancing through the serried lines. 'Thanks me over and over again for all I have done, and will never, never, never forget it. But I've done nothing! Well, I congratulate you, Mr. Sinclair. You have won almost an ideal nature—excuse me, sir.'

'Look here, inspector,' exclaimed the young man—' my conscience smote me, just now, when I was keeping back a portion of the story from you. The last time I saw her was the day before her departure for Paris. I didn't know she was coming on here so soon. We met by appointment at a registrar's office—and—the fact is, inspector, I am married to Miss Knollys !'

'Married to her !'

'Yes. And I haven't seen her since. Her maid accompanied her ; and we parted when the formalities were gone through. And that's what made me frightfully apprehensive.

She bears my name now. Any dishonour to myself means dishonour to her. It's the same maid who has come on here with her, and she had exhibited the greatest affection for Miss Knollys—indeed, devotion.'

'A devoted confidential maid!' commented the inspector incredulously. 'A confidential maid devoted to her mistress! Why, when will women know one another? A confidential maid: well, now, I've been looking for the link, and perhaps I've found it. Do you know anything about this devoted confidential maid?'

'No; can't say I do,' answered Mr. Sinclair, startled. She's a girl of rather striking personal appearance, and her name is Murdoch—Lydia Murdoch.'

That grim smile of the inspector's broke over his face.

'Hah! just so, just so!' he murmured; 'I should have got at it scientifically. Mayfair case—divorce proceedings Montmorency Vane—Vine, *alias* Grainger—good! I should have been glad of an interview with the handsome Miss Murdoch, but can't spare the time. Toppin must see to it. If I were you, Mr. Sinclair, I should send that confidential maid about her business. Her antecedents are deplorable.'

'You don't mean that?'

'Yes. There's nothing she can be directly charged with that I can see. She's too clever for that. But let her carry her devotion somewhere else; let her get into somebody else's confidence. She has had a pensioner with very expensive tastes, and I dare say she'd replace him even if we managed to relieve her of the pensioner. Where there's one, there's two. And honest people get victimised. Lady-like girl, too, Miss Murdoch! Do me the favour of breakfasting with me, Mr. Sinclair. My colleague will be here presently; and you will be able to testify to Mrs. Bertram how hurriedly I have been obliged to leave. I shall ask you to make my excuses.'

An earlier visitor than Toppin, however, arrived to say a few farewell words to Mr. Byde.

Grandpa called while they were at breakfast. He seemed quite hurt that the inspector should refrain from ntroducing him to the strange young gentleman seated at his left hand.

'Your friend might like to know a vicomte,' he hinted.

'Don't insist, Benny,' urged the inspector soothingly—
'I'd really really rather not. And, besides, *he* knows better
than *that !*'

Monsieur de Bingham then drew a large pill-box out of
his waistcoat pocket, and screwed it up tightly in paper.

'A little memento from Finch and myself,' said he; 'but
don't look at it until you get on your journey.'

'If they are antibilious, Benjamin, I assure you——'

'Well, never mind; that's our present, and I give you
my word that you can accept it. That's right—put it in
your pocket. You know very well I wouldn't ask you
to commit yourself to anything incompatible with your
position. How we do understand each other, you and
I !'

'Where *is* Master Finch ?'

'Not up yet. Too early for him. But he sends you his
compliments, and wants to know whether he can go back
to Soho for his Christmas ?'

'So far as I am concerned, certainly. And he can
take a walk up Oxford Street on Boxing-day. We start
fresh.'

'I may as well tell you,' added grandpa, grasping the
inspector heartily by the hand — 'that the present is
Bartholomew's rather than mine, although he might
not have brought himself to offer it to you, but for
me.'

'That's very kind of you, Benjamin, I'm sure. Silver-
coated, are they ?'

'More than silver-coated they are. And now, old friend,
good-bye, good-bye.'

The inspector was escorting his visitor.

'Oh, we shall meet again soon, I dare say,' he replied—
'but I hope it won't be professionally, Benjamin. Keep
out of it.'

'Old friend,' exclaimed grandpa, with a change of manner
which recalled his outburst in the Rue des Petits Champs—
'I respect you—I do, indeed. I should grieve to hear that
you had met with accidents.'

Grandpa looked as fresh and spry and dignified as ever,
but you would have said his eyes were moistening.

'I hope that there are no serious accidents in store for
me, Benjamin ?'

Mr. Bingham hesitated, and then spoke out impulsively.

'Between this time and to-morrow,' said he, averting his glance, 'accidents *might* happen to you, old friend—they *might*, they *might !'*

'I see you did rejoin your friends last night after all, Benny?'

'How we do understand each other, don't we !' repeated grandpa.

A fresh grasp of the hand, and he was gone.

'Well done, Benjamin,' mused the inspector, gazing after Mr. Bingham; 'I really don't think he would like to see me hurt !'

Toppin came up presently, and his colleague made ready to supply him with the final instructions. Mr. Toppin's countenance, however, wore a crestfallen expression that was quite painful.

'A mishap,' he began. 'No lack !'

'In a few words——?'

'Got the Anarchist's address from the hotel, and collared him in his lodging. Hinted at the Prefecture of Police, and put the matter to him as a fellow-revolutionist. My suspicions perfectly well-founded. He wouldn't lie. Told me he had forced Neel's portmanteau because Neel seemed to be a priest-*bourgeois*, the worst kind of *bourgeois* for the working man. Had meant to restore to the working man something of what the *bourgeoisie* had taken from him. Searching the special receptacles of the portmanteau, had found six loose diamonds, twisted up in a kid glove. Had meant them as a donation to his lodge. Resigned them on my representations. Said there were plenty of jewellers' windows to be smashed in, whenever the Anarchists chose, along the Rue de la Paix and in the Palais-Royal.'

'Well, where are the stones?'

'Infernal mishap! Went to the Grand Circus to pass an hour, last night being *the* night of the week—and—well, there, I must have lost them. Extraordinary! Can't imagine how it happened. Haven't slept a wink all night.' Toppin did look very much upset. 'Ran against that old friend of yours there, by the way, and had a talk with him,' he added—' the Vicomte.'

'Oh, ah, yes,' observed the inspector; 'the Vicomte—just so! You must have had your pocket picked, friend Toppin.

'There's no French thief could pick *my* pocket,' declared Toppin somewhat indignantly.

'It was an English thief, perhaps? They do come over, you know.'

'Yes, they do come over. But I'd like to see the man, English or anything else—— No, I must have dropped them somehow!'

The inspector turned to take his leave of Mr. Sinclair. They exchanged addresses, talked for a moment or two about the future, and then parted; and, from their cordial bearing, Toppin judged them to be old acquaintances.

Mr. Byde's conference with his subordinate dealt more particularly with the affairs of the I.O.T.A.

Brother Bamber was to be carefully kept in view. That was a personage, remarked the inspector, who might some day have to cut his long, fair, silky beard off, dye his eyebrows, 'stop out' his front teeth, and get away. The Yard might possibly, one of these fine mornings, send a word to Toppin to look after him; and the Yard might be 'a day behind the festivity;' unfortunate contretongs of that description had occasionally occurred. It would be a good thing for Detective Toppin if he could be present at the festivity, or anticipate it; that was how men rose in the profession.

Brother Bamber, Paris agent of the I.O.T.A., was playing at two or three games simultaneously. Did the inspector, as he threw off these suggestions, feel much confidence that Toppin would rise rapidly in the profession?

The inspector stood there quite inscrutable. The sculptured features of his meerschaum Sphinx could not have been less instinct with opinion than his own. We know, however, that Toppin did show great improvement in a sensational case which he conducted not long afterwards.

With regard to the position of Brother Neel, nothing in that matter would require Toppin's notice. Mr. Toppin might do well to make a visit to the Avenue Marceau, No.

95, and ascertain the movements of one Lydia Murdoch, lady's-maid in the service of Miss Knollys. If he could strike up an acquaintance with her, it might prove useful. Friend Toppin had better lose no time about it. A good ' fake' for him with the party in question would be the superior betting-man, down on his luck a bit—' you know —nothing loud or horsey—nothing common or flash : the scrupulously-dressed betting-man, with only one ring ; the fellow who can talk, without forcing it, about the sporting baronets and noblemen he meets on English racecourses. See ?'

Mr. Toppin said he saw, and that he fancied it was just what he could do. In fact, he caught at the mission eagerly. What he saw more vividly than his own metamorphosed figure, thus outlined roughly for him by Inspector Byde, was the other figure which his duty now commanded him to approach. An imperial shape, in one fleeting, statuesque attitude, again defined itself before his gaze, as he stared unintelligently at his superior officer. Toppin, the practical Detective Thomas Toppin, felt absolutely nervous as he seemed to see once more the clear pale face—the large dark eyes—the dark blue, large, perturbing eyes.

' And here's a message to the Yard which I've written out for you,' proceeded the inspector ; ' and I want you to hand it into the telegraph-office as soon as my train starts. We separate here ; and now, mind, I want you to watch the station until——'

They were standing in front of the terminus, to the right of the main entrance under the clock. Cabs, with travellers and their luggage, bound for the morning-mail to England, had already driven up to the left side of the station, and disappeared through the iron gateway. Looking at Toppin as he addressed him, the inspector paused in his observations to follow the direction of that officer's fixed regard.

One of the cabs had driven up behind them, and had there stopped. A female form, clad in a stylish travelling costume, had alighted, and that form had suddenly embodied Mr. Toppin's mental picture. It was—' the party in question.'

' '*Cré nom de noms de noms*,' muttered Toppin, disappointed and crushed, ' she's going away !'

' She's going by the mail,' said the inspector, ' then it's a rendezvous. Be off, Toppin ! Hand in the message. We can't bring the Remington case home, but, by the Lord Harry, I'll have the man on another charge before I eat my Christmas dinner !'

CHAPTER XXI.

OPENING the small packet placed in his hands by Mr. Bingham, the inspector found exactly what the circumstances of his colleague's misadventure led him to expect. They were not antibilious pills, nor any pharmaceutical preparation in coating of either silver or gold ; they were finely-cut brilliants of the purest water, and in number they were half-a-dozen.

The inspector satisfied himself upon the point without attracting the attention of his fellow - passengers. He stowed Mr. Finch's present away in the pocket rendered secure by the row of buttons ; and as he reflected that he was now carrying back the recently-stolen Wilmot diamonds, in all probability not one missing, he set himself, as was his wont at the conclusion of successful inquiries, to review his progress step by step, and to examine at every successive step the environing possibilities of error.

The sudden remark of a fellow-passenger that they might be traversing at this very moment the actual scene of the unexplained railway murder, broke into his analytical exercises. And then all the passengers got up from the places where they had comfortably ensconced themselves, and crowded towards the windows, as though the crime had not yet been committed, and might be just about to begin ; or as if they were unable to resist the notion that the assassin had remained ever since upon the spot, but at the side of the line, out of danger of the passing trains, and that, as they dashed by, he would settle his feet in the third position, and make his bow.

Creil left in its rear, the mail-train rushed onwards to Amiens. It was a ' gray-day :' not too cold, the passengers commented, for the season of the year—and dry. Darkness

would have set in some time before they steamed into
Victoria, thought the inspector.

He had his programme determined for the evening.   That
in an unknown portion of the train there was a man who
meant to steal upon him with the dusk, he did not for an
instant doubt—a man who, if they sat alone, they two, by
chance, would bound upon him when he looked aside, or, if
the vicinage of others held him back, would watch him at
arm's length ceaselessly and in silence until they reached
their journey's end—a man who meant to dog his footsteps,
and at the first dire opportunity to stay them—a man who at
the last resort would check him at the threshold of his goal,
and seize him with a reckless fury by the throat—he did not
doubt that, somewhere in the train, that man lurked and
calculated.

Amiens and Abbeville ; Boulogne ; Calais.   The inspector
had not changed his place while the mail-train sped over
French soil to its destination on the coast.   Here lay the
Calais pier, however ; the Channel boat placidly awaited
them ; and he should now learn whether, as he hoped, a
murderer was resolutely following in his path.

Yes—as he had planned it, so would be the *dénouement :*
oh, well enough he recognised the man who with bent head
pushed into the midst of the last voyagers embarking !   The
tall shapely woman whom the inspector likewise eyed with
recognition—was she or was she not, wondered half-a-dozen
of the Irresistibles grouped near the gangway, the appurten-
ance of that same personage who, with his head down,
walked a little in advance of her, and never spoke ?

The Irresistibles, French or English, in commerce or
diplomacy, were always ready to assist the unprotected
siren ' going across.'   Periodical travellers ' by this route,'
they knew how to secure precious comforts for any quaking
Circe who might have recompenses to bestow subsequently.
When they met again together, after good actions of this
sort, they would while away the tedium of an uneventful
passage by relations of their subsequent rewards.   From the
jocularities of their narrative style, it might then have
seemed to Circe that the piece of magic recorded in an
ancient chronicle were being turned against herself.   The
disappointment of the Irresistibles proved great, indeed,

when the handsome *soubrette* of the Mayfair scandal, looking, as they put it, like a duchess in disguise—an infelicitous
locution—passed them all by as though they were not, and
took another's arm, the barely-proffered arm of that
Marquis-de-Rouge-et-Noir sort of customer over there—the
gray-eyed, Roman-nosed beggar who was now making his
way towards the extreme end of the boat—the swaggerer
who, as an Adonis of Gaul, quite a dazzling Adonis, phrased
it in a plaintive tone, had scanned them momentarily with
l'air de se fichcr du monde.

At Dover, making his way from the landing-stage to the
railway platform, the inspector met one or two men, in the
attire of civilians, who stared very hard at him, but did not
either speak or nod, and at whom he also stared hard for an
instant, without speaking or nodding, either. They were
squarely-built men, with beards and round felt hats, and
they carried plain walking-sticks. They did not appear to
have any business to attend to, and they never seemed to
be looking at the people close to them.

The inspector knew each of these civilians, however, and
they knew the inspector likewise, notwithstanding their
reciprocal obliviousness of social usage. He turned back to
ask the hindermost of them a question as to Sergeant Bell.
On the Dover platform, Mr. Byde became a decidedly conspicuous figure. He loitered in front of the carriage he had
chosen, until the moment before the departure of the train.
That ' Marquis de Rouge et Noir,' who ignored or forgot the
disguised duchess, his companion, must assuredly have perceived the inspector, as he hurried into a compartment lying
at no great distance from Mr. Byde's.

There was no lack of fellow-passengers for Inspector
Byde on his through journey to Victoria. He had pointed
out in his last words to Sir John, on the previous evening,
that the most convenient point for Tudor Street, W., would
be Victoria, and, when delivered at this destination, he
loitered in a singularly aimless manner about the most
brightly-illuminated portions of the terminus. One other
traveller—not two ; the female form had disappeared—
lingered about the premises at just the same time, though
not in the most brilliantly-illuminated portions.

It was the 'witching hour for London clerks. Their office

work over till the next day, they were pouring into the
terminus in multivious streams. Any unobtrusive watcher
could escape attention. But why should the inspector
lounge in a railway terminus instead of proceeding to the
Department at once, there to report himself? For the man
who meant to dog his footsteps it was a stroke of luck,
perhaps, that the inspector—arriving at his resolution, by
the way, with an odd abruptness—told the cabman, whom
he ultimately summoned, to drive not in the direction of
Scotland Yard, but through by-streets to the main thoroughfare in which stood the Silver Gridiron, hostelry famous for
its discomfort as for its excellent larder. The cabman had
unwittingly undergone a swift, keen scrutiny as he prepared
to depart with the inspector in his vehicle. Not one of
' ours ' had pronounced the implacable watcher. A second
vehicle took the same road as the inspector.

The Golconda Club, as they are well aware at the
Criminal Investigation Department, lies just out of Soho,
on the north side of Oxford Street. To this club may
belong ladies as well as gentlemen ; and no proportionate
membership of the two sexes has been fixed by any statute
drawn up by a committee, nor by any edict of the pro-
prietor. What the fees imposed in the Golconda Club may
happen to amount to, nothing in the shape of public announcement would enlighten the inquirer. There are no
tariffs displayed upon the walls ; there are no printed papers
to be obtained on application at the secretary's office; no
manifolded circulars in violet ink, no stamped receipts, no
ledgers, no account book. There is a secretary's office, with
a bureau, writing materials, a waste-paper basket, railway
guides, postal directories, and fine Ordnance maps. There
is no secretary, however; nor has any member of the
Golconda Club ever thrown into the waste-paper basket
scraps of writing paper with characters inscribed thereon.
Externally, the club presents the aspect of both the adjoining Queen Anne houses, respectable and repellent, in
weather-beaten brick.

One of the contiguous buildings is a private institution for
the treatment of renal disorders ; another has its ground-
floor windows filled with the fasciculi of the music publisher :

its first floor rented by an Italian singing-master; and its higher stories occupied by medical students up from the country to attend the Middlesex Hospital, close at hand. Within these dingy Queen Anne structures lie spacious and solid apartments, their carved and moulded panellings and cornices reserving for the stranger an artistic surprise.

The large room of the Golconda Club had its panels in white and gold. In the florid colours of the ceiling it was no difficult task to discern the story of a mythological incontinence.

When Inspector Byde, after a protracted sojourn at the Silver Gridiron, drove to the dark street in which the Golconda Club had flourished, to his knowledge, for three years, the members, male and female, had already begun to drop in. Some of the gentlemen were in evening dress, others were in a judicious costume for the afternoon, one or two wore shooting-jackets, check-shirts, and gaiters to their boots. A subdued tone pervaded their sustained, easy, and general intercourse. The mild air of implicit faith which sat extremely well upon a few of them, not so long ago mere striplings, would have marked these out for jam tarts or bread and marmalade, in any company infested by the young suburban rakes who, having been to Paris, Vienna, and Madrid, come back to their mothers and sisters, but more particularly to their sisters' schoolfellows, with the unapproachably appalling manner of the *homme blasé* whose horrors of debauchery are all mysteriously implied, and all fictitious. *Blasés* young men, with capitalist papas attending businesses ' E.C.,' were welcome guests, and ready prey, to members of the Golconda.

The male members of the club would not unfrequently be well born; but, base or noble of blood, most of them possessed and traded upon that ' air of native distinction ' which has been commonly supposed to exist specially for lovers in decayed circumstances, and for virtuous people (of attractive personal appearance) wronged. All these men were scoundrels. One or two of them had been in foreign and transatlantic prisons; for others, deserving the same experiences, the latter remained yet in store; the greater number would never meet with their deserts.

Among the ladies, not one could be pointed to as honestly

exhibiting a plain face, a deficient figure, or a shabby toilette. What they deserved—the lady members of the Golconda Club—had not assuredly been measured by themselves; what their deserts might be could not be measured by even the 'sterner' sex, their victims: till the crack of doom it was the divine secret of the Recording Angel.

Pending the hour for settlements, the green baize tables had been set in the great room. The Golconda was believed to figure in the books of the police as merely an illegal and licentious gambling-club, tolerated for reasons which have their scientific counterpart in pathology. None of the gamblers, therefore, concealed their money stakes when the inspector was heralded as a visitor, and when he entered. He had been in the habit of looking in at the Golconda for a hand at whist, and he was known by sight to all the members. On the present occasion he declined to play, although urged with lavish blandishments by the large blonde, who had been Countess of Ulvermere. (She was divorced, upon the husband's petition, some eighteen months before.) He lounged from table to table, moved listlessly from group to group, and mingled in such conversations as did not cease at his approach. The company thinned, however, in a curious way, to-night. Inspector Byde had come there for someone, it seemed: for whom? The company thinned; with no unseemly haste, but still with haste. He had not come alone, it was remarked.

The inspector presently found himself with no companions but a slim, fair gentleman, who limped, and two ladies who slowly paced up and down with their arms about each other's waists. In the slim gentleman, now talking deferentially to Inspector Byde, the Chetwodes of Radhampton would have recognised their cousin, Wybert Rae, expelled from his university just before he took to the turf as a 'gentlemen-jock.' His limp would remain with him for life, a souvenir of absolutely fearless cross-country riding. His banishment from the turf had been due to other causes. At the present time, his means of livelihood were undefinable—that is, in the nomenclature of polite definition. He could be met with, however, wherever Mabel Stanley, the taller of these two ladies, might be met with; and wherever Mabel Stanley might be met with, there also could be met this other lady, Alphonsine Moireau, the disowned daughter of a French optician established in Marylebone Lane.

The noiseless folding doors behind the inspector opened gradually. Two men were standing on the threshold. One of them entered. The doors folded noiselessly upon the other. The man who entered, reeled and swayed in his walk.

' Raphaël !' exclaimed in a low tone Mabel Stanley (once Eva Grey, once Alma Vivian).

' *Gare !*' muttered Mdlle. Alphonsine, rapidly to the newcomer, as he stopped and gazed before him stupidly ; ' *Gare !—y a du monde ! !*'

' Professor Valentine restored to us from the mansions of the opulent,' drawled the slim, fair gentleman. ' And the black art—how goes it, Valentine ?'

The new-comer took a devious course towards the last speaker. Face to face with Mr. Rae, he solemnly picked a sovereign from that gentleman's left shoulder ; immediately, without uttering a word, changed it into a gold ring before his eyes ; as seriously blew the ring back to the left shoulder, and there transmuted it into a silver locket. He then turned up his wristbands as if to prepare for more elaborate feats of prestidigitation.

' Bertie !' called the voluptuous Mabel sharply.

The ladies waited at a side-door while the ex-gentleman steeplechase-rider waved a jaunty salute to Inspector Byde, and, with his rather interesting limp, rejoined them.

The visage of the voluptuous Mabel wore an expression of alarm. They pushed through the side-door ; it closed after them noiselessly, like the larger doors beyond.

' A-ha—a-ha, friend Raphaël,' said the inspector musingly, as he returned from a saunter among the tables—' A-ha—a-ha !—with talents like those you are a dangerous thief. Take my advice, now. Keep to the conjuring line, and get along honestly. Advertise Professor Valentine as free for penny readings, birthday - parties, and temperance fêtes.'

The inspector shot out both arms as he spoke, and appeared to be pulling himself together.

Raphaël swayed in the direction of the inspector, and bent a melting Oriental look upon him.

' Theen my new trickth ?' he asked gravely.

From the inspector's right shoulder he apparently extracted the same silver locket, which he at once changed into a Japanese fan.

' Watch thith,' he continued, agitating the open fan gently in the air.

An artificial bird alighted on the fan from some one of the aërial regions known to all prestidigitateurs.

The inspector was watching—and he was listening, too. He had held his hands down unclenched. Suddenly his lips parted, and he moved his arms almost imperceptibly upward from the elbow.

' Theen my trick with the handkerchief ?' demanded Raphaël, just before him, producing one.

' No,' replied the inspector. . . .

· · · The swaying form before him had not advanced. He could distinguish vaguely the white object which Professor Valentine still grasped, and which he had not raised.

The inspector staggered, and for a second or two the white object in front of him whirled round and round, and seemed to be whirling everywhere.

Raphaël had not advanced, however. He still stood there, stupidly gazing to the right and to the left, and balancing his body with the starts and jolts of intoxication.

Would it be credited—through the inspector's unhinging mind there flashed at this juncture the regret that he had come back from the Continent without a new dish for the Camberwell *cuisine!* . . .

. . . The handkerchief had been dashed against the inspector's face from behind. One hand held it tightly across his mouth and nostrils; another gripped him at the back of the head. It was no doubt whilst in the very act of breathing that he had been seized. Had he not allowed for such a contingency as this ? Of course he must have allowed for this contingency, as well as for others. His respiration stopped. He clutched at the arm in front of him, and once more staggered. The vice in which his head had suddenly been taken, relaxed with the movement. . . .

' Now, boys !' shouted the inspector—in a deafening voice

as it resounded in his own ears, but very faintly to the ears of others. He had drawn a breath, however; and, as with both hands he fastened upon the arm in front of him, during the brief and silent struggle which ensued, he inhaled the air again, again, and again, eagerly and greedily, his face averted from the cloth or coarse ample handkerchief whose sickly fumes had swept into his lungs, thence to drive liquid lead into the contracting veins.

'Now, boys!' called the inspector, this time more loudly.

His assailant used his utmost efforts to free himself, but in vain.

Lady and gentlemen members of the Golconda Club had crowded in at the noiseless doors, and were blocking the entrances. They looked on at the struggle without comment, and without concern.

The inspector's assailant dragged him furiously towards the principal exit. At a sudden commotion, audible from outside, Raphaël hurried to the side-door. Vine, *alias* Grainger, dropped the handkerchief; growling almost like a wild beast, and his face perfectly livid, he grappled with the inspector with immense power. It was too late; the exertion availed him nothing now.

Inspector George Byde was recovering, and he met his antagonist as he had met in times past many a murderous and hardy criminal.

Sir John gasped out an appeal for rescue. None of the bystanders moved or spoke. In the Golconda Club there were few comrades, fewer friends, and no rescuers.

A detonation rang out as the group at the side-door parted. Vine, *alias* Grainger, tore himself partly free, and then fired again. But two men rushing from the side-door were upon him. For a moment, perhaps, he might elude these men, but escape from them would be impossible.

'Take him, boys!' urged the inspector, who had sunk to his knees.

Vine, *alias* Grainger, levelled his revolver at the two men, and they hesitated. A bystander, whom they called on to secure him, shrugged his shoulders. Officers

of the law possessed no allies among members of the
Golconda.

'Take him,' repeated Mr. Byde feebly, 'it's murder!'

An oath, a reckless gesture, a third and a fourth report.
Sir John had turned the weapon against himself, and he fell
with a bullet through his head.

'I'll go for trial, then,' he pronounced laboriously, as
one of the two men stooped, and lifted him into a sitting
posture.

The other of the pair aided the inspector to regain his
feet, and stood supporting him.

'I want you,' murmured the inspector, as his gaze encountered the unsteady figure of Professor Valentine. 'You
are not drunk, you know.'

'Me drunk—me!' Raphaël hiccoughed, with a dislocating
shock. He seemed to be positively collapsing under a
seismic disturbance. 'Who thayth I'm drunk? Me
drunk!' He held himself erect by an ostensibly miraculous
feat of equilibrium. 'I'd like to thee the man who thaid I
wath!'

'Mind he doesn't escape,' said the inspector faintly to his
companion. 'We shall want him.'

Blood was falling in large drops to the carpeted floor at
the inspector's feet. His left arm hung loosely from the
shoulder, and the palm and fingers of his left hand, now
relaxed and open, glistened in a thickening crimson stream.
He leant upon his companion for support, and his features
contracted in a momentary spasm.

'Serious?' demanded his companion in a low tone
anxiously. 'Hope not, sir?'

'Two places,' replied the inspector, composing his features
with an effort; 'left arm and shoulder. Nothing serious,
though, I feel sure. Just support me to where that man is
lying.'

They approached the prostrate body of Sir John. The
latter had closed his eyes, and was moaning in his struggles
to breathe freely or to speak.

The gentlemen of the Golconda Club looked on, impassive,
silent, callous. Each for himself, and self-reliant; not one
willing to aid his neighbour—not one capable of trusting to
his neighbour's aid; all—the bandits, corsairs, wreckers of

society. As the ladies and gentlemen of the Golconda—cheats and Delilahs, confederates and informers—stood in stony groups around the lofty and spacious apartment of the club, the tragic scene so rapidly enacted appeared unreal, a show, a piece of mere undisquieting make-believe — the rehearsal of a stage play in a vast and brilliant drawing-room—the actors, intense masters of their art—the spectators, dullards.

It was blood, however, that tracked the inspector's uncertain progress, as he and his companion advanced slowly to the spot where lay the prostrate form : blood that rained in clinging, viscous drops through his numbed fingers, from his nerveless arm : blood that flowed into the shining, irregular, red patch underneath the dying man's head, and swelled the red patch there into a vermilion pool.

'If we could have hindered that ——,' murmured the inspector regretfully. 'The case would have led up to sensational evidence. Ah, what I could have brought out ! The public might have had a glimpse of what goes on beneath the surface.'

'He's done it too well,' said Mr. Byde's companion. 'But yourself—how do you feel yourself, inspector ?'

'Running down fast. But it's only a faint, I'm sure. Hit in the shoulder. Tell Marsh to prop that man's head up. I can't speak loudly enough.'

The other of the two strange men had knelt by the side of Sir John, and was loosening the latter's garments at the neck. In obedience to the direction, he at once gently placed the prone figure in a recumbent posture, which afforded the dying man almost instantaneous relief. His respiration became less laboured, and he unclosed his eyes.

'Vine !' called the inspector, summoning up his energies.

The gray eyes turned mechanically in the direction of the sound. They encountered the inspector's face, and they travelled no farther. A look of recognition dimly lighted them up, and dawned through the lines of the pale, convulsed visage. It seemed as though the ebbing spirit had been arrested on its path—arrested by that peremptory summons, and, for an instant, recalled.

'Vine !' repeated the inspector more loudly; 'if I put a question to you—can you answer ?'

Marsh bent forward to catch the whisper from the blood-less lips. With the whisper issued from the blanched lips a thread of vivid crimson, which gradually broadened in its downward course. ' Yes,' came the answer, followed by words only audible to the man stooping forward.

' He says he's going for trial,' said Marsh.

' Are we to take Finch for the railway murder ?' demanded Mr. Byde. ' Are we to take him—come ?'

' No !' was the distinct reply.

' You are very ill, you know,' pursued the inspector. ' I am afraid you have hurt yourself seriously. Come !—who shot that man, and got away so cleverly ?'

Still fixed upon the inspector, the gray eyes had never-theless a gaze in them that went beyond him, elsewhere, far away. Once more, it was the constable in plain clothes, Marsh, who interpreted the barely articulate sounds.

' He says he'll take his trial—— upstairs.'

' Listen to me, Vine !' commanded the inspector, with a failing voice. ' Are you guilty, or not guilty—you hear—guilty, or not guilty ?'

' Guilty,' whispered Sir John. His eyes wandered from Inspector Byde to the man who was supporting him, and who had picked up the revolver ; and as the light from above flashed along the bright metal chambers, the gray eyes rested for a moment upon the firearm itself, and then, with a vacant expression, drooped and closed. ' Guilty,' he sighed, whilst a frown appeared to gather about his brow— ' and cleverly—but—I shot him—and—he is waking— must——'

The crimson stream sluggishly trickling from his mouth welled forth in a sudden volume, and from his forehead the gathering frown faded. As the head fell on one side, the muscles of the visage no longer at their painful tension, a slight stir from the surrounding groups proved that, among the silent members of the Golconda Club, there were some, at any rate, who had attentively followed the scene. Indeed, a few fans were fluttering vigorously before a few white faces ; and the large blonde whose affability with Inspector Byde has been alluded to, belied her brazen smile and stare by an abrupt gesture of repugnance, and by a smothered phrase of pity. She had herself been the cause of blood shed, as she would complacently recount to other ladies, and to gilded youth about the town. The sight of blood, however, endure she could not—she could not, really !'

'Gone,' pronounced the constable in plain clothes, Marsh, allowing the lifeless body to sink at full length to the ground —'gone, as he said, for trial !'

'How is it you were twice late ?' complained the inspector in a feeble tone. 'The telegram I told Toppin to send off must have reached the Yard early in the day ?'

'Sergeant Bell thought that Toppin must have been under a misapprehension when he telegraphed.'

'Sergeant Bell thought ?   Sergeant Bell thought ?' muttered the inspector, leaning heavily against his companion. 'There are two many Sergeant Bells at Scotland Yard. "Sergeant Bell thought!" Take care of that revolver. I want it for the Remington affair.'

'How do you feel, sir ?' asked the plain-clothes constable, Marsh. 'Let me get some brandy for you, here ?'

'Not here—not here ! And don't leave me, either of you. They know that I have valuables in my possession. Don't leave me !' Upon uttering which injunction, Inspector George Byde lost consciousness.

Some of the gentlemen members of the Golconda began to stroll towards the police-officers.

'Stand back, you ——, all of you !' exclaimed Constable Marsh savagely.

Christmas Day had passed ; Mr. Finch had reaped his harvest from the popular revelries of the succeeding forty-eight hours, and the same, in riotous living, had partially expended : and Inspector George Byde found himself permitted by his medical adviser, by Mrs. Byde, and by the weather, to repair at easy stages to the offices of the Chief, opposite Whitehall.

The inspector was much paler than we have seen him since the outset of his mission on the subject of the Wilmot (Park Lane) inquiry, 'with confidential instructions as to possible issues therein involved.' He wore his left arm in a black silk scarf ; and the Chief, after a keen glance at him, pushed an easy-chair forward with his foot, and invited Inspector Byde to sit down.

The Chief stated in brief, metallic accents that he had had the report of the Departmental surgeon before him, and that he had been pleased to know that from the inspector's injuries there would be no complications to be feared. He had just gone through the report dictated by the inspector to an amanuensis, on the previous day. The suggestions relating to matters extraneous to the inquiry entrusted to him should be duly noted; prompt action would be taken upon them whenever apparent necessity should arise.

When identifying the abstracted valuables recovered for him by the Department, Mr. Stanislas Wilmot had expressed very great astonishment that any officer should have been able to secure the missing property absolutely intact, and had requested that the officer who had conducted the case with such signal success might call upon him to receive some personal reward. He (the Chief) need not say that Inspector Byde would be fully aware of the Departmental regulation on this point.

With regard to Mr. Stanislas Wilmot himself, facts which had been quite recently communicated to them, would render it advisable to pay some attention to the business dealings of the Wilmot firm in Hatton Garden. A supervision would be arranged for, and if active measures should turn out to be necessary, Inspector Byde would be consulted.

As to the original robbery from the strong-room of the Park Lane private residence, it was incredible that Sergeant Bell should have allowed the man Forsyth to elude him. Forsyth had been supposed to fill a place in Wilmot's employment as butler. That appeared to be only nominally the state of the case. Forsyth possessed some sort of hold upon this Mr. Stanislas Wilmot.

' We found the locksmith to whom Forsyth took certain keys, a few months ago, with an order for duplicates,' continued the Chief; 'but Bell entirely broke down in the supervision he was told to exercise, and when we wanted the man Forsyth, he was well out of the way. We have reason for presuming that he made a dash for Holland. The Remington affair has been explained by telegram and correspondence to the Paris authorities. One or two of the French newspapers, just to hand, deal with the murder in a style that is worth your looking at. I have ordered the papers to be put by for you. A narrow escape you ran, it seems, at the hands of our worthy friend, Michel Hy. He is publishing a little work, by the way—a book of wild theorising, for the use of visionary Continental detectives; I have an advance copy from him somewhere about, and if you like to look at it while you are away from duty——'

The inspector, who knew his Chief to be a man of the very fewest words, inferred from the unaccustomed length of the observations vouchsafed to him that 'the Yard' rated his expeditious return, with the whole of the missing valuables, a greater achievement than either his colleagues or his superiors would be willing to admit explicitly.

Wild theorising! That was the spirit in which they met originality—that was how they dismissed any conscientious searching after improved methods! They would be describing him—Inspector George Byde—as a wild theorist, next!

Whilst awaiting his interview with the Chief, he had proved the theorem that if one side of a triangle be produced, the exterior angle shall be greater than either of the interior opposite angles; that any two angles of a triangle are together less than two right angles; and that the greater angle of every triangle is subtended by the greater side. He had been interrupted in a languid examination of the problem: To make a triangle of which the sides shall be equal to three given straight lines; but any two whatever of these must be greater than the third. If anyone went into his room downstairs, during his absence, thought the inspector, and found his book upon the table—his book, and the scrap of paper covered with diagrams—they would laugh at him and his exercises, no doubt! And yet how those exercises had cleared his head and braced his mind up for this interview!

'We shall have to reconsider the position of the Golconda,' continued the Chief. 'As you have seen from the memoranda furnished by Sergeant Bell, the woman who applied at the Knightsbridge post-office for letters addressed "Adelaide," to be left till called for, was the Jane Clark, of South Bank, St. John's Wood, who has undergone terms of imprisonment for "long firm" swindles under the aliases of Daisy Dacre, Violet Vere, etc.; and there is not the slightest doubt that she has been allowed to go on using the Golconda, in spite of their pledge to us. We trace that woman to various resorts in company with the man Remington. Among other of her exploits, she proved as his principal creditor in the liquidation of his estate last year. Nothing connects her directly with this case, although the name and address noted upon the morsel of paper found near the body of the deceased had evidently been agreed upon between them, the handwriting being, so far as we can pronounce, that of the deceased himself. She must have formed the link of communication with Forsyth, but we cannot prove that. Your hint to explain the intervention of the man Vine would appear to be well founded. Somebody about the premises, or having access to them, must have been watching Forsyth, and must have been cognisant of his relations with Remington. Who? That is more than we can say. Not, at any rate, the Brother Neel with respect to whom you have reported favourably. And that reminds me. We shall put this Maëlstrom business under your charge. One of these so-called Good Templar leagues, professedly created for ' reclaiming ' the English artizan of the manufacturing towns, but unquestionably a Socialist organization of the most determined character, is latterly in correspondence with both Paris and Vienna. Their programme and methods are expected to form new departures. You will be good enough to give your attention to this, inspector; we think you are just the man for the work.'

By that barely perceptible shake of the head, the inspector betrayed a misgiving. He knew his bias. It was too bad to be thus constantly exposed to the temptation of endeavouring to atone by a public triumph for his one mistake. Ah—certainly it would be sweet to strike a blow at all these canting fellows; but, as he impressed so often upon his son, Master Edgar, ' where the prejudice is strong, the judgment will be weak.' His own prejudice ran very strong, in the particular domain of the I.O.T.A. brethren, and their like. He could not stand them. Weren't they always posing for the monopoly of the Christian virtues ; wouldn't you think, to hear them prate, that all these dear-friend, brethren-fellows were heaven-sent teachers of a patented morality? Yes; and when he remembered what he possessed at home, tied up with red tape, endorsed, and put away in pigeon-holes—ha !—it made him smile to hear them prate, some of them, and to see them pose. There were a few of the hierarchs whose private lives had oddly strayed within the ken of Scotland Yard. If they owned the monopoly of the Christian virtues, why could they not let bygones be by-gones—why did they cherish rancour and bear malice—why was that money-making enterprise, the organ of the I.O.T.A. in the press, endlessly to be girding at himself, George Byde, because of a single mistake? Well, they must go on as they might deem proper. Let them gird! In the future Brother Neel had better keep his hands clean.

It was much more soothing to think of Mr. Sinclair and Miss Adela Knollys. Their course of true love had run smooth; and the course of true love ran too often in rough, dark, and tortuous ways; channels that the frailest or most foolish obstacle would sometimes part for ever; sources that would brusquely separate, diverge, flow on—the one unruffled, pure, and bright; the other clouded, acrid, and impetuous—flow on, diverging ever, to never, never re-unite. They both flowed into the sea, at last, these water-courses, mused the inspector wisely; alas ! too often they were different seas, wide as the poles asunder, but salt, each of them, with tears. How she reminded him, Miss Adela Knollys, of his own dear fair-haired little daughter, May ! If she could have lived—ah ! if their poor child only could have lived——

'And now, inspector,' concluded the Chief, wheeling his chair round to his bureau, with an air which the inspector understood—'it is only due to you to add that the Depart-ment have full confidence in your abilities.'

'I have done my best, Sir Roland,' answered the inspector, on his feet at once, and erect, 'and if I have only been partially successful in the matter of the supplementary confidential instructions—another time——'

'What?—Oh—Why, we've nothing to complain of ! Your direct instructions were to recover abstracted property, and that was all—a packet of loose diamonds—exceedingly difficult undertaking, given the circumstances. Well, you've done so, haven't you?'

'Thank you, Sir Roland,' answered the inspector, saluting. He crossed the room, closed the door behind him, and stood for a moment on the threshold, meditating.

'Well, yes,' he added, in a tone of corroboration—'Q. E. F.'

A CATALOGUE OF SELECTED DOVER
BOOKS IN ALL FIELDS OF INTEREST

CONDITIONED REFLEXES, Ivan P. Pavlov. Full translation of most complete statement of Pavlov's work; cerebral damage, conditioned reflex, experiments with dogs, sleep, similar topics of great importance. 430pp. 5⅜ x 8½.
60614-7 Pa. $4.50

NOTES ON NURSING: WHAT IT IS, AND WHAT IT IS NOT, Florence Nightingale. Outspoken writings by founder of modern nursing. When first published (1860) it played an important role in much needed revolution in nursing. Still stimulating. 140pp. 5⅜ x 8½.
22340-X Pa. $3.00

HARTER'S PICTURE ARCHIVE FOR COLLAGE AND ILLUSTRATION, Jim Harter. Over 300 authentic, rare 19th-century engravings selected by noted collagist for artists, designers, decoupeurs, etc. Machines, people, animals, etc., printed one side of page. 25 scene plates for backgrounds. 6 collages by Harter, Satty, Singer, Evans. Introduction. 192pp. 8⅞ x 11¾.
23659-5 Pa. $5.00

MANUAL OF TRADITIONAL WOOD CARVING, edited by Paul N. Hasluck. Possibly the best book in English on the craft of wood carving. Practical instructions, along with 1,146 working drawings and photographic illustrations. Formerly titled *Cassell's Wood Carving*. 576pp. 6½ x 9¼.
23489-4 Pa. $7.95

THE PRINCIPLES AND PRACTICE OF HAND OR SIMPLE TURNING, John Jacob Holtzapffel. Full coverage of basic lathe techniques—history and development, special apparatus, softwood. turning, hardwood turning, metal turning. Many projects—billiard ball, works formed within a sphere, egg cups, ash trays, vases, jardiniers, others—included. 1881 edition. 800 illustrations. 592pp. 6⅛ x 9¼.
23365-0 Clothbd. $15.00

THE JOY OF HANDWEAVING, Osma Tod. Only book you need for hand weaving. Fundamentals, threads, weaves, plus numerous projects for small board-loom, two-harness, tapestry, laid-in, four-harness weaving and more. Over 160 illustrations. 2nd revised edition. 352pp. 6½ x 9¼.
23458-4 Pa. $6.00

THE BOOK OF WOOD CARVING, Charles Marshall Sayers. Still finest book for beginning student in. wood sculpture. Noted teacher, craftsman discusses fundamentals, technique; gives 34 designs, over 34 projects for panels, bookends, mirrors, etc. "Absolutely first-rate"—E. J. Tangerman. 33 photos. 118pp. 7¾ x 10⅝.
23654-4 Pa. $3.50

THE AMERICAN SENATOR, Anthony Trollope. Little known, long unavailable Trollope novel on a grand scale. Here are humorous comment on American vs. English culture, and stunning portrayal of a heroine/villainess. Superb evocation of Victorian village life. 561pp. 5⅜ x 8½.
23801-6 Pa. $6.00

WAS IT MURDER? James Hilton. The author of *Lost Horizon* and *Goodbye, Mr. Chips* wrote one detective novel (under a pen-name) which was quickly forgotten and virtually lost, even at the height of Hilton's fame. This edition brings it back—a finely crafted public school puzzle resplendent with Hilton's stylish atmosphere. A thoroughly English thriller by the creator of Shangri-la. 252pp. 5⅜ x 8. (Available in U.S. only)
23774-5 Pa. $3.00

CENTRAL PARK: A PHOTOGRAPHIC GUIDE, Victor Laredo and Henry Hope Reed. 121 superb photographs show dramatic views of Central Park: Bethesda Fountain, Cleopatra's Needle, Sheep Meadow, the Blockhouse, plus people engaged in many park activities: ice skating, bike riding, etc. Captions by former Curator of Central Park, Henry Hope Reed, provide historical view, changes, etc. Also photos of N.Y. landmarks on park's periphery. 96pp. 8½ x 11. 23750-8 Pa. $4.50

NANTUCKET IN THE NINETEENTH CENTURY, Clay Lancaster. 180 rare photographs, stereographs, maps, drawings and floor plans recreate unique American island society. Authentic scenes of shipwreck, lighthouses, streets, homes are arranged in geographic sequence to provide walking-tour guide to old Nantucket existing today. Introduction, captions. 160pp. 8⅞ x 11¾. 23747-8 Pa. $6.95

STONE AND MAN: A PHOTOGRAPHIC EXPLORATION, Andreas Feininger. 106 photographs by *Life* photographer Feininger portray man's deep passion for stone through the ages. Stonehenge-like megaliths, fortified towns, sculpted marble and crumbling tenements show textures, beauties, fascination. 128pp. 9¼ x 10¾. 23756-7 Pa. $5.95

CIRCLES, A MATHEMATICAL VIEW, D. Pedoe. Fundamental aspects of college geometry, non-Euclidean geometry, and other branches of mathematics: representing circle by point. Poincare model, isoperimetric property, etc. Stimulating recreational reading. 66 figures. 96pp. 5⅝ x 8¼.
63698-4 Pa. $2.75

THE DISCOVERY OF NEPTUNE, Morton Grosser. Dramatic scientific history of the investigations leading up to the actual discovery of the eighth planet of our solar system. Lucid, well-researched book by well-known historian of science. 172pp. 5⅜ x 8½. 23726-5 Pa. $3.50

THE DEVIL'S DICTIONARY. Ambrose Bierce. Barbed, bitter, brilliant witticisms in the form of a dictionary. Best, most ferocious satire America has produced. 145pp. 5⅜ x 8½. 20487-1 Pa. $2.25

UNCLE SILAS, J. Sheridan LeFanu. Victorian Gothic mystery novel, considered by many best of period, even better than Collins or Dickens. Wonderful psychological terror. Introduction by Frederick Shroyer. 436pp. 5⅜ x 8½. 21715-9 Pa. $6.00

JURGEN, James Branch Cabell. The great erotic fantasy of the 1920's that delighted thousands, shocked thousands more. Full final text, Lane edition with 13 plates by Frank Pape. 346pp. 5⅜ x 8½. 23507-6 Pa. $4.50

THE CLAVERINGS, Anthony Trollope. Major novel, chronicling aspects of British Victorian society, personalities. Reprint of Cornhill serialization, 16 plates by M. Edwards; first reprint of full text. Introduction by Norman Donaldson. 412pp. 5⅜ x 8½. 23464-9 Pa. $5.00

KEPT IN THE DARK, Anthony Trollope. Unusual short novel about Victorian morality and abnormal psychology by the great English author. Probably the first American publication. Frontispiece by Sir John Millais. 92pp. 6½ x 9¼. 23609-9 Pa. $2.50

RALPH THE HEIR, Anthony Trollope. Forgotten tale of illegitimacy, inheritance. Master novel of Trollope's later years. Victorian country estates, clubs, Parliament, fox hunting, world of fully realized characters. Reprint of 1871 edition. 12 illustrations by F. A. Faser. 434pp. of text. 5⅜ x 8½. 23642-0 Pa. $5.00

YEKL and THE IMPORTED BRIDEGROOM AND OTHER STORIES OF THE NEW YORK GHETTO, Abraham Cahan. Film *Hester Street* based on *Yekl* (1896). Novel, other stories among first about Jewish immigrants of N.Y.'s East Side. Highly praised by W. D. Howells—Cahan "a new star of realism." New introduction by Bernard G. Richards. 240pp. 5⅜ x 8½. 22427-9 Pa. $3.50

THE HIGH PLACE, James Branch Cabell. Great fantasy writer's enchanting comedy of disenchantment set in 18th-century France. Considered by some critics to be even better than his famous *Jurgen*. 10 illustrations and numerous vignettes by noted fantasy artist Frank C. Pape. 320pp. 5⅜ x 8½. 23670-6 Pa. $4.00

ALICE'S ADVENTURES UNDER GROUND, Lewis Carroll. Facsimile of ms. Carroll gave Alice Liddell in 1864. Different in many ways from final Alice. Handlettered, illustrated by Carroll. Introduction by Martin Gardner. 128pp. 5⅜ x 8½. 21482-6 Pa. $2.50

FAVORITE ANDREW LANG FAIRY TALE BOOKS IN MANY COLORS, Andrew Lang. The four Lang favorites in a boxed set—the complete *Red, Green, Yellow* and *Blue* Fairy Books. 164 stories; 439 illustrations by Lancelot Speed, Henry Ford and G. P. Jacomb Hood. Total of about 1500pp. 5⅜ x 8½. 23407-X Boxed set, Pa. $15.95

AMERICAN ANTIQUE FURNITURE, Edgar G. Miller, Jr. The basic coverage of all American furniture before 1840: chapters per item chronologically cover all types of furniture, with more than 2100 photos. Total of 1106pp. 7⅞ x 10¾.   21599-7, 21600-4 Pa., Two-vol. set $17.90

ILLUSTRATED GUIDE TO SHAKER FURNITURE, Robert Meader. Director, Shaker Museum, Old Chatham, presents up-to-date coverage of all furniture and appurtenances, with much on local styles not available elsewhere. 235 photos. 146pp. 9 x 12.   22819-3 Pa. $6.00

ORIENTAL RUGS, ANTIQUE AND MODERN, Walter A. Hawley. Persia, Turkey, Caucasus, Central Asia, China, other traditions. Best general survey of all aspects: styles and periods, manufacture, uses, symbols and their interpretation, and identification. 96 illustrations, 11 in color. 320pp. 6⅛ x 9¼.   22366-3 Pa. $6.95

CHINESE POTTERY AND PORCELAIN, R. L. Hobson. Detailed descriptions and analyses by former Keeper of the Department of Oriental Antiquities and Ethnography at the British Museum. Covers hundreds of pieces from primitive times to 1915. Still the standard text for most periods. 136 plates, 40 in full color. Total of 750pp. 5⅝ x 8½.
23253-0 Pa. $10.00

THE WARES OF THE MING DYNASTY, R. L. Hobson. Foremost scholar examines and illustrates many varieties of Ming (1368-1644). Famous blue and white, polychrome, lesser-known styles and shapes. 117 illustrations, 9 full color, of outstanding pieces. Total of 263pp. 6⅛ x 9¼. (Available in U.S. only)   23652-8 Pa. $6.00

CATALOGUE OF DOVER BOOKS